THIS COLLECTION INCLUDES:

Like a Winter Snow

Like a Christmas Dream

Like a Silver Bell

THE PORT WILLIS HOLIDAY COLLECTION

LINDSAY HARREL

LIKE A WINTER SNOW

A PORT WILLIS ROMANCE

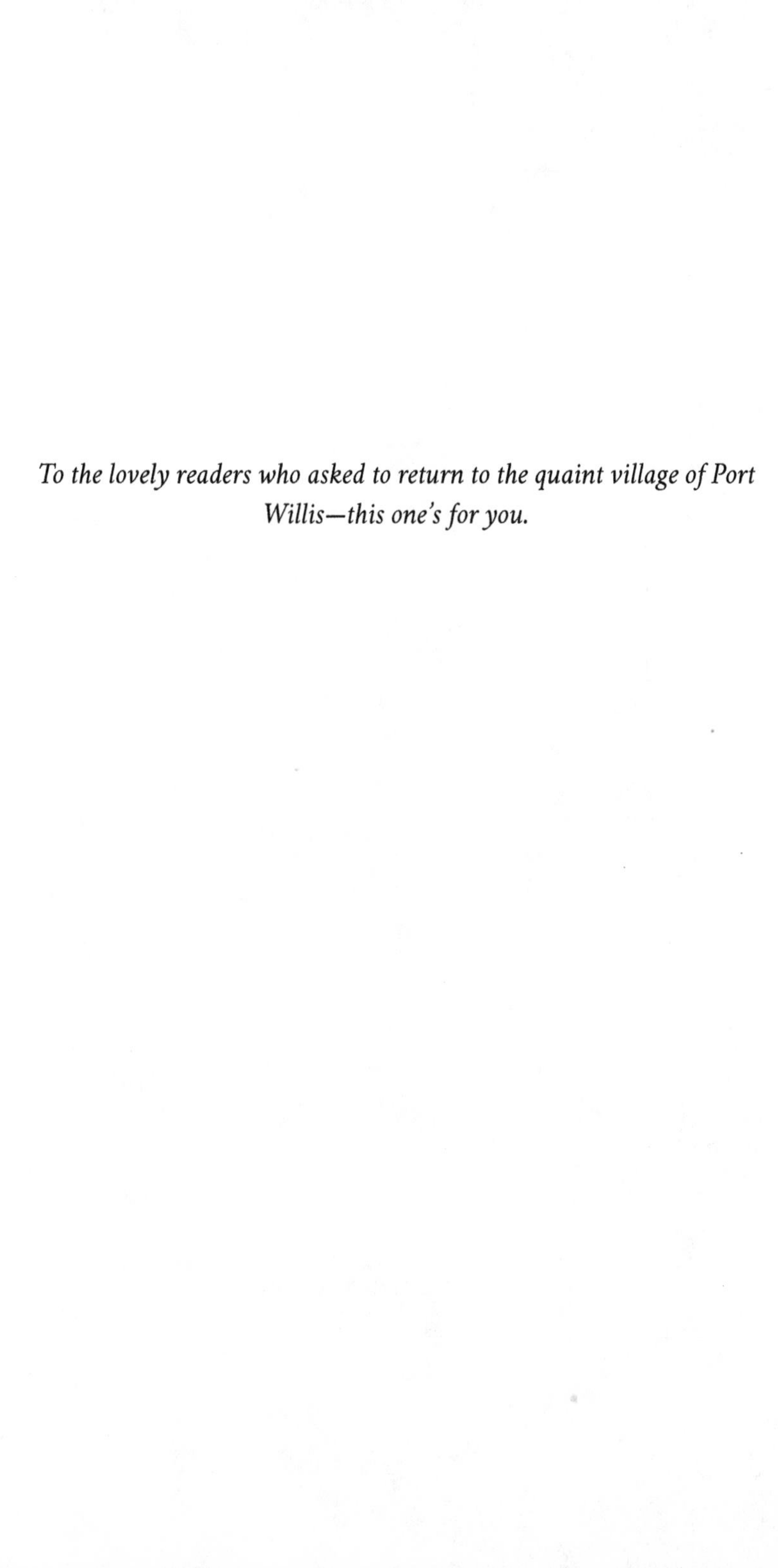

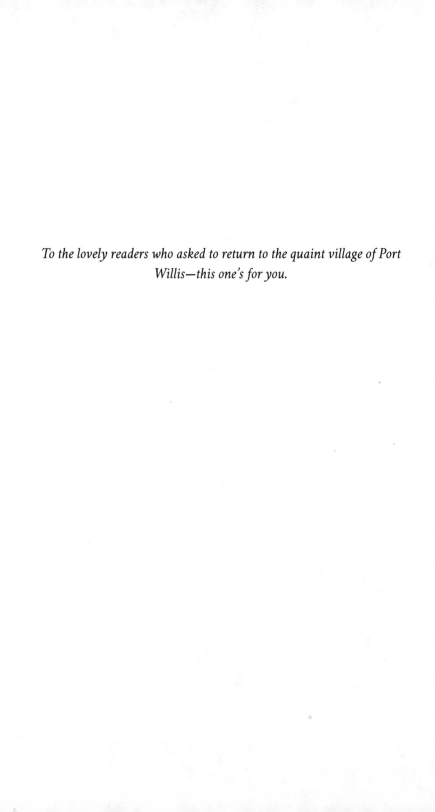

To the lovely readers who asked to return to the quaint village of Port Willis—this one's for you.

CHAPTER 1

If it were anyone but Sophia Barrett getting married, Joy Beckman wouldn't dream of getting on a plane tomorrow.

She stepped from the elevator onto the polished laminate flooring of one of the top skilled nursing facilities in New Port Richey, Florida. At least if she had to leave town, she knew that her mom was getting the best care possible while recovering from her broken hip and subsequent surgery.

"Rockin' Around the Christmas Tree" played softly from a speaker as Joy made her way toward her mom's room. She flashed a smile at the few residents in wheelchairs she passed in the hall, her insides twisting at the way their faces lit at the small kindness. How she wished she had time to sit and talk with each one, especially those whose families didn't live nearby. Any time of year, that would have gripped her, but especially now—no one should be alone at Christmas.

Still, all her focus today was on Mom. Joy had been dreading saying goodbye for the next two weeks, but it was time. She prayed the pep she was about to force into her voice would be enough to fool her mother.

Of course, if it were one of Mom's bad days, it wouldn't matter.

"Knock, knock." Joy peeked her head through her mom's open doorway. The room was small but comfortable, with pale blue walls and several framed garden photos bursting with pastel colors. An essential oil diffuser in the corner dispensed a lavender scent throughout the room.

Mom's nurse, Linda, blocked Joy's view of the bed as she took her patient's vitals. She looked up at Joy's greeting. "Good afternoon, Dr. Beckman." She kept her drawling voice low.

Joy approached the bed and finally spied her sleeping mother, tucked in and looking so frail under a bright pink and yellow quilt she'd made years ago. Betty Beckman had once been as vibrant as the colors in the quilt, with thick brown hair that gleamed, high cheekbones, and green eyes that had always hinted at some secret joy within. Now, her gray hair hung limp around her shoulders, combed and neat but lacking its former luster. Her cheekbones protruded from her thin face. She'd lost so much weight just in the sixteen months since she'd received her Alzheimer's diagnosis.

And then there were her eyes. Instead of looking at Joy like the light of her life—the miracle baby Betty had been given forty-two years ago after so many losses—she sometimes viewed her as a stranger.

Joy cleared her throat. "I've told you, Linda. You don't have to call me Dr. Beckman. Joy is fine." Though she'd once taken such a thrill at the title bestowed upon her when she'd received her PhD more than ten years ago, her work in counseling women from all walks of life had ended when she'd sold her practice in Arizona last year and moved here to help Dad care for Mom.

She'd made the right call then. Was she making the right call now, traveling so far away a week and a half before Christmas to perform maid of honor duties?

But the plans were made. Her flights booked. And Sophia was counting on her to help with some last-minute details. Joy couldn't abandon her best friend.

Then again, she was needed here too. She'd already failed her parents once. And potentially doing it again ... not an option.

"All right then, Joy." Linda finished her observations and draped her stethoscope over her neck. The plump woman angled a look at her. "I hear you're leaving town for a spell."

"Yes, for a wedding." Had Dad told her, or had Mom had one of her lucid moments? "How is she today?"

Linda's brows knit together. "Her recovery from surgery is going well, though it will most likely be another two to three weeks before she's released. As you know, it was a bad fall."

Joy tried not to let the words bring a sense of utter devastation, but no matter how hard she fought, they bulldozed her heart. Because if only she'd been doing her duty instead of sleeping ...

No. Negative self-talk did no good.

She straightened her spine. "And her memory? How's that been today?" Joy sat in the chair next to the bed and took Mom's wrinkled hand, running her thumb over two veins rippling across the top. Mom's simple one-carat circle diamond winked from her ring finger.

"You know how it is. Good moments mixed with the bad. She was telling me about your trip, and when I asked a question about your friend—Sophia, is it?—she suddenly didn't know who I was referring to."

"Sounds about right." Joy had counseled several women through the loss of parents after dementia and Alzheimer's had consumed their loved ones' minds, so she'd known what to expect from the progression of the disease. But her heart hadn't been prepared to experience it herself.

Working to control the tears beginning to gather in her eyes,

Joy blinked quickly then changed the subject. "I expected Dad to be here."

"He left, maybe an hour ago or so. Went to lunch but said he'd be back in a jiffy." Linda gathered a few empty containers of Jell-O and plastic spoons from Mom's movable bedside table and tossed them into the small trashcan under the nearby sink. "He told me about the assisted living facility he's considering. I told him I know many patients who live there and love it."

"What are you talking about?"

Linda's cheeks paled. "Oh, dear. I ... never mind. Please forget I said anything." She started for the door.

"Linda."

The nurse turned, frowning. "I figured you knew. I shouldn't say anything else. Talk to him about it. But ..." She studied Joy. "Get all the facts before you form an opinion one way or the other."

Turning on her heel, Linda left. Joy slumped in her chair.

Dad was thinking of moving Mom into a full-time facility after rehab was complete?

She needed to talk to him. Now. Joy dug in her purse and pulled her phone from within, noticing a text from Sophia on the lock screen.

LESS THAN THIRTY-SIX HOURS! EEK!

Joy dismissed the notification, unlocked her phone, and dialed Dad's number. It went straight to voicemail. When was the man going to learn to keep his phone turned on? At nearly eighty, Dwight Beckman hadn't seen the need for a cell phone, but Joy had convinced him of its necessity. After all, she had to be able to communicate with him about Mom twenty-four seven.

She shoved the phone back into her purse, hopped up, and paced.

Fifteen minutes of fretting later, her father walked in sipping on a fifty-ounce Big Gulp. "Don't worry, it's diet."

"I wasn't going to say anything." She'd learned to hold her tongue when it came to her diabetic father and his eating habits. All she could do was provide good meal options and ensure he regularly saw his doctor. And pray. A lot.

Dad lowered himself into the chair Joy had vacated, his belly hanging over his belted pants. He set his drink on the ground, wincing a bit at the movement. "Did you finish packing?"

"Yeah. I came to tell Mom goodbye, but she's been asleep since I arrived."

"We had a good chat this morning before she dozed off." He turned and gazed at Mom with the most loving eyes.

Once upon a time, Joy had dreamed of a love like her parents had. Devoted despite heartaches. On the same page in all the ways that mattered. Individual and allowed to thrive in the areas where they were different.

But she'd come to realize that it wasn't the plan for her life. That, instead, she was meant to be a friend and helper to all. And she had found peace in her place.

Still … in times like this, when life seemed so fragile, it would be nice to share the burden with someone else. To have a shoulder to lean on. Yes, she had Sophia, but her best friend had moved to England more than a year ago after meeting the love of her life, William Rose.

And of course, Joy had God, who would never leave her. But sometimes, having a flesh-and-blood partner in life sounded appealing.

Appealing … but not likely.

"What did you chat about?"

When Dad didn't answer right away, Joy moved to the opposite side of the bed and pulled up a second chair. "Linda mentioned something about an assisted living facility."

He frowned and pushed his large plastic frames up the bridge of his nose. "She shouldn't have done that."

"She thought I knew." Mom stirred, and Joy lowered her voice. "Why didn't I know?"

But the answer was obvious. Dad didn't feel like Joy could be trusted to help them anymore.

"Nothing is decided, JoJo." His voice softened at the use of his nickname for her. "Your mom and I are just evaluating our options." He fiddled with some papers on the side table. Pulling a brochure from the bottom of the stack, he held it out to her.

She reached across the bed and took it. The glossy cover read *Glenn River Assisted Living and Memory Care,* and beneath the title, several grinning elderly residents played cards around a table.

"At this place, we'd be able to live in the same apartment. Your mother would receive the elevated care she needs, and I could pay room and board until I get to a point where I need more assistance as well. They'd cook and clean for us and take care of all of our needs."

"But I do all of that for you." Joy couldn't help the tremble that had crept into her voice. "You want to leave your home?"

"You've done a wonderful job, and we couldn't be more grateful, but maybe it's time for you to get back to doing what you love."

All of his kind words couldn't erase the truth—Dad wouldn't even be considering this move if Joy hadn't, literally, fallen asleep on the job.

She set the brochure down on the quilt and eyed her father once more. "I *am* doing what I love—taking care of you guys."

"As I said, it's just one of many options we're considering. I don't want you to worry about it. Go and enjoy your trip."

"Sure. Okay." She'd endure the time away for Sophia's sake.

And when she returned in two weeks, Joy would get right back to where she was supposed to be—helping Mom and Dad in the difficult days to come.

CHAPTER 2

A piercing squeal met Joy's ears as she exited the gated area of Cornwall Airport Newquay.

Following the group of passengers into the airport's main lobby, she raised up on her tiptoes to try to catch a glimpse of Sophia. Some days, being five two had its advantages. Today was not that day.

Finally, the person in front of her broke off to the left, and Joy had a clear view of the room just in time to see a pair of arms closing around her.

"You're here, you're here!" Sophia let go and pulled away, her grin carefree and strong.

Joy laughed. "I am."

"Did you have a good flight?"

"Long"—she exhaled some of the stress from her shoulders —"but good." She'd actually managed to sleep a bit on the long stretch from Tampa to London—a miracle considering the man next to her snoring the entire way as well as her stormy conscience hurling accusations at her. The moment she'd landed, she'd called to check on Mom. Linda had chided her, said they'd take good care of her mother in her absence.

But would they? Could anyone care for a mom better than a daughter?

"So glad to hear that." Sophia wove her arm through Joy's. "Let's grab your luggage and hit the road. I can't wait to show you Port Willis."

Be upbeat, Joy. Don't ruin this for Sophia. "And I can't wait to see it." Joy was supposed to have visited last Christmas, but her mom had been worse than anticipated. Sophia had come to Florida instead nine months ago, and they'd spent a lovely week together catching up face-to-face.

They walked toward the baggage claim area, and while they waited for her bag to be unloaded, Joy studied her friend. Soft black waves fell to Sophia's shoulders, framing her face, including her bright blue eyes. As always, she was dressed stylishly but simple. Her white sweater fit her long, thin frame well, and she wore her favorite pair of comfy black slacks. She'd exchanged her usual flats for boots, and wrapped around her neck hung a soft yellow infinity scarf. Her best friend rarely wore colors.

At least, she hadn't before moving here—before finally healing from an abusive past relationship and all the yuck that went with it.

Finally, the carousel started moving, and bags of all shapes and sizes whirred by until Joy spotted hers. When it moved close enough, she stepped forward and lugged the leopard-print suitcase off the conveyor belt.

Sophia chuckled. "That bag is so you."

Yes, with her blond bobbed hair and bright and mostly vintage clothing, Joy's style definitely contrasted with Sophia's. "Whatever do you mean?" Joy's laughter joined her friend's, shaking her long earrings to a tickle along her neck.

It felt good to laugh. The last year hadn't provided much opportunity.

Sophia led her through the doors of the small airport, and a strong wind nearly knocked Joy back against the door, leaving her cheeks tingling. "Whoa. It's a bit chilly out here."

"I warned you it'd be colder than Florida."

They high-tailed it through the parking lot.

"You said the average temp would be fifty degrees." A glimpse at the sky showed full gray clouds threatening to burst. Hopefully the weather would make a turn for the better on Sophia's wedding day.

Sophia clicked a button on her key fob, and the lights of a blue sedan flashed. She popped the trunk and slid Joy's luggage inside. "The operative word being 'average.' It's rained nearly every day this month so far. I don't know what I was thinking, having a wedding in December."

They both climbed into the front seats of the car. How strange to see the wheel on the right side of the car. Sophia started the engine, and heat began to pour from the vents.

Joy buckled her seat belt. "You wanted a Christmas wedding. The most romantic time of year and all that."

"Yeah, but the weather is the most gorgeous here in the summertime. At least, that's my favorite season so far. But maybe that's just because it's when I first moved here."

"And met William," Joy teased.

A small smile quirked at the corner of Sophia's lips. "That too." The lemon air freshener dangling from the rearview mirror gently swung as her friend pulled out from the parking lot. "Oh well. If it's overcast and gloomy on my wedding day, or rains all day, or whatever the case may be, at the end of it all, I'll be Mrs. William Rose and that's what matters."

"Exactly. And then you'll have a lovely ten-day honeymoon in Italy before William has to start the spring term." Given her love of books and that she owned a bookstore, Sophia marrying a literature professor was perfect.

"It'll all work out." Sophia kept her eyes on the road, but

despite her own tiredness, Joy didn't miss the tremble in her friend's lips.

"What's wrong?"

"Can't keep anything from you, can I?"

"No, and you'd better not try." Joy spotted a sign for an overlook. According to Sophia, Port Willis was only about a half hour from the airport, but once they arrived at the small village, she suspected they'd be overrun with "curious" neighbors and local gossips out to meet the newcomer. "Pull over here and let's talk."

"Bossy as ever, I see." But Sophia did as Joy had asked.

"As your best friend and maid of honor, I'm allowed to be." Not only that, but considering their nine-year age difference, Joy had always looked at Sophia as the younger sister she'd never had.

When they reached the lookout point and climbed from the car, Joy had to keep her jaw from dropping. The Gulf back home was beautiful in its own right but nothing like the view in front of her. They stood on a grassy bluff, and the ocean pounded the cliffs below so hard that water misted her face. The roar of the ocean was strong but not angry—a reminder that Joy was a part of this world but not its driving force.

She breathed in the fresh air and hunkered into her newly purchased neon orange parka. The pockets warmed her hands as she turned to Sophia. "Well? Spill."

Sophia folded her arms across her chest. "It's nothing big, really. Just stress, I think. Running a bookstore during the holidays and planning a wedding is just much more than I anticipated."

"Hasn't your mom helped?" Sandy Barrett was a well-known event planner who specialized in weddings.

"As much as she can, but there's only so much she can do from Phoenix. She doesn't have contacts over here, and she's busy with her own events. In fact, she won't even be out here until the day after Christmas because she has a major event on Christmas Eve that was already planned when we chose our wedding date. She offered to hand it off to another coordinator, but I insisted she keep the engagement for the bride's sake." Sophia rocked back and forth on her heels. "I've kind of regretted being so generous, though. There's still so much to do before the wedding, and I just feel like there's no possible way to get everything done in time."

"When is Ginny getting into town?" One of the other bridesmaids—and the groom's former sister-in-law—American Ginny Rose was now a culinary student in London. She'd been Sophia's first friend in Port Willis.

"This weekend. In time for the bachelorette party."

"I can't wait to meet her." Joy nudged Sophia with her hip and slid a hand around her waist. "And I'm here now, so just give me a list and I'll go to town."

"Really?"

"Of course. What did you think I came here to do? Lounge around and eat bonbons all day?"

"What is a bonbon anyway?" Sophia's arms came around Joy once more and she squeezed. "I don't know what I'd do without you. Seriously. Even though I love my life here, I've missed you so incredibly much."

"I've missed you too. Life has been ..." Joy quieted as thoughts of her mother, her father, and assisted living facilities spiraled through her mind. But she was here for Sophia, not to have a pity party about the direction her own life had taken. Her own failures. "So, now that that problem's solved—"

"Not so fast. I'm such a terrible friend. I didn't even ask you how your mom is doing. Just plowed ahead with my own problems. Please forgive me."

The smell of rain and wet earth tinged the air. "You have a lot going on."

"But you do too. So, how is she?"

Joy just shrugged. "About the same as the last time we talked. Dad is considering moving them into an assisted living facility."

"And what do you think about that?"

She didn't want to discuss this, or her guilt over leaving Mom would become evident. "I—"

A fat drop of water hit the ground in front of them followed by a hundred more.

They ran back to the car, ducking inside as fast as possible.

Sophia reached in the backseat and handed Joy a towel. "I've gotten used to these spur-of-the-moment deluges by now. I come prepared."

"Nice." Joy used the towel to dab her face and hands dry. "So, this list of last-minute things. Is it stuff I can handle on my own?"

Sophia's forehead scrunched. "Most of them, I think. It's just a lot of random little things that simply have to be done, like picking up the groom's gift I ordered for William, meeting with the venue coordinator to run through the order of events for the ceremony and reception, calling all of the vendors and confirming the details. But with this huge holiday sale I have going at the bookshop, I'm swamped with orders and trying to get them shipped out in time for Christmas. Not to mention working the front desk. My seasonal employee had a family emergency, so William's been filling in when he can, but ..."

"Have no fear, friend." Joy handed her the towel. "Together, we've got this."

Yes, a to-do list was the perfect way to remind herself of why she'd come—and to justify leaving her parents to do so.

CHAPTER 3

No wonder Sophia was stressed.

Joy took the wedding to-do list in hand, stuffed it into her jacket pocket, and stepped out of Rosebud Books's front door. Despite the sun shining through a lightly clouded sky, the air whipped against her coat and gave her a reason to hurry. Still, she didn't want to miss any details of this small fishing village on the Cornish coast.

Port Willis seemed everything Sophia had described—quaint, with shops new and old lining the main thoroughfare, stunning views to rival the most breathtaking of locales, and affable townspeople who had come to greet their bookshop owner's best friend the moment they'd arrived in town the day before. But even more than its physical structure and residents, there was something remarkable about its essence. Somehow this centuries-old place that smelled of salt spray and fudge breathed newness into Joy's spirit.

"Hullo! Pleasant day, isn't it?" A male grocer tipped his head toward Joy then returned to tidying his display of apples and oranges in the wooden crates outside his store.

"It's beautiful."

Moving past Trengrouse Bakery and the local bank, she continued walking down High Street—or up, rather. The road led from one end of town to another, ending at the docks, which were currently behind her. Last night, Sophia and William had taken Joy to a favorite restaurant down that way, and afterward they'd stood on the short pier in the moonlight. Despite the cold temperature, there had been something soothing in the sway of the dock, the gentle rocking of the boats. And when William had slipped his arms around Sophia's shoulders, and her friend had leaned back against him, Joy's heart had nearly burst with contentment. How she had wished for such a man for her friend, who had suffered so much pain.

And now, to focus on helping her friend have the wedding day of her dreams. Joy shook herself from the memory and continued climbing the steep road toward the antique shop where Mrs. Mavis Lincoln was holding Sophia's groom gift for William.

Seeing the sign for the store, Joy hustled across the road and pushed her way through the door. Instant warmth greeted her, as did Mariah Carey singing about what she wanted for Christmas. The upbeat but modern tune seemed a jarring contrast to the shop, which was stuffed to the brim with treasures from every bygone era. In front of her, a large wardrobe that reminded her of the one from those Narnia movies appropriately welcomed her into this other world. Surrounding that, knickknacks of all kinds called to her—everything from a stack of ceramic chinaware to mid-century chairs and a collection of antique purses, including one vintage beaded bag that practically screamed her name.

To her left sat an artfully arranged display of Victorian Christmas cards. Joy's fingers itched to flip through them. But no, she had a job to do …

Okay, a few moments wouldn't hurt anything.

She removed her gloves and stashed them in her purse then

slid her fingers over one card with rounded edges and a now-faded but once-vibrant picture of Santa feeding grain to a flock of hunting geese. Flipping to the next card, she couldn't hold in a giggle at the strange illustration that depicted two large mice fighting over a piece of hard candy the same size as them.

As she held up the card to see it better, a small yip startled her into dropping it. Joy turned around to find a medium-sized white dog sitting on its haunches and staring at her. He wasn't menacing at all, just curious, his head cocked, one ear standing on end.

Joy bent slowly to pick up and replace the card in its case then knelt once more near the dog, holding out her hand, palm down. "Hi, boy. Are you the local guard dog?"

"More like lap dog."

Her head rose to find the owner of the British accent—and Joy nearly did a double take.

Behind the dog stood a forty-something man around six feet tall, with broad shoulders, a neatly trimmed beard, and rich brown eyes that reminded her of her favorite coffee beans. He wore a nice pair of dark blue jeans and a long-sleeved, collared shirt underneath a black sweater vest. On anyone else, his style would have appeared boring to Joy, but on him it seemed classy. "H-hi."

H-hi? Seriously? She was forty-two, not fourteen.

But when a woman saw a man who was a cross between Henry Cavill and Gerard Butler, apparently it rendered her unable to speak.

Especially when that man wasn't wearing a ring on his left hand. Yeah, she hadn't been able to stop herself from looking.

Don't be ridiculous, Joy. Focus on the dog.

Right. The dog. She swung her gaze back to the adorable little mutt, who looked at the man as if waiting for a cue. Finally, he sniffed the air then rose to approach. He was missing a back leg and hopped over to her.

"Oh my goodness, you are just the cutest, aren't you?" she murmured.

The dog bumped his head against her hand and she was a goner. "What's your name, sweetness?"

"Don't let him fool you." The man came closer and lowered himself into a squat.

The scent of his cologne—an Oriental mixture of cinnamon, vanilla, and something else she couldn't quite name—drifted toward her. Joy bit her lip to hold in a sigh of pleasure at smelling the extremely masculine and yet cultured fragrance.

Oy vey.

He continued. "His name is Rascal, and he owns it. He will steal you blind if you ever happen to leave your food unattended. Isn't that right, old chap?" As the man scratched between Rascal's ears, the dog's tongue lolled out.

"Well, I don't blame him. Dog food just isn't that appealing when there's a burger to be had, right, Rascal?" She ran her hand down his soft fur, the motion bringing pricks of tears to her eyes. It had nearly broken her heart to give up her dogs when she'd moved in with her parents, but she'd managed to find good homes for all of them.

At the man's lack of reply, Joy snuck a glance at him.

He studied her for a moment then cleared his throat and stood. "Sorry he interrupted your browsing. Can I help you find something specific?"

Joy followed suit, brushing off a few strands of dog fur as she rose. "It's no trouble at all. And, actually, I'm here to pick up an order."

"All right. If you'll just follow me, I can get you squared away." He whistled and Rascal was at his side in seconds.

She followed as he threaded his way through the tiny aisles of the shop, finally arriving at a desk with a register.

The man pulled a stack of order cards from a box. Wow, old-fashioned—how appropriate for an antique store. "What name is the order under?"

"Sophia Barrett."

He looked up and a grin split his chiseled face. "Ah, the bride to be. It's a pleasure to meet you."

A laugh sputtered from Joy's lips. "She is indeed a pleasure to meet, but I'm not her." She offered a handshake. "Joy Beckman. The maid of honor."

Something twinkled in his eye. "My mistake. Oliver Lincoln." He took her hand and for a moment, she thought he might bend forward to kiss it.

She held her breath until he released his hold.

O-kay. Time to cut back on the BBC miniseries episodes, then.

Joy folded her hands in front of her. "Lincoln, you said? So, you're related to the owner?"

Oliver dug through the stack of cards. "She's my aunt. I live in London, but she's been having some health difficulties the last few months. Her gout is taking its toll, I'm afraid. Since I'm a groomsman in the wedding, I was already planning to come to town, so I decided to make an extended holiday of it to get my aunt back on her feet." He pulled a card from the stack. "Here it is. That took long enough. I've tried convincing her to upgrade to a computer records system, but she won't hear of it. I'll return in a moment."

As he wandered through a curtained door, Joy blew out a breath. A man who owned a three-legged dog *and* gave up time to help a sick aunt. Whew.

She absolutely, 100 percent could *not* mention this little meeting to Sophia, or Joy would never hear the end of it. No man had turned her head in … well, never like this. In her twenties, she'd been busy with school. She'd tried some online dating in her thirties but quickly decided that was not for her. One too many dates had spent the entire dinner whining about their exes, and Joy—therapist that she was—had helped them figure out the root of their relationship woes. Each time, they'd been back into their ex-girlfriend's good graces before dessert had arrived.

A long time ago, Joy had come to realize that singleness was her lot in life. And for the most part, she was actually okay with being everyone's friend. A helper to all.

So why was she reacting so strangely to Oliver?

"It must be the jet lag."

"What's that, love?" The man himself returned to the room just in time to hear Joy muttering to herself.

"Uh, nothing." And there she went biting her lip again at the way he'd called her "love."

Stop it, Joy. It's just something the English say.

She zeroed in on the item in Oliver's hands. "Is that the gift?"

"It is—and a nice one at that." He slid the rosewood case across the desk and popped it open to reveal an antique fountain pen.

"Oh, that's perfect for William. He's going to love it." Joy had spoken to Sophia's fiancé a lot over the last year—several times when Sophia wasn't around—so she could ascertain whether he truly had her friend's best interests at heart.

Every time, he'd passed her tests with flying colors.

"Absolutely." He snapped the box closed and placed it in a bag for Joy. "My mate sure does love his books and writing."

"How long have you been friends?"

"I grew up here in Port Willis before my parents moved us to London when I was in year eleven. William is five years younger and was friends with my brother Ben. But then he and I ended up at uni together when I was a postgrad student and stayed in touch even when he moved back here and I stayed put." Oliver handed the bag to Joy.

She did the math in her head as well as she could. William

was thirty-six or thirty-seven, so that would make Oliver in his early forties. Just like her.

Move along, Joy. "That's wonderful. Friendships are everything." She took the bag from him, and her fingers brushed his.

Nat King Cole serenaded her from somewhere up high.

Oliver's eyes locked with hers. "Yes, they are."

A moment passed before she could eke another word past the lump in her throat. "So I guess I'll be seeing you around?"

"I hope so."

"Me too. I'm sure we will, with the wedding activities and such."

And as she turned to leave, one thought worked hard to poke through the romantic wall she'd built around her heart—friendships were important, indeed.

But sometimes, they weren't quite enough.

And other times, they simply had to be.

CHAPTER 4

"And this is the main street." Joy flipped the camera on her iPhone so her parents could see her surroundings. It was only 7:00 p.m. on a Thursday, but the streets were deserted, nearly everyone having gone home or into a pub for dinner.

Every storefront glimmered with an assortment of twinkle lights hung round their doors and framing their picture windows. Wreaths with red bows had been pinned to most of the streetlamps—the historical wrought-iron kind, with a hanging inverted cone of glass. The only thing missing was a blanket of snow, and Joy would have sworn she'd stepped into a town from one of those cheesy Christmas movies she secretly couldn't stop watching.

She maneuvered the phone to face the ocean then toward a prominent hill overlooking the village. "Just up that way is the local lighthouse. It doesn't work anymore, but apparently it's open for the public to explore."

"Where did she go?" Her mom's voice drifted from the phone. "Why can't I see her anymore?"

Joy hit the reverse button on the screen and switched back to selfie mode. "I'm here, Mom."

"Oh, hon, I was just telling your dad that you'd disappeared." Her mother sat up in the hospital bed, her eyes clear. A good day after several bad ones, according to her dad's daily report.

And Joy was missing it.

She continued walking down High Street toward Sophia's cottage, located just behind the bookstore. Thanks to finishing up yet another item on her friend's to-do list, Joy had already been running late for dinner before calling her parents. But she couldn't stand going another minute without connecting with them.

"Sorry, Mom. I was just trying to show you the town. I'll take lots of pictures and send them to you. It's kind of dark now." The Cornish sunset was obscenely early in December—it began around four fifteen, with nightfall complete by five thirty or so. But tonight a heaven full of stars glittered above her, a thousand diamonds rejoicing in anticipation of Sophia's nuptials approaching in nine short days.

"That'd be nice, dear." Mom's voice started to drift, her eyes to dim.

No, stay with me. "I miss you guys. I'm so sorry I'm not there."

Dad poked his head into the frame. "We miss you, but it sounds like you are having a wonderful time."

"Wonderful time? Where is she? Joy? Honey? Why aren't you here?" Mom's wail projected from the phone and flooded the nearly empty streets—and Joy's heart.

"Mom …"

"We're going to go, all right, JoJo? Talk to you soon." And with that, Dad hung up the phone, leaving Joy in the silence.

Her lips trembled and she shut her eyes for a moment, breathing in, out, deep, strong. There wasn't anything she could do for Mom from here but pray Dad could get her calmed down.

Joy pocketed her phone and increased her speed, feet aching as she walked downhill. Maybe her yellow T-strap heels hadn't been the most practical choice for a day of running errands in a town nearly as hilly as San Francisco, but they went so well with her black A-line pocket dress dotted with pictures of tiny cacti and tied at the waist with a large yellow belt. Accented by black leggings, a red cardigan, and dangling cactus earrings, the outfit was one of her favorites.

Too bad she'd had to slightly diminish its effect by throwing her puffy parka on top, but Joy was smart enough to forego fashion for warmth when necessary, especially since they'd already experienced a dip in the temperature since she'd arrived two days ago. In fact, according to Sophia, temps would continue to decrease during Joy's visit. Meteorologists were even calling for snow around Christmas, which hadn't happened in fifteen or so years.

A door closed and a bell jangled somewhere nearby as she hurried toward her destination.

"Joy. Hey! Hold on."

She stopped so abruptly at the sound of Oliver's voice that a small smattering of loose gravel caught her unaware. Joy twisted on her heel and fell onto her rump. In moments, a wet tongue licked her face.

"Thanks, Rascal." She nuzzled the dog and looked up into Oliver's face—the one she hadn't been able to get out of her mind since she'd first seen it yesterday.

"Are you all right?" He offered his hand to her.

She took it, and he hoisted her upright. "Other than a little wounded pride, yeah. I'm good." Joy inspected her leggings and found a small hole near the ankle. She pointed to it. "I take it back. My day is ruined. I will never recover."

Oliver's lips twisted in humor. "You must allow me to buy you another pair."

Joy laughed. "That's sweet, but these can't be replaced, unfortunately."

"They're that expensive?" His question wasn't one of concern, just curiosity—not surprising, considering his blue sport coat looked as if it cost a pretty penny.

"No, they were probably two dollars at Goodwill. But it's the memories surrounding them that can't be replaced." Like when she and Sophia bought them and tried to have a *Sisterhood of the Traveling Pants* moment … and they'd been more like long shorts on her friend. Oh, how they'd laughed.

Or the time when she'd spilled salsa on the leggings during a recent movie night with Mom. Joy had chosen *You've Got Mail,* one of Mom's favorites, and they'd curled close together on the couch until her mother had fallen asleep.

Yes, that was a memory she'd be going back to over and over in the coming months, something to hold onto when the grief and trials seemed fiercest.

Hands in his pockets, Oliver leaned against a lamppost. "Your smile turned quite serious just then."

"I was just thinking about my mom."

His silence in response urged her to continue.

Huh. That was usually *her* tactic to keep clients talking. Funny thing was, she wanted to share her heart with this almost-stranger.

He was throwing her off balance in more ways than one.

It really was getting cold out here. She folded her arms across her chest to try to get warm. "I'm sorry. I'd love to chat, but I need to get going. I'm late."

"Are you heading to Sophia's by chance? Because so am I."

"Really?"

"Really." He eased off the lamp and started walking, whistling for Rascal to follow. "So if you don't mind the company …"

"No, not at all." *I'd enjoy it quite a bit, actually.*

Oh, brother.

Rascal flew past them. The dog navigated the steep hill just fine despite his missing limb, somehow managing much better than Joy in her heels. Her toes squished at the front of her shoes and burned.

"Can I assist you down the hill?"

How was it he'd noticed her difficulty but hadn't made her feel bad about her silly choice in footwear? This guy was racking up the points.

Points that meant absolutely nothing, because, well, she was leaving in ten or so days. And despite that it had already literally happened, she would *not* allow herself metaphorically to fall head over heels for the first time in forever—not with someone who was un-keepable.

But still. She appreciated his thoughtfulness.

"Considering I don't want to end up with a scraped face or broken limb just before I have to stand in front of a hundred people at my best friend's wedding ... sure. Thanks." Joy took his arm and allowed him to support her down the hill. Her head only came to his shoulder, but their arms rubbed against each other as they maneuvered toward their destination.

Maybe she should pat herself on the back for selecting these shoes after all.

He's just being nice, Joy.

Right. Back to reality. Again. "So, you said you were in town to help your aunt. How is she?"

"She's doing a little better. Thanks for asking."

"Are you caring for her alone?"

"My parents are coming down after Christmas and staying for a few weeks, but for right now, I'm all she has. Which isn't much, I'm afraid. I don't know quite what to do other than ask her what she needs and fetch it for her."

"And help keep her business running." They passed a fudge shop and Joy inhaled. The smell of the chocolate wafted outside despite the CLOSED sign on the white door. "That's vital for a small business owner."

"As I well know."

"Oh?"

Oliver cleared his throat. "I own my business as well."

"Yeah? I used to own a women's counseling practice."

"Two peas in a pod, then, eh?"

She couldn't help the grin that overtook her at the old-fashioned idiom her mom used to say all the time. "What kind of business do you own?"

"An accounting firm."

"Oooh, yeah, so I don't think we're the same after all. I hate math."

"Pity. What was your favorite subject in school?"

"Does recess count?"

A guffaw rent the air. "You like socializing, do you?"

"I mean, I *did* choose a career where I listen to people talk all day, right?"

"I'm quite the opposite. If I could stay tucked away in my office all day long, I would. So long as I had Rascal with me, that is."

"He's such a sweetheart."

At that, Rascal stopped and turned then yipped in agreement. Oliver and Joy laughed.

"You're a dog person, I can tell."

"I used to have six dogs. Each one was a rescue next on the list to be euthanized before I took them home." She sighed, her joviality gone. "I may never have children, but those dogs were my babies. I couldn't bring them with me when I moved—"

"Moved?"

They reached the bottom of the hill. Oliver released her arm.

See? Just being a gentleman.

A breeze ruffled the bottom of Joy's dress, bringing a chill with it that left her shivering for a moment.

"I left Phoenix about sixteen months ago and moved to Florida to help care for my mom after she was diagnosed with Alzheimer's. My parents are seventy-nine and eighty, so it was difficult but necessary. And six dogs wouldn't have brought the peace my mom needs right now."

Oliver squeezed her elbow, and Joy was struck with the sudden desire to snuggle deep into his arms, to see if he'd be as warm and gentle as he appeared. "That's amazing."

"My parents are the amazing ones. I'm just blessed I get to be there with them."

He shook his head as if in disbelief. "I'm in awe and I barely know you."

"Don't be too impressed. Remember, I'm also the one who can't walk down a hill by herself. So …"

His eyes roamed her face. "I think I could learn a lot from you."

"And I'm sure I could from you too." She said it casually, though with his eyes searching hers, she felt anything but.

"Then ask. Whatever you'd like. I'm an open book."

She tilted her head. "Why do I get the feeling that's not always true?"

His strong jaw clenched as if she'd hit upon a nerve with her words. "It may not be always true, but it's true right now. You're easy to talk to, you know. Must be the therapist in you." Oliver paused. "Or maybe it's just you." The whispered words floated toward her on the breeze.

They stood under another lamppost outside Sophia's house, and the glow hid half of his face in shadow. The moment felt private, hidden … theirs.

She needed to lighten said moment. Now.

"I get that a lot." Joy forced a smile and pointed to Sophia's house behind them. "Shall we?"

"Indeed."

Rascal led them across the road, and when they reached the front door, Joy let them in. "Soph! Sorry I'm late."

Sophia's head popped around the corner. "Hey! Oh good, you found Oliver." Her friend's eyes lit with interest as she looked between them.

Busted.

Joy strode forward. "How can I help with dinner?" Once she was in the kitchen, she noticed William chatting with a red-headed man at the tiny table.

"You didn't think I actually cooked tonight, right?" Sophia leaned forward and pulled three pizza boxes from the oven.

"I know you better than that. But you guys could have eaten."

William and the man at the table stopped talking. Sophia's fiancé stood and walked toward them, stooping way down to give Joy a hug. "Hey, mates. Good of you to come." He adjusted his glasses before reaching over to slap Oliver on the back then slipped his arm around Sophia's shoulders.

The red-haired man stood as well, his jeans and hoodie making him seem underdressed next to Oliver and William, who was never without a collared shirt or sweater of some sort. "I don't think we've met."

"Ah, yeah, sorry." William ran a hand through his dark blond curls. "Joy, this is my mate and groomsman Steven Applegate. Steven, this is Joy Beckman, Sophia's maid of honor. And you know Oliver."

"Pleasure." Steven shook Joy's hand.

"Likewise. I've heard a lot about you."

"All good things, I hope."

"Of course." Joy turned and lifted her eyebrows at Sophia, whose lips twitched. Yes, good things, indeed. According to Sophia, Steven and her friend Ginny were perfect for each other but weren't in a relationship beyond friendship.

"How about we eat and talk? I'm starving. The bookstore

was a madhouse today." Sophia kissed William on the cheek then opened the top of the pizza boxes.

"I see you got a sausage and pineapple." Joy pinched Sophia's side. "Weirdo."

"She's not weird. Just unique." William winked at Joy.

"Toe-may-toe, toe-mah-toe." Joy snagged some paper plates from the counter, handing one to each person in the room. They all dug in.

William lifted his soda water in the air. "A toast."

"What are we toasting?" Sophia asked.

"Love—and all the unlikely places it can lead."

Everyone clinked cups and cans together.

Joy felt eyes settle on her. Lifting her head, she met Oliver's gaze.

"Hear, hear." He threw back his soft drink with abandon.

Even though she knew she probably shouldn't indulge the butterflies fluttering their tiny wings in her stomach, Joy smiled, nodded, and took a hefty sip of her drink.

CHAPTER 5

"Girl, he couldn't keep his eyes off of you the entire night." Sophia slapped a label on a box of books headed for London then scooted it aside to make room for another on the bookstore's front counter. "He's single, you know."

Despite the guys staying at Sophia's until eleven the night before, the two women had risen early and headed to the bookstore before it opened. Overnight, twenty more orders had come in for rare books—Rosebud's specialty—and Sophia was determined to get the local ones shipped in time for Christmas.

Joy rolled her eyes and ran her finger down a printed inventory list. "You're just in matchmaker mode thanks to your almost-wedded bliss." Finding the title she sought, she crossed it out with a Sharpie.

As she took a sip from her third cup of coffee, her eyes roamed the store. Joy had never been much of a reader—movies and TV shows were her jam—but there was something calming about being here, in a place that honored story.

Classy Christmas decor enhanced the already peaceful feeling of the shop's cozy, small-town atmosphere. A medium-sized tree perched in the front window display, and books wrapped with large bows were stacked artistically underneath the lowest limbs. On the front counter to the left of the register, Sophia had placed a simple Willow Tree nativity—understated but in a place of prominence. The crowning touch was the continuous strand of fairy lights strung from bookcase to bookcase, creating a soft glow that hummed in the pre-dawn hours.

"That's not true. There was something there." Her best friend blew a strand of hair out of her face as she taped up a new box and set to carefully wrapping two books with frayed covers. "Don't even try to deny it."

Joy clutched the list of orders in her fist. "I'll be right back."

She whisked away from her friend's knowing gaze. Bookcases surrounded her, towering over her short frame. As she took another look at the list in her hand, jazzy Christmas music spilled from well-hidden speakers.

Joy wandered the bookshop's aisles until she found the first book on the list. As she delicately plucked it from the shelf, an expanding ray of morning light drew her eyes upward to the large windows over the loft area, where customers flocked during business hours to study, chat with others, or simply enjoy reading. The rising sun streaked beams of light through the store, adding a new depth, a new perspective.

Things always looked different in the light.

Because last night, she might have actually agreed with Sophia about Oliver's eyes on her. She'd felt a warmth, like the soft glow of sunrise, from his gaze. When she'd look his way, there was this quiet connection between them—like he understood her.

Of course, this morning she felt nothing but foolish. How could he understand her? They'd met a grand total of two times.

With quick steps, she found two more books and hauled her load back to the counter, glancing at the clock as she passed. The shop was set to open in forty-five minutes, and after helping Sophia here, Joy had to make numerous phone calls to confirm vendors. Enough thinking. They'd better get cracking.

Sophia's hands waited by the printer to snatch a label as it slid out. "I didn't get a chance last night to ask how your parents are doing."

At least she'd changed the subject. Though a supportive friend, Sophia had never understood Joy's acceptance of the single life. A few years ago, she'd even threatened to create a profile for her on an online dating site. Thankfully, Joy's stink eye had been enough to scare Sophia away from that scheme.

"Mom actually had a good day yesterday. So that was encouraging." Joy slid the books she'd collected onto the front desk then snagged the order list.

"Did they say anything else about the possibility of assisted living?"

"Thank goodness, no." Inspecting the order list, Joy grabbed the first corresponding book then slid it inside a mailer envelope. She located the right printed label and stuck it onto the front of the package.

"Do you think they're still considering it?"

The heater clicked on, whirring somewhere above them. "I hope not." She secured the mailer closed.

"Why don't you want them to move? I know you'll miss living with them, but. . . . "

"It's more than that. Why should they pay thousands of dollars to get the same care I can give?" She pushed away the nagging thought that the levels of care were not as alike as she wished she could claim.

That if her mom had been in a facility with constant professional attention to begin with, she'd never have broken her hip.

"But don't you think it may be good for all of you to have your own space? And for your mom to get some specialized care?" Putting down the book she was holding, Sophia rounded the counter and clasped Joy's hand between her own two.

"You're wonderful, Joy, but you have a PhD in counseling, not medicine. And don't you miss working? You are so talented and you've helped so many people."

"Of course I miss working, but it's just not an option right now. I'm still helping others—my parents." Joy squeezed Sophia's hands and tilted her head, forcing a grin. "I've just found a different path, like you have."

"Yeah, but this path makes me come alive." Sophia's eyes roamed the bookstore, taking in the books, smiling at them like treasured friends. Her gaze rambled back to lock onto Joy, penetrating deeper than anyone else's ever could. "Yours ... well, I think it may be breaking you. I know better than anyone how difficult circumstances can change us, but I worry that yours are dragging you down, and you won't fight it because you feel like you're supposed to go down with the ship."

Joy's lips trembled. "They're my parents."

"I know, friend. But this ... I think maybe it's beyond you."

"No, it's *because* of me." The words popped out before she could stop them. Boo for Sophia and her insightful heart.

"What do you mean?"

Joy pulled away. She had to busy her hands. Now. She snagged the next book and started packaging it.

Sophia rounded the counter and worked alongside Joy in silence. Waited.

Her friend had experienced heartache Joy couldn't imagine, yet she hadn't allowed it to turn her bitter. She'd found a way through the pain, the mess.

And she'd allowed Joy to walk with her through it.

Why did Joy have such trouble allowing Sophia to do the same for her?

She picked up an old copy of *Sense & Sensibility*, brought it to her nose, and inhaled the musty-but-not-in-any-way-disgusting smell of paper and ink that had been forged with story. Sophia believed the written word could heal.

And Joy knew from experience the spoken ones could too.

"It's because of me that Dad wants to move Mom into assisted living."

Sophia's hands stilled and she turned toward Joy, eyes filling with her trademark compassion.

Joy took a breath and continued. "It was my day to be with Mom. Dad was exhausted so I told him to run errands, see his doctor, do whatever he needed to do. That we'd be fine." Joy's thumb ran from the bottom to the top pages along the open edge of the book in her hand.

After she was quiet for half a minute, Sophia tucked her hair behind her ears and softly prodded. "What happened?"

Joy set the book down again. "I guess I was more tired than I thought." Memories of that day flooded in, and the story flowed from her lips.

The terror she'd felt at waking from an unintended nap to find her mother vanished. The mounting panic when Mom was missing for one hour, then two, then five. The overwhelming relief at getting a call from the police that they'd found her nearly a mile away—but then the crashing weight of guilt when they told her that, just before being discovered, Mom had stepped off a curb.

She'd broken her hip from the fall and been scheduled for surgery the next morning.

Joy couldn't wipe away the remembrance of her mother's whimpers of pain in the following weeks as she'd recovered, of her mother's confusion over her physical limitations and surroundings, especially once she'd been moved into the skilled nursing facility where she now resided.

"Oh, Joy." Sophia's arms came around her, and her friend's tears dripped onto her neck. Or maybe those were Joy's own.

Finally, Sophia released her hold and snagged a box of tissues from under the counter. She pulled one out for herself and offered the box to Joy, who grabbed a tissue and wiped her eyes.

Her friend studied her. "Do you remember what you told me time and time again when I blamed myself for David's abuse?"

"That it wasn't your fault."

"Yes." Sophia balled the tissue in her fist. "And it's not yours either."

"It's different, though. This is my responsibility. My privilege. And I'm so afraid ..."

"Of not being needed?"

"What? No." Joy paused. "Maybe. I don't know." She looked down at her hands. Little flecks of white tissue stuck to her damp fingertips.

"Joy, you're always taking care of other people. It's who you are. But you also need to take care of yourself."

How many times had she preached that same thought to her clients? Joy sighed. "I recognize that. But I have no idea how in this case. Doing one kind of negates the other."

"I can see how you might feel that way, but I think it's still possible."

"How?"

"First, by telling yourself the truth. Fight against the notion that you're to blame for all of this. Alzheimer's is an unfortunate part of life, and I can't imagine how hard it is to watch your mom and dad go through that. Is it okay to embrace the sadness of the situation? To be angered by the injustice of it? Yes, of course. But don't take on guilt that you weren't meant to wear."

The ever-empathetic Sophia sniffled and her voice shook. "And second, maybe do something small for yourself. You could apply for a few jobs, just to see what happens."

"I don't know ..."

"Well, I do." That stubborn lift of Sophia's chin reminded Joy a bit of herself when she knew she was right about something. "And I also know that we can't see all the doors opened to us if we aren't looking or only focus on the path we've set before ourselves. Look around, friend. Explore. See what's out there."

That seemed impossible. Still … "You're right."

"Yes, I am." Sophia's eyes sparked. "And I'm not just talking about a job, you know."

Of course she wasn't.

Visions from last night replayed in Joy's mind. Of Oliver watching her as she'd joked with Sophia. Of his quiet smile that communicated so much more than a loud laugh ever could. Of the way her stomach had bottomed out when he'd leaned down to hug her goodnight.

It'd been a quick embrace—that of a new friend—but it had nearly knocked her off her feet. Again.

There was no denying she was attracted to him, but how did he feel? And what did it matter? She was leaving here before the year was up, going back to her parents who needed her.

Her path *was* set and no amount of Hallmark-laced notions of romance would change that.

Joy screwed her face into an appropriate glare and tossed her tissue at Sophia's face. "Hey, I'm supposed to be the older, much wiser friend, remember? Stop telling me what to do." She winked then turned to snatch the mailing labels from the printer. "Now, let's finish up here, or you're never going to get all of these mailed today."

Her friend opened her mouth as if to say something then snapped it shut. Shaking her head, she joined Joy in packaging the last of the orders.

CHAPTER 6

Out here, her troubles seemed far away.

The ocean roared in her ears as Joy walked with arms outstretched, shoulders back—finally loosened. Her fingertips skimmed the tall brown grass as she headed up the hill toward the lighthouse that stood sentinel over Port Willis.

After picking up some peanut butter fudge from Betty's Fudge Shoppe for the bachelorette party the next night, Joy's feet—and, she supposed, her heart—had led her here.

Here, where the darkening sky of late afternoon met the grassy bluffs that boasted a picturesque view of the foamy Atlantic waters. Joy stopped and veered off the dirt path just slightly, stepping close to the cliff's edge and peering down. More white than blue, the water swirled close to the rocky land below.

Gray clouds rolled across the horizon, gathering like soldiers ready to march. It looked like rain might find her again, but having lived in Arizona for fifteen years before moving to Florida, she welcomed the moisture, loved the way it fed the beauty of the land around her.

Wind whipped her short hair back and forth across the tops of her ears, rendering her bobby pins useless.

But the cold outside couldn't match the warmth inside her. The day had been a busy one, with all the calls she'd made and errands she'd run for Sophia, so she hadn't had much time to consider what her friend had suggested this morning at the bookstore. Now, though, she'd spent the one-mile walk from town to the lighthouse praying, seeking.

Sophia had always spoken of this place with reverence, saying it's where she'd first started to hear God speaking to her again last year. And Joy could believe it—here, away from the village, it was so quiet. Made it easier to listen. Easier to hear.

She still didn't have any of the answers, but maybe that wasn't the point.

Joy turned and continued her ascent toward the lighthouse. After the last rise, the land flattened and the lighthouse soared over her. The round tower structure jutted into the sky, the stark white calm of its bricks a contrast with the battering ocean that threw itself violently against the lighthouse's outer walls.

As she approached, she noticed a wooden sign hung on the bright red door. Squinting in the waning light, she read its carved words.

Port Willis Lighthouse
Open sunrise to sunset
The lighthouse is no longer in service, but exploration is welcome so long as you have a care.
Please mind your step and enter at your own risk.
Maintained by the Port Willis Historical Society

Eyeing the clouds, Joy frowned. She should probably hurry back to the bookstore before the storm broke—Sophia undoubtedly could use her help with the last few hours of a fire sale—but something pulled her toward exploring, just as the sign had suggested.

Her friend's words from this morning drifted back to her. Sophia was right—she *was* always taking care of others. Her heartbeat quickened just a bit at the thought of crossing the threshold into the lighthouse, of enjoying a few moments for herself.

Maybe just a quick looksie wouldn't hurt. Still, she should let Sophia know she'd be along soon. Joy dug around in her canvas messenger bag, pushing aside the box of fudge before she finally found her phone. She snapped a picture of the lighthouse and shot Sophia a text. Then, after shoving the phone back inside her bag, she opened the door and stepped inside.

The air felt like it'd been trapped inside a freezer for weeks and only just released. Joy hurried toward the winding stone staircase. The bottom step was chipped, and no handrail guarded visitors from falling, though only ten to twenty steps were visible from below before they curved and connected with two walls on either side. This place had to be at least a hundred years old if not more.

She walked the steps, which were taller than most conventional ones. They clearly hadn't considered short people when designing this lighthouse. Joy had to pause a few times when she got off balance from the strain of constant rising, but eventually the steps ended and a medium-sized watch room opened before her. Joy strode toward the huge window that seemed to take up the entire wall opposite the steps. From here, she could see tiny Port Willis nestled into the bluffs, its harbor outfitted with bobbing fishing boats of all colors and sizes.

As she turned her gaze toward the ocean, one large plink of rain turned into several and then hundreds within seconds. Waves rolled in from the outer rims of the ocean, higher than she'd seen in the three days she'd been here. Despite being encased in rock and steel and whatever else comprised the lighthouse, she heard the whistle and whine of the wind as it whisked between the cracks of the old place.

Joy placed her hand against the window, cold penetrating her skin. She closed her eyes and listened.

"Joy."

Her eyes popped open and she turned to find Oliver standing at the top of the steps, drenched. His thick hair that had been neatly gelled in previous encounters now hung limp across his forehead in curled brown strands. Water fell from his slick black jacket onto the floor where he stood, panting slightly.

"Oliver." Joy rushed toward him. "Are you all right?"

"Just a bit chilled is all."

That had to be an understatement. "What are you doing here?"

His lips curved into a grin even as a shiver seemed to overtake him. "Rescuing you from the storm … or so I thought. But here you are, by all appearances perfectly dry and content." He began to shrug out of his coat.

"Here." She unzipped her parka, slipped it off, and offered it to him before he could protest.

He folded his coat and placed it over a railing underneath the window. Amusement lit his features. "You don't think that will fit me, do you?"

"Well … it's better than freezing." Joy tilted up her chin in playful defiance.

"If I *were* freezing, that may be the case." He waved his hand up and down his body, causing her to look at his clothing for the first time since he'd taken off the coat. Totally dry. His jacket must have been waterproof. "But it was nice of you to offer."

"Oh. Right." Her cheeks flamed as she put on her jacket. "And it was nice of you to come find me. But how did you know I was here?"

"I was in the bookstore shopping for my aunt when Sophia

got your text. I volunteered to make sure you got home in one piece."

He peered down at her, a look on his face she couldn't quite define, just like she couldn't define the twisting of her gut.

She was used to taking care of herself. And totally capable of doing so too. But having someone else looking out for her … she kind of liked it.

Joy shook away from his gaze and pivoted toward the window. "I appreciate it. I know I should have headed back when I saw the storm coming, but I couldn't resist coming up here. I'm glad I didn't miss this view."

Waves pounded against the window, joining the rain in a song with an irregular drumbeat.

"Cornwall is known for its epic storms. Storm watching is actually quite popular in the wintertime." He eased beside her at the window, and his presence filtered heat her way.

"Whenever we get a big storm in Florida, we have to batten down the hatches, as they say. We've only had to board up for a hurricane one time while I've lived there, but I was just thankful it fizzled out before reaching us."

Mom hadn't done well during that one. Her shrieks of terror still reverberated in Joy's consciousness.

"Not a good memory, I take it?"

Was she really that readable, or was he just that perceptive? Joy sighed. "No. My mother … well, it's just difficult to switch roles with her. Going from clinging to her strength to being the rock in the storm."

"I'm sorry for what you're going through." No platitudes, no advice. Just sympathetic words that did more to soothe her heart than he could know.

Her chin quivered and Joy exhaled. "She's always loved storms, my mom. When I was young, she'd come to my room and wake me in the middle of the night, get me all gathered up in blankets, and take me to this big picture window we had. The lightning would zing across the sky, and the thunder would rumble, and my mom would say, 'Look at how powerful our God is. You never have to be afraid of anything because there's not a lightning bolt he doesn't know about, not a drop of rain he doesn't allow to fall.'" Joy fought against the tears. "But guess what? I'm afraid."

Her hand flew to her mouth, trying to stop the words before they came. This was too much to share with someone she'd met only days before, wasn't it?

Oliver tucked an arm around Joy's shoulder, giving her a light squeeze. A steady heartbeat thrummed beneath his chest.

It felt even nicer than she'd imagined.

For just a moment, she allowed herself the comfort, to lean into his embrace. Her eyes tried to peer through the sheets of rain, but Port Willis had become a blur in the deluge. It was only her, Oliver, and this lighthouse.

A pocket of safety in the storm.

She continued. "The thing is, I've always been able to see that the bad things that have happened in my life were somehow blessings in disguise. I can logically recognize that the rain falls on the evil and good alike. Even that our perception of rain and lightning can be flawed. We see only the chaos and destruction, the inconveniences, the way they ruin our plans. But fire and water, they bring life too. Refining. Rejuvenation." Joy shook her head. "Still ... this time, I don't think I want what God seems to have planned for my life."

Oliver squeezed her shoulders tighter, resting his chin on the top of her head, and they stood like that for seconds ... minutes ... Joy lost track. His steady breathing anchored her as the storm slowly abated.

Finally, he spoke. "'None of us can see the way forward in the fog. We simply must take the next step—'"

"And trust that the light will lead us where we need to go." Joy craned her neck up to see Oliver. "You know *The Fog Rolls*

In? That's one of my favorite movies." And it was totally obscure, a film she'd stumbled across on cable one Saturday evening a decade ago. But the story of two best friends who fall in love and then find themselves on opposite sides of a war had grabbed her attention from its first moments.

"I don't even own a copy of it, yet I know every word." Oliver loosened his hold on her shoulders and looked her square in the eyes. "I can't believe you've heard of it."

"Same."

"That quote has always meant a lot to me."

She'd opened up to him but to ask him to do the same meant something different. As a therapist, she always felt bonded to her patients after she heard their stories. And she knew what she asked next might set her up for heartache.

But she asked it anyway. "Why?"

He didn't even hesitate in replying. "There have been times in my life when I didn't know which way to turn. Everything from relationships that led me away from God, to business decisions that I feared making. I lost my first business because of that fear. It took years to rebuild, and now I have dozens of employees who depend upon me to lead them. It's quite a responsibility and one I don't take lightly. One I don't always know how to navigate. But I've promised myself I won't allow fear to be the reason for standing still again."

His Adam's apple bobbed as he swallowed.

Good gravy. She was melting into a puddle of mush. Never in her life had she connected with a man in such an effortless way. In past relationships, it'd been like pulling teeth to get a man to open up emotionally, to share his heart—and it had certainly never happened this quickly.

What was going on?

She opened her mouth to respond to his vulnerability but thanking him didn't feel quite right. What she should do is ask him to go on because she sensed there was more he wanted to tell her.

But if she already felt this close to him after a few days, what would learning *more* about him, his thoughts—his feelings—do to her? Especially when they'd be going their separate ways in a little over a week?

Joy stepped back a bit. "Oliver, I ..." She pursed her lips. "Thank you for coming here. And for listening. But we probably should be heading back."

Though close to setting, the sun had reappeared as if the storm had never happened.

Oliver frowned but nodded. He followed her down the steps and out the door, into the light.

As they walked back to town in silence, one question poked at her. Why in this moment did the sunshine feel almost more frightening than the rain?

CHAPTER 7

Sophia's guest room sat at the back of the tiny house, but Joy could still hear the door bell when it peeled out a jaunty version of "Jingle Bells," the music floating down the hall and under the crack of her closed door.

The bachelorette party was about to begin.

Joy took a deep breath and clicked the SUBMIT button on her laptop before she could change her mind. A confirmation popped up.

THANK YOU FOR SUBSCRIBING TO JOB ALERTS IN YOUR AREA.

Leaning back against the bed's headboard, she closed her laptop, balancing it on her outstretched legs. She didn't know where her attempt at moving forward would go, but she'd taken Sophia's advice.

And now, it was time to attempt to have some fun.

With a renewed sense of gusto, Joy pushed the laptop onto the soft padding of the pillow-top mattress and stood. A quick glimpse in the mirror confirmed her mustard-yellow, high-waisted cigarette pants and tucked-in chevron knit sweater hadn't wrinkled. Joy popped in her favorite pair of green hoop earrings and slipped on some red pumps before she dashed down the hall.

Sophia was in the kitchen with a tall brunette clutching a suitcase. An excitement brewed between them as they spoke in hushed tones.

The clip of Joy's shoes against the wood floors announced her entrance and both women turned.

The brunette, who wore a blue sweatshirt that read THE LONDON CULINARY INSTITUTE, broke out in a huge grin that lit up the room as she rounded the counter and dropped her suitcase to the floor. "Joy!"

Joy laughed, the woman's warmth contagious. "So nice to finally meet you, Ginny."

They hugged as if they'd known each other for years, even though they'd never met in person. But Sophia had connected them from across the ocean.

The bride-to-be threw her arms around them, creating a group hug. "I'm so happy to have you both here with me."

The hug ended and Ginny fairly bounced in her purple Chucks. "And I'm so glad to have that last course behind me."

"Are you almost finished with your program? You're going to be a pastry chef, right?" Joy dug her hand into a bowl of pretzels she'd set out on the counter, along with other snacks essential for a girls night. They were just waiting for Mary—Sophia's third bridesmaid, whose family owned her favorite pub in town—and then they'd head to dinner and come back here afterward for a movie marathon. Joy and Ginny had wanted to do more for Sophia, but she'd said what she really wanted was a quiet evening with her best friends.

Ginny snagged a piece of fudge. "Yep. Just finished, actually, but I have a three-month internship that begins next month. Then I'm done and the sky's the limit."

"I'm so proud of you." Sophia threw her arms around Ginny.

"Maybe once you're done with that, we will see you more often, huh?"

"I wish. That's when the real craziness will begin. If I can do what I want, anyway." Biting into the fudge, Ginny leaned back against the counter.

"And what's that?" The pretzel crunched in Joy's mouth, the saltiness coating her taste buds.

"I'd love to open my own bakery. I can have complete creative control. And I already have experience running a business." She shrugged. "It seems ideal, really."

"I've been trying to convince her to do it here. The Pottery Club next door to the bookstore is closing—the owner is retiring—and it'd be perfect."

Ginny fidgeted and reached for a napkin. "And that sounds amazing, really. I'm just not sure what my future holds, and I don't want to lock myself down." She wiped her fudgy fingers.

"And what you mean by that is ... you don't know what's happening with Steven. Is that it?" Sophia poked Ginny's arm. "Because you promised you'd keep me apprised, yet I've heard *nada* from you on the matter since the last time you visited."

"And when was that?" Joy watched the two women, the ease they had together, and a sharp emotion ensnared her. Not jealousy, exactly. She was glad for them. It was more like wistfulness because Joy had to leave here soon but the two of them would be able to stay.

They had the world in front of them. They'd chosen their paths. Had been transformed by them. They were free.

Joy wanted that for herself but she shouldn't. Because that freedom might take her away from the two people who needed her most right now. And that was a high calling. One worthy of sacrifice.

The memory of Oliver's arm around her the day before at the lighthouse flitted through Joy's mind.

She nudged it away without hesitation.

"September." Pushing off the counter, Ginny sauntered to the couch—only a few steps away, being that the cottage was only a thousand square feet—and sank down onto its soft blue-linen cushions.

Joy and Sophia joined her in the living room, which was surprisingly absent of Christmas decor besides the tree in the corner. Sophia had likely used most of her personal decorations at the bookstore.

"I would have updated you if there were anything to say. Steven has come up to see me in London several times in the last year, and I've come here. And I don't know ... I really like him. Like, I ..." Ginny's lips screwed up on one side, brow furrowed. "I don't know. I may even love him, you guys. The way chocolate chips love cookie dough. But I've been so busy and honestly, I'm scared. He's not Garrett, but I don't want to make any of the same mistakes I made with him either."

Sophia reached over and squeezed her friend's hand. "You're right. Steven is *not* like your ex-husband. And you are not the same woman you were when I met you. You know your own mind, Gin, but you've got to move past the fear. He's a good man, and I'm pretty sure he loves you too."

"I know." Ginny tugged at her ponytail. "I'm spending some time with him and his family for Christmas, so we'll see how things go. Either way, I need to decide what I want to do. If I do move back here, I want it to be for me, not for him. Not this time."

Joy admired the strength she saw in the women in front of her. "I think it's really wise of you to not rush things."

A weak smile ghosted across Ginny's face. "Thanks. And sorry, Soph, but to be honest, I've been dreading this trip a little bit. As much as I'm excited to see you and William tie the knot, I know Steven and I need to have a talk. And then there's the whole matter of seeing Garrett again. I'm guessing he'll have his new wife with him ..."

At Sophia's nod, Ginny grimaced. "Of course, I completely understand. And I'm glad that he and William have reconciled. William *should* have his brother at his wedding, especially since both of their parents are gone."

"You could have said no to coming—I would have understood—but it means the world to me that you're here anyway."

"Of course, girl. You're my best friend and William was my brother-in-law for five years. I love you both so much." Ginny exhaled and straightened. "But enough about me. What's going on with you guys? How are wedding plans coming?"

As they discussed whether the color of the baby roses in Sophia's bouquet would match the tabletop arrangements at the reception, Sophia's phone buzzed. She read the text and frowned. "It's Mary. She's running late and will meet us at the restaurant. You guys ready?"

Ginny stood and popped another piece of fudge in her mouth, swallowing quickly. "Do you mind if I freshen up a bit?" She eyed Joy and Sophia. "Next to you two, I look like a complete train wreck."

Sophia laughed. "You do not. But go ahead. We're in no hurry."

"Five minutes. Be right back." Ginny snatched her suitcase and took off down the hallway.

Joy stood and wandered back to the kitchen. Ginny's mention of chocolate chip cookies had made her hungry. She snagged a bag of "chocolate biscuits"—close enough—and pulled the tab along the top to open it. "I really like her."

"I'm so glad." Sophia followed her and climbed onto one of the kitchen bar stools. "You, Ginny, and Mary are my people. I couldn't do life without you."

"Yeah, we're pretty great, aren't we?" Joy scrunched her nose as she opened the cookies and offered the bag to Sophia, who waved it away, seemingly deep in thought. "What is it?"

Sophia's gaze focused in on her. "You were pretty quiet when we were talking."

"Just observing. Sitting back and figuring out how all the pieces fit together."

"Yeah, but other than when you're working, that's not you. You're always the first one to dive into a conversation." Sophia bit her lip. "Did we make you feel left out with our talk of love and relationships?"

"Soph, no. Of course not." Joy reached her hand into the bag, the plastic crinkling as she rummaged. Triumphant at last, she pulled an unbroken cookie from inside and took a bite. Sugar danced on her tongue and she sighed.

"Are you sure? I know you always play it off as cool and independent, but don't you ever get …" Sophia shrugged.

"Lonely?"

"I guess. Maybe?"

Joy swallowed and licked the front of her teeth before she spoke again. "Look, I am really happy with where I'm at. I've told you that a thousand times—I've embraced the single life. Even like it. I have a lot more freedom to do what I want to do. Independence." The irony of what she'd just said slapped against her cheeks as the words tumbled out. But it was true, in a way. She wouldn't have been able to uproot her life and move across the country to be with her parents so easily if she'd had a husband, a family.

"And anyway, I doubt I'd be able to find a man who could put up with my idiosyncrasies. I'm set in my ways. I like to stay up late watching *Dr. Who* one night and *Pride & Prejudice* the next. I'm a strange mix of vintage and modern, and I like it that way. No man would be able to figure me out. And I'm not changing. So I think I'm better off as I am—everyone's friend. I'm good with it. Really."

The look that flitted across Sophia's face personified doubt. "And what about Oliver?"

"What about him?"

More cookies. She definitely needed more cookies. Her fingers snagged a few from the bag, and she shoved a broken one into her mouth.

This time, the chocolate tasted bitter.

Sophia hopped down from the stool, took the cookie bag from Joy, and lifted an eyebrow. "That's what I thought."

CHAPTER 8

Eight in the morning was way too early to be up, especially after such a late night.

But Joy couldn't sleep. She padded in her bare feet from the guest room toward the kitchen, the wood chilling her toes. The delectable smell of coffee wafted down the hallway. Either Sophia was also awake or she'd set the automatic timer on the coffeepot.

Rounding the corner, she discovered Ginny nursing a mug of Joe at the counter. The woman slumped forward in her seat, frowning, staring out the small kitchen window. First light trickled in, dark enough to make Joy wonder if it was going to be another cloudy day.

She cleared her throat as quietly as possible.

Ginny's head shot up and pivoted, eyes wide. "Oh, Joy. Hey."

"Morning." Joy walked around the counter to the coffeemaker and pulled a mug from the cabinet above. "Did you sleep?"

"Not well."

Pouring herself a cup, Joy took a sip. Ahhh. Liquid clarity. "Any particular reason?" As for herself, she'd collapsed into bed at 3:00 a.m. after a huge dinner at Village Pub—an adorable nautical-themed restaurant—followed by two different chick flicks, lots of popcorn and cookies, and chatting until they were so tired they started mumbling nonsense and descending into fits of laughter unbefitting their age.

"Oh, not much. Just the whole what-do-I-do-with-my-life-after-this stuff."

"So, really minor then." Joy grinned and stood at the counter opposite Ginny's seat, leaning against the gleaming granite.

"Yeah." Ginny cocked an eyebrow. "Why are you up so early?"

"Kind of the same reason."

"Really?"

"M-hmm." After another sip, Joy told her about Mom and Dad, the potential of working again—she'd already received five job notifications in the last twelve hours—and even the guilt she felt over being away.

She started to say something about Oliver too then stopped. It wasn't the same as Ginny's relationship with Steven. Joy had no room to commiserate. It was ridiculous to even consider.

Because Ginny and Steven would end up together, once Ginny saw what the whole rest of the world saw—that Steven was crazy about her. He'd snuck up to their table last night during dinner to give her a hug hello and to kiss her cheek. The heat between them had sizzled more than the large stone fireplace crackling in the corner of the pub.

But Joy and Oliver … even if she wanted to explore that, it really could go nowhere.

Commiseration, no. Encouragement, she could offer. "You'll figure it out, Ginny. You are smart and capable and have an amazing man who supports you and wants the best for you."

A smile tugged at the corner of Ginny's lips. "You're right. Thanks, Joy. I'm so glad you're here. Be praying for me today, all right? I have lunch with Steven and his parents and afterward, we're going out to dinner. To talk."

Joy leaned close and wrapped her in a hug. "Absolutely."

"Aw, why are we hugging?" Sophia waltzed into the room, her black hair pulled back from her smiling face.

The two separated and Ginny laughed. "I just needed some therapy, and Joy was happy to oblige."

It *had* felt good, helping someone again. "I'm always glad to listen." She turned to Sophia. "So, what's on the docket for today?"

Snagging some coffee and a chocolate cookie, Sophia sat at the eat-in table. "I was going to open the bookstore at ten for a few hours. I know it's Sunday and a lot of people don't venture out, but since it's the weekend before Christmas, I thought it may be a good idea to be available."

"Makes sense. What do you want me to do?"

"Actually, William offered to cover the store for me, sweet man. So I was thinking you and I could start packing up a bit around here?" After the wedding, Sophia was going to move into William's house since it was bigger. She hoped to rent her cottage in the new year when they returned from their honeymoon. "There's more last-minute stuff to do but the majority of shops will be closed around here."

"That sounds great to me."

"I'll help too until I need to leave for lunch." Ginny took a final swig of her coffee and hopped off the stool. "Besides, I've been dying to see your wedding dress, and it sounds like now is the perfect time for you to model it for us."

"Ooo, yes." Joy clapped her hands. "Great idea."

"It's a bit of a monstrosity to get into. I'll need some help."

"We can practice for the real deal."

Sophia bit her lip then squealed. "Six days until I'm Mrs. William Rose. Can you guys believe it?" She stood. "All right, let's go see it."

They followed Sophia down the hallway to her bedroom, decorated in delicate whites, pinks, and greens. A floral quilt lay across the top of the king-sized bed, and a vase of silk pink roses adorned the white shabby chic side table. On Sophia's closet door hung a large white garment bag that nearly reached the floor.

Sophia lifted the hanger from the top of the door then placed the bag on the bed. A hot pink tag at the top declared the bag the property of S. Barrett.

Her friend glanced at Joy and Ginny, eyes sparkling. "Ready?"

"Girl, yes." Ginny wrung her hands in anticipation.

Sophia unzipped the bag ... and gasped.

"What's wrong?" Joy stepped forward, certain she'd see some sort of stain marring the dress's fabric. But the white beaded bodice—rather low-cut considering Sophia's modest nature—and flowing Georgette maxi skirt appeared in perfect condition.

Yet Sophia shook her head, tears filling her eyes.

"Soph?" Joy pinched her friend's elbow.

Sophia jolted then pointed at the bag and its contents. "That is not my dress."

"What do you mean?"

"*My* dress has cap sleeves, a sweetheart neckline, gorgeous embroidery, and tulle lace. This"—she pointed again—"is not that." Her breathing grew ragged.

"Here, sit down." Joy helped Sophia lower herself onto the edge of the bed. "Just call the dress shop, tell them there's been a mix-up, and demand you get your dress ASAP."

"It's in London."

"So it's their mistake, right?" At Sophia's nod, Joy continued. "They can figure out a way to get it to you same day. And like you said, we still have six days to figure this out. It's going to be fine."

Sophia blew out a breath and unclenched the fists she'd started making. "You're right. Can you find my phone?"

Ginny located it on the dresser and handed it to Sophia. "Here."

"Thanks." Sophia found the shop's phone number and called, standing to pace while she waited. After a minute, she hung up. "It just kept ringing and ringing. No way to leave a message."

"Maybe we can tweet them or contact them via email," Joy offered.

"It's this little hole-in-the-wall shop, so I honestly don't know if they have a website. I was in London dress shopping when I happened across it." Sophia rubbed her forehead. "Should I just keep calling and hope that eventually the owner will answer?"

"That's not a bad idea. Let's start packing and you can call every ten minutes and pray you get through." Joy zipped the bag and waltzed to the closet door, eyeing it then turning on her heel. "Sorry, but unless you have a chair in here, one of you will have to hang this."

Ginny snatched it from her and replaced the dress where it belonged.

For the next several hours, the three of them packed Sophia's bedroom. Eventually, Ginny left and lunchtime faded into afternoon. Sophia's attempts to contact the dress shop proved futile, with Sophia growing more and more discouraged every time her calls remained unanswered.

Argh. Her friend did not need this—did not *deserve* this—especially after all she'd been through.

Joy's head spun with details of a forming plan as she dug into the back of Sophia's closet. She crammed a pair of black flats into a moving box. Reaching for sandals decorated with red jewels, she tossed them in as well and snagged some white wedges in the next breath.

"Something on your mind?" Sophia's voice piped up from her spot across the room.

Did her friend know Joy well or what? "I could drive to London and exchange the dress in person. Then we'd be guaranteed to at least know what's going on and get the deed done."

Sophia, who had been tossing piles of lounge shirts and sweats into a box, froze. "That's actually a great idea. But you can't go. You don't know how to get there."

"It's called GPS, silly. I'll be fine."

"But you'd have to drive on the opposite side of the road. It took me a few months to feel okay with that. And London is a five-hour drive from here."

"I've taken plenty of road trips." The thought of driving on the left was a bit nerve-wracking but nothing Joy couldn't handle. "I'd have to borrow your car, though."

Sophia bit her lip and turned once more to stare at the dress. "I should be the one to go."

Joy set down a pair of white ankle boots and walked toward her friend, placing a hand on Sophia's arm. "You have a bookstore to run and last-minute details that only you can accomplish. I really don't mind. I'm here to help. Let me."

"I'll call William and see what he thinks." Sophia got on the phone and dialed her fiancé.

While she did that, Joy stepped out of the room and snagged a few water bottles from the fridge. Uncapping one, she allowed the cool liquid to flow down her parched throat. Who knew one could sweat in the middle of a British winter?

Sophia emerged from her room a few minutes later and found Joy in the kitchen. She placed her phone on the counter. "William said there's snow in the forecast for London and its surrounding areas. It may be a bad storm. The forecasters aren't certain but road conditions could be sketchy. Neither of us think it's a good idea for you to go."

"But—"

"Alone, that is." Sophia tilted her head, worry evident in her eyes. "You can say no to this, Joy, but Oliver was there with William and offered to take you. He said his aunt was feeling a bit perkier and could handle the store for a day if you leave at first light tomorrow."

A whole day with Oliver? Alone?

She chided herself for the tiny thrill racing up her spine. A. Friend. He was just a friend.

A handsome, amazingly insightful friend who …

Stop it, Joy. Just … stop.

Joy must have waited too long to respond because Sophia shook her head. "That settles it. I'll just keep calling the shop and hope that someone answers tomorrow. It's probably closed for Sunday or something to that effect."

"Didn't you initially go there on a Sunday?" That was the only day Sophia ever closed the bookstore for part of the day.

"Yeah, but—"

"I'm going, Soph. You have to have your wedding dress. That's a nonnegotiable. And I for one am not willing to trust that the shop will get it here for you." She paused, mulling. "That's really nice of Oliver to offer to come with me. I guess, to be safe and ease your mind, I'll let him."

CHAPTER 9

Twenty hours later, Joy stood triumphant at the front of the wedding dress shop. In her hand she held Sophia's dress along with a two-hundred-pound refund.

Oliver followed her out to the car and whistled. "I can't believe the verbal thrashing you gave that woman—and all without yelling or saying one rude thing." He opened the back door to his silver SUV, took the dress from her, and set it inside with care. "That takes talent."

She rounded the vehicle and opened the other back door. "All I did was remind her she had a duty to her patrons to ensure they looked beautiful on their wedding day, and that it's a bit difficult for the bride to do when she doesn't have the right dress." Leaning in, she pulled the top of the garment bag toward her so it lay flat across the seat. "I still can't believe she didn't label the dresses more clearly. We're just lucky that Samantha Barrett hadn't picked up Sophia's dress and taken it to who-knows-where."

"Indeed."

She laughed at the simplicity of his reply. Last night, Sophia had said something about Oliver being on the introverted side, but with Joy, he'd never really seemed that way unless in the presence of other people. In fact, he'd been downright chatty this morning on the drive—during which she'd learned that he loved sushi but salmon (her favorite) revolted him, that he played a mean game of Yahtzee and dabbled in guitar strumming when he had a few spare moments, and that his ideal day consisted of walking and playing fetch with Rascal at Hyde Park.

When he'd asked about her, she hadn't known what to say. Even though she liked herself, she just didn't feel that interesting, not when most of her time was spent hanging out with her parents. So she'd gushed about her love of everything movie-related and confessed her secret addiction to the British royals —even that she'd stayed up all night when she'd lived alone in Arizona to watch William and Harry's weddings and all the preceding festivities live on television.

She'd never even told Sophia that particular fact, afraid her friend would have teased her mercilessly for her romantic sentiments. But, really, it was more than that. One of her first memories was watching Princess Diana's wedding while snuggled up with her mom in the early hours of the morning.

Either way, the time passed with Oliver in the car on the way to London had been entirely too pleasant for Joy's good.

They closed their doors and climbed into the car. Oliver started the ignition and glanced over at her. "Where to now?"

"What do you mean? We need to get this back to Soph." Heat poured from the SUV's vents, and Joy lifted her hands to warm them.

"You can't tell me you came all the way to London and aren't going to see a few sites. That just isn't right."

"Believe me, I'd love to. Do you know how many movies set in England I've seen? How often I've wanted to visit?" She still couldn't believe she was here. The skies were drearier than in her favorite films, and evidence of previous snowfall decorated the gutters. Even so, icy streets and storefronts strung with lights added a certain holiday spirit, enough to bring the magic of being here to life. "But we've got to get back. Sophia needs my help with a ton of stuff."

"I refuse to allow you to come to my city and not take in at least one place of notoriety."

The man was stubborn but so was she. "What about the snow headed this way? Sophia said there was a good chance of it."

Oliver whipped out his phone and messed with it for a moment. "Ah. Looks to be several hours out. We'll be gone before then." Replacing it on his center console, he looked her square in the eyes. "So, what's it to be?"

Joy huffed, smiling to show him he'd won—and that she didn't hold a grudge. "Why don't you pick?

"I know just the place."

Half an hour later, he'd parked and walked them into Westminster Abbey. Joy took in the Gothic style of the centuries-old church where British coronations and some royal weddings were held. "This is a dream." She glanced at Oliver, who'd shoved his hands inside the pockets of his gray trench coat.

"You said you loved the monarchy and that you watched the Duke and Duchess of Cambridge's wedding, so ..." He shrugged.

"It's perfect." She reached out and squeezed his arm. "Thank you for bringing me here."

They ventured inside and purchased tickets to a guided tour. Their verger—a caretaker of sorts who acted as a tour guide through the church—was an older man with a thinning pad of hair up top and a long black robe. He led them throughout the abbey, from Poets' Corner to the royal tombs and every other notable location within. Joy's fingers itched to take photos, but the abbey's policy didn't allow it. Part of her was glad because it meant she could simply observe, pray, and enjoy her surroundings.

At the far eastern end of the church, the verger walked through large brass gates into what he called the Lady Chapel, or Henry VII's chapel. His spectacles caught the light flickering through the gorgeous high stained-glass windows as he described the late medieval architecture, evident in the fan-vaulted ceiling, where curving wood was carved equidistantly, creating the effect of ladies' fans spreading across the ornate ceiling.

Joy's neck hurt from straining to make out the designs on the dozens of banners hanging from above. According to the verger, these banners represented the Knights of the Order of Bath, and the nearly one hundred statues of saints interspersed between them displayed the largest surviving figure sculpture collection from Tudor England. Beneath the banners on either side of the main aisle, rows of mahogany stalls contrasted with the light-colored walls and ceiling.

"This is the resting place of fifteen monarchs, including Mary the First, Elizabeth the First, and Mary, Queen of Scots." The verger walked around the cavernous chapel with his hands behind his back.

Now that he mentioned it, she saw tombs scattered about the room. On the east side of the space rose two large gilt bronze effigies of Henry VII and his wife. The marble effigy of Elizabeth the First depicted a somber woman lying in her regal finery across the top of the tomb.

The soaring ceiling, the elegant details, the way the light swooped through the entire chapel—it all brought a beauty she couldn't describe, embedding it down deeply in her soul. This place that memorialized the dead was so gorgeous in its rendering, and it made Joy feel ... alive.

How ironic.

Oliver leaned toward her. "Amazing, isn't it?" His whispered words brushed against the top of her ears.

"Hmm ..."

"That's all you have to say?"

Her eyes found his, but although she saw teasing glinting beneath his lashes, she couldn't joke in this moment—not when, for the first time in a long time, she didn't feel so burdened. So frightened of what was to come. This monument to the Creator, meant to honor life even in death, gave her something physical yet other-worldly to cling to.

So yes, words wouldn't come. Joy could only express her gratitude to him for bringing her here by reaching out her hand and lacing her fingers between his.

Surprise lit his face but he didn't pull away. In fact, his hand grasped hers with a firmness that said he wasn't going to let go.

And something about this place and whatever was happening inside of her ... well, she was okay with that.

Her gaze left his and traveled upward, finding the light once more. And when she closed her eyes in reverence, it continued to shine even then.

The trip to Westminster had taken much longer than she'd expected, and she wasn't the only one who had lost track of time.

As they made their way to the front of the abbey, Oliver checked his Orient dress watch. "Oh, wow. It's already half past three. How did that happen?"

"It was just so mesmerizing." And she didn't just mean the church, though it was deserving of that adjective. After their tour had ended, they'd wandered hand in hand, room to room, taking in the sights. Despite her usual affinity for talking, she found herself bound in a spell that she feared would break if they spoke, a spell she didn't want to emerge from until absolutely necessary.

Necessary had finally arrived.

Joy dropped Oliver's hand and dug in her purse for her phone. "How's the weather?" Her weather app should tell them, though it was never too reliable. She powered up her phone as they rounded the last corner toward the massive entrance. Other visitors exited and a blast of icy air hit Joy when she got close.

She dropped her phone into her bag. No weather app needed.

Snow fell from the gray sky at an alarming rate.

Joy turned to Oliver, whose brow furrowed. "You okay to drive in this?"

"I'm fine driving in snow, though this looks a mite heavy." Oliver buttoned his jacket and reached for her hand once more. "Come on. Let's get to the car, and I'll check the weather reports just to be sure."

She nestled her hand in his and ducked against the wind. By the time they reached his car, her head was wet from the falling flakes of white, her fingers stiff from the cold.

Oliver cranked the car heater and defroster, using his wipers to rid the windshield of the precipitation already gathering on the glass. "Wait just a moment while I take a look." He pulled his phone from his pocket, and his thumb danced across the screen.

Joy took the opportunity to text Sophia and let her know they'd been waylaid a bit but that she'd report in when they left.

A text came back immediately.

I've been trying to call you. It's only snowing a little here, but between Port Willis and London, the storm looks pretty fierce. It's way more intense than they thought. You should stay there until it clears.

Joy's fingers flew as she typed a reply.

But we have your dress. And you need my help.

Moments later, her phone dinged in response.

Your safety is way more important than any dress. Stay

PUT FOR TONIGHT. YOU CAN COME TOMORROW ONCE THE ROADS ARE PLOWED AND IT'S SAFE.

A groan escaped Joy's throat. "Sophia said she's seen bad reports—"

"I think we should stay in town tonight," Oliver said at the same time.

This was not the plan. But some things couldn't be helped. "I just can't believe the weather stations didn't warn us how bad it would be."

Through the windshield, Oliver peeked at the sky. "I'm not sure how great American forecasters are, but here they get it wrong all the time."

"Good point."

"So we're agreed then? We shouldn't venture back to Cornwall today?"

"Yeah, I think so."

He put the car into DRIVE and eased onto the road, which was already crammed with cars. To their left and up the street a bit, a double-decker tour bus driver honked.

"So where are we going?" There must be a dozen hotels within walking distance, but based on the rate of snow coming down, they didn't have long to find shelter.

When he didn't answer, she glanced over. His face was a mask. "Oliver?"

He cleared his throat. "How would you feel about going to my place?" After a brief pause, he hurried on. "You can take my room, and I'll take the sofa, of course."

Unease rippled through Joy's stomach. But why? It was a practical solution, and she certainly didn't fear being alone with him.

Oh, please. She knew why and Joy couldn't lie to herself. Being with him in the car was one thing. Seeing his home, being among his things, sleeping in his bed—innocent though it might be—would only get her closer to stepping over the friendship line that stood between them. And once they'd crossed it, she knew there would be no going back.

Not with him.

But staying at his place was the best choice they had, right?

She forced a smile. "Sure. Sounds great."

CHAPTER 10

When they reached the tall black door of apartment 404, Joy held Sophia's dress while Oliver inserted a key into the lock. Opening the door, he flicked on the lights, took the garment bag from her, and invited her in.

Attempting to conceal the deep breath she inhaled, Joy stepped into Oliver's flat, the scent of something sweet greeting her. "Did you bake before you left?"

He kicked the front door closed and deposited the garment bag into a hall closet. "It's a candle my mum gave me. Warm biscuits or some such thing. It seems to give off a scent even when it's not lit."

They both removed their damp coats and hung them. Joy's sweater was blessedly dry, and her jeans were mostly so. They wouldn't be the most comfortable clothing to sleep in, but she'd make do.

The entryway connected to a hallway that opened on one side into a great room and kitchen with gorgeous stainless-steel appliances and a white marble countertop with swirls of gray. Joy's boots clipped along the real-wood plank flooring, a rich chestnut brown that shimmered as if it'd just been polished.

From the open-concept kitchen, she could see a four-person wood table and chairs set in front of a floor-to-ceiling window granting a full view of Hyde Park, which was quickly becoming whiter by the moment.

How different his flat was from her former house in Arizona—all vintage and bright. But though it screamed designer, his home also gave off cozy vibes.

"Your place is lovely." Joy slipped off her shoes, not wanting to ruin the gorgeous Persian rug as she stepped up to the window to study what lay beyond. Her fingertips grazed the glass as she watched the lowering sun slip behind the clouds and snow swirl in the light of lamps that had turned on only moments before.

"Thank you." Now he stood beside her. "Make yourself comfortable. Please. My home is your home."

She pressed a hand to her chest. He had no idea how those words affected her.

Because she didn't have a home anymore. Not one of her own, anyway.

She shook herself from the melancholy thought. "I will. Thanks." Treading from the rug back onto the wood floors, she found her way to the leather tan wraparound couch that sat opposite a white brick fireplace flanked by elegant white bookcases. Before she sat, she flipped a switch on the wall and artificial flames leapt to life.

While Oliver rummaged in the kitchen for something to eat, Joy casually studied the rest of the living room. A home was often a good way to get to know people. It took her a moment to realize that he had no Christmas decor of any kind. Hmm. A dog bed lay in one corner, so out of place in the refined bachelor pad that she had to smile. She bet Rascal—whom Oliver had left behind with his aunt—was allowed on the couch, however much money it had cost.

On the mantle sat several framed photos. One displayed

Oliver with his parents, younger brother, and a woman in a bridal gown—his sister-in-law, she'd guess. Another showed him hugging two young girls to him, his smile easy. In the last one, Oliver stood with his arm around a beautiful woman whose black dress showed off her long, tan legs.

A twinge of something Joy didn't want to address sliced through her.

She turned her attention from the pictures to a thick book beside them. Joy approached but had to rise on her tiptoes to make out the book's title. *The Holy Bible* on the spine gleamed back at her in silvery letters.

"How do water biscuits, cheese, and ham sound for dinner?"

She turned to find him with a tray. "Water biscuits?" Glancing at the food selection, she laughed. "Oh, crackers."

Oliver grinned. "Crackers, sure. Do you want to head to the table?"

The warmth of the fire was so inviting, the rolling flames so soothing. "Would you mind if we ate over here?"

"Not at all." He glanced at the couch but lowered himself to the ground in front of it, which was covered by a silk rug. Setting the tray down, he patted the spot next to him. "Join me?"

"Of course." Joy sat on the soft rug and snagged a cracker from the platter, placing a thick slice of Gouda on top. "*Bon appétit.*" She lifted the cracker as if in a toast.

Oliver quickly grabbed a cracker of his own and hit it softly against hers. "I'm sorry it's not more of a feast."

"Are you kidding? It's perfect. Pretty much how I eat at home, especially when it's just me. And that's fairly often since Mom went into the rehab facility."

"How is she?"

Joy thought back to the call she'd made to her parents before she and Oliver had entered Westminster Abbey. "Pretty good, all things considered. She's making progress with the physical therapy, and they think she could be home by just after New Year's."

"I'm sure that's a relief to hear."

"Yeah, it is."

A silence fell between them as they ate and watched the fire. Oliver turned on the radio, and soft Christmas music lilted through the room.

Joy used her napkin to wipe her mouth. "I noticed you don't have any Christmas decor."

"It's just me and Rascal here, and I knew I'd be gone for the actual holiday." He took the empty platter from between them and placed it on a side table next to the couch. "It seemed a waste to spend time decorating when I'm the only one who would see it."

Considering his words, she stared into the fire. Whether intentional or not, the orange flames in the fireplace provided the only light in the room, creating a soft glow that didn't reach the shadowed corners. The halo effect surrounded them, limiting the outside world.

"I don't think beauty is ever a waste. And to me, there's nothing better than sitting in front of a Christmas tree as its lights sparkle, thinking about the magic of the season, the fact that love came down to us when we least deserved it."

"I see your point. And maybe I can't think of anything better." He paused. "But I can think of something that's just as good."

She felt the heat of his gaze on her. When she swiveled to look at him, his eyes drank her in.

They'd ended up close together, the sides of her right leg and arm just brushing against his. The air pulsed with emotion.

Get up. Leave. Say goodnight. Nothing lasting can come from this.

Joy should listen to her inner self. But instead, she spoke, the words nearly strangling her. "And what's that?"

Slowly, methodically, Oliver twisted to face her more

directly and lifted his hand to her face. His thumb trailed her cheekbone upward. "It's good to be sitting here, with you, listening to holiday music, eating a pathetic excuse for a dinner. I'm loving every moment of it."

"Hey, the food wasn't that bad."

He smiled. "And there you go joking, but I'm serious. Joy, I've never met anyone like you before, with such a zest for life and such a heart for others. I feel more alive just being near you. And to be quite honest … I'm mad about you."

She couldn't force her eyes off him, couldn't speak. All her objections and questions swirled away with the snow that fell outside.

He saw her. He understood her. He … wanted her.

And she wanted him.

It might not be a winning scenario, but right now, she almost didn't care. Kicking the last shred of doubt to the momentary curb, she allowed herself to speak the truth. "I feel the same way."

With a smile, he moved his face nearer, and before she could close her eyes, his lips skimmed hers.

And then, the fire died.

Joy jolted awake.

Despite the socks on her feet and the pile of blankets Oliver had loaned her, she shivered.

What time was it? The darkness outside the curtains indicated it was still the middle of the night. Had she slept long? If so, it didn't feel like it. Maybe that's because subconsciously she'd spent the time lying on Oliver's pillow smelling the remnants of his extremely manly shampoo and thinking about the kiss that had only lasted a second.

Joy pulled the comforter tighter around her. If only they

hadn't been interrupted by the power going out last night. It had certainly broken the magic of the moment. When they'd been plunged into darkness, Oliver managed to locate two flashlights and call the power company using his cell phone. The storm was to blame, of course, so who knew when power would be restored.

Maybe the interruption had been for the best.

She tried rolling over and going back to sleep, but her brain and her freezing body wouldn't let her. Maybe moving would help. Or eating. That was supposed to warm you up, right? Worth a shot. She didn't want to wake Oliver, who had bunked in the living room, but maybe she could quietly scrounge for something in the kitchen.

Rising from the bed, she pulled one of the thick quilts around her shoulders, grabbed the flashlight, and clicked it on to its lowest brightness. As she opened the door to Oliver's bedroom, a squeak resounded from the hinges. She winced and continued, passing his office on the way. When she reached the kitchen, she glanced over at the couch where Oliver was supposed to be sleeping.

"Couldn't sleep either?"

Joy whirled, dropped her blanket, and shone her light toward the eat-in-nook. Her gaze landed upon Oliver shading his eyes with his hand. Joy quickly clicked off the flashlight and waited for her eyes to adjust to the dimness.

He sat bundled in one of his kitchen chairs, which was turned toward the window. Everything remained dark out there except for a small sliver of moonlight somehow breaking through the clouds. It appeared as if someone was tossing white confetti from the sky. The snow fell at all angles: straight downward, diagonally, some nearly perpendicular to the ground she couldn't see but knew was there.

And other than Oliver's question, the room was devoid of sound.

The fact the storm had not abated did cause her some temporary distress—what would happen if they couldn't make it back to Cornwall soon?—but the tranquility of the moment was too great to allow such a thought to ruin it.

In reply, Joy simply pushed her feet forward and pulled up a chair next to Oliver.

He opened his blanket and wrapped it and his arm around her shoulders, insulating her in his warmth.

She laid her head in the crook of his arm.

"Happy Christmas Eve." He whispered the words against her hair, sending a shiver down her spine.

"It's past midnight?"

"According to my battery-operated wall clock, yes."

She attempted to adjust the blanket, and her hand bumped against his. Feeling brave, she wove their palms and fingers together. "Where were you this time last year?"

"Probably in bed."

Her laughter spilled into the silence. "Okay, not sometime between midnight and morning, but Christmas Eve. Mom and I decorated cookies. My parents and I attended the candlelight service at church, grabbed some delicious takeout for dinner, and ended the night by watching *White Christmas*. The perfect day." Her lips arced upward at the happy memory. "Christmas Day was another story. Mom had a meltdown and so did I. But Christmas Eve … that was one for the books."

"I'm glad for that." His thumb stroked the top of hers and he sighed. "As for me, I spent the day with family. But it was supposed to be my wedding day."

She straightened and pulled away to face him. The blanket keeping them wrapped together drooped. "Supposed to be?"

He took a moment to finish his thought. His fingers pressed against her hand as if wanting to anchor it there. The clouds broke a bit, allowing more starlight through. Joy could make out the contours of Oliver's face, his mouth falling into a frown. "My fiancée ended things a year ago in October."

"I'm sorry. What happened, if you don't mind me asking?"

"I don't mind. That's why I'm telling you." He shifted. Was he itching to pull her close again like she hoped he would? But she needed to focus on his words, not on how wonderful it felt to be enveloped in his embrace.

"Jana and I dated for three years before I finally worked up the nerve to propose. We were extremely busy people—she an interior decorator and me a business owner. After I proposed, things were good for a while but business picked up. A lot. So I dedicated more hours to growing it, maybe partially because I wanted to be successful when my previous venture had failed but also because so many employees depended on me. I went from five to twenty in a span of a few months. Those people had spouses, children, elderly parents to care for. The pressure was intense."

"That's understandable." She squeezed his hand in a show of support.

"Even so, I lost Jana because of it. She got tired of me showing up late and canceling on her for dates, wedding planning appointments, you name it. I even stopped going to church because I could squeeze in a few extra hours of work if I did. I had the right motivation but the wrong priorities."

"You were putting others first. That can't be wrong."

"It was if I started to see myself as some kind of savior. And I did. I thought it was solely on my shoulders to save my employees from ruin the way I'd been ruined years before that. But it wasn't. Because I forgot to factor in one thing." He paused. "I forgot to factor in God."

Something jabbed her spirit, and she turned her eyes back to the snow—the thing that was keeping her from "saving" Sophia. "I think I can relate to that sentiment."

"Maybe we're two peas in a pod after all then, eh?"

That got a laugh. "Maybe so." A sudden thought came to her, unbidden. Joy bit her lip. "Is Jana the woman in the photo on the mantle?" The one who made the Oliver beside her look so happy?

"Yes."

"So ..." How did she ask the question on her mind without coming across as insecure and ... well ... petty?

"So does that mean I'm not over her?"

"I guess so. Yeah."

"I'm not going to lie. When she ended our engagement, it nearly broke me. There were several mornings that the only thing that got me out of bed was that my employees depended on me. But then, the Lord woke me up, reminded me that the sun keeps on rising and setting, that his mercies are new every morning."

"That's a great revelation ... but why keep her photo on the mantle where you're going to continue seeing it? Why subject yourself to that pain?"

"I suppose it's a reminder. That sometimes, the things God has planned for our lives aren't what we expect. But they're good. Somehow, they're good." Oliver lifted their connected hands, pulling them from underneath the blanket. He brought his lips to the top of her hand, kissing it with all the tenderness of an English gentleman in one of her favorite films. Then, his eyes found hers. "And I didn't expect you, Joy Beckman."

The breath whooshed from her. This was it. The moment of no return—the moment her heart would start its descent toward, eventually, fully breaking.

But with the snow coming down just outside, the promise of a new day on the horizon, and the beautiful words he'd just spoken, Joy couldn't do anything but fall.

With her free hand, she stroked his disarray of hair, pushing her fingers through it, then curving them down around the back of his head, her thumb grazing his ear. She scooted sideways in her chair toward him and lifted her face, inviting him into her sphere.

He dropped her hand and cupped her chin, staring at her through the darkness, the intensity in his gaze not lost on her despite the lack of light. And then he leaned forward and brushed his lips against hers once, twice, three times before he deepened the kiss.

Joy looped her other arm around his neck, pulling him to her. And in that moment, they became like two falling snowflakes that were drawn to each other—impossible to separate.

CHAPTER 11

"This is quite possibly the best egg casserole I've ever tasted in my life." Joy almost moaned as she placed the last bite of Ginny's Christmas morning dish into her mouth, chewing, relishing the way the sausage mingled with the egg.

"It's a really simple recipe," Ginny said from her spot on the carpeted floor next to Sophia's Christmas tree.

"You say that, but I'm sure I'd find a way to screw it up." Sophia set her fork onto her empty plate and plopped back against her couch cushions. "Joy is right. That was amazing. I know you specialize in baked goods, but you really should just open a restaurant."

Ginny pulled her legs into her chest and wrapped her arms around her knees. "I already have a bazillion items I want to add to my bakery menu. An entire restaurant would make it impossible to narrow down."

Outside, as the sun proclaimed it a cloudless day, the sky had already forgotten the storm that had nearly caused Joy and Oliver to miss Christmas in Port Willis. But, the snow had stopped the previous morning—though it was due to start again today in London and Cornwall—and by afternoon, the plows had done their thing. Whatever the reason, Joy had felt a strange mixture of gratitude to be heading back to Sophia and sadness over the beginning of the end as it concerned her relationship with Oliver.

If cuddling and kissing a bunch and talking about anything and everything for less than a day constituted a relationship.

Joy sipped the hot apple cider Ginny had simmered on the stovetop early this morning. The toasty liquid warmed her lips and throat as she snuggled under a blanket, her eyes roaming Sophia's beautifully decorated tree and landing on the framed painting of a couple cradling a baby thousands of years ago—a baby who would become King.

The steam from her mug filled her lungs. Between whatever she had going on with Oliver and her mom's deteriorating health, Joy had much to worry about. But today was a day for thankfulness. A day to remember that hope would always trump the things that troubled her.

"So how about we open a few gifts before the guys get here?" Sophia stood and knelt beside the tree, sorting through the gifts until she located a large bag and a medium-sized box with a glittery gold bow.

William, Steven, and Oliver were joining them for Christmas lunch before the latter two joined their families for dinner. Joy was nearly giddy at the thought of seeing her man again.

My man. Oh, brother. Slow your roll, Joy.

"You guys, I feel like the worst friend in the world. I didn't have a chance to go shopping yet." Ginny ran her fingers under her eyes. "I haven't purchased a single item for anyone … not even Steven."

"Girl, don't sweat it. We know you've been busy." Sophia handed her the gift bag and set the box on the oak coffee table in front of Joy. "And I have a feeling Steven doesn't need some store-bought gift to make him the happiest man in the world on Christmas."

Curling her fingers around her mug, Joy leaned forward in her seat. "Did I miss something?" With all the commotion over retrieving the dress and getting stuck in London, she'd forgotten to ask Ginny how things had gone with Steven.

Ginny's cheeks turned a delightful shade of pink. "He and I had a nice chat the other night."

"Uh, details?"

"Sophia's already heard it all. I'd hate to bore her—"

"As if you could." With a happy sigh, Sophia sank back onto the couch and hugged a red, fringed pillow. "I mean, I never get tired of watching *You've Got Mail*, so why would hearing about my friend's romantic exploits be any different?"

"Oh, this sounds good." And if the attention were on Ginny, it wouldn't be on Joy and *her* romantic exploits—the details of which she had yet to divulge to either woman. To anyone, actually. She'd been too exhausted when she'd slipped in late last night. "You've definitely got to dish now."

Light spilled from Ginny's smile. She tucked a strand of hair behind her ear. "After I left here on Sunday, I had lunch with Steven and his parents, as you know. We've met several times before, and they're lovely people."

"The loveliest. Now, skip to the really good part."

Ginny stuck her tongue out at Sophia. "Ha ha. Fine." She turned her attention back to Joy. "For dinner, I thought we'd go to this eclectic diner we like to visit every time I'm in town. But instead, he took me to his houseboat, where he made spaghetti."

"Ah, a man who can cook. I like it." *Does Oliver cook?* Joy pushed away the thought because a detail like that didn't matter. She probably wouldn't be involved with him long enough to find out.

"Well, he tried, anyway. Let's just say it was adorable." Ginny bit her lip, smiling at the memory. "After we ate, we moved to his couch and chatted about our plans for Christmas, a little about the wedding, and about my plans for the bakery. Basically, everything but what we really needed to talk about. Finally, I got up my courage and told him how I felt."

"What does that mean? What did you say?" Joy usually allowed others to tell a story without interruption but couldn't seem to contain her questions today.

Ginny's fingers rustled against the red tissue paper sticking out from her gift bag. "Kind of what I said to you guys the other day. I told him I wanted to move back and open a bakery here, but I was afraid it was for the wrong reasons. He asked what I meant, and I said, 'I'm afraid I want to do it because you're here.'" She paused, a tear sliding down her cheek. "Then he turned to me and said, 'Ginny, open the bakery wherever you want. Don't you know that I'd move to London, Paris—even back to Boston, if that's where you wanted to go?" She paused. "Which I don't, by the way. Even though part of me would love to show my parents how successful I'm going to be. But I digress. He basically said if I wasn't going to open a bakery here, he'd uproot his life and go wherever I was. The only reason he hasn't done it yet was to give me time to decide what I wanted to do. Time to heal from Garrett's betrayal and the divorce. Time to find God and become secure in my knowledge of who I really am."

Now Sophia and Joy both had tears in their eyes too.

Joy's tears originated from happiness for Ginny and Steven. But she recognized another source as well. An ache had formed in the pit of her heart, and it had everything to do with how she'd perhaps finally found such a man for herself but eventually would have to let him go. How could he possibly fit into her life?

She'd considered it at all angles. If things ever came to the point where they fell in love, fully and completely, how would they be together? Joy's parents needed her, so there was no way she could move half a world away. And Oliver's employees and the success of his company meant everything to him. She wouldn't be the woman who took him away from that.

"And that right there is the sign of a good man." Sophia nearly bounced in her seat. "Tell her the rest."

"Yes, please." Joy steadied her voice. "And don't leave anything out."

"All right, all right." Ginny laughed, wiping away her tears. "What he said stunned me, frankly. And it made me realize that even though I initially came to Port Willis for a man—Garrett—it's still home. The people I love the most in the world are here. And yeah, I could bake anywhere, but I want to bake here. It was just fear keeping me from admitting that before. So I have a meeting scheduled tomorrow about renting the space next to the bookstore. And Soph and I have already started talking about opening a wall between the two so customers can flow between our stores. We'll have to talk to the city about it and get the permits and everything, but ... yeah. It's super exciting."

"That's fabulous, Ginny. I'm so happy for you."

"Yes, super-duper exciting." Sophia looked pointedly at Ginny. "But if you don't tell her what happened with Steven, I'm gonna do it for you."

Joy nudged her best friend. "Man, when did you get so bossy?"

"Been hanging around you too much, I guess."

Joy and Sophia laughed then returned their attention to Ginny.

"After he told me that, he took my hands in his, looked me straight in the eyes, and said, 'Ginny Rose, you've done amazing things over the past year. Simply amazing. And even though you said you didn't know who you were, I did. And I love that woman. I love you.'"

Joy and Sophia sighed at the declaration.

Now Ginny was full-on happy crying. "I know, right? How did I get so lucky? So then I blubbered and blabbered on, I don't really know about what—you know me—but eventually I said I loved him too."

Joy's fingers drummed against the gift on her lap. "That's pretty much the best story ever." *Will I ever have one like it?*

She'd never asked that before, not for years, anyway. When Sophia and William had gotten together last year, she'd felt nothing but joy for them. Nothing. Not one iota of comparison or jealousy or anything.

Now, though?

She wished she could pause time so this week would last forever.

No. She knew her future, and she'd always been okay with it. One romantic holiday with a guy she barely knew wouldn't change that. If she could just stay focused on how this was temporary and try to enjoy herself anyway, then maybe it would be a nice story to keep for herself if she ever gave loneliness an inch in her life.

"Yes, it is. Now." Sophia swung her gaze toward Joy. "Don't think you're getting out of telling us about what happened in London." Her eyebrows rose and her lips quirked.

At that moment, the doorbell chimed. The guys had arrived.

Joy released a sigh—saved by the bell, literally—and hopped up. "That will have to wait, I guess."

No, she couldn't put off Sophia forever, but for now, her heart raced in anticipation of spending time with Oliver again. *Merry Christmas to me.*

How was this her life? Joy felt as if she'd walked onto the set of a Christmas movie.

A gentle snow fell where she stood just outside Sophia's house, caressing her cheeks and eyelashes. It had been fluttering down since lunch time, so a few inches covered the ground.

According to Sophia, the dusting would melt rather quickly once it warmed up, which was supposed to happen tomorrow—just in time for the wedding in three days.

Oliver stood beside her, one arm looped around her shoulders, Rascal at his feet. Together, they watched the slow fluff twirl to meet the sleepy town. The street remained quiet, not a car or person about. Chimneys puffed out curls of smoke, and the lamppost she'd begun to think of as "theirs" emitted a soft glow.

Once again, it was just the two of them in a world of subtle color and peace.

"What are you thinking?" Oliver's breath warmed her ear.

Joy pulled her gaze from the sky and connected it with his. "That this has been such a lovely day." Feeling bold, she snagged his free hand. She'd have tugged him to sit on the bench next to the lamp, but snow covered the wooden slats. "And that this is the perfect way to end Christmas Day."

He leaned down to give her a kiss—too quick but still potent. They'd managed to sneak a few pecks here and there, but with so many of their friends crowding into Sophia's tiny house to celebrate the holiday, there hadn't been much occasion to be alone until now. "And it's not quite over yet."

"What do you mean?"

He lowered his arm and opened his thick gray coat. From the inside pocket, he plucked something flat wrapped in tissue paper. "It isn't much, but I thought you may fancy them."

Joy carefully took Oliver's gift in her purple-mittened hand. The paper crinkled as she unfolded it from what felt like cardstock of some sort. As soon as she saw the picture of two large mice, Joy couldn't help the laugh that fell from her lips. She flipped through the same vintage Christmas cards she'd been eyeing in the antique shop the first day they'd met—ten in all—each one more ridiculous than the last.

"Thank you." Biting her lip, she glanced at him again. "But I didn't get you anything."

"I'm sure you can think of something." Humor glinted in his eye.

"Hmm." As Joy slipped the cards inside her jacket, she turned to face him. "How about a nice pat on the back?"

"That'd be great—if I were Rascal."

"A hug, then?"

Oliver stepped closer and put his hands around her waist. "Getting warmer."

"Yes, a hug *would* make me warmer, thanks." Despite the chill of the snow against her face, her lips twisted into a full-on grin. This was too fun.

He pulled her to him, and she snuggled against his chest. How did she fit so perfectly here in a place she hadn't known existed more than a week ago?

After a few moments of delicious heat, she glanced up and quirked an eyebrow. "I do have one more idea ..."

"And what's that?"

"A kiss, of course."

"I suppose I could accept that."

"You have to come closer, though. A girl can only lift on her tiptoes so much."

He complied and their noses nearly touched.

Joy's arms encircled his neck as she grazed her lips against his cheek. "There you go. Merry Christmas."

His chuckle shot joy right into her heart. "That's probably the best gift I'll receive this year or any other."

And somehow, she believed he meant it. "Challenge accepted."

"What challenge is that?"

Looking at him with mock sincerity, Joy blinked rapidly. "The challenge of giving you an even better gift every year, of course."

Something shifted in his eyes, from joking to serious in two seconds flat. Then she realized what she'd said. How she'd sounded. What she'd presumed. Joy swallowed hard. She hadn't meant to ...

But trying to explain away that she'd made some giant implications would only be awkward, so she did what she'd been longing to do all day.

She snagged his lips with her own.

His arms tightened around her back, and her arms dragged him closer so there wasn't much between them other than her questions. But with every moment locked in his embrace, Joy steadily released her doubts. A continual ebb and flow of deepening and lightening kisses continued as the passion mounted inside her, an aching need pulsing, begging to escape. She felt it all the way to the toes curled inside her pink boots.

Finally, she broke away, needing to catch her breath. Her head spun and her pulse galloped as Oliver crushed her to his chest. The rapid beating of his heart proved she wasn't the only one affected by their chemistry.

"I very much look forward to seeing how you top that in future." His whisper sent a thrill of longing and sorrow through her.

What future?

Maybe she could banish the thought if she lingered here, anchored in the beauty of the present. Joy closed her eyes and inhaled the scent of him.

Oliver's fingers played with a short strand of her hair as he continued holding her. "I need to go but I don't want to." Dinner with his aunt and a few of her friends was supposed to begin at six, and it had already been five forty-five when they'd come outside.

"And I need to go inside." Sophia's mom would arrive in the morning, and Ginny had headed off to spend the evening with

Steven's family, so tonight it'd just be her, Sophia, and William. "But I don't want to either."

"I suppose I'll be the responsible one then." Icy cold met Joy's cheeks upon his release. The twinkling lights strung along Sophia's roof illuminated his teasing smile. "Will I see you tomorrow?"

"I hope so. Thank you again for the cards. I love them."

"You're welcome. And I think it will come as no surprise that I loved your gift as well—and the enthusiasm with which you gave it."

Surely she'd left him in no doubt of her feelings. "Merry Christmas, Oliver."

"Merry Christmas, Joy."

With that, she spun on her heel and hightailed it inside the house, leaning against the door after she'd shut it.

"Well, well, well. Looking a bit flushed, are we?" Sophia stood in front of her, arms crossed, a huge grin plastered on her face.

Joy peeled off her mittens and parka, which she hung on the coatrack before moving into the living room. "It was cold outside. Where's William?"

"He said he's taking a nap in my room, but I think he just wanted to give us a chance to catch up. And don't change the subject." Sophia followed her into the room and plopped onto the couch. On her television, she'd queued up a Christmas station that featured a roaring fire and played holiday tunes at a low volume.

In the bleak midwinter, frosty wind made moan. Earth stood hard as iron, water like a stone ...

"Who, me?" Joy couldn't bring herself to sit just yet, so she wandered to the front window next to the Christmas tree. Peeking through the curtains, she could just make out Oliver and Rascal's retreating forms.

Snow had fallen, snow on snow, snow on snow. In the bleak midwinter, long ago.

"You really like him, huh?" Sophia's voice had dropped all teasing.

Joy turned to face her best friend again. "Yeah."

"I haven't seen you this gone over a guy since … well, never, actually. There was Chase, but even he only lasted three dates."

"I know, Soph, but there's no future between me and Oliver thanks to the small matter of my parents and his job. It's just not realistic." But oh, how right it had felt being in his arms. That had been real enough.

In the bleak midwinter, a stable-place sufficed. The Lord God Almighty—Jesus Christ.

"That's what I thought when I first started to fall for William. I didn't think it would work out. But look at us now." Sophia patted the spot next to her on the couch.

Dragging her feet, Joy walked over and slumped against the cushions. She snatched a pillow and hugged it to her chest, focusing her gaze on the undulating flames flickering on the TV. "It's different for you. You didn't have anything tying you down in the States." Joy cringed. "I don't mean it like that. I love my parents."

"Of course you do." Sophia snuggled close to Joy, each woman supporting the other—a symbol for their friendship if ever there were one. "Did you consider what I said last week about applying for some jobs?"

"Yes. I subscribed to a site with job postings." She thought about the notifications she'd received already for therapist jobs in her area. None of them had been quite what she'd be looking for, but Joy had to admit a flicker of longing at the thought of returning to counseling women who needed help.

"That's a great step."

"Thanks for encouraging me to do it. All of this with Mom

and Dad, the move to Florida, selling my practice ... it's just been an overwhelming time."

"I'm sorry I haven't been there with you. And to throw a wrench in things with my wedding."

"Stop it." Joy nudged her with an elbow. "There's nowhere I'd rather be."

"I'm guessing part of that has nothing to do with me."

Joy groaned. Her friend wasn't going to let up with the Oliver stuff, was she? "You got me. Obviously, I'm enjoying the scenery too."

"I'll bet you are."

They laughed and the fire on the television danced.

What can I give Him, poor as I am?

"Joy." Sophia's words came out soft, cautious. "Are you ever going to tell me what happened between you and Oliver in London?"

Yet what I can I give Him, give my heart.

"Of course. I'll tell you everything, friend."

CHAPTER 12

"Hey, Mom." Joy slipped from the warmth of the giant manor where Sophia's rehearsal lunch was in full swing.

Though it was a surprising fifty-two degrees and the recent snow had never reached the town of Wendall where the wedding venue was located—about fifty miles from Port Willis—the air still vibrated with a chill. She stepped into a gorgeous garden that wound from the house down toward a magnificent, ancient-looking tree that overlooked a bluff. Many plants in the garden lay dormant, but other flowers and trees of all colors and varieties decorated either side of a crushed gravel walkway.

Joy stared at a pink rhododendron bush as she tried to focus on her mom. "How are you feeling?"

"Oh, just fine, dear." The vague tone in her mother's voice indicated that she might not remember who she was talking to—despite that *she* had called Joy—but she was putting on a good show nonetheless. A wet cough rattled across the phone.

Joy straightened. "That didn't sound good."

"It's just this cold I've had. It's been bothering me for days."

"You have a cold?" She'd called her parents two days ago on

Christmas, but Mom hadn't been up to talking, and Dad hadn't mentioned Mom was sick.

If Joy had been there, she'd have known. Instead, she'd spent the time helping Sophia with last-minute details and fitting in as much time with Oliver as possible. She should have tried calling them again before now.

"Are the nurses taking good care of you?" Joy stuck her free hand into her parka pocket.

"Of course, of course."

Another cough put Joy on high alert. "Mom, are you sure you're okay? Has Dr. Lieberman been to see you yet? He should check your lungs, make sure they're clear."

"Stuff and nonsense. I'll be right as rain after a few nights of rest."

"Can I talk to Dad, please?" She started walking in order to stay warm. As she rounded a bend in the garden path, the sun popped out of the shade and warmed Joy's cheeks.

"No, he ... well, I don't remember where he went."

"That's okay, Mom. Don't worry about it." Joy breathed a sigh of frustration. In about three days, she'd be back in Florida, monitoring Mom's care more closely. She simply had to trust that her mother would be fine until then and that others were capable of caring for her in the interim.

Yeah, right. There was nothing *simple* about that.

After a few minutes of sharing the wedding plans for the next day, Joy came into view of the tree where Sophia and William's rehearsal had been held an hour ago. The wedding party had stood along the cliff, which offered a stunning prospect of the ocean but also wind that had pummeled them. Thank goodness for a blessedly brief ceremony and strategically placed outdoor heaters, or Joy would have frozen solid.

Now that same wind howled across the phone, making it difficult to hear Mom. "Sorry, what was that?"

"I'm tired."

"I'll let you go. Thanks for calling. Love you."

Mom hung up without saying another word. Even though Joy knew the disease was the reason Mom rarely acknowledged her love anymore, it felt like rejection and rejection always stung.

She stuck her phone into the back pocket of her jeans and leaned against the tree, watching the swirling depths of the ocean below. Her chaotic hair tickled the tips of her ears as it twirled with the gushes of air being sent upward.

"There you are." Oliver's comment nearly got lost on the crazy gale as he joined her at the tree. "The bride was looking for you. Apparently it's time for them to say a few thank-yous."

"All right." Joy couldn't keep the sadness from tingeing her words. With every moment that passed, normal life beckoned her back. Never had she been one to run away from her problems, but if she could only slow time …

"What's wrong, love?"

She bit her lip, tears nearly finding her eyes. "I just talked to my mom."

"Ah." His arm slipped around her shoulders, and she felt safe there, buffeted from the roiling draft coming up from the sea. Amazing how he understood her—that she didn't necessarily need to talk out the pain again. That she simply needed a companion to walk through it with her.

Oh, goodness. She really was going to full-on cry if she didn't get out of here and back to Sophia, so she put her arm around Oliver's waist and directed them toward the garden.

As they neared the house, Oliver stopped, holding Joy with him. He dropped his arm and framed her face with both hands, stroking her cheeks with his thumbs. "I'm sorry for your pain, Joy."

And that was all it took. Big plops of salty water streamed from her eyes onto his fingers. He took her into his arms and held her while she sobbed, soaking his brown cashmere sweater in the process.

After her tears died down, she pulled back slightly and looked up at him. "Thank you." Her nose felt nearly blocked and her makeup was sure to be in shambles. "You wouldn't happen to have a handkerchief, would you?"

"I'm not *that* old."

A smile flitted across her face at the tease. "But it would be British of you, wouldn't it?"

"I'm sorry to disappoint."

"Guess you can't believe everything you see in the movies." She knuckled away the excess moisture from under her eyes as she laughed.

"Real life can be better than the movies." He swooped in for a kiss that was over far too quickly. But the look in the depths of his brown eyes speared her. "This is madness, Joy."

"What?" Her words were soft as the petals of the Christmas roses blooming in the bush to their right.

"The way I feel about you."

She was afraid to ask what he meant by it.

He snatched her hand in his. "It came on like that winter snow the day we were in London. So quick, I'm not sure either of us saw it coming. And I don't know about you, but I've never experienced something this powerful before."

That certainly couldn't be true. "What about with Jana?"

"Jana and I were childhood chums, and things between us developed slowly. Looking back, I'm not sure I loved her in the right way, as a husband should love a wife. It was more like best mates who settled into a romance."

"My favorite romantic movie trope is friends-turned-lovers." Anne and Gilbert. Harry and Sally. Emma and Knightley. "I always imagined that's how my story would go."

You don't have a story. This is it. A chance encounter. A winter romance. Nothing more.

But she wanted it to be more.

For the first time, she allowed herself to dream. What would it be like to leave responsibility in the dust and pursue a relationship with Oliver after Sophia's wedding and beyond? To see it through?

Ugh, she was a horrible daughter to even consider it. Her parents had always been there for her when she needed them. How could she possibly do any less?

They began to saunter down the path arm in arm. Oliver's cologne wafted toward her, the scent fresh and deep. "What's going on in that brilliant mind of yours?"

"Just thinking."

"About ..."

"The future."

The pressure of his arm around her increased slightly as he kissed the top of her head. "Don't borrow trouble."

Might as well say it. Break the bubble now. "What are we doing, Oliver? There's no future between us."

"You don't know that."

She gently disengaged herself from him. "I like you, Oliver. I really do. But that doesn't change the facts. And we're too old to play make believe." Her throat burned with the admission because that is just what she'd been doing—allowing herself to be swept away by the magic of the season, of Sophia's fairytale ending.

"I'm not pretending, Joy." Oliver moved toward her again, his boots crunching the gravel.

If only he'd stop looking at her like Charles Bingley looked at Jane Bennett, like Joe Fox looked at Kathleen Kelly, like Luke Danes looked at Lorelai Gilmore. "I'm not saying there's nothing between us. Clearly, there is. But it's just not realistic. There's nowhere for it to go. I'm not the kind of woman to pursue a relationship that's impossible before it begins. And you don't strike me as that kind of guy either."

"Why is it impossible? Simply because we live in different countries?"

"Don't you see that as a problem?"

"I admit it's not ideal, but it doesn't make things impossible. Just more complicated. But Joy, you're worth *complicated*."

Why did he have to be so wonderful and smooth and … wonderful? Clearly, her brain was mush around him. She closed her eyes at the thought, focusing on the problem at hand. "I appreciate you saying that. But there's no way I can abandon my parents. They depend on me, and I won't let them down." Not again, anyway.

"And you have no idea how much I admire you for it."

Her eyes opened again, and she tilted her head. "Then you wouldn't ever ask me to do it. And unless you're willing to leave your business behind …"

His jaw clenched.

"Exactly." She softened her voice and squeezed his upper arm.

"You're not leaving room for another possibility."

Was there really something she hadn't considered? "And what's that?"

"That there's some other solution that neither of us can see right now because it's *not* the future. Only God knows what will happen, and he can work anything out."

"I know that God *can* work things out but he doesn't always." Case in point—instead of Mom and Dad living out their retirement traveling the world as they'd always intended, they were stuck in the clutches of Alzheimer's and a slow, agonizing separation thanks to the disease. "We have to make the best decisions we can with the information we have right now."

"Normally I would readily agree to using logic in decision making. But sometimes the heart can't be told how to feel." Behind him, a radiant display of yellow flowers adorned an evergreen shrub. "Joy, do you know the last time it snowed in

Cornwall? It's been years. And do you know the last time it snowed here at Christmas time? Even longer. Yet, it happened. A year ago, we couldn't have predicted it. In fact, a year ago it was unusually warm at Christmastime. So, we can't tell the future, true. But you're forgetting one thing about the information we have right now."

"And what's that?" She couldn't keep the tremble from her voice.

"That what we're feeling for each other, it's rare. And it's a gift."

This was crazy. She'd always scoffed at the movies in which a couple met and fell hard for each other in a matter of days, yet that's what had happened.

Oliver looked at her with such longing that it stole her breath. All she wanted to do in the moment was burrow into his arms, forgetting that such things as Alzheimer's and oceans and responsibility even existed. But what good would it do? In a matter of days, she'd return to the United States. He'd return to London. And their time together would be nothing but a lovely and picturesque memory she'd hold onto when times got even tougher.

Joy swallowed, hard. "You're right. It's a beautiful gift. And I don't want to ruin the memory of it by arguing. It'd be easier to end it now instead of allowing things to grow bitter between us."

"Joy."

"I'm sorry, Oliver. I have to focus on Sophia right now. I'm supposed to be here for her, after all."

Then she rose up on her tiptoes, kissed his cheek, buried her hands into her jacket so she wouldn't reach for him again, and headed inside the manor.

CHAPTER 13

There couldn't be a more beautiful day for a more beautiful bride.

Joy's heart snagged at the sight of Sophia standing before a floor-length mirror in her A-line dress with beaded appliqués and capped sleeves. The basque waistline, tulle skirt with a lace hem, and chapel train worked together to perfectly highlight Sophia's allure. Her bright eyes and red lips popped even more than usual against the white of the dress. Tendrils of black curls framed her face, and her mouth pulled into a soft smile as she allowed her mom to hug her shoulders from behind.

She was Snow White about to marry her prince, and despite Joy's woes in the love department, she couldn't have been happier for her best friend.

"You are lovelier than any bride I've ever seen—and I've seen a lot." Sandy Barrett's voice wobbled as she squeezed her daughter. Stepping away, she straightened the portrait neckline of her elegant silver gown. Not many women of sixty-one could pull off the asymmetrically ruched bodice, dropped waistline, and cascading ruffles, but Sandy wore it well.

Sophia batted away the beginning of a tear before it could fall. "I won't cry. I won't cry."

Joy flounced past fellow bridesmaids Ginny and Mary with a box of tissues extended. "Yeah, right. We all know better than that. Stick some of these in your bouquet."

"Good idea." Sophia pulled a few tissues from the box then leaned forward to embrace Joy. "Thank you for everything you've done since you've arrived. I couldn't have accomplished this without you."

"Anything for you." After the rehearsal lunch the day before, they'd returned to Sophia's so her friend could pack luggage for the honeymoon. Joy had spent the time gathering everything they'd need to bring to the wedding venue today. Of course, during the packing, Sophia had demanded to know the reason for Joy's smudged mascara—the woman was way too observant—and Joy had spilled everything. At least she'd managed to reign in her tears that time.

"You look absolutely amazing." Ginny pushed forward in her ice-blue lace, empire-waisted gown. "Like the perfect chocolate truffle layer cake. Ooo, or better yet, a black-tie cheesecake with a raspberry topping. Elegant and classic but decidedly delicious."

"Uh, thank you?" Sophia's laugh sounded like tinkling glass as she embraced Ginny.

Mary, who was six feet tall but not intimidating in the slightest, slid a final bobby pin into her blond updo. "Now you're just making us all hungry."

"Good thing your family is catering today, then, because it means we're in for the best food ever." Sophia lowered herself daintily onto the edge of a chair.

"Between them, me as a bridesmaid, and my brother as the photographer, you couldn't have gotten married without the Hammett family." Mary slid a white faux fur wrap over her bridesmaid dress. Even though William and Sophia had rented portable heaters for the outside ceremony, Joy was grateful they'd have some extra coverage from the wind.

A knock sounded on the door of the bridal suite.

"Come in," Sophia called.

A handsome man stuck his head into the room, a camera slung around his neck. He was even taller than Mary with brown curls and the same bright green eyes as his sister. "If you're ready for photos, we can begin."

"Great, thanks, Michael."

"Sure. Would it be possible to grab the rings from you? I'd like to take some shots with them in the foreground and you and William in the background."

"Of course." Sophia turned to Joy. "Where are they?"

"They should be in the box with all the other things we brought with us today." Joy strode to the back corner of the room where she'd placed the box. Though it was normally the best man's job to hold on to the rings, William's brother Garrett hadn't been available to participate in the pre-wedding festivities. When Joy had volunteered to be in charge of the rings instead, the bride and groom had gladly agreed.

The box was kind of tall, so Joy had to strain to see into it. She sifted through the contents—a sewing kit, stain-remover wipes, breath mints, pain relievers, floss, extra buttons, deodorant, and more—and was about halfway done before a slow panic built inside her.

She remembered grabbing the rings and placing them on the dresser when she was gathering items the day before. But had she actually placed them in the box?

Or had she been too distracted by her break-up with Oliver that she'd forgotten?

"No." The word whooshed out and clanged an invisible bell that signaled doom.

"What's wrong?" Sophia appeared at her side.

Joy's hand skimmed the bottom of the box for the third time but didn't come up with anything else.

She'd failed her best friend. How was this possible?

"Joy? Are you okay?" Sophia's gentle touch was way nicer than Joy deserved.

Determined to stand her ground though faintness threatened, her eyes flitted to Sophia. "I forgot the rings."

Sophia's jaw went slack.

"I'm so sorry, friend. I can go get them—"

"You'd never make it back in time." Sophia chewed her bottom lip, leaving imprints in the red color. Her friend bravely straightened her shoulders and visibly shook off the concern. "It'll be fine. We just won't do the ring exchange part, or maybe we can find some twisty ties or something like that."

"On it!" Ginny took off out the door and down the hall, presumably toward the kitchen.

Sophia deserved so much more than twisty ties for rings. She didn't even have her engagement ring to show off because she'd chosen to have it soldered to the wedding band the week before.

How could Joy have allowed herself to become so inattentive to the people who mattered most in her life? First, she'd failed Mom. Now her best friend.

This was a disaster.

"Don't worry." Sophia tilted her head and smiled. "There are bound to be things that go wrong today. But remember—in the end, I'll be William's wife, and that's all I care about."

Dad had tried to soothe Joy too, telling her that Mom's escape and fall were almost inevitable at some point. That was one of his arguments for moving to the assisted living facility—so the likelihood of future occurrences would be lessened. But Joy had shut that down, reminding him Mom had always valued family and home and that staying together had to be a top priority.

Oliver's words from their conversation on Christmas Eve floated back to her. *"I started to see myself as some kind of savior.... I thought it was solely on my shoulders to save my employees from ruin the way I'd been ruined years before that. But it wasn't. Because I forgot to factor in God."*

Was Joy doing the same, inserting herself into a role she wasn't meant to play?

But employer and daughter were different things. A daughter was forever. And yes, she needed God's help in caring for her mom, but she also recognized that God wasn't going to just provide another way. *Joy* was the way he was providing.

"Joy? It'll be fine, okay?"

She forced a smile at Sophia's words. "Okay."

But she knew that wasn't true. Not one bit. And as soon as she had a chance, she'd do what she could to right the wrong she'd committed against her friend.

❄

If she timed it just right, she'd be able to get to Sophia's and back before her friend departed for the honeymoon.

Joy swiped the mascara sure to be dripping from her eyes and headed toward the ballroom's exit. She'd just delivered the sappiest of all maid of honor reception speeches, leaving both her and Sophia in tears. Now the dancing was in full swing as the bride and groom made their way around the room to greet guests.

Stopping a moment, Joy turned and peeked back at her best friend. Sophia was radiant standing next to William, who looked dashing in a peak-lapel tuxedo and simple black silk bowtie. The way he only had eyes for his bride, whose laugh fluttered through the manor's ballroom as she clutched a flute of non-alcoholic cider and talked with abandon—well, Joy's heart nearly burst at the sight.

But then her attention caught on the hand holding Sophia's drink. Instead of a gorgeous princess-cut diamond that should have reflected the holiday lights strung from the ceiling, her ring finger featured a red twisty tie from a bag of bread Ginny had managed to locate in the kitchen just minutes before the ceremony.

The audience had laughed along with the bride and groom as they'd twisted them onto each other's fingers, joking about never taking them off. But the entire time, Joy's gut had roiled, her face flaming. It had been difficult to push aside her guilt and enjoy the sacred ceremony, even her two favorite parts—when Sophia had cried as she'd walked down the aisle toward the man she loved, and when William pledged to love and care for Sophia.

And if that hadn't been enough to make Joy sick to her stomach, she'd spent the entire wedding thus far avoiding Oliver—first his gaze, which had tried to catch hers more than once throughout the ceremony, and then his presence during the reception, when he'd attempted to talk with her. Fortunately, as maid of honor she had several duties to perform, so she had plenty of excuses for not having time to chat.

Focus, Joy.

Right. She left the noise of the hundred or so guests and classic love songs like "My Girl" behind and entered a hallway that eventually led to steps converging with another set of stairs to form the grand staircase.

Amid the goings-on, she'd formulated a plan—slip out after speeches, borrow Ginny's car, get the rings from Sophia's house, and return before the newlyweds left. She'd miss the cake cutting, but she hoped Sophia would be too busy to notice her absence.

From the bottom of the stairs, a man approached. Oliver.

Seeing him again—especially in his tux, ice-blue vest, and matching straight tie, his hair and beard trim and neat, his eyes sparkling with concern—nearly collapsed her lungs. He stopped just shy of her, putting them momentarily at about the same height.

"I'm sorry, but I don't have time to talk. I've got to go." She picked up the hem of her gown and continued past him down the steps. "I have to get those rings to Sophia and William before they leave for their honeymoon."

Oliver caught up to Joy and matched her pace. They reached the foyer, where tall tapestries decorated the walls and sconces lit the cavernous space filled with columns and grandeur. "They're staying at a B&B tonight then flying out to Italy early in the morning. They won't have a chance to swing by home on their way to the airport."

"But—"

"Ginny said I could borrow her car. I know I don't have any driving experience here, but it's mostly a small road and not too far. Daylight is almost gone, but I've driven at night plenty of times, so I'll be good."

"Joy."

She zipped her parka over the blue dress, preparing to face the cold. "I'm sorry, Oliver, I have to go."

But his hand on her arm halted her midstride. "If you'd just listen for a moment, there's something I need to tell you."

"Sophia has to have those rings. They can't go off on their honeymoon without them. It wouldn't be right." Turning, she finally allowed herself to peek up at him. Mistake. His warm gaze nearly drove her into his arms. How she wished she could hide there. But she was a grown woman who needed to buck up and handle her own problems. She'd made a mistake. And she'd set it right. "She deserves perfect. I already screwed that up for her wedding, but I can at least make sure her honeymoon starts off on the right foot. She needs those rings."

"I agree."

Joy tugged out of his grasp. "Then why are you trying to stop me?"

A smile slid easily across Oliver's lips. "If you'd let me get a word in, you'd know."

"Sorry." She blew out a breath and crossed her arms over her chest. "What are you trying to say?"

He stuffed his hand into his pants pocket. "I have the rings."

"What?"

He produced the two circular objects, and Joy nearly yelled in exultation.

"My parents arrived in Port Willis this morning, so when I heard the rings had been left behind, I called them. My dad drove them down as soon as he could. I was just coming from the parking lot to give them to you." Holding the rings out to her, he waited until she opened her palm. Then he dropped them in.

The metal felt cool as her fingers curled around them. She'd better stick them in the pocket of her jacket for safekeeping. "But how did he get into Sophia's house? How did he know where they were?"

"My aunt has a key for emergencies. I asked William, and he asked Sophia where she thought they may be. He was only there a handful of minutes before locating them."

"I don't know what to say." Though her mind was spinning, her mouth couldn't keep up. "I guess we should head back up."

Oliver followed along as she made her way to the ballroom.

But just before re-entering the wedding, she turned. "Thank you."

"Of course. I care about William and Sophia too. And you." For a few moments, Oliver just stared at her. "I knew you'd try to sneak away. And that Sophia cares more about having you here than having her ring."

Even after less than two weeks, he knew her well.

He continued. "You know that, right? People don't want you around simply because you do nice things for them or help them out. It's because you're you. You light up every room you're in. You live up to your name more than anyone I've ever known."

She sucked in a quick breath. How was she supposed to leave him standing here, pretending indifference?

From inside the ballroom, "Unchained Melody" began to play. One of her favorites. So soulful, so full of longing. It fit her mood perfectly right about now. "Dance with me?"

Without breaking eye contact, he took her hand and led her inside. Then, after helping her out of her parka, his gentle tug brought her with him to the dance floor. Taking her right hand in his left, and placing his other around her waist, he pulled her close.

She leaned into him, the wool of his tuxedo jacket surprisingly soft against her cheek. They fit so well together—and not just in the way their bodies moved fluidly around the dance floor, but also in the way he'd come to her rescue without her even asking him to. The way he'd anticipated her moves and decided to act in aiding her.

Simply put, he'd become her hero when she hadn't even been looking for one.

And that was the best kind.

"Joy?"

"Hmm?"

"I didn't get a chance to tell you how smashing you look tonight. Simply gorgeous, love."

Do not look up, do not look up, do not look up.

If she did, she'd be a goner.

Not that she wasn't already. But the fragile seam holding her heart together would finally break completely if she let him kiss her again.

"Thank you," she mumbled. Joy forced her eyes to roam the room, at the other couples swirling around them.

There were Mary and her husband, Blake, dancing comfortably and talking.

And Ginny and Steven, heads together, smiling.

Nearby, William twirled Sophia and dipped her then leaned in for a kiss.

Pop. There went a stitch. Joy tightened her hold on Oliver's hand and he did likewise. She closed her eyes and allowed herself this moment.

Pop. Another.

The song ended more quickly than she'd hoped, and the DJ replaced it with something upbeat. Despite the change in pace, Oliver kept rocking Joy back and forth for a few moments longer. He must know what she did—this was their last chance to be together.

Her heart hung on by a thread.

Groaning, Joy pushed herself from his arms. "That was great. Thank you."

"Joy—"

"I … can't." Holding in a sob, she maneuvered around guests and raced to her jacket. She had to return the rings before she completely lost her mind and focus.

But as she felt in her jacket pocket for the rings, her phone vibrated against her hand. Tugging it from the inner pocket, she studied the screen. She'd missed a call from Dad. And he'd left a voicemail.

It was probably nothing. But why, then, did she have this sinking in the pit of her stomach? Cold dread wrapped itself around her heart, jerking at the last stitch holding Joy together.

With her jacket flung over one arm and her phone clutched in hand, she hurried from the room to the relative quiet of the hallway and pressed the button to listen to her voicemail.

Dad's voice filled the line. *"Hi sweetie. I don't want to worry you, but your mom has developed pneumonia. They're going to keep monitoring her here and move her to the hospital if she gets any worse. I'll keep you informed about what's going on when I know more. Love you. I hope the wedding is going well."*

Pneumonia? People died of pneumonia, especially the elderly. Especially those with weakened immune systems or those in hospitals.

She dialed Dad's number, but the call went to voicemail. "Dad, it's me. Call me when you get a chance. I have a few questions about Mom."

What now? She wasn't supposed to leave town until Monday, but she couldn't wait around while Mom suffered. Who knew the severity of her condition?

The rehab center. They'd know how Mom was really doing. Joy dialed and the front desk connected her to Mom's nurse, Linda. Joy's voice shook as she asked the question she feared speaking aloud. "Linda, hi, it's Joy Beckman. How is she?"

"Tolerating treatment at the moment. Sleeping when she's not coughing."

"She's stable, then?"

"Yes, but you know how quickly someone can turn."

"Okay, thanks, Linda."

"I'm sorry I can't give you a more definitive answer."

"It's all right. I'll be there as soon as I can."

As she ended the call, Joy shoved the phone back into her jacket and snagged the rings from the other pocket. Then she hauled herself through the ballroom doors again and scanned the room, spotting Sophia talking to her mom and Ginny.

Her heels clicked on the wood floors as she crossed as fast as her short legs would carry her. Upon her approach, Sophia's smile flattened. "What's wrong, Joy?"

"My mom. Pneumonia. Too early to tell what's going on. But …"

"You need to go."

Joy's chest heaved from the exertion of almost running in three-inch heels. And there was the emotional exercise too, what with her insides flipping all over themselves. "I don't want to abandon you."

"You're not." Sophia drew Joy into an embrace. "I love you. You're the best friend a girl could ask for. I'm so glad you were able to share this day with me."

"Me too."

Sophia released Joy. "Now go."

"I can drive you if you need me to," Ginny said. "Unless you'd rather have Oliver do it. I'm sure he wouldn't mind."

"No." That would just be ... too much. "I'd appreciate that, though I'd hate to pull you away from here."

"The most important thing is you getting back to your mom." Sophia placed a hand on Joy's arm and squeezed.

"Thanks, friend. Oh! I almost forgot." She opened her palm and held out the rings.

Sophia let out a joyous gasp. "Where did you get those?"

"Oliver."

Her friend's brows knit together. "Are you sure—"

"Yes. I'm sure." After so many years of friendship, she knew what Sophia was thinking. "Mom needs me. And I have to let him go."

Pop. The last stitch burst. Joy hurried from the room before she could ruin Sophia's happy wedding with her sobs.

CHAPTER 14

She couldn't remember ever feeling so exhausted or emotionally spent.

Joy stood outside her mom's room at the skilled nursing facility, fingers trembling as her hand hovered over the door handle. Why couldn't she make herself go inside? Maybe because she didn't know what she'd find. That Mom was still here and not in the hospital should be a good sign. But what if the facility hadn't been taking good care of her while Joy had been gone? Was Dad enough of an advocate? This place had the best reviews of any of the skilled nursing facilities in the area, but ...

Just go in, Joy.

Inhaling as deeply as she could manage, she pushed open the door. The room was on the dark side, the evening sun barely peeking through the window. As Joy approached the bed, her legs wobbled from exhaustion. Thank goodness she'd taken the time to change into comfy clothes and flat shoes at Sophia's house before taking off for the airport last night. Of course, she probably smelled like airplane and no doubt her expertly applied wedding makeup had worn off. Plus, her leftover curls were probably as flat as a savanna by now.

But Joy hadn't been able to reach her father at all since he'd left that voicemail, so she'd come straight here from the airport.

As her eyes adjusted to the dimness, she could make out her mother lying in bed, eyes closed. A cough erupted from her lips, and she fidgeted, moaning.

"Mom." Joy rushed forward.

"JoJo?" Her dad spoke from the chair next to the bed. He reached beneath his glasses to rub his eyes. "What are you doing here? I thought you weren't supposed to be home yet."

"I got your message and hurried back."

A frown marred his normally jolly face. "You didn't have to do that. I only meant to keep you informed. Your mother—"

"Needed me."

Her dad studied her, frowning. "Let's go into the hallway so we don't disturb her."

With a glance back at Mom, Joy followed Dad out of the room. Her tired eyes ached against the glare of the bright fluorescent lights. She and Dad made their way into the unoccupied waiting room at the end of the hall. A TV hanging on the wall crackled with the evening news. On a side table in the corner rested a Charlie Brown Christmas tree decorated half-heartedly with a few tiny red bulbs.

"She's fine, JoJo. The antibiotics are working and she's responding."

"That's good to hear." Joy's muscles protested as she plopped into a not-so-comfortable seat. "I know how bad pneumonia can be, and when I couldn't get ahold of you, I came as quickly as I could."

Dad sat next to her. "Did you miss the wedding?"

"Only the last few hours of the reception. Sophia understood."

But did Oliver?

She couldn't think about that now, about how she'd left without saying goodbye. Was it duty or fear that had led her to do such a thing?

Maybe a bit of both.

Joy hurried on. "But I'm back now and things are going to be different than before. You guys have my full focus again. During the plane ride, I started researching how we may be able to get a little more help with Mom at home. That would give us both a bit of a break from caregiving on a regular basis, which would allow us—"

"I've decided to move."

A distinct buzzing filled Joy's ears, and it had nothing to do with the television meteorologist reciting the weather report for the following day—sunny with a high of seventy-four.

She must not have heard him right. "Come again?"

His features softened and he leaned his head back against the white wall. "The Glenn River facility. I showed you the pamphlet, remember? They have an immediate opening, and I've decided to take it for your mother and me. We can live together in the same apartment. It's often difficult to find a situation like this, especially one as affordable as Glenn River."

He couldn't be serious. "But Dad, you don't have to spend the money. You have me." Joy gripped the wooden armrests until her fingers pulsed and pressed white.

Dad placed his hand over hers.

He was putting on a brave front, Joy could see that. There's no way he could actually want to leave the house he and Mom loved and move into a tiny apartment. To have strangers inside his home every day, multiple times a day. To give up the life he knew.

"I'm sorry." A tear slid down Joy's nose as she bent forward in her chair, placing her elbows onto her knees, her head into her hands. "This is all my fault."

"What are you talking about?"

"If I hadn't fallen asleep, let Mom leave the house unattended . . ."

"JoJo, look at me."

"No." She couldn't bear to see the pain in his eyes.

Dad sighed and ran his hand down her back in light circles like he had so many times when she was a child. "I was already considering the move before your mother broke her hip. You know as well as I do that it would have eventually come to this, that we wouldn't be able to care for her at home for the rest of her life. It has nothing to do with you and your capabilities. Having you here has been so helpful—you'll never know how much—and we've made some wonderful memories this year. But it's time to let someone else carry the burden."

Her head popped up. "Mom's not a burden."

"No, but caring for her is. One that you were never meant to take on your shoulders forever. And it could be a long road yet."

"But I'm her daughter."

"And I'm her husband. In sickness and in health, until death do us part, remember? This is my life, and this is my choice. I choose to be with her, for as many days as we have left together. That may be ten months, or it may be ten years. No one but the good Lord knows. But you still have your whole life ahead of you. In the moments when she's lucid, she's told me that she feels awful that you've thrown away your career to be here with her. And she doesn't want you throwing away your chance at happiness, whatever that may include."

"I'm not throwing anything away." Oliver's face flashed in Joy's mind, which only made her chest tighten more. "This is my life and my choice too, Dad. I don't want to have any regrets."

Then why did you leave him without saying goodbye?

She nearly growled in frustration. Why couldn't her inner voice just take a day off for once?

Joy stood and wiped the moisture from under her eyes. She steeled her petite frame. "I need to see Mom again. Once she's past this pneumonia business—and I'm not dead on my feet after nearly a day of travel and no sleep—we can discuss this like two rational adults."

Then she charged down the hallway toward Mom's room before Dad could get out another word.

CHAPTER 15

The whole world was preparing for the start of something new. Why couldn't Joy get on board?

She walked the brick pathway winding along the banks of the river in downtown New Port Richey, which was just up the road from the skilled nursing facility. Having spent every waking moment in her mom's room since she had arrived the day before, she'd finally stepped outside for some air.

And as she passed the facility's front desk, that's when she'd remembered—tomorrow was New Year's Eve. The day after that, New Year's. A time for making resolutions. For welcoming change.

Joy didn't want to do either one. She wanted to keep things exactly as they were.

But why?

Inhaling the scent of steaks cooking on a charcoal grill nearby, Joy meandered the path, passing plenty of couples and families taking advantage of the seventy-degree weather. No need for a parka here, just a linen long-sleeved red blouse, cuffed jeans, and white Keds. In grassy areas beside the river, people biked, tossed Frisbees, and picnicked under the sycamore and redbud maple trees. Nearly every bench along the path was filled.

Her phone rang from her back pocket. Joy nearly fumbled it in her rush to remove it. As she glanced at the Caller ID, she did a double take and answered. "Uh, excuse me? You're only two days into your honeymoon. Why in the world are you calling me?"

Sophia laughed. "Well, hello to you too."

"Sorry, I was just so shocked to hear from you." Joy let up on the teasing. "Everything okay?"

"Oh, yeah. Great, in fact. Italy is absolutely breathtaking. There's so much history here in Rome."

"I can't wait to hear all about it. When it's over. Does your husband know you called me? I'm surprised he doesn't want you all to himself right now."

A man with Oliver's build walked toward her, a leashed dog beside him. The terrier barked at Joy as they passed.

She sped up.

"It was his idea." Joy could picture Sophia sticking out her tongue in that playful way that only her closest friends ever saw. "I know we've texted a bit, but I have a few minutes before we head out to dinner and wanted to check in. How's your mom? How are you?"

Joy released a breath and some tension from her shoulders with it. "Mom's doing good, actually. Much better than I thought she'd be. In terms of the pneumonia, anyway." The confusion seemed to be at an all-time high—or maybe Joy had just forgotten in her nearly two-week absence how bad things really were. So far, Mom hadn't recognized her once since she'd come home. It had been all Joy could do not to break down at the polite distance in her eyes. "And me … well, I'm hanging in there. Dad decided to move them into that assisted living and memory care facility once Mom's released from rehab, so I'm currently devising ways to convince him that he's making a mistake."

Her friend grew silent on the other end for a few moments before speaking again. "Is he, though?"

"Soph, we've talked about this."

"I know, but …" Sophia sighed. "Never mind. Have you gotten any job leads?"

"No." The temptation not to tell the whole truth came and went. "To be honest, I unsubscribed from the job alerts."

"Why?"

"I can't pretend that my reasoning is entirely well thought out. It may have occurred yesterday after my dad told me his decision." She'd been so emotional, so determined to do her part in clinging to the future she knew to be right.

"Ah."

"Don't 'ah' me."

"Like you haven't had many, many occasions to 'ah' me over the years."

"Older, wiser, remember?" Joy stood aside for a mom pushing a double-wide stroller along the path. The woman thanked her, and Joy continued on her way to, well, wherever she was going.

A metaphor for her life, perhaps?

"Joy, in all seriousness, though … how are you feeling about being there? About leaving England?"

The question hung between them for longer than it should have. But Joy simply didn't have an answer. "I'm trying not to think about it."

"That won't work for long."

"I know." She spied an unoccupied bench and stopped walking. Sliding onto it, Joy stared out across the river. A kayak glided by, paddles piercing the sparkling water. "How was he?"

"Oliver?"

"Yeah."

"You sure you want to know?"

"No. And yes." Her teeth nipped the inside of her lower lip, and the metallic taste of blood collided with her tongue.

"He was devastated, Joy. He couldn't believe …"

"That I didn't say goodbye?"

"Yes. And, I think, that it was really over." Sophia exhaled. "I know you told him you didn't see a future together. But I think he hoped you'd change your mind somehow."

"But I had to leave."

"Except …"

Joy straightened. "Except what?"

"Well, your mom was actually okay, right?"

"I didn't know that at the time." She sounded defensive, yes, but really. After all that Joy had been through with her mom, Sophia had no right to doubt her decisions.

"True—and I would have probably done the same thing. It's just that …"

"Spit it out, Sophia." Oh, hostility wasn't a good look on her, but in a way, it felt good. "How would you have handled *your* mom being sick? I know it's hard to imagine since she's never had any health-related issues, but please, tell me how I *should have* behaved."

The quiet on the other end told Joy she'd gone too far.

"I'm sorry, friend. I know you love me." She groaned and closed her eyes momentarily as she massaged her forehead. "What were you trying to get through my thick skull?"

"I *do* love you, and that's the only reason I'm saying this." Sophia's voice shook.

Joy had spoken to her friend on the phone enough to know she was on the verge of tears. Guilt welled up in her throat.

"I'm just wondering if you being there with your mom has actually done anything to help her recover more quickly."

The gentle words carried with them a force that left Joy feeling slapped. "I guess not but it's only been a day. And even if it hasn't helped her, it's helped me to be close. Being away from her right now would be torture."

"Why, though?"

What was Sophia getting at? "Because I love her."

"Of course you do. That's not the issue. That's never been the issue. You love more fiercely and more completely than anyone I know. You hear someone you love is in trouble and make a snap decision to drop everything and help them."

"And there's something wrong with that?"

"No. But I think you sometimes assume that you're the only one who can help."

"That's not true." Right? "I just have a lot less going on than other people. More time available to help. No spouse, kids …"

"Is that why you couldn't let yourself accept the possibility of something with Oliver? Because you'd have to sacrifice the ability to help others? Do you think that just because I'm married now means I no longer can be there for those I love?"

"Of course not."

"Then maybe fear is what really stopped you from being with him."

"You have no idea how much it killed me to walk away from him." Joy couldn't sit anymore. She hopped up and pumped her legs as she headed back toward the nursing facility. Sophia's words—however lovingly spoken—pummeled her. But no matter how quickly she moved, she couldn't outrun them. "What do I have to be afraid of? The worst has already happened. I lost him."

"I'm so sorry, friend. I'm not trying to add to your pain."

"I know." Joy swallowed a few sobs. Ugh, she was so tired of crying. The last year had probably produced more tears than all the rest of her life combined.

"But think about it. It's less scary to choose your parents over Oliver. There's no risk of potential heartbreak. And you figure you have the backing of the Bible, right? The idea of 'putting others before yourself'? You don't even have to consider whether you made the right decision because it's ultimately God's will for us to help others."

"Isn't it?"

"Yes, but I think sometimes God wants us to be stretched. To choose the thing that's frightening and unsure. To live boldly. To take a chance on the unknown."

"I understand that. I do. But I can't just abandon my parents, even if Dad wants me to."

"It's not abandoning them to have a job and a relationship. And it's what your parents want. Don't they get a say in their own lives? Or do you think that you know better than them?"

Joy opened her mouth to protest, but stopped herself—because yes, without realizing it, that's exactly what she'd thought.

"And besides all of that, don't you trust God to take care of those you love without you?"

Joy huffed into the phone, her breath coming in short bursts as the questions drilled closer and closer to her heart. "I don't know, Sophia. I don't know anything anymore."

Except she did.

Joy Beckman knew two things—that she loved her parents with all her heart and that, if given the chance, she could feel love of a different sort for Oliver Lincoln.

Two hours later, Sophia's words still rattled around in her brain. *Don't you trust God to take care of those you love without you?*

Joy sat in the wooden chair next to Mom's bed while she slept, laptop balanced on her propped legs. The cursor hovered over the Subscribe button. Should she sign up for job alerts again? Stop fighting Dad's decision? Willingly and graciously give up her role as Mom's caregiver?

For so long, she'd known her place. Was God asking something different of her now?

Without making a decision, Joy groaned and shut her laptop then glanced at Mom. She had more color in her cheeks and was already coughing less than she'd been the day before—and apparently a lot less than earlier this week. Everything she'd seen indicated that the nursing staff had done a fabulous job of caring for Mom in Joy's absence.

Mom's eyes drifted open as Joy contemplated Sophia's words further. Joy shouldn't stare at her—her mother tended to get flustered under others' watchful gazes if she was having a less lucid moment when she awakened—but she couldn't help it.

"Hi, sweetie. Why the long face?"

Sweetie. Did Mom recognize her at last? Joy swallowed the lump in her throat and put her laptop aside. "It's nothing, Mom. How are you feeling?"

At Mom's push of a button, the bed lifted to sit her upright. "Much better, I think."

"You seem like it." Joy snagged Mom's cup off her movable side table. "Here's some water."

"Thank you." Mom took it from her hand and sipped through the tiny straw. "What were you doing on the computer? Something for work?"

It wasn't worth it anymore to point out her mother's lapses in memory. "Kind of."

"How was the wedding, dear? You haven't shown me photos yet."

Actually, she had, but Joy grabbed her phone anyway and swung her chair closer to Mom.

"Why don't you climb up here with me? It'll be easier to see them."

"Really?" The last time she'd snuggled in bed with her mom,

it hadn't been two minutes before Mom had freaked out about a stranger lying next to her. But in this moment, Joy craved the closeness. "Okay." She settled into the spot beside Mom then navigated her phone to photos of her time in Port Willis.

Just like she had the day before, she flipped through the photos, skipping quickly over one of her and Oliver in front of Sophia's Christmas tree. Oliver had plopped a Santa hat onto Joy's head, taken her phone, and kissed her cheek while snapping the selfie. The goofy grin on Joy's face said more than words ever could.

"Who was that?"

"Uh, no one."

Mom looked down her nose pointedly at Joy. "Sweetie, that wasn't no one. That was an attractive man giving my daughter a kiss. One she seemed to enjoy very much."

My daughter … The words were sweeter than any of the treats Ginny had made last week. If only this moment could last forever. "It doesn't matter, Mom." Joy leaned her head on Mom's shoulder and inhaled the scent of her eucalyptus mint shampoo. Being here, with her—that's what mattered most.

"Of course it does."

Joy couldn't hold in the tears any longer.

Instantly, Mom wrapped her thin arms around her daughter, and Joy clung to her, burying her face in Mom's embrace. No longer was she a forty-two-year-old woman, but a little girl with a scraped elbow, a middle schooler who'd been teased, a teen who'd failed. Regardless of how much Mom forgot about her life and who she was, no matter how feeble and withdrawn she became, she'd always be the wiper of tears, the encourager of dreams, and the best woman Joy knew.

Joy would keep holding onto that and to moments like these —when Mom was just Mom.

"Shh, there, there, baby. Whatever it is, nothing's so bad the sun won't shine tomorrow."

"But it is, Mom. It is." And the entire story poured from Joy's soul—every last detail, even the ones she probably should have filtered out. But she didn't know how to be the one taking care of her mom anymore. And perhaps it was selfish, but right now, she wanted someone to take care of her.

"Oh, my darling girl." Mom pulled back so she could look into Joy's eyes. Hers were shining too. "I never should have allowed you to move home."

"I didn't give you much choice. And I wanted to be near you."

Snagging a tissue off her side table, Mom used it to dab the moisture from Joy's cheeks. "Ultimately, that's why I let it happen. I knew I was drifting away from you little by little, and I wanted any time with you that I had left. But now I see how selfish I've been."

"You've never been selfish a day in your life."

"Well, that's a load and we both know it." Mom chuckled. "You have always been an example to me of selflessness."

"Me?" That couldn't possibly be true. She curled once more against Mom. This could all end at any second, and she wanted to soak up every bit of Mom she could before she left Joy again.

"Yes, you. You've always been my little helper, and I've taken it for granted that you would be there if I needed you." Mom gripped the tissue. "But I never wanted you to do so at the expense of your heart. Love is a gift, my darling. Don't chase it unnecessarily, but if it finds you, hold on tight. That is not a selfish thing to do. Frightening? Oh, yes. But not selfish."

"What we're feeling for each other—it's rare. And it's a gift." Oliver's voice resonated in her heart.

Joy shook her head. "I've only known him for a few weeks."

"Love has grown in far less time than that. I only knew your father for a day or so before I realized he was the one for me. Of course, I didn't tell him that, and he didn't tell me he loved me until months later. But I knew early on."

Joy had always written off that notion, called it silly. Now, though … "But how do we overcome the real obstacle of living in two places?"

"Have faith. If God is calling you to this, if he is giving you this blessing, then he will make a way. You don't have to see what that way is to believe it exists."

Could it be true? Was faith enough?

Yes.

The word vibrated deep within her, and she knew what she had to do. "Mom, I have to go." Joy kissed Mom's cold cheek. "Please be here when I get back."

"I'll try, sweetie. I'll try."

CHAPTER 16

She wasn't going to make it.

Joy pulled onto High Street then let loose a tiny screech as a car barreled toward her. She jerked the wheel of the rental toward the left side of the road, where she was supposed to be. At least it wasn't snowing. The mist she'd encountered while driving from Cornwall Airport Newquay to Port Willis had been difficult enough.

Her heart beat wildly—and not just because of her near accident but because of what she was about to do.

Despite the late hour, Port Willis was more alive than usual tonight. The windows of a few popular pubs glowed as she drove past, loud music spilling from inside as patrons entered and exited. According to Sophia, Port Willis didn't host an official fireworks display at midnight, though some residents set off sparklers and smaller fireworks from their homes to celebrate bringing in the new year.

Joy glanced at the clock on the car's dashboard, which flashed 11:45 p.m. She hadn't come this far—and endured two layovers and a long wait in Newquay for a rental car—to be late. The car growled as she accelerated as much as she dared.

Finally, she turned onto the quiet street where Oliver's aunt lived. Cutting the engine, she climbed from the tiny Smart car, clutching a package in her hands. The biting chill—and the fact she'd forgotten to pack gloves—reminded her she wasn't in Florida anymore. Joy pulled her knit cap down around her ears and stared at the two-story fisherman's cottage with gray slate siding and custom hardwood windowsills.

Propelling herself forward, Joy pushed open a gate leading to an adorable courtyard. A lit Christmas tree peeked from behind thin curtains in the front window, and shadows moved in the same room.

Her tongue fastened itself to the roof of her mouth. What if he didn't want to see her? What if she was blowing this all way out of proportion, making some grand gesture, and he was in there with someone else?

Joy nearly pivoted on her booted heel, but the words of her and Oliver's favorite movie came back to her: *"None of us can see the way forward in the fog. We simply must take the next step and trust that the light will lead us where we need to go."*

The light had led her here. It was up to her to trust.

She stood firm and knocked.

It took a few long, agonizing moments, but the door eventually opened, letting out the sound of conversation and guffaws.

A woman with a head full of white hair and a sunny smile gazed down at Joy. Her eyes twinkled in a way that reminded Joy of old vintage postcards of Santa Claus. "Hullo, dear."

She'd met Oliver's aunt only once before, when running errands the day before Sophia's rehearsal. "Hi."

Suddenly, the talking behind Mavis Lincoln ceased.

"Joy?"

Oliver.

He appeared at the door behind his aunt, eyes wide. "You're here."

"I am."

"Who's here?" A disembodied voice piped up behind Oliver and his aunt, and a sixty-something woman with shoulder-length blond hair and a clear sense of fashion snuck into the space next to Mavis.

"Uh, hi." How awkward. Now even if Oliver didn't want to see Joy, he would likely feel obligated to invite her in. She should have called or texted … but that never happened in movies.

Note to self—reality did not always line up with film.

"Mum, this is Joy Beckman. Joy, my mother, Tabby Lincoln."

The woman tilted her head, studying her. "Hello."

"Hi." Ugh. It's like she didn't know any other words tonight.

"For goodness's sake, let her in so she doesn't freeze," Oliver said.

Mavis chuckled. "Of course. Sorry, dear."

The two women backed away from the door as Joy stepped through.

Instant warmth settled into her bones, and the scent of pine and cookies surrounded her. The tiny room was stuffed to the brim with furniture that had obviously been clustered together to make room for the giant tree Joy had spied through the window. Tinsel and ribbon dripped from its branches, and someone had painstakingly hung hundreds of mismatched ornaments, everything from homemade popsicle photo frames, to tiny red baubles, to what appeared to be chocolate coins.

Two men—one older, one younger, both of whom looked a whole lot like Oliver—lounged on the sofa, staring at her. A woman Joy recognized as Oliver's sister-in-law hunkered over a dining table putting together a puzzle with her two young daughters.

On the coffee table sat several flutes and a bottle of unopened champagne. The family had clearly been preparing to celebrate the start of a new year together and Joy had interrupted. "I'm sorry if this is a bad time."

Oliver's entire family shifted their gazes to him, but he couldn't possibly have noticed. Not with the way his gaze remained riveted on her, a hunger burning in his eyes. "What are you doing here?"

Joy's cheeks flamed. "I came back. To talk to you." Then she remembered the package in her hand. "And to give you this."

A muscle in Oliver's cheek flinched, and he seemed to mentally shake himself from a spell. "Come on then. Let's go talk."

"No, dear, we'll leave." Mavis cast a knowing look around the room, and the rest of Oliver's family shuffled out, directing a few hurried glances back at him. His youngest niece whined about wanting to finish the puzzle.

When they were alone, Oliver stepped closer. "What's that?"

Joy swallowed. "I never got you a Christmas gift."

"Yes, you did." A tiny ghost of a smile haunted his lips.

Right, the kiss. "I got you something a bit more tangible."

"That was plenty tangible."

She couldn't help the slight laugh. "You know what I mean. Here." Shoving the package into his hands, she waited.

The thick brown paper barely crinkled as he opened it to reveal his gift. "*The Fog Rolls In*."

"You said you didn't own it." On such short notice, she'd had to snag her own copy from her DVD collection. But even if all of this went badly, she liked the idea of him owning something that had once belonged to her.

"I don't."

"Well, you do now."

"Thank you."

"You're welcome."

Silence fell between them. What was he thinking?

Joy turned to the tree and fiddled with a soft angel ornament.

"How's your mum?"

"Okay, actually. I mean, the pneumonia was nothing to worry about. And my dad has decided to move them into a facility."

Oliver sidled up next to her. "Is that a good thing or not?"

"I thought there was no way it could be a good thing, but I'm coming around to it." Joy chanced a look up at him and found him already watching her. "I don't know if you've realized this about me, but I can be a bit stubborn."

"Not you." The tease in Oliver's voice brought a grin to her face.

She hip-bumped him. "I know. It's one of my many charms." Joy sobered. "But sometimes, it means I think I know what's best. And I stick to that even when others—or even my own heart—tell me differently."

"So just what are you trying to say, Joy Beckman?"

Her eyes wandered until she located a clock on the mantle. 11:57 p.m. Not much time if she wanted to do this right.

Here it went. Everything she'd been feeling the last several days spilled out of her heart and onto her lips. "I'm sorry I left without saying goodbye. And I don't know where this is going, Oliver Lincoln, but I can't stand the thought of walking away from you again. I ... I want to take the next step, wherever it may lead us."

His arms came around her lightning fast, and a laugh bubbled from his throat. "That's what I was hoping you'd say." And he leaned down, clearly aiming to kiss her.

"Wait!" She wriggled from his grasp and looked frantically around the room before spotting a wooden chair. Joy stalked toward it and tugged it back toward a bewildered Oliver.

"What are you doing?"

"Hold on. It'll make sense in a minute." When she had the chair positioned where she'd been standing, she climbed on it and tugged the green sprig from her jacket pocket. It was slightly squished and tiny, but it was enough.

"Is that mistletoe?" Thanks to her increased height, he now glanced slightly upward.

"It just may be." Joy placed one hand around Oliver's shoulder and leaned toward him. Then she held the mistletoe above them. "And look. We're standing under it."

The adoration in his eyes nearly melted her, but she stood her ground.

Behind them, the clock chimed midnight.

"Happy New Year's, Oliver."

"Happy New Year's, love."

Then she swooped in for the kiss she'd been anticipating—and determined that, yes, reality did indeed beat the movies.

She may not know how the next scene would play out, but if she continued trusting, continued loving, continued risking, then this was not an ending after all.

It was, instead, the most beautiful beginning.

LIKE A CHRISTMAS DREAM

A PORT WILLIS ROMANCE

For my sons, Elliott and Theodore.
I love you up, down, around, and back again.

CHAPTER 1

One fire down, a thousand and one to go.

Sarah Bentley leaned away from her computer and stretched her neck from side to side. How long had she been tucked away in her office with the door closed this morning? Not that she really needed the privacy. All the other in-house counsel for Bentley & Co were spending the day after Thanksgiving with family.

If Sarah really wanted to be with her family, she'd simply take the elevator to the thirty-first floor and find her father in the CEO's massive corner office. Or she could head home and be roped into helping Mother plan their annual Christmas Eve soiree.

No thanks. She'd take pointless, stressful work any day.

Of course, she wouldn't have minded spending the day with her siblings, but Benjamin was likely working too—being vice-president at a Bentley & Co subsidiary was just as demanding as Sarah's position, if not more so—or out for drinks with his friends or flavor-of-the-week girlfriend.

And Ginny … well, her younger sister lived halfway around the world, and Sarah hadn't seen her in more than seven years.

Then, out of the blue, last week, Sarah had received that email. An invitation …

She sighed and glanced out of her office's large picture window across downtown Boston. Though the snow from earlier had stopped falling, clouds on the horizon threatened a repeat. Instead of glistening like it did in the summertime, the Charles River looked still and somber. And The Pru, a skyscraper that had first made its mark on the Boston skyline in the sixties, appeared much taller, more intimidating, than usual.

The weather matched her mood quite perfectly.

But if she could just work for a few more hours, then maybe she'd be able to fully enjoy her second date with Warren this afternoon.

As Sarah prepared to jump back into the proverbial flames, her cell phone's ringtone pierced the quiet.

She didn't recognize the number, and a little flutter lifted her chest. "Hello?" No one spoke, but ragged breathing filled the line.

Most people would get annoyed at what appeared to be a crank call, but over the last three years, Sarah had received more calls like this than she could count. She gentled her voice. "Who am I speaking to?"

"S-Sarah?"

Sarah tried to place the woman's voice. Was it Brittany, the young fireman's wife she'd met with last week to discuss her options? But no, the voice sounded more mature than that.

Suddenly, it clicked. "Elise, is that you?"

More silence.

Elise Gentry. Oh, wow. So many implications if this was indeed the woman she thought it was.

So many ways Sarah could help.

So many ways she could fail.

She pushed away from her desk and stood to pace. "Please,

tell me how I can help." When she placed her hand against the cold pane, Sarah's palm burned at the contact.

This was the hardest part—being powerless to do anything but wait.

"Yes, it's Elise. And I'm ready. To leave him." A determination rang through the words. "He's never going to touch me again. And I won't give him the chance to hurt Rose. I … I have to be strong. For her."

And no matter how many doubts assailed Sarah at the moment, *she* had to be strong for Elise. "Elise, I'm proud of you. I know that cannot have been an easy decision. We can talk more at my office, but first I need to know where you are. Are you safe?"

"Yes. I spent the morning packing. Jeff is out of town on business until next week." An audible gulp. "My s-sister is with me. I'm calling from her phone."

"Good. You've done so well. I can be at my office in fifteen minutes. Are you able to meet me there?"

"I can be there in about forty-five minutes." A pause. "Thank you, Sarah."

Hopefully Elise would still be thanking her in weeks, months, even years from now. "Of course. You know where it is?"

"I do." With every word, the woman sounded a tiny bit stronger, an amazing feat for what Sarah suspected she'd been through.

She had first encountered Elise Gentry at a charity event a year ago. They'd been casually chatting—Sarah telling Elise what she did as an attorney at Bentley & Co, Elise regaling her with details about life being married to one of the city's most prominent businessmen—when Sarah had told her about her *other* job. Her passion project, the one that had first settled in her heart during her nonprofit law class at Yale nearly ten years ago.

Elise's eyes had told Sarah everything she needed to know. But up until now, the woman had never come right out and confirmed Sarah's suspicions.

"See you then. And Elise?"

"Yes?"

"It's going to be okay. We're going to help you." *Please let that be true.*

Sarah hung up, snatched her purse, threw on her coat and scarf, and practically sprinted from her office. Once she made it down the long hallway and the twenty stories to the bottom floor of Bentley & Co's building, it should only take five minutes to walk to the offices of New Dawn Women's Council, a non-profit Sarah had founded with her best friend Melissa. Their organization provided women in abusive relationships free legal counsel in custody and divorce proceedings. They also put them in touch with shelters and other services they might need during the transition period.

Most often, New Dawn helped low-income women who had nowhere else to turn. Occasionally, however, they provided services to women from well-to-do families whose husbands controlled the pursestrings. And them.

But those cases—where judges could be paid off, where the court of public opinion could ruin a wife's reputation thanks to a few well-placed rumors, where money could often buy the best lawyers in town—were much more difficult to win.

And these women, they depended on Sarah. She couldn't afford to let them down.

If only she could give more of herself to New Dawn. But Father still expected twelve-plus-hour workdays at Bentley & Co. She should be grateful that he'd agreed to fund New Dawn in the first place—even if she knew exactly why he'd done it.

After all, Father never did anything without a calculated reason.

No wonder Ginny had run far away from Boston—all the

way to England—and not looked back. If only Sarah were that brave.

The wind tousled Sarah's carefully arranged hair and blew against her favorite Michael Kors red ruffle belted wool trench coat as she trudged toward the nonprofit. Despite the fact it was after the lunch hour and threatening to snow again, people jostled for position on the sidewalk. Car horns cursed in short beeps, and vendors hocked their wares from lime green and silver carts that lined the street.

It took Sarah a few minutes longer than usual to reach her destination, but finally, she arrived, stepping inside the building and taking the elevator to the fourth floor. Her Prada heels clicked on the travertine as she entered Office 405, discreetly labeled as NDWC. She bypassed the small but stylish waiting area, waved hello to the receptionist Jackie, and headed to her own office—only a fourth the size of her space at Bentley, but everything she could want or need: a comfy chair, a filing cabinet in the corner, and a mid-sized but well-appointed desk, on which rested a photo of her and Melissa, who ran this place when Sarah couldn't be here. The room still smelled like the lavender essential oil she'd diffused the last time she'd been here, meeting with a client. Today, it did nothing to calm her nerves.

As Sarah peeled off her coat, Melissa popped her head inside the door. "What are you doing here?" Her friend's dark skin and curly hair had always contrasted Sarah's pale complexion and straight auburn locks, and her style was much more casual—as proven by the flannel shirt and faded jeans she currently sported. But in all the ways that mattered, especially regarding New Dawn, the two fell into complete sync.

"Elise Gentry is on her way in."

Melissa's eyes went wide as she moved into the office. In her hands she held a Hershey's kiss, most likely from the giant bowl on her own desk. "Looks like you were right."

"Unfortunately."

The kiss's tiny foil jacket crinkled in Melissa's fingers as she unwrapped the chocolate. "I'll make sure Jackie brings her straight back when she arrives." She slipped the kiss inside her cheek.

Sarah had been so busy considering all the details that she'd forgotten to alert Jackie herself. "Thanks, Mel. You're a gem." Moving to her file cabinet, she slid open the top drawer and pulled a few pamphlets from a folder. The pamphlets would describe what was ahead.

Elise might think that leaving was the hardest part, but winning custody and getting what she deserved—more than deserved—from a man as well connected and respected as Jeff Gentry?

Sarah would be gentle but honest—it was going to be the most difficult thing Elise had ever done.

Maybe Sarah too.

"Hey." Melissa's hand pressed against Sarah's shoulder.

Sarah turned and found her friend's eyes on her, radiating concern.

"You're going to do great."

"Maybe you should take this one." Despite Mel's relaxed exterior, she was a shark in the courtroom. Having been first years together at Yale, they'd been practicing law for the same amount of time. But instead of wasting away in corporate law like Sarah had been forced to do, Melissa had spent her days fighting against child abuse at the Department of Children and Families.

"You've cultivated trust with the client already."

"You know who Jeff Gentry is, though, right?" Sarah closed the drawer a bit more forcefully than she'd intended. The snap reverberated in the room. "Owner of Gentry Pharmaceuticals. Philanthropist. Voted Boston's Mr. Congeniality two years in a row."

"And, apparently, we can add abusive jerk to his resume."

Sarah blew out a breath and tried to quiet the bees buzzing around in her chest. "Elise deserves the best against a guy like that."

"And who better to give her that than someone who knows that world so well? I'm just a poor kid from Philly. But you … you're Sarah Bentley. Of the Boston Bentleys."

Her friend's voice teased, but Sarah wasn't in the mood to deal with thoughts of who everyone assumed she was just because of her family connections. She rolled her eyes as she sat and arranged all the necessary paperwork on her desk.

Melissa plopped into the chair across from her and waited until Sarah looked up. "Look, I know you hate everyone thinking you're this spoiled princess who only got a job at Daddy's firm because of your name—"

"Gee, thanks."

"But obviously, you're someone who deeply cares about others. And you're wicked smart to boot. So stop doubting yourself, get inside this case, and do what you do best. Advocate."

"I just wish I could be here more, you know? Give more of myself to this."

Melissa arched an eyebrow. "Whenever you feel like standing up to Daddy dearest, you know I'm behind you one thousand percent."

"It's not that simple. The moment I do, we're out of funding." Sarah snapped her fingers. "Just like that."

"We'd figure it out."

"And in the meantime, women and children would suffer while we waited for donors to come through. I'll just have to work harder."

"You're already running yourself into the ground. Maybe what you actually need is a vacation. Have you thought of that?"

"Bentleys don't take vacations. Not real ones, anyway."

"You know, bringing work with you kind of defeats the purpose of a vacation."

"Exactly. There's no escape."

"What about your sister's bakery thing? You could reconnect with her and get a vacation out of it. Bam. Two birds. I can help cover this case while you're out."

"The only thing Father would hate more than allowing me time away from work would be me visiting Ginny."

To her parents, Ginny Bentley Rose had been all but disowned when she'd dropped out of school, followed a Brit to a tiny village in Cornwall, and married him at the age of twenty-one. A few years ago, he'd divorced her, but instead of falling apart and coming home, according to her social media accounts—which, yes, Sarah followed—Ginny had gone to culinary school in London. Now she was back in Port Willis and opening her own bakery just before Christmas.

And even though her family had scorned Ginny, she had extended a peace offering in the form of an invitation to her grand opening.

Part of Sarah longed to go ... but the rest of her knew how impossible it would be.

Not that it mattered what Sarah wanted. It never had, not to her parents, especially her father. The only thing he'd ever caved on was allowing her to open New Dawn—but in order to do it, she'd had to promise never to leave Bentley & Co.

And, as the oldest child, to eventually replace her father as CEO.

When you were a Bentley, everything came with a price.

"Why do you give in to him?" Melissa's voice was tinged with frustration.

"Because I've seen what happens when people defy him." Father'd always had a soft spot for Ginny, his youngest, but when she'd rebelled, he hadn't hesitated to cut her out of his life—not just out of his will, but out of his heart too.

As much as Sarah despised his way of doing things, he was still her father. The only one she had. If she was nothing to him, then who was she to everyone else?

That's why New Dawn was so important. It was the only thing that made Sarah feel like herself. Or at least, the person she wanted to be.

Straightening her spine, Sarah adjusted her blouse. Elise would be here any moment. Time to focus. Time to fake the confidence she had to feel in order to tackle this case and win it. Not only for Elise and women everywhere just like her.

But also, for Sarah herself.

❄

If Sarah had written the perfect man into existence, he would probably look and act a lot like Warren Kensington.

Warren put his BMW into Park in front of her parents' home and studied Sarah from behind his thick black frames. "I had a really nice time with you this afternoon."

Sarah fidgeted with the strap of her purse. "Me too." And she had. After pulling herself together enough to take the meeting with Elise Gentry, she'd needed a distraction, and Warren had provided it in spades. He wasn't just handsome to look at, with his nary-a-lock-out-of-place tapered haircut, his piercing brown eyes, his square jawline, and impeccable style in clothing. Warren also possessed a true kindness in his spirit, something that Sarah hadn't seen in a man she'd dated in a very long time.

That was what happened when she went out with guys from her circle, which was why Warren had surprised her. She might not feel tingles up her spine when he held her hand, but they got along well.

And best of all, her father had nothing to do with her decision to date him.

"I'd better let you get inside." Despite his words, the wistfulness in Warren's eyes told her it was the last thing he wanted to do.

"Yeah, I shouldn't be late for dinner. Mother will never forgive me if the food that Betsy made gets cold." Sarah quirked one side of her lips. "I mean … talk about tragedy."

A smile flitted across Warren's lips. "I won't be party to that for sure." Tentatively, he lifted a hand and swept a strand of hair back from Sarah's face, his finger tracing a line down her cheek. Was he thinking about kissing her? Did she want him to? It had been so long since she'd really been kissed. Working crazy long hours didn't leave much room for a social life. "When can I see you again?"

"I'd love to say soon, but I'm just not sure." As a look of doubt crossed Warren's features, she rushed to reassure him. "I mean it. I've got so many projects. Even if I work from now until New Year's, I won't complete half of them. And then there's New Dawn …" Her initial meeting with Elise had gone well enough, and they planned to meet again on Sunday once her new client had time to get settled at her sister's house and gather some documents.

"I admire the work you do there so much."

If only Mother and Father could see it the way Warren did. "Thank you."

Her phone buzzed from her purse. A quick glance showed Mother's name on the screen. "That's my cue." Sarah reached for the door handle.

"Here, let me get that." Racing around to her door, Warren popped it open and gave her a hand. A breezy chill hit her legs, and her heels crunched on the snow left over from this morning's storm as she climbed out.

She looked up into Warren's eyes. "Thanks again for a great time." It may have only been cappuccinos and pastries at her favorite bakery, but the conversation had been just as pleasant as the treats. "I'll text you when I get an opening in my schedule."

"I'll be waiting." His gaze drifted momentarily to her mouth, then back to her eyes, and before she knew what was happening, he had met her lips with his. The kiss was brief, but nice.

As Warren straightened again, Sarah smiled. "I'm glad you finally asked me out."

The Kensingtons and Bentleys had been friends for ages—having met during summers spent in Nantucket—but Warren had only ever been friends with Benjamin, who was two years younger than Sarah. Earlier this year, Warren had taken over the Boston branch of Kensington Corporation, a multi-faceted organization based in New York that specialized in everything from technology to pharmaceuticals. Sarah and Warren had reconnected at a charity event to raise money for victims of domestic violence.

"Me too. I was surprised when your father suggested it, but—"

"What, wait?"

Warren scratched behind his ear. "Your dad and mine have been meeting at least once a month for a while now. I thought you knew. During one of his visits to our offices, he mentioned that you were single and looking to ..." His cheeks reddened. "Anyway, I'd always thought you were beautiful, but figured I didn't stand a chance with you."

The blood pumped faster through Sarah's veins. "My father set us up?"

"I wouldn't say *set us up,* but—"

"I can't believe this." Did he think he had a say in every area of her life? First, where she'd go to college, then what she'd major in, then where she'd work after college, then where she'd spend her career. And now he was trying to interfere in her love life too?

"I didn't mean to upset you."

Sarah exhaled through the tightness in her chest. It wasn't Warren's fault he'd been a pawn in George Bentley's machinations.

He had a reason for every move he made. This wouldn't be an exception.

Wait. "You said he's been meeting with your dad regularly?"

Warren nodded. "I think they're in early discussions about a merger."

Of course they were. Sarah ran a gloved hand across her forehead where a headache had started to form. "Thanks for the information." She cringed at the cold, informal tone of her voice—but at the moment, she couldn't muster any warmth.

Was she overreacting? Probably. Still, she couldn't stop the tremble that shook her hands as she gripped her purse.

Her parents could have her career in exchange for their affection. Fine.

They might be able to coerce her into following their intended trajectory for her life.

But they could not have her love life. No matter how many times she'd backed down on what she wanted in the past, she wasn't giving *that* up without a fight. "I need to go."

"Have I screwed everything up?" Warren looked miserable, his brow knit in confusion, lips pushed to one side.

She reached out a hand and touched his arm gently. "No, it's just—" Words fled her brain, and Sarah simply squeezed. "I need to get inside. I'll … text you."

Turning on her heel, she strode from the circular brick driveway toward the massive front door of the hilltop Georgian manor in Boston's Metro West suburbs. Stepping inside the home where she'd lived all her life, warmth enveloped Sarah—warmth that had nothing to do with the people who lived here, but rather the fact that a fireplace near the entrance roared and crackled.

Since she'd left for work this morning, the servants had

decked the grand entrance with Christmas decor. A sixteen-foot Christmas tree sparkled with lights and gorgeous designer ornaments from all over the world. Garland circled the banister of the curving wooden staircase, and the mantel of the fireplace in the front sitting room displayed a fancy Advent calendar that had delighted Sarah as a child—that is, until her mother had caught her sneaking chocolate and paddled her so hard that even seeing the calendar now made her backside ache with phantom pain.

As Sarah shrugged out of her coat and scarf, one of the maids raced around the corner. "I'm so sorry for not being here when you arrived, Ms. Bentley." She took Sarah's things before Sarah could allay her concern, and took off toward the coat closet.

Sarah steeled herself for the dinner ahead. Still sorting through her feelings about Warren, she walked toward the formal dining room.

Mariah Bentley sat at one end of the table, George Bentley at the other—a queen and king presiding over their subjects, aka Benjamin and now Sarah. Salads adorned each of their plates, but no one was eating.

Mother's head snapped to attention the moment Sarah set foot into the room. "Nice of you to finally join us." Her regal attire tonight consisted of a red long-sleeved blouse that fluttered from shoulder to wrist and black Dolce & Gabbana slacks that complemented her trim figure. Even her hair—sleeked back in a brown-and-no-trace-of-gray bob—seemed perfectly suited for a crown.

"You could have started without me." The words popped out, surprising no one more than her. She never talked back to her parents. But with Warren's revelation, something unusual had lit inside of her, burning her gut.

Mother recovered quickly, though one eyebrow remained arched. "*We* didn't want to be rude."

Sarah pursed her lips together and slid into a chair across from Benjamin, catching the amused look in his eyes. She'd kick him but her legs didn't reach underneath the sixteen-person table. "I was simply saying good-bye to Warren."

Now that she knew his motives, it wasn't hard to catch the quirk of a smile on Father's lips. "I suppose we can forgive her then, can't we, Mariah?" He forked a cucumber with his fork and put it to his thick lips. At age fifty-five, George Bentley struck an imposing figure with his full head of salt-and-pepper hair and six-foot-four frame. Though slightly rotund around the waist, her mother's efforts to stave off his diabetes had been largely successful. He'd discarded his Armani suit jacket but still wore his yellow shirt and black tie, and his Rolex winked from beneath his left cuff.

Snatching her cloth napkin from the table, Sarah fluffed it onto her lap. "I won't be seeing him again." She could feel Mother's sharp gaze boring into her, but picked up her fork and shoved some salad into her mouth anyway. The bite of garlic in the dressing took her by surprise, and she forced a swallow.

"And why is that?" How was it possible for Father's voice to boom across the room louder than usual?

Sarah straightened her spine, but refused to look at either of her parents. "Because I draw the line at an arranged marriage."

Benjamin guffawed across the table, and Sarah speared him with a glare that left his bright blue eyes laughing. He ran a hand through a textured crop of brown hair that had always made his sisters envious.

"Excuse me?"

Sarah's gaze flitted to Father. "I know you suggested he ask me out. I'm assuming it's because you're considering a merger with his family and want an 'in,' but *I* want no part of that." Oh goodness. When was the last time she'd spoken this way to him? Her insides trembled as she stabbed a cherry tomato with her fork, and the juices oozed out onto the lettuce underneath.

"You're clearly overreacting, dear."

"No, Mariah, she's right. I do think it'd go a long way in Scott's mind. You know how family-oriented he is." His words twisted at the end, as if they represented something odious.

So he wasn't even going to deny it. Maybe he had a shred of respect for her after all. "I have no interest in using Warren to make your goals come to fruition." What was wrong with her? Why couldn't she stop the flow of anger spewing from her lips?

The mutilated tomato slid into her mouth and she choked it down with a gulp of water.

Silence filled the room for a full minute before her father spoke again. "I think you should reconsider."

Of course he did.

Sarah looked to Benjamin, her only potential ally in the room. With her eyes, she pleaded with him to change the subject.

"So, how about that invite from Ginny, huh? Will you be going, Mother? Father?" Her brother's eyes twinkled.

Troublemaker.

Sarah stuffed more food into her mouth and peeked at Mother from the corner of her eyes.

Mother's pursed lips pulled her whole face taut. "It's ridiculous—opening a bakery just before Christmas Eve. She's losing out on an entire holiday season's worth of profits. And to think she went to Harvard business school ..."

"Soooo, you're not going then?"

"No, Benjamin, of course not. You know we have our annual Christmas Eve party."

Nice excuse—as if they'd have gone otherwise. No, Ginny had been disowned, and for what? Daring to follow her heart?

The subject changed and the family descended into inane conversation—and with each moment, Sarah's chest grew tighter. Who were these people to try to dictate their children's every move? Didn't they have a right to their own lives?

But no, Father had always ruled his household with a firm fist and sound "logic." And Sarah had let him. Not since she was thirteen years old had she truly rebelled against anything he'd asked of her—until now. And suddenly, refusing to date Warren didn't seem like enough.

Maybe in order to break free, to show her parents that she was her own person, Sarah needed to make an even bigger stand. Who knew? Perhaps they'd even respect her for it.

"The only thing Father would hate more than allowing me time away from work would be me visiting Ginny." Sarah's own words from earlier today floated back to her.

What if ... was it completely crazy?

Before she could really consider all the ramifications of her idea, Sarah's mouth betrayed her once again. "I'm planning to go to England for a few weeks. For Ginny's bakery opening."

Mother's fork clattered to her plate, and one glance at Father proved she'd been delusional to think he might ever respect her for being her own person. The tips of his ears were turning red. He placed his fork on his plate, pushed it away, and folded his hands on the table, staring Sarah down.

She swallowed hard.

At last, he nodded. "Fine."

Huh? "Fine?"

"Yes, fine. I'll grant you the leave. You can represent our family and bring back news of Ginny's endeavors. If you'd like, you can bring work with you. Better yet, I'll hire someone temporarily to take on some of your projects. And why only go for such a short time? Take the whole month. Leave this week."

This week? Could she really do that? Her head spun with the details. She'd need to talk to Melissa about whether she could handle everything at New Dawn, especially with Elise's case, but her friend had sat in on the initial meeting and was as aware as Sarah for now. Besides, legal proceedings usually slowed down in the month of December anyway ...

And then there was the chance to reconnect with Ginny. More time meant more reconnection. Of course, it also granted more time for awkwardness and pain between them.

Her gaze narrowed. "What's the catch?" There was always a catch.

"You may go, but you must be back for your mother's Christmas Eve party. With the time difference, that means that you should be able to leave directly after the grand opening and return in time."

It would be tight, but Sarah would make it work. "Done."

"And"—the light from the chandelier above them caught a gleam in Father's eyes—"you will attend the party with Warren Kensington."

So that's what he was playing at. Well, fine. She could attend one party with him. That didn't mean she was going to continue to date him. And it's not like she despised his company.

Sarah fisted the napkin in her lap and ground out a reply. "All right." The legs of her chair screeched against the polished wood as she stood abruptly. "Guess I'd better get packing."

CHAPTER 2

It had been three—no four—days, but Sarah had finally arrived in the small Cornish fishing village known as Port Willis.

"I can drop you at the car park or harbor, miss. Which do you prefer?" The chauffeur she'd hired at the Cornwall Airport Newquay watched her from his rearview mirror as he idled, waiting for her answer.

"Do you know where the local bookstore is?" Sarah didn't know much about Ginny's new life, but she did know that the soon-to-open bakery was somehow connected to the bookstore she used to own with her ex-husband Garrett. According to the bookstore's website, a woman named Sophia Rose was the bookstore's current owner. "My phone is dead or I'd look it up on GPS." How she'd managed to forget her charging cord was anyone's guess. Might have been the nerves threatening to take over whenever she thought about being reunited with her sister.

"Sorry, miss. My reception isn't what I'd like. I need a new phone myself." The sixty-something man's eyes twinkled underneath his bushy gray eyebrows.

"No worries. The harbor is fine. I'm sure I can find someone to help."

People strolled along the small sidewalks past storefronts that looked to be something out of a Robert Appleton novel. Even from within the vehicle, she could feel the history in this place thrumming, a living, ever-evolving thing. Through the car doors, Sarah caught whiffs of a variety of smells all swirling together as they passed a fudge shop, a bakery, and several pubs. Raucous laughter greeted her ears as they drove by a restaurant with big windows revealing walls lined with televisions broadcasting some kind of sport.

The sun was just setting over the water as the car approached the harbor, where a handful of sailboats and dinghies bobbed.

"Here we are." The car rolled to a stop in front of a restaurant.

Sarah leaned closer to the window and made out the restaurant's name on its weathered blue sign. "The Village Pub."

"Might grab myself a nice warm supper before I head back out. Would you care to join me?"

"Oh." She'd murmured the words to herself, not expecting a reply. "That's very kind, but I need to find my sister. She lives here."

"And she didn't arrange to pick you up from the airport herself? It's only a half hour's drive."

"She doesn't know I'm coming."

"Ah, a surprise visit. That sounds lovely." The man clambered from the car and popped the trunk to the four-door sedan.

Sarah scrubbed a hand across her face. It would be a surprise, all right. Lovely? One could only hope.

But after seven years of nearly radio silence between them … Well, it might not be a bad idea for Sarah to get a room at the local inn, just in case Ginny's welcome was not as warm as the invitation to her bakery's opening had seemed. For all Sarah knew, Ginny had been inviting her family out of spite—to show them that she'd done what they'd all doubted she could do.

Follow her dreams and actually succeed.

The chauffeur opened Sarah's door and greeted her with a cheery smile. "Here you go, miss."

"Thank you." She took his offered hand and stepped from the vehicle. Her eyes trekked up the hill. Oops. The four-inch pumps she wore may have been her go-to for business dealings and airport travel, but they would make traversing the cobblestone street under her feet fairly challenging. At least the rest of her was properly attired with her scarf, gloves, and parka. A quick glimpse at the weather forecast a few days ago had shown an average of forty degrees, and while snow wasn't overly common in December, it did happen on occasion. But after the bitter cold snap Boston had just experienced, this was nothing.

She paid the man his tip and snagged her rolling suitcase from him. As he disappeared inside the pub, she took the opportunity to finally be alone and get her bearings. There were many lit windows down here by the water, but most seemed to be private residences. The street where she stood—appropriately labeled High Street, according to the adorable wrought-iron streetlamp—ended at the harbor and cut through the middle of town, rising, rising, rising, until it curved away from her eyes.

As she faced the harbor, Sarah got the sudden urge to climb aboard one of the boats and sail away. A breeze tickled her nose and sent strands of hair skimming across her lips. She closed her eyes and inhaled the briny air. *Courage,* it seemed to whisper. Or maybe that was her own heart, begging.

"If I had my camera with me, you'd make a pretty picture indeed."

Sarah whirled, finding a well-built man with a mop of brown curls and cable-knit sweater standing outside the pub, hands shoved into the pockets of his worn jeans. There was something so casual and self-assured about his stance, and the smile on his face only added to his small-town charm.

Of course, the way the British accent glided from his lips didn't hurt his appeal either.

And here Sarah was, gaping like a wide-mouthed fish. She straightened. "Excuse me?" The words came out sharper than she'd intended.

"I'm sorry, didn't mean to startle you." He moved a step closer and glanced at her suitcase. "We don't get many visitors in the winter months. Certainly not as many as in the summer."

"Right." She swallowed a lump that had formed in her throat. How was it possible she could stare down sharks in the courtroom, but this man she'd laid eyes on moments ago flustered her? "I'm visiting my sister, Ginny Bentley—I mean Rose. The trouble is, I'm not quite sure where to find her."

"Oh, I know Ginny. Of course, in Port Willis it's difficult to not know everyone, especially when you've grown up here." The man's easy grin unlocked a certain brightness in his eyes—which, if she were looking, she'd have to admit were the most gorgeous seafoam green color she'd ever seen.

Good thing she wasn't looking.

"Would you mind telling me where I can find her?"

"I'll do you one better. I can take you there."

She shifted, her feet pinching in the toes of her heels. "Thank you, but you can just tell me how to get there."

"It's no trouble. Actually, I've been meaning to pop in to discuss some food photography for the bakery anyway."

His comment earlier about a camera made sense now. "You're a photographer?"

He shrugged. "Professionally, only on the weekends. The rest of the time, I work at the pub." He gestured behind him. "My family owns it."

Sarah peered inside the windows of the Village Pub. Though it was only five o'clock on a Tuesday evening, the bright interior appeared fairly well filled. A fire roared in one corner, and from her vantage point, Sarah could make out a long wooden paddle and anchor hanging on the wall. "It's adorable."

"I'll tell my mother you appreciate her decor."

Sarah gripped the handle of her suitcase. "Please do. And forgive me, but I didn't catch your name."

The man stared at her for a moment before breaking into another grin. "Michael Hammett at your service."

"Sarah Bentley." She held out her hand as she would when making anyone's acquaintance.

But when he reached out, and his large hands enveloped hers, she couldn't help but think she should have allowed a breach in etiquette just this once. She shivered despite the glove that kept her from actually touching his skin.

"Very nice to meet you, Sarah. But I'm an idiot for making you stand here in the cold. Want to make our way to the bookstore?" He turned toward the steep road.

High Street, indeed. Sarah pictured snapping an ankle in her ridiculous shoes and grimaced. But it was too late to turn back now.

For the first time, he eyed her shoes. "It's not far, but I'm happy to get my car and drive you if you'd like."

"That won't be necessary. Just lead the way."

"At least let me take that for you." Before she could protest, he snatched the suitcase gently from her fingers.

"Thank you." They began the uphill trudge, and soon, Sarah's breaths came in short puffs, her toes burning. But at least she hadn't fallen. Yet.

Beside her, Michael struck an impressive figure against the night sky, where thousands of stars twinkled above them. Had she ever seen this many stars at once? Maybe at their Nantucket home, but she'd been too busy going and doing to notice.

At a break in the buildings, the cliffside opened up to a view of rolling grassy hills and a distant lighthouse that appeared to be guarding the little village nestled into the bluffs.

"Ginny doesn't know you're coming, does she?"

The abrupt question made Sarah stumble. In an instant, Michael was grasping her forearm, his hold supportive but not restrictive. Sarah couldn't help being drawn into his worried gaze. Up close, she could see a slight sheen of stubble dotting his cheeks.

"Are you all right?"

What must this man think of her, falling all over herself—and him? Sarah pulled away from his gentle grasp and forced a smile. "Thanks. I clearly wasn't planning for such a hike in these shoes."

He chuckled. "I guess you weren't."

They continued the climb, passing a few others. But the street was fairly deserted. Perhaps this was one of those small towns that mostly shut down at dusk when it wasn't tourist season.

Sarah assessed her words before speaking. "How did you know?"

"Most people don't wear heels around here."

"Not that." Sarah cleared her throat. "That Ginny doesn't know I'm here."

"Ah. Simply because Ginny isn't one for secrets and she hasn't mentioned her family coming. Considering none of us has met any of you, well ..." He shrugged. "There would be lots of excited chatter spilling from her, I imagine."

Memories of her sister and her "chatter" warmed Sarah's chest. "She is the most genuine person I know." And yet, Father and Mother had never seen it that way. They'd tried their best to change Ginny—to make her "more like Sarah."

She was relieved to know their efforts had been in vain.

"Here we go." Michael pointed across the street to a building that looked to be hundreds of years old—essentially like everything else in this town. Several shops lined the storefront, but the bright yellow door and the sign above it indicated which was the bookstore. The store next to Rosebud Books looked to be undergoing construction.

Sarah crossed the road and read the sign in the window: *Coming Soon: Once Upon a Time Bakery*. Her fingers twitched as she traced the letters.

Michael joined her, shielding his eyes to look inside. "Doesn't seem like anyone is here. Maybe they're at Gin's home. It's just around the corner." He led her to a quaint little cottage.

Her feet ached at this point, but not as much as her heart. Would Ginny be happy to see her, or throw her out on her ear?

Only one way to find out.

She reached out and knocked on the cottage door. The wind snickered around her as she waited. Maybe Michael sensed her anxiety, because he remained silent.

Low voices floated from inside, and finally, the door creaked open.

The woman on the other side of the door was tall and slender, with stick-straight hair just past her shoulders and warm chocolate eyes that were older and wiser than the ones Sarah had known so well. Her jeans and Beach Boys T-shirt were dusted with flour, her feet bare.

And tears streaked Ginny's cheeks.

A redheaded man sidled up next to Ginny, slipping his arm around her shoulders. His face brightened when he saw Michael. "Hey, mate. Who's this you have with you?"

"Sarah?" The name burbled from Ginny's throat, a mix of astonishment and joy—or so Sarah hoped.

"Hey, Gin." Sarah chewed her bottom lip. "It's good to see you."

CHAPTER 3

In many ways, it was as if the last seven years had never happened.

Sarah sat on Ginny's worn couch as her sister banged around in the kitchen. It was just the two of them in the tiny house. After an awkward hug and round of introductions, Steven—the redhead—and Michael had left the women to chat.

Ginny hadn't said much, had simply taken Sarah's luggage and wheeled it back to her guest room, then told Sarah she could sit while Ginny prepared some tea.

The kitchen sat adjacent to the living room, so Sarah caught glimpses of her sister bobbing in and out of view as she pulled things from cabinets and talked to herself. Meanwhile, she nestled into the couch—such a bright yellow that their mother would surely cringe at the sight of it. The thought made Sarah smile. *Good for you, Gin.*

Boxes filled the room, most without labels. An undecorated Christmas tree stood in the corner by a window that gave a lovely view of the street.

"I've been too busy to decorate it." Ginny balanced two mugs as she padded across the rug.

"What?"

Her sister deposited one of the mugs into Sarah's waiting hands, and Sarah murmured her thanks.

"The tree. One of those boxes—I'm not sure which at the moment—has all of my Christmas decorations and ornaments, but I've been much too wrapped up in moving back from London to Port Willis and getting the bakery ready to open. Steven put up the tree for me, but I just haven't found a spare moment."

And here Sarah was, taking up precious time. Hopefully she could make up for it over the next three and a half weeks by lending her assistance. Not that she was an expert in opening a business by any means. Melissa had done much of the initial setup for New Dawn. But surely she could find some way to help, even if it were manual labor.

"Be right back." Ginny was gone only minutes before she returned with a platter of chocolate chip cookies, which she placed on the coffee table in front of the couch. "These are fresh out of the oven as of an hour ago."

Sarah hadn't had her sister's sweets in so long. Memories of them playing in their large kitchen at home assailed her. The cook used to swat them out if she were there, so Sarah and Gin would sneak back in the evening. That's when Ginny practiced her baking skills—and Sarah showed her support by eating them.

She took a cookie and bit into it, moaning as the heavenly decadence hit her tongue. "Wow. You've gotten even better, if that's possible."

"Well, I did go to culinary school." Ginny's tone betrayed her amusement.

"Right." Sarah polished off the cookie and took a sip of her tea. "Mmm, did you add cream to this?"

"I did. You're drinking that the true British way."

"Nice." Sarah placed both hands around the mug, soaking in its warmth.

Silence settled between them as they both sipped their drinks. Finally, Ginny tilted her head and worried her bottom lip. "So, you just in the neighborhood, or …?"

Nerves rattled in Sarah's stomach. She swallowed. "I wanted to come to support you. I can stay till the twenty-third."

"Does that mean you'll be here for the opening?" Her sister's questioning eyes bore into Sarah.

"My return flight is that evening, but yes, that's the plan. If it's okay with you. I can always stay at a hotel." Sarah averted her gaze.

"Of course you're not staying at a hotel. That's as ridiculous as … well, serving grilled cheese with chocolate chips."

"Really, Gin?"

"I'm just saying." A pause. "But I must admit, I'm surprised Dad let you come."

Gripping the mug handle, Sarah stood and paced. "I didn't give him much of a choice. He just …" She blew out a breath and walked to the window. Outside, a streetlamp burned a beacon into the starry night, illuminating a wooden bench below it. The sight filled her with calm. Here, the Bentleys seemed so far away, as did the life they had planned for her.

Suddenly, Ginny was beside her, sliding her arm through Sarah's. "I know."

The quiet way she said it … she *did* know.

But enough about Sarah.

The band around her lungs finally began to ease. If Ginny held any sort of grudge for Sarah's silence over the last seven years, it wasn't apparent. But how could she let it go?

"So how are you, Gin?" *I've missed you.* Why couldn't she say the words? Sarah extricated her arm gently and moved back to the couch.

Her sister stayed at the window a moment longer, then

turned and smiled that kid-on-Christmas-morning grin that lit her whole face. "I'm good. Really good." She snagged a cookie from the platter and sank onto the cushions. "Life isn't perfect, but God's blessed me with so much."

Since when did her sister believe in God? They'd grown up with wishy-washy religion, going to church whenever it made their parents look good. Easter, Christmas, that sort of thing.

Of course, there had been those few short years in her teens when Sarah had snuck away to youth group with her friend Rachel. There, she'd found an acceptance she'd been yearning for all her life. But Father had beaten that fledging faith out of her little by little a long time ago. *"It only makes you weak to believe in someone other than yourself."*

Clearly, Ginny's experience had been different. Maybe Sarah would ask her about it sometime.

She cleared her throat. "I'm really proud of you for attending culinary school and opening a bakery. That was always your dream." Even when their parents laughed at her, as if the idea was truly so out of the question.

"Thanks, Sarah. That means a lot." Ginny chewed, her face relaxed as she studied her sister. "It means a lot you're here too. I still can't believe it."

"Yes, well." *I should have come sooner.* "So, Steven … he looks to be more than a friend?"

A blush attacked Ginny's cheeks and she swatted at some flyaway strands of her hair. "Yeah, for about a year now. Well, we've been dating a year. Before that, he was a friend, then kind of more than a friend, but I wasn't ready to date anyway for a while after Garrett and I divorced, and …" She bit her lip. "I'm rambling. Sorry, I do that sometimes."

Sarah laughed. "You don't think I remember? Mother used to scold you all the time."

"My one great weakness." Ginny stuck her tongue out.

"Along with fidgeting, daydreaming, somehow always dirtying my clothes ..."

"I'm sorry about you and Garrett."

"Thank you. It was definitely a difficult season in my life, but I grew a lot from it. Learned a lot too. About the way I see myself. About the real meaning of success. And about God too."

There it was again—God—sliding right off Ginny's tongue as natural as could be.

Sarah studied her sister. Ginny had always wilted under other people's censure and bloomed under praise. Now that she considered it, the idea of Ginny being able to laugh at all the things their mother had found "wrong" with her was really quite incredible.

She was the older sister, but maybe Sarah could learn a thing or two from Ginny.

"From our brief interaction, Steven seems really nice." Sarah's fingers drummed along the ceramic mug. "How is everything going with the bakery?"

A shadow flitted across Ginny's face. "Mostly well. We've hit a few snags with deliveries and such. Delays in getting my industrial ovens installed, that sort of thing. But we are still on schedule to open. Only ..." Her smile dimmed.

"What?" Sarah leaned forward slightly.

"Just before you got here, I received a letter. It was tacked to my bakery's front door." Ginny set the mug down and stood to snag an envelope off the mantel.

"And? What does it say?"

"That apparently there's some parish law that says competing businesses can't be opened within a kilometer of each other." Ginny's finger slid along the edge of the envelope as she stared absently at the bare Christmas tree in her living room.

"Can I see it?" Sarah put her mug on the coffee table and held out her hand.

Ginny shrugged and handed it over, then fiddled with the tree branches while Sarah looked over the bundle of papers. Sure enough, someone had printed out a copy of the local code of ordinances. Several pages in, a thick black marker had circled a specific code referencing business regulations within the parish. Sarah skimmed the regulation and her attorney's brain went to work.

She glanced up, gripping the paper in her fist. "Why would someone send you this?"

"I guess I'm in violation of an ordinance I wasn't even aware of." Ginny sank onto the couch, her head in her hand.

"How?"

"Trengrouse Bakery is less than a kilometer away."

Sarah raised an eyebrow. "I passed that on the way here. You're opening a bakery with clear competition so close?"

Ginny pushed her hair from her eyes and sat up straighter. "I'm not dumb."

"I didn't say you were."

"You're right." Her voice softened. "I'm sorry."

The last thing in the world Ginny should be doing was apologizing to Sarah, even if she *had* snapped at her. Not only was the possibility of losing her dream bakery understandably upsetting, but Sarah's seven-year absence from Ginny's life made Sarah the sister with far more to be sorry for. "So what's going on?"

"Mr. Trengrouse has been in business forever, and I didn't want to step on any toes, so I paid him a visit. When I asked him his thoughts on me opening a bakery, he almost seemed relieved. He said he had been considering retirement for a while now, but didn't want to leave the town without a bakery."

"Did he change his mind or something?"

"His daughter Rebecca took over for him about three months ago. She grew up here, but moved away for university or something. I don't really know her, to be honest. I figured she was coming in to help out while her dad closed up shop, but maybe she changed his mind."

"Don't panic. I'll take a look at this and try to get it sorted out. I'm sure there's a loophole." Sarah winked, attempting to feign more confidence than she felt. "There's always a loophole." Sure, she didn't know British law that well, but she was a Bentley, right? Bentleys got things done, no matter what.

Maybe *this* was how Sarah could make up for the past seven years. The idea settled into her heart and warmed her.

Jaw slack, Ginny stared at her. Then, without warning, she jumped forward to hug Sarah around the neck.

It took a few moments before the shock wore off and Sarah hugged her sister back.

CHAPTER 4

Two days into her investigation about the code in question, and Sarah still didn't have any answers for Ginny.

She groaned and shoved her laptop away from her.

"Bad day?"

At the sound of the masculine British accent, her head swiveled to the door of Ginny's cottage. Michael stood in the doorway, a brown vintage leather jacket worn open over a henley sweater, a camera bag slung over his shoulder.

Whew. She'd never found "casual" so attractive.

"Hi. Nice to see you again." Why did she have to sound so formal, as if preparing to take a deposition?

"Sorry to let myself in, but I knocked and no one answered."

"In most places, that would be considered breaking and entering." She tried to infuse teasing into her voice, but it came out stilted and almost accusatory.

And there was that infuriatingly crooked-yet-perfect grin again, the one that had melted her defenses on Tuesday when they'd first met. "Ah, but you're in Port Willis now, and that means you can enter when your friend is expecting you and doesn't answer. Most would consider it a politeness, to make sure that friend is in fact all right and not in dire straits."

Sarah slid from the stool that sat under the granite countertop bar of Ginny's kitchen and ran a hand down the red tunic covering her black leggings. With her hair pulled back in a bun and her oversized reading glasses pushed high on her nose, she wasn't exactly dressed for company. "I wasn't aware I was expecting you." She removed the glasses and placed them on the counter.

Michael closed the door behind him and came closer, his smile held in place. For goodness's sake—how had she not noticed those dimples before? But it had been dark last time. "I meant your sister. She asked me to take some photos for her website, remember?"

"Oh. Right." That made sense. Ginny had been baking up a storm since yesterday morning, filling platters with an assortment of cookies, muffins, and other pastries. The kitchen still smelled of cinnamon and nutmeg. She must have been preparing for the shoot.

Of course, Ginny being Ginny, she'd used the opportunity to ply Sarah with sweets—and to try to get her to open up about her life. But what right did Sarah have to drown Ginny in her sorrows when she'd not been there to hear her sister's over the years? So, she'd stuck with the safest of topics: work, particularly the work she was doing at New Dawn. Her sister had been so incredibly supportive of her dream.

When she'd asked if Sarah planned to do it full time someday, Sarah had changed the subject. Of course, she'd wanted to ask Ginny how she'd been so brave as to leave. But leaving wasn't the answer, not for her. It couldn't be or New Dawn wouldn't survive.

"Is she here, then?"

And there Sarah had gone, staring off into space, thinking of how nice it had been to connect with Ginny, to hear her hopes and dreams for the bakery and her future with Steven. Michael must think Sarah a dunce for her inability to focus. "She's at the bakery right now. I can shoot her a text to see if she's coming back, if you'd like."

"Nah, that's all right. It's around the corner, remember? I'll just head over there." He cocked his head. "You *have* seen it, right?"

"Yes, you pointed it out when I arrived." Sarah picked at a fingernail that she'd worn down to the nub. Mother always fussed at her whenever she went more than a few weeks without a manicure, but there hadn't been time before she came here.

"But surely you've been inside? I figured you'd come early to help her get everything ready."

"I haven't toured it yet." Sarah closed the lid of her laptop and snatched it off the table. "And I'm helping in other ways. Now, if you'll excuse me, I need to get back to it." Turning on her heel, she started toward the guest room, but Michael was in front of her in an instant, blocking her way.

"I'm sorry if I offended you."

The contrition in his voice brought her attention to him. Mistake. From here she could see flecks of gold in his eyes. That must be why they shone—

Oh brother. She couldn't allow herself to get distracted, even if it were by a handsome man with a pair of fine eyes. She had too many other things to accomplish during her visit—namely, reconciling with her sister. And that meant finding a way around this ridiculous law.

Of course, being rude to her sister's friends was uncalled for. Sarah shifted the laptop to her other arm. "You didn't. I'm just trying to solve a problem for Ginny using my specific skill set, but things are not going well."

"Sad to hear that. What do you do?" Michael leaned against the wall in the dim hallway, which was lined with various photos: Ginny and Steven, Ginny and a bride with black hair and arresting blue eyes, even an old family portrait from when Sarah, Ginny, and Benjamin were teens.

If Sarah had been treated like her sister had been, the last thing she'd want hanging in her hallway was a photo of the people who had scorned her and her dreams. Was this what forgiveness looked like? And how had she managed to forgive them at all?

Sarah cleared her throat. "I'm an attorney for my father's company and work on the side for a nonprofit that provides counsel for women leaving abusive relationships. Ginny's having a legal issue of sorts with her bakery and asked me to look into it. Well, I volunteered."

Michael watched her, and his silence urged Sarah to continue.

She explained in short detail what was happening with Ginny's bakery and the parish code. "Regardless, I can't seem to find much information about the ordinance, other than that it was instituted something like a few hundred years ago. There was probably a reason for it back then, but maybe it's an old forgotten law that's no longer applicable. Anyway, someone—presumably Trengrouse or his daughter—has dug it up to keep Ginny from opening her bakery."

"Have you tried contacting the parish council?"

"Yes, but I haven't received an answer yet." Sarah sank against the wall next to Michael. The air around them was quiet, still. "There's a parish council meeting in a week and a half, but I'd love to give Gin some peace of mind in the meantime. If I can't, though, I'll see if we can add an item to the meeting agenda."

"Maybe you just need to talk to Rebecca about it. I've known her my whole life. We grew up in the same grade in school. She's a bit of a tough nut to crack but not unreasonable. Maybe all of this can be solved with a simple friendly conversation."

"Well, it wasn't *friendly* of her to just leave that note on my sister's door, was it?" Sarah ignored Michael's amused smirk and inhaled. "But you're right. Going directly to the source never hurts." She glanced at her watch. Late afternoon. "Rebecca is probably still at the bakery, unless it closes early in the afternoon. Do you know?"

Quick as a flash, he reached out and pinched Sarah's elbow. "Hold on there, Iron Lady. Maybe you want to take some time to think of how to approach her in a less ..."

"Intense way?"

"Exactly." Michael pushed himself off the wall. "And I know just the thing to distract you. Would you like to come with me to the bakery and take that tour?"

Sarah considered him for a moment. Perhaps a change of scenery would be good for her. "All right. Give me just a minute and we can go."

They stepped inside the bakery, and Sarah observed the small area where booths and tables lined the walls and filled in the open space, providing seating for thirty or so patrons. The neutral white paint and blank walls gave the room an impersonal feel, though the fun gray-and-white diamond pattern that traversed the entire front of the bakery granted it some charm.

A wraparound display case met the polished marble counter where the cash register sat, and behind it, a currently empty gray wooden built-in boasted plenty of rows and nooks for decor, mugs, and the like. White subway tiles lined the wall surrounding the built-in. There should have been a menu somewhere, but Sarah couldn't locate one. Maybe Ginny was still finalizing it.

As she took in the surroundings, Sarah cringed at the

obvious ways her sister was falling behind schedule. Then again, Ginny had never been as fastidious as Sarah. At least this meant there were numerous ways Sarah might be able to help Gin, especially since she wasn't making much progress with the legal assistance.

"I think she's back that way." Michael's words interrupted Sarah's thoughts.

They headed through a swinging door to the back of the bakery and found Ginny and Steven staring at each other like adorable, lovesick fools as Ginny shoved a beignet into Steven's mouth. He chewed, his eyes rolling back playfully in his head. "Brilliant. Absolutely brilliant."

"You think so?" Ginny's squeal evidenced her delight.

"You did it. Somehow, you made a better beignet than you have ever done."

"I want to try one." Michael's booming voice made Steven and Ginny turn.

A blush crossed Ginny's cheeks. She dusted powdered sugar off her hands and pulled a platter from the countertop, holding the golden drops of heaven under Michael's nose. "Have at it."

He took one from the platter and popped it into his mouth. "You're right, mate. It's perfection."

"Sarah? You want one?" Ginny's eyes turned shy. Maybe there was something in her that sought her big sister's approval after all.

Full from all the pastries yesterday, a beignet was absolutely the last thing she wanted, but Sarah stepped forward and snagged one anyway. "You're going to make me fat, little sis."

"I honestly doubt that." Michael's words floated toward her in a soft cadence, but Sarah heard them nonetheless.

Something inside her swelled at the thought. Did he find her attractive?

Why does it matter? You're kind of still dating Warren.

The thought rankled. She hadn't even had time to do much

more than text Warren about her last-minute trip, though she had remembered to ask him to her parents' Christmas Eve party. Of course he'd said yes. Did that count as dating?

Sarah finished off the beignet, which melted in her mouth in seconds, and washed away the crumbs in the sink. She turned her attention back to Ginny. "Michael is here to take photos for you."

"Yes, sorry. I forgot to let you know we'd be here instead."

"No worries." Michael placed his camera bag on the white quartz countertop that gleamed under the recessed kitchen lighting. Shrugging out of his jacket, he began to pull out camera parts and assemble them.

"I've put everything I'd like you to photograph over there." Ginny indicated the far counter under a window, where natural light from the slightly cloudy day drifted in. "Arrange them however you think they look best. Do you need me to stay and help?"

"Whatever you'd like. I'm happy to free up your time if you need to do other things, but if you want to stay and make sure you're happy with the result, that's okay too." Michael placed an expensive-looking lens onto the camera. Sarah couldn't take her eyes off the way his fingers moved. Quick but sure.

He caught her staring, and she swiveled so hard to the right that her knee banged against a lower cabinet. She clenched her teeth to keep from crying out.

"Great. Steven was going to go over the website with me, and then Sophia and I were going to review details for opening day."

Sarah had yet to meet Sophia, Ginny's best friend and soon-to-be business partner. They had commissioned a door between the bookstore and bakery so patrons could easily flow from one to the other. She needed to poke her head inside Rosebud Books soon. How had she done so little with her time here so far?

But before she could open her mouth to ask if she could

accompany Ginny, Michael spoke up again. "Sarah, would you like to stay and help me with the shoot?"

"Me?" Sarah dashed him a confused look. What did she know about photography?

But her gut felt sucker-punched at the pure … something … in his eyes. What was it? Admiration? But why? There wasn't much to admire in the way Sarah had acted toward him so far. Not cold exactly, but definitely not warm.

And yet, everything about this man screamed at Sarah to trust him. Maybe it was in the way he seemed to really see her—and to be quiet enough to really listen.

But that was unnerving because it meant she'd have to speak. To share her heart. And in her experience, doing that only warranted cold glares and the silent treatment. Melissa was the only person who really knew Sarah anymore. For some reason, her friend hadn't gone running the other direction. Melissa was brave like that.

Still, Michael wasn't asking for Sarah to reveal her deepest, darkest secrets. He just wanted her to stay and help him out. She could do that. It was better than beating her head against the laptop looking for answers. "Sure."

"Great."

Ginny and Steven scampered out—but not before her sister shot Sarah a questioning arch of her brow.

Taking a white ceramic plate, Michael stacked four brownies in the foreground, twisting each one slightly to make a more artful arrangement. Next, he positioned the other brownies around the pile in a way that seemed random to Sarah, but—judging by his furrowed brow—made sense to him. There was something mesmerizing about watching him work.

The end result of his efforts made her crave … the brownies.

Just the brownies.

Liar.

Michael stared at the plate for a moment. Then, he picked up a brownie and turned to her. "Would you mind taking a bite out of this one?"

Sarah jerked a step back, blinking hard. "What?"

He walked the few feet toward her then held the brownie up to her mouth. "The picture. I'm going for a certain effect." He winked.

"Um, sure." She leaned in to take a bite, and he pulled it away. Sarah should have been annoyed. Instead, a smile flitted across her lips. "Really? The last time someone did that to me, I believe I was in seventh grade."

"You were that young the last time someone flirted with you?" He shook his head. "What a pity."

The words struck a match to something buried deep inside of her, but she pushed the feeling of light away, cocked a hip, and threw on the sassiest tone she could muster. "If this is you flirting, then I suppose I should prepare for you to pull my pigtails next?"

"I would if you had pigtails and not that endearing little bun." Michael angled toward her, and the spicy bergamot scent of him enveloped her. How had he managed to get so close? They stood toe-to-toe, and as she glanced up, the teasing look in his eyes turned to something more serious.

Ignoring it, she placed her hand against his solid chest and pushed back. "Fine." Leaning in, she took a small bite of brownie. After savoring the chocolate, she swallowed, licking her teeth for any remaining bits. "Satisfied?"

"Perfectly." He set the dessert on top of the stack on the plate, and the air around her that had been so warmed by his presence cooled as he moved on to his next task.

This was getting ridiculous. Of course, he was attractive, and many women would take the opportunity to flirt and have a good time with him. But Sarah had never been one of those women. She'd dated, yes, but it had mostly been for show. Warren Kensington was the first guy in a good long while who had seemed interested in more than dating "George Bentley's daughter," but had *that* even been real?

When had finding a guy who saw past her family's money to who Sarah was ever happened? Never, that's when.

The thought that it could happen here was just laughable. Michael was a handsome guy who, yes, made her feel a bit unsteady. But in Sarah's experience, flirting and forever didn't go hand in hand. She'd be better off with someone like Warren. At least she'd know what to expect with that kind of guy, even if they quite possibly lacked the spark she'd always dreamed of for her love life. But sparks had grown from mutual respect before, and if she could learn to trust Warren's intentions, then perhaps …

Settling in, Sarah watched Michael work for a full hour, helping him arrange things, even lending her hand for a few shots. Finally, he straightened. "I have an idea, if you're amenable."

"Need me to take a bite out of something else, do you?" Somehow, Sarah's laugh came easier now after time spent in his presence. "You people are seriously trying to blow me up like a blimp." Eyeing a cake batter cookie on the top of a pile Michael had just finished photographing, she reached around him—her hand skimming his side—snagged it, and popped a bite into her mouth.

At his raised eyebrow, she swallowed and shrugged. "What? You were finished, weren't you?"

He chuckled. "I was. And I do like watching you taste Ginny's sweets. They seem to have a way of breaking down your defenses."

"What's that supposed to mean?"

"Don't take offense. You just get this relaxed look on your face, and it's clear you're enjoying yourself." He paused, then in slow motion lifted his hand to her lips.

Sarah stilled. What …

But his thumb merely brushed the corner of her mouth and was gone. "Sorry. You had a crumb on your face."

For a moment, neither of them moved. The rush of blood in her ears blocked everything out around Sarah until all she could focus on was the man in front of her.

Michael coughed. "Uh, I had a thought about your legal problem. That's what I was going to say."

"Oh?" She blinked her focus back into view.

"If you'd like, I can go with you to chat with Rebecca. Perhaps a friendly face will make things less awkward and … less intense."

Less intense. She could use some of that. "That would be great. Thank you."

"So … tomorrow, then?"

"Okay. Tomorrow."

CHAPTER 5

The word "charming" perfectly described Trengrouse Bakery, with its striped awning and window display case full of artisan bread, scones, croissants, and Victoria sponge cakes.

However, the same could not be said of its owner's daughter.

As Sarah stepped into the crowded bakery on Friday morning, with Michael beside her, her gaze narrowed on a woman with dishwater blond hair who was bustling around behind the counter. Everything about her was small, from her petite stature to her nose, ears, and mouth. But the most striking thing about her was the scowl she wore as she pulled a wrapped pastry away from an elderly man with a cane who was standing at the front of the line.

"Roderick, you are one pound short again. This is not a charity!" Her voice carried across the space, which wasn't difficult since the small room covered maybe a few hundred square feet for standing, at best, with a few tables along the wall.

One little boy pressed his face against the glass case of sweets connected to the counter, and customers waited in line chatting among themselves. Most seemed to ignore Rebecca's outburst.

"But Rebecca, your da' always let me put it on me tab."

A pinched expression flashed across Rebecca's features. "As you can see, it's just me. And I require payment now." The bagged pastry in question was in both their grips, the man's wrinkled and spotted fingers beginning to loosen.

"Oh, for goodness's sake. This is not how people should treat their customers." Without waiting for Michael to follow, Sarah dug in her purse and pulled out her wallet. Circumventing the line, she found herself face-to-face with the woman who wanted to run Ginny out of business before she'd even begun. "Here." Whipping out a credit card, she gave it to Rebecca. "It's on me."

"Thank ye, lassie. Tis verra kind." Roderick took the pastry and hobbled away.

Rebecca glared at Sarah but ran her credit card through the register all the same. "He'll never learn if people keep paying for him." Pulling the printed receipt from the machine, she shoved a pen into Sarah's hand. "Sign here, please."

Was this woman always this pleasant?

"Hullo, Rebecca." Michael joined Sarah at the counter as she signed the receipt and handed it back to the unfriendly blond. "How's business?"

"Michael." Rebecca jabbed the receipt onto a spike where a stack of others rested beneath it on the counter. "It's fine, as you can see. People still know where to go in this town to get the best breakfast and desserts around."

"Great. We—this is Sarah Bentley, by the way."

Rebecca narrowed her eyes but nodded.

"We wanted to talk with you about the letter you sent to Sarah's sister, Ginny Rose."

"I'm a little busy if you hadn't noticed."

"We won't take much of your time. Can you call Louise out here to give a hand at the counter while we chat?"

Considering him a moment, Rebecca finally turned to a window that showed through to the kitchen. "Hey, Louise! Get out here, will you?"

Sarah couldn't hold back her grimace. How was she ever going to talk some sense into this woman? At least the attorneys she dealt with on a daily basis back home pretended to have some manners.

Once a rotund middle-aged woman ambled out from behind the door, Rebecca indicated a table in the corner that a young couple had just vacated. She and Michael followed Rebecca to the table then followed her direction to sit.

"Well? You have three minutes."

Sarah took in a breath of air scented with warm blueberries, cinnamon, and coffee. Her body relaxed at the delicious smells that contrasted with the sour expression this woman wore. "About the letter you sent to Ginny. I just have to ask—"

"Why I'd do such a thing?" Sarcasm dripped from her tone.

"Yes, actually. It seemed—" *Immature. Rude. Overdone.* "A bit hasty."

"Hasty? That little tart thinks she can run my dad out of a business he built from the ground up, and *I'm* the hasty one?"

Tart? "Excuse me?" Sarah lifted a finger, a sudden desire to jab it in Rebecca's face racing through her veins, but Michael snagged her hand and pulled it beneath the table before she could. The movement—and subsequent stroking of his thumb against the top of her knuckles—took Sarah so off guard that her next words flew completely out of mind.

Michael beamed at Rebecca. "How long have you been back now? A few months? What were you doing before this?"

"Three and a half months, actually. And why the sudden interest? You haven't talked to me since high school." Folding her arms across her chest, Rebecca leaned back in her chair.

High school? Michael had made it sound like Rebecca was at least a friend.

The air crackled with intensity. This was getting them nowhere. Sarah would just have to deal with Rebecca the same way she dealt with any threat to her family's business—as a ruthless attorney. Not who she liked to be, but who she had to be.

Sarah leaned forward, lowering her voice. "Look, Rebecca, you don't know me, and I don't know you. But here's the thing I do know: My sister talked with your father, and he was OK with retiring. So why do you suddenly seem to have a score to settle?"

"My father is sick and not in his right mind at the moment." Talking between clenched teeth, Rebecca growled her words. "So forgive me if I don't much believe that he's willing to just give up the bakery he loved more than anything. And I do mean anything."

Sympathy shot through Sarah. How well she understood one's father loving work and money more than his own family. But Rebecca couldn't be allowed to play dirty just because she had daddy issues.

Michael squeezed her hand. Or was she squeezing his? Did he sense what she was feeling? But how could he possibly?

Time for this to be done and over with. Sarah pushed herself abruptly away from the table, her chair squawking loudly in the enclosed space that had grown warmer and warmer the longer she sat—and not only from the large convection ovens holding numerous trays of cookies, croissants, muffins, pies, and other delectable baked goods she'd spied just behind the door to the kitchen.

Towering over Rebecca, Sarah leaned forward. "You know that law you dug up won't hold water in court. I'm an attorney and I'll make sure of it."

A smirk crossed Rebecca's lips as she stood. Though she

barely came to Sarah's shoulders, the woman held her ground, fists clenched at her sides. "From what I hear of her, Ginny Rose won't open that bakery if there's the slightest chance she'll upset people. And even if the law is declared illegitimate, by the time that's declared, her loan will come due, and she won't have the funds to pay without a working business, now will she?" Rebecca turned on her heel and stomped back to the counter, head held high.

Sarah stared after her. The woman was infuriating but she was also right. If the case got tied up in court, Ginny might not be able to open a bakery for months or even years past her original planned date. And by then …

Perhaps Sarah could wrangle the money for the loan. She didn't yet have access to her trust fund, not until she "married appropriately," but—

"We should probably go." Michael's whispered words breathed warmth against Sarah's ear, sending a shiver up her spine.

Her attention turned from Rebecca to the other patrons openly watching and discussing the American who'd just been verbally smacked down by one of their own. However horrid a person, Rebecca was the insider here and Sarah the outsider.

Sarah nodded and allowed Michael to lead her from the bakery.

The wind whipped at the bottom of her jacket as they exited. Morning light streamed through the clouds. Down the hill, the water in the harbor bubbled and rocked the boats in a jaunty dance. A mom with her three children examined fruit in the boxes out front of the grocer's storefront, and the scent of cooked fish steamed from the vents of a local eatery.

Port Willis was indeed a lovely little community, a few citizens notwithstanding. No wonder Ginny wanted to make a life here. But if Sarah couldn't find a way to roust Rebecca Trengrouse, then her sister would have to sacrifice her dream.

"I can't believe that went so poorly." Sarah buried her face in her hands.

"Rebecca has definitely grown tougher over the years."

She peeked at him, studying the way he tugged at a few curls at the nape of his neck that had slipped from underneath his beanie. "I'm used to tough. You should see the people I've had to go up against in court."

Michael started walking down toward the bay, and Sarah matched his steps. "And you like that? Being an attorney?"

Folding her arms across her chest, Sarah sighed, her eyes focused on the horizon. Clouds dotted the crystal-blue sky, fluffy like an abundance of cotton balls falling all over themselves. "No. I mean, I hate the constant fighting. But it's sometimes rewarding."

"In what way? Financially?"

"No."

He stopped midstride at her sharp retort, and a flush warmed her cheeks.

"Sorry, that came out … Well, here's the thing, OK? I don't know if Ginny told you this, but our family is quite wealthy. And I hate it. I've always hated it, but never more than now. Because …" Oh, there she went, dangerously close to the edge. Wanting to step over, just to see what it felt like to reveal a piece of herself to someone other than Melissa.

But also terrified of what might happen, of what might crumble beneath her feet if she did.

They had reached the water. Seeming to sense Sarah's need for some quiet, Michael pointed to a path off to one side that led up to a grassy bluff overlooking the harbor. They hiked upward for a few minutes then stopped at the crest. From here she could see what seemed like the entire village, and even though there was a sharp drop-off less than ten feet away, she somehow also felt safe, secured away from all the world.

Sarah drew in a deep breath and sat, her knees pulled into

her chest. Michael lowered himself beside her, their shoulders brushing, together watching a boat glide past the harbor's quay into the open sea, free from its constraints. With him beside her and the sun burning overhead, the slight chill in the air didn't affect her quite so much.

"Thank you for trying to help me with Rebecca."

"My pleasure." He plucked a strand of the grass that surrounded them, folding it over and over in his fingers. "You know, it's funny. Though I would never say you're rude like her and would most definitely say you're much more charming, I have to admit that the two of you are rather alike, in that you're just women trying to protect their loved ones."

"Are you chastising me?" Despite the light accusation in her tone, she genuinely wanted to know. In fact, her stomach twisted at the thought he might say yes.

Why did this man's good opinion mean so much to her?

Michael tossed the grass away and scooted back so he faced her, pinning Sarah with a look that turned her bones into liquid. "No. I just always find it helpful to look at things from another's perspective."

"Oh." Sarah's hold loosened and she allowed her legs to straighten in front of her. "Yes, I can see the value in that."

"What I want to know most is why you feel such a need to protect Ginny."

"She's my sister."

"Yes, and I'd feel the same way about my sister Mary. But you're carrying it like a burden. It's not your problem to solve."

"But it is. I'm the one with a law degree." Sarah watched as the boat from earlier disappeared over the crest of the horizon.

"True. But Ginny seems content to trust God to work it all out."

So Michael believed too. That made sense, really, he with his constant smile. Sarah remembered that fleeting happiness, how it had felt to relish trusting in someone other than herself to make things happen.

But she'd seen too much of the world since then. People would chew you up and spit you out if you let them.

"I don't know about God, but I let her down once. I'm not going to do it again."

CHAPTER 6

If Sarah couldn't solve Ginny's legal problems, she'd do her best with the other stuff.

"Which one do you like more?" Sarah held up the two sample paint cards while her sister sorted through all the knick-knacks spread across the white countertop in the front of the bakery. They'd spent all day yesterday shopping in Port Willis and surrounding towns in an attempt to find the perfect decor to complete the modern look Ginny was going for at Once Upon a Time.

Ginny glanced up and waved her hand. "Whatever you think."

Studying the canary yellow card next to the light teal, Sarah shook her head. "This is your bakery. You're going to have to live with the accent wall color every day, not me."

Blowing some errant wisps of bangs from her eyes, Ginny pulled out her ponytail holder and smoothed her hands over her long locks. "Yeah, but I really don't know. Like, I absolutely love the yellow. It feels bright and most like me. But is it too much for an entire wall? And what if I choose the wrong color and then hate it and have to stare at it forever and ever because it would be such a pain to repaint it?" She looped the elastic band around her hair.

Sarah couldn't help it. Laughter burst forth. "Okay, Miss Dramatic." Closing her eyes, she tried to imagine both colors up on the long wall opposite the door.

As she stood there picturing it, the utter quiet struck her. It was Sunday, and according to Ginny, that's when Port Willis just about shut down, especially in the wintertime. Everyone spent the day with their families—some even attended church—then tucked themselves away, resting before things began again on Monday.

In Boston, noise always surrounded the city. Horns honking. People shouting. Sirens blaring. Music bopping. Sarah usually enjoyed the constant movement—maybe because it kept her from thinking too hard about things and the way she wished they were. But wishing didn't make things happen. Doing did.

"You OK, sis?"

Ginny's question brought Sarah back to reality. She opened her eyes. "Just trying to think about what color I'd choose if I were you." Sarah set the cards on the counter, along with the assortment of candles, tea canisters, white and yellow mugs, and the rest of the items they'd bought yesterday. Their biggest and best score had been a set of three large metal pendant light fixtures made from vintage bakery whisks that they'd purchased from an antique store in town. Steven planned to stop by later today to hang them above the front counter.

They were modern and different from Sarah's taste, which made it more difficult for her to help Ginny with her vision. "Maybe you should forego an accent wall and just use accented decor instead. You can always change that out without too much hassle."

"Oh, that's a great idea." Ginny ran her fingers over a few other knickknacks they'd picked up. "I think I like the yellow, then."

"Good choice." Sarah held up a mini chalkboard. "This feels more shabby-chic."

Ginny touched a finger to her chin, pondered the sign, and agreed. "I thought I may go that direction at first. You know, because of calling it Once Upon a Time."

Sarah snagged a few yellow mugs and studied the built-in behind the counter before placing them on one in the middle. "Why did you choose that name?"

"Partly because we're adjoining the bookstore with it. Fairy tales and all that."

"That makes sense." Sarah grabbed a knife and sliced the tape from a sealed box. Nestled inside was a yellow- and white-spotted tea kettle and matching strainer—all for display since Gin would be using her fancy other tools to make hot tea. "So why not go shabby chic, then?"

"Don't you remember the room I had growing up?"

"Yes. It was gorgeous and I was jealous. I would have loved a pink room with a lacy white comforter." The Styrofoam surrounding the tea kettle squeaked as Sarah pulled the delicate item free. "Instead I got a nautical-themed room with clean, angular lines." She held the kettle out to Ginny, who took it and arranged it on one of the shelves.

"Mother never really cared what we wanted, did she?"

"Still doesn't. Neither does Father." Sarah shoved the empty box shut and moved it to the ground. At her sister's silence, she turned.

Ginny continued to unpack colorful plates and cups and place them onto the shelves. What was she thinking? In the five days since Sarah had arrived, they'd had pleasant conversation. Sure, it was surface level, but that suited Sarah just fine. Because what was she going to say? She couldn't change the past. All she could do was use her time here to help Ginny now.

She still couldn't believe her sister hadn't been more upset yesterday when Sarah had finally gathered the courage to tell her she couldn't figure out her legal problem. But maybe that was because she'd grown so used to her family disappointing her that it didn't surprise her anymore. Or maybe Ginny had more faith in Sarah than Sarah did in herself. After all, they still had a shot at addressing the law at the parish council meeting. But that wasn't for eight more days. At least Sarah had been able to contact the council and add a motion to the meeting's agenda.

Finally, Ginny turned to Sarah and leaned against the built-in case. "You know why else I chose the name Once Upon a Time Bakery?"

"Why?"

"Because I used to believe in fairy tales. Before Garrett destroyed that belief. And now ... well, I believe again but in a different way."

"How is it now?" Sarah joined her sister behind the counter, leaning a hip against the counter.

Ginny smiled. "Before, I thought a heroine had to go out and make her own destiny. Like, if I didn't save the business and get my husband back, then I was a failure. But now, I know that so much of a fairy tale ending is about trusting God to fight for me."

Huh. "So, you just wait around for God to do things for you?" When Sarah had first found her faith, she'd been so young, but she'd still read through the Bible at a voracious pace —the Bible she'd found tucked away on a dusty shelf in their Nantucket estate's massive library.

One day, she'd returned to her room to find the Bible missing and a biography about "strong women" in its place. A note in her father's handwriting said, "If you're looking for inspiration, find it here."

Sarah hadn't thought about that moment in a long time. About the way her teenage heart had plummeted with the loss of that precious book. About how, to avoid a confrontation, she'd read the biography cover to cover and had never gone searching for the Bible again.

But now, she couldn't help wondering—what if she had? Might things be different?

Might *she* be different?

Ginny fiddled with a snagged thread at the end of her sleeve. "No, not at all. We still move forward and follow our dreams—our dreams, not the ones people have for us—but we don't take things on our own shoulders. We know that God works all things together for good and that even when we feel like we've lost control, he hasn't. So even if this bakery fails, *I* won't be a failure." Ginny's lips twisted. "I am probably not explaining that very well. I'm still pretty new to this having-faith-thing. We definitely weren't raised that way, were we?"

"No, we weren't." Her sister had never known about Sarah's clandestine trips to her friend's youth group. How would she, when Sarah hadn't told a soul … until she'd heard a sermon about sharing faith with those you love, and something had stirred in her spirit. She'd gathered her courage one night to finally tell her parents about her new belief.

Instead of agreeing to try out church as a family, her parents had grounded her for "sneaking around" and had implemented a schedule that was so full she no longer had time to attend youth group.

Sarah shifted. How had Ginny come to her newfound beliefs? "Gin—"

"Hello!" The door between the bookstore and bakery opened, and Sophia Rose stuck her head inside. "Can we come in?"

Ginny straightened and squeezed Sarah's arm. "To be continued." Then she turned to Sophia, whom Sarah had met last night at dinner. "Come on in, you guys."

Sophia Rose, the gorgeous raven-haired beauty from the bridal photo on Ginny's wall, waltzed in with her shoulders high and a smile highlighting her cheekbones. Behind her came her husband, a tall and lean man with curly blond hair and thick glasses. William fit the literature professor persona better than anyone Sarah had ever seen, with his sweater vest and collared shirt rolled to reveal his forearms. Sophia's adorable slightly rounded belly whispered of the couple's upcoming blessing, due in April, if Sarah remembered correctly.

William carried what appeared to be a casserole dish wrapped in a towel. "Where do you want this, Gin?"

"This way." After giving Sophia a quick hug, Ginny led them into the kitchen, propping open the door so everyone could scoot inside.

William deposited the dish onto the counter. "Be right back." He headed through the swinging door once more, leaving the three women alone.

"What's all this?" Ginny peeked under the foil covering the casserole dish. Sarah caught a whiff of onion and roasted meat. "You didn't ..."

Sophia laughed and placed her hand on her stomach in the way pregnant women did without seeming to realize it. "Of course I didn't make that. Becoming a wife hasn't changed my culinary skills." She turned to Sarah. "What your sister is so delicately pointing out is that, of my many talents, cooking and baking belong to her and her alone."

A former social worker and victim of domestic violence, Sophia now volunteered at a crisis center for other victims when she wasn't running the bookstore. When they'd learned of their shared passion for helping victims, she and Sarah had fallen into easy conversation last night.

"I'm with you there." As Sarah's stomach perked up, she nudged Ginny away so she could glance at the food. "Are these Cornish pasties?" The shortcrust pastry was golden brown with a flaky texture and braided cooked dough along one edge where it had sealed in the filling.

"It is indeed. Mrs. Lincoln dropped them by for all of us."

"Oh, that was so sweet and considerate." Ginny replaced the foil on the dish and moved to pull some plates from her cabinet.

"She's the one who owns the antique shop, right?" Not even one week here and Sarah had already met half the town. "Wasn't her brother there too?"

"Yes, he and his wife moved back to town recently to help her out. She's got gout, poor thing, but she still finds time to serve everyone else in town." Sophia tucked a strand of hair behind her ear and joined Ginny in getting out what they needed for the meal.

"Speaking of the Lincolns"—Ginny ducked behind the massive refrigerator door and emerged with some water bottles and soda—"when are Oliver and Joy coming into town?"

Sarah scurried over and took a few from her arms. "Who are they?"

"Oh, sorry. Joy is Sophia's best friend from America. She came here last Christmas for Sophia's wedding and fell in love with a Brit."

Glancing between Sophia and Ginny, Sarah quirked an eyebrow. "I'm sensing a theme."

The women burst out laughing.

Sophia winked at her. "Be careful or it'll happen to you too."

Michael's face flashed in her mind. Not only that but the way he'd sat with her on Friday, enjoying the quiet and the view. She'd thought about that way too often during the last few days.

But fall in love? No way. She didn't even have the luxury of a flirtation, not with Warren waiting in the wings and the weight of her father's expectations on her shoulders.

A water bottle tumbled from Sarah's hands and rolled across the floor. She set the rest of the drinks on the counter and picked the chilly plastic container off the ground.

Would it be too much to hope that Ginny and Sophia would just think she was clumsy?

Clearing her throat, Sarah placed her hands on her hips. "Sorry, I distracted you from Ginny's original question."

After a confused look passed across Sophia's face, she smiled. "Oh yeah. Pregnancy brain." She stuck out her tongue just slightly and turned to Ginny. "Joy and Oliver are planning to come to your opening and stay through New Year's."

"They don't live here?" Sarah asked.

"No, she's from Florida and her parents are there," Sophia said. "She didn't want to leave them because her mom has Alzheimer's. So they did the long-distance thing for a while then got married about six months ago. Oliver moved to Florida and travels back to London about every other month for work."

"That's sweet how they worked it out."

William returned with a side of peas and gravy and placed it onto the counter next to the pasties. He snagged a plate then handed it to Sophia, stealing a quick kiss before he released it.

With all the horrible relationships Sarah constantly saw back home—men who treated their women like garbage or even people like her parents who never showed affection and treated each other as indifferent acquaintances—she could definitely appreciate the change in scenery.

And as she dished up her Cornish lunch and joked and laughed with her sister and her friends, the natural warmth of the kitchen seemed to reach out and wrap Sarah in its arms, beckoning her to lean into this place.

If she weren't careful, Port Willis and its people were going to be hard to leave come December 23.

CHAPTER 7

This was never going to work.

Sarah paced the length of Ginny's hallway, turned on her heel, then paced back the way she'd come. Studying the stack of papers in her left hand, she sipped from a coffee mug using her right. The words on the page blurred together, which was unsurprising considering how late she'd been up the night before writing her notes.

Hair hung in her eyes and she blinked in rapid motion. "Just keep going, Sarah. Just keep moving, moving, moving."

Great, now she was talking to herself. But someone had to motivate her. Since Sarah had spent last Sunday decorating, her sister was one week closer to the opening date of her bakery but no closer to actually being able to open it. Yes, Sarah had helped apply some paint, hang the menu, arrange the decor, and select some more last-minute trinkets to enhance the character of the space, but Ginny's legal problems were not just going to go away.

And unless Sarah wowed the parish council at tomorrow night's meeting, Ginny could kiss her dreams of owning a bakery goodbye.

As much as she said she trusted God to fight for her, Ginny had to be worried. Sarah saw the more prominent crease in her brow, the way her lips drew taut when she didn't think anyone was looking. Yet, still she acted like she believed in God's ability to handle it.

If only Sarah were as confident.

"Argh." She threw the papers against the wall. Instead of a satisfying thud, the papers fluttered to the ground as slow as they pleased.

"Wow."

Sarah glanced up at the sudden intrusion, the movement sending her coffee sloshing over the rim of the mug and all over her white sweater.

"Oh man." Michael strode forward from the doorway, snatching a towel from the kitchen counter as he came closer to Sarah. He held it out as if a peace offering.

"Don't you ever knock?" Tears welled in her eyes as she jerked the rag from his hands and ran it along the front of the cashmere. But what was the point? It was clearly ruined by her clumsiness. She dropped the towel onto the floor and sighed. "I'm sorry. That was rude."

"No, I barged in here again without thinking about how it might interrupt your work." Michael watched her for a moment, and she took the time to study him too. It had been days since she'd seen him, though they'd texted a bit here and there. He'd been working and so had she, and Sarah had declined Ginny's invitation to attend church that Sunday morning, where she would have seen him.

There was no sense in denying it. She'd missed him—his infectious laugh, that eternal optimism he seemed to possess.

She could tell him, but what would that do?

"I'm not getting anywhere with it anyway."

Michael scooped up the fallen papers and handed them to

Sarah. "Is this work-work, or help-Ginny-save-the-bakery work?"

The paper crunched in Sarah's fist. "The latter. I haven't done any actual work since leaving Boston. It's been strange." Yes, she'd checked in with Melissa almost daily regarding New Dawn work and called Elise several times since their first meeting two weeks ago, but that didn't feel like work. She'd kept busy trying to help her sister, but something deep inside craved working toward something with purpose.

Not that a bakery didn't have purpose. She just didn't feel like she was doing much to truly help Ginny. Anyone could paint and decorate.

It all came back to tomorrow night's meeting. And the papers in her hand were proof that she didn't have any leverage, no matter what angle she tried.

Her jaw ached and head pounded. The answers should have been there, but if they were, Sarah couldn't find them.

"Hey, so I know I can't help much with it, but I do know when someone needs a break. And you are definitely there." Michael eased the papers from Sarah's hands and laid them on the kitchen counter. "Go get changed. I've got just the thing."

"No, I need to figure this out. It won't get done if I do something else."

"Actually, I've found when I'm having a creative block, doing something else is the exact thing I need." Michael placed his hands on her shoulders, his lightly twitching thumbs shooting a spark through her insides.

Sarah's breathing hitched at his nearness. "What did you have in mind?"

A grin spread across his face. "You'll just have to trust me."

That was the trouble. She did. But why? She'd only known the guy a few weeks.

She held up her forefinger. "I'll give you one hour."

"It's going to take longer than that."

She scolded her stomach as it flipped at the thought of spending extended time with him. "I'd better change then."

"We'll be walking a lot, so just maybe don't wear heels, yeah?" Michael chuckled.

"Ha ha." Sarah shoved him playfully then ducked and squealed as he tried to snatch her waist. A minute later, she found herself in Ginny's guest room, laughing and shaking her head as she threw off the soiled sweater. Reaching for her emerald green belted wrap blouse—a favorite that she'd been told made her eyes pop—her hand switched directions at the last second and landed on a long-sleeved T-shirt. She tossed it on with a pair of faded jeans and threw back her hair into a messy bun.

With her tired red eyes and casual clothing, at least no one could accuse her of trying to impress Michael.

Because she definitely wasn't. Nope.

She joined him in the kitchen and, after slipping on her parka, they headed out. Soft gray puffs clouded the sky, and the crisp air bit into her cheeks with a winter reminder of the possibility of snow coming before she left Port Willis.

The thought of returning to Boston sat sour in her stomach.

No. She wouldn't think about that. Not today. Instead, she'd focus on the gorgeous scenery as they drove.

And yeah, maybe even the gorgeous company.

Throughout the hour-long drive, Michael snuck glances at her and asked her a slew of small-talk questions. Sarah relaxed into her seat as they chatted, her eyes taking in the peaceful countryside. They passed several other tiny villages, though none could compete with the charm of the seaside Port Willis.

Trees surrounded and arced over the road along several stretches. And even though many of their branches hung bare, there was something wondrous about them—the way they hedged the road in, almost like they were protecting it.

Eventually they arrived at what Michael said was a two

hundred-acre estate with massive gardens famous in the area. He got out and opened her door for her. She climbed from the truck, taking his offered hand, which he didn't relinquish as he led her through the front office and paid for their entrance. Tugging her along one of the many trails, Michael strolled with his camera around his neck, gazing at the trees surrounding them and naming various plant life.

She should have tugged her hand away, but the way it nestled so perfectly inside his thrummed a constant glow through her—silly, considering they both wore gloves. Her cheeks heated despite the cold air turning them pink.

Their shoes crunched the gravel underneath their feet. "And that is a cluster of snowdrops." Michael pointed to a drift of low-growing plants with sturdy-looking stalks. Each stalk played host to one small white flower that drooped downward.

Currently, the flowers were closed tightly, but Sarah imagined them as they would be in their rightful glory—their petals spread wide and arching over one another.

With a little sun and patience, these beauties would bloom. What a sight that would be.

If only I could see it. But she'd be gone by then.

"They're gorgeous."

He looked from them to her, a smile quirking the side of his lips. "Yeah, they are." He squeezed her hand, dropped it, and pulled his camera from its bag. Then he snapped a few shots of the snowdrops up close. "You ever learn anything about photography?" Michael kept taking photos, but somehow she sensed he was just as attuned to her as she was to him.

"No. I had to learn how to play the piano like any good Bentley would, but that's about where our artistic education stopped."

"Pity." He straightened and turned to look at her. "You want to learn?"

She hesitated. "I don't want to drop your camera."

He tapped the strap hanging from the back. "That's what this is for."

Bits of light had started to break through the clouds and filter down, combining with the canopy of trees to create soft spotlights all around them. Here, she felt hemmed in, safe, but not trapped—finally free from the eyes constantly watching the oldest Bentley daughter and future CEO of Bentley & Co.

Here, with Michael, she was simply Sarah.

And Sarah wanted to learn a bit about photography.

She took off her gloves then stepped closer to him. "Would you mind showing me a few things?"

"I'd love to." He slipped the camera strap around her. The camera's weight strained against her neck as if the thing was trying to escape—surprising, given the effortless way Michael had held it like it weighed nothing more than a tissue.

She took the precious tool from him, her fingers brushing his. "What do I do first? I mean, I know the basics of how these work, but how do you get a good photo?"

"It's all about lighting. If you can find the right light, you're halfway to a decent photo."

"How do you know what the right light is?" Holding the camera to her eye, she squinted through the tiny viewfinder. The world narrowed but somehow that didn't make it any smaller. Instead, it allowed her to focus. She moved the lens closer to the snowdrops, zooming in to see the tiny bladed leaves on each stalk.

"When shooting outside, the early morning or a few hours before sunset are really the best times when it comes to light. You want soft, not harsh, but not so soft that there are a lot of shadows."

"Harsh is bad, soft is good. Got it." Sarah lowered the camera and found Michael staring at her. Glancing away, she bit her lip and studied the cluster of buttons on the back of the camera.

"But it looks like there are a lot of settings on this thing. I'm thinking there's more to it than you're letting on."

"Here, may I?"

"Of course." But before she could unloop the camera from her neck, he stepped up beside her and took the camera in his right hand while she kept hold of it in her left. Their shoulders pressed against each other, and his left arm slipped around her shoulders as he leaned in, making adjustments to the buttons on the camera.

Sarah could hardly breathe with his nearness as she watched his thumb fly.

"There. It's ready for you. Just aim and shoot."

She swallowed, afraid to look up at him—of what she'd see there and of what she'd reveal of the butterflies tumbling about in her chest. "But you didn't teach me anything." Not that she could have really focused on any lessons at this moment anyway.

"My first lesson is that you just need to feel it out. Find joy in the doing before getting bogged down in all the details. Just have fun."

She nearly laughed. Fun. What was that?

"I'll try." Taking the camera fully in her possession again, Sarah repositioned the viewfinder. Michael stepped back to give her space. The tension in her shoulders dropped with the distance, but so did her heart at having him farther away.

But it put her alone with the camera—just her and a world of possibility. In this moment, the only thing that mattered was *her* perspective, how she saw the world. That's what would be recorded. Nothing more, nothing less.

She framed the snowdrops and clicked the button to take a photo, a sigh whooshing from her lungs.

After snapping several more, she glanced up. Michael leaned against a tree, hands in his jacket pockets, watching her, an indiscernible look in his eyes. "May I see them?"

Sarah managed only a nod.

He reached for the camera, his eyes not leaving hers until the last possible moment. Then he studied the photos. "These are really great, Sarah."

She looked down at them, shrugged. "They're amateur."

"They're yours and *that* makes them perfect. Don't let anyone ever tell you any differently."

A tear spilled from her eyes, and she swatted it away, praying he hadn't noticed.

Goodness, this man. If she didn't get away from here right this second, she was bound to leap into his arms and make a complete fool of herself.

Her fingers tingled as she tugged her gloves back on. "I think I'll leave the photography to the professionals. But thank you, Michael." *Thank you for seeing me.*

She started down the garden path once more, shaking the fallen leaves from her shoes.

CHAPTER 8

The best thing about being an attorney was helping people. But when Sarah failed, she once again became that green first-year law student who didn't have a clue about how things really worked.

And right here, in this moment, she was desperate to avoid that feeling.

Sarah uncrossed and recrossed her legs for the thousandth time as she listened to a local parish citizen drone on about her dislike of chickens.

Really? Chickens?

"Bottom line, I'm waking up far too early because of the noise. I'd like to propose a zoning change." The forty-something placed a hand on her ample hip and harrumphed into the microphone set up in the middle of the floor. Seven council members sat up front, the chairman in the middle, and the rest of the small room was filled with townspeople from Port Willis and a few surrounding villages.

Across the aisle, Sarah spied Rebecca Trengrouse lounging in her seat, arms crossed over her chest. No one sat with her.

Trying to keep herself from rolling her eyes at Chicken Lady,

Sarah gripped the folder in her lap and smoothed the top sheet of paper that contained her outline. To her right, Ginny sat with Steven, her bobbing knee the only sign she was nervous about today's outcome. On Sarah's left sat Michael, who'd insisted on coming as moral support.

She'd received no massive revelations during their day out together yesterday, but one thing was for certain—if she spent much more time in his presence like that, she was going to kiss the man, plain and simple.

And though that idea was altogether much too pleasant, she knew it could lead nowhere. Nowhere real, anyway. What was she going to do? Run off to England like Ginny had?

And what about Warren? He'd texted her several times during the last few days to let her know how excited he was to spend Christmas Eve together. Not that they'd ever said they were exclusive. But still.

A sigh escaped Sarah's lips, and Michael's hand slipped over one of her own, giving it a quick squeeze before releasing her. She looked at him and mouthed *thank you*. Leaning toward her, he whispered, "You've got this, Sarah. I believe in you." His breath warmed her ear and neck, sending shivers up her spine.

The council voted to retain the current zoning, much to Chicken Lady's loud dismay, and moved on to the next agenda item. "Next, we have Ms. Ginny Rose with a motion to discuss and dismiss Ordinance Five Two Six Eight."

Ginny and Sarah stood and walked to the microphone, which Ginny snagged and adjusted to fit her height. "Hello, esteemed council."

If this hadn't been such a serious matter, Sarah would have snickered at her sister's formality. Ginny had never been one to enjoy speaking in public, and Mother had constantly been on her about her use of "slang." Really, it was just further proof that Ginny had always been different than the rest of the Bentleys.

But while their parents saw that as a bad thing, Sarah

wished she had what Ginny possessed—a surety inside herself. Ginny knew who she was, with or without the world's approval.

With or without her family's approval.

Ginny stepped back and looked expectantly at Sarah. Oops. Sarah must have missed her introduction. No matter. She squared her shoulders and took her sister's place behind the microphone. "Thank you for allowing us the time to come before you to discuss this outdated ordinance that, if allowed to remain as part of the law, will inhibit my sister from opening a bakery in Port Willis. You see ..."

Sarah filled in the council on the ordinance, Ginny's history with Mr. Trengrouse, and his apparent wishes before his daughter took over. "Digging up this ordinance—one that I have, in fact, seen broken by no less than three local businesses —is a last-ditch attempt by the owner's daughter to keep a monopoly over the baked goods industry in town." Glancing from council member to council member, Sarah could see she'd swayed at least three of them to her side. Most of them were, after all, businesspeople. They had to understand that monopolies were bad for villages, driving up prices and lowering quality.

"Why is she afraid of a bit of honest competition? And why is she trying so hard to maintain the business her father was fully in favor of letting go?" Maybe that last part was a low blow, but Rebecca had to take it if she was going to dish it out, right? Next to her, Ginny shifted and pressed on Sarah's arm.

Had Sarah gone too far? Perhaps. She inhaled a deep breath then leaned toward the microphone. "Thank you."

The chairman covered his microphone and conferred with one of his colleagues then nodded and looked back at Sarah and Ginny. "We appreciate you bringing this to our attention. Is the aforementioned business owner or his daughter in attendance tonight?"

"I am." Rebecca stood and waltzed to the front of the room, squeezing in beside Sarah and nudging her out of the way.

Sarah's hands curled, but Ginny grabbed one of her fists and led them back to their seats.

"Miss ..."

"Trengrouse."

"Miss Trengrouse, please enlighten the council as to why you took it upon yourself to find this law and use it in what seems to be a scare tactic."

"Sir, that is not at all what this is." Rebecca put on a slick tone that dripped with syrup. "I simply want justice to be done. This is a law, and I feel the law should be followed. Don't you? As for the other businesses that Ms. Bentley referred to, I actually have documentation that shows they agreed amicably to disregard the ordinance in question." She held up a piece of paper.

Sarah wanted to groan. Why hadn't she investigated further?

Her face must have revealed her inner angst because to her left Michael's hand encased hers. As she listened to Rebecca go on and on about how her family had established Trengrouse Bakery in 1909 and how her relationship with her family and all her fondest memories centered around kneading bread and frosting cinnamon buns and how all of that might be ruined if the council allowed an American with no regard for Cornish tradition to come in and plow through them all, the desire to weep came harder and faster.

Not just crying. No, tears wouldn't do the feelings welling up inside of her justice.

This was a soul-deep cry from her heart, one that was watching her sister's dreams die second by second—like seeing a hangman first knotting the noose, then testing it for its strength and ability to kill, then fitting it around the dream's neck ...

"Thank you for your input, miss. You may take your seat."

The chairman glanced at his fellow members. "All in favor of dismissing Ordinance Five Two Six Eight, raise your hands."

Only one member—not even one of the ones Sarah had thought she'd snagged earlier—raised their hand.

"All opposed, raise your hands." The other six members, including the chairman, lifted their hands.

A smile twitched on the chairman's lips as he located Rebecca in the crowd. "The motion to dismiss Ordinance Five Two Six Eight is denied. And with that, our meeting is adjourned."

Although the room burst to life at that moment, to Sarah, everything stopped. The increasing volume reminded her of bees buzzing around a hive. She leaned forward and buried her face in her hands.

Ginny rubbed her back. "It's okay, sis. We'll find another way."

How was her sister the one comforting Sarah? Where was she drawing her strength, her optimism, her trust from? Certainly not from the family who had raised her then spit her out.

"But now, I know that so much of a fairy tale ending is about trusting God to fight for me." Gin's words from last week flooded back to Sarah.

It must be God, then.

What would it be like to return to the faith of her youth? What must God think of Sarah, who'd basically abandoned him in favor of her parents' religion of self-sufficiency? In their world, the only way for a person to get what they wanted was to outsmart others or work with them. It was the strategy Sarah had chosen with Father: give him herself as future CEO in exchange for New Dawn's funding.

Maybe it was too late for her. But it was not too late for Ginny. Sarah wouldn't allow someone—Rebecca Trengrouse, in this instance—to shatter her sister's faith, her spirit, her dreams.

"You're right. We will."

Sarah kept her gaze averted from Michael's, though the intensity of his eyes on her powered through the air. If she looked his way, he'd surely see the trembling, the self-doubt, the guilt. Pressing her lips together, Sarah stood and anchored herself with the only resource she had available—resolve to find a way, no matter what.

A steady rain paddled the window, plinking with abandon.

Though she tried to ignore it, the sound of every drop, like fingers tapping the glass, rang above her head. She rolled over and glanced at the clock gleaming red in the darkness—3:24 a.m. Only five minutes past the last time she'd looked.

Groaning, she rolled out from beneath the comforter, the cold floor greeting her toes before she could stuff on her slippers. Might as well get up. Her thoughts wouldn't let her sleep.

She wrapped herself in a robe Ginny had lent to her and opened the door with a quiet touch, flinching when a squeak resounded through the dim hallway. Sarah snuck past Ginny's room and into the kitchen where her sister had left a light on above the stove. As she filled a kettle with water from the refrigerator, her mind continued circling back to earlier tonight—or should she say, last night?

Rebecca Trengrouse had made fools of them all, but that wasn't what bothered Sarah most. The thing she kept coming back to wasn't really about the parish council meeting at all but rather a question Michael had asked her when they'd visited the Trengrouse bakery: *"What I want to know most is why you feel such a need to protect Ginny."*

After she turned on one of the stove's burners, she lit the gas. Once the tiny blue flame fluttered into being, Sarah placed the kettle on the range, and, after removing a mug from the cabinet and placing a bag of chamomile tea inside, leaned against the counter with arms folded across her chest.

Michael hadn't even known their family's history when he asked that question. He still didn't know everything, though bits and pieces of the story had fallen into place during their long day at the garden. Yet even he could see that something wasn't right in Sarah and Ginny's relationship.

Why *did* she feel this burning need to protect Ginny—and Ginny's dreams? She hadn't done so in the past. So why now?

The kettle whistled, startling her from her thoughts. She flicked off the burner, pulled the kettle from the stovetop, and poured the liquid into her cup. The steam curled against her cheeks as it lifted and dispersed.

Taking the mug in hand, Sarah wandered into the living room and caught sight of the bare Christmas tree. Ginny still hadn't decorated it and probably wouldn't. Christmas was what … ten days away? Nine? The bakery opening would be here before they knew it.

If it came at all.

Fighting the urge to hurl the mug of tea against the wall, Sarah set it down onto the coffee table instead. She strode toward the boxes under the tree and pulled open the tabs of the top one. A sparkling assortment of ornaments greeted her.

After a successful search for hooks, Sarah began to take ornaments from the box. One after another, she pressed the hooks through the caps of dainty glass icicles, porcelain balls, and sparkling snowflakes. Then she hung them on the tree, ensuring that each one shone from the perfect spot, yes, but also that they all blended into one picture, working together to create something one couldn't make on its own.

Her tea grew cold as she worked.

A noise sounded behind her, so Sarah turned. There stood Ginny, mouth slightly open as she watched. After a moment, she walked to a small stereo and turned on its radio. Kenny G or some such musician spun a soft Christmas tune throughout the room as Ginny joined Sarah at the box and lifted out an ornament. They worked in tandem, not speaking, the only sound that of a silky saxophone surrounding them.

After a while, Sarah reached into the box and felt around. Only one ornament left. She tried to hand it to Ginny, but her sister just smiled. "You do the honors."

"I don't deserve to." Heat, sudden and fierce, hammered the back of Sarah's eyelids.

Ginny's face softened and she stepped closer. "Sarah, please. Don't beat yourself up over this."

A tear escaped. "I didn't protect you, Gin. I should have. I … I'm so sorry."

"Oh, sis." And there came Ginny's arms around her again. "The bakery is my dream and my responsibility, not yours. If it's meant to be, it'll be. God's got a plan. I may not know what that is, and I may not even like it, but …" She shrugged.

Sarah shook her head, tears now falling much more freely, soaking the shoulder of Ginny's long-sleeved pajamas. "I'm not talking about the bakery." Her words came out muffled, so she pulled herself back from her sister's embrace. When Sarah looked Gin in the eyes, her sister's tears mirrored hers. "I'm talking about when Mother and Father disowned you. I should have stood up for you. I should have told them how ridiculous they were being. I should have—"

"Stop. Just … Sarah, come on. I don't blame you. I know the hold they have over people. They had the same hold over me."

"But you were strong enough to get out."

"Not really. I just fell in love and that was stronger than my fear." Ginny gripped Sarah's upper arms. "I don't blame *you*. I never blamed you."

"You should have, though. I've been a horrible sister." Sarah lifted the star ornament in her hand closer to examine it. Her finger traced the golden spires, following a trail of glitter across its surface.

"I was the one who left, not you." Ginny gently nudged Sarah in the ribs. "And you're here, aren't you? You've bent over backward to help me these last few weeks. You put your life—your work—on hold to be with me. And whatever happens with the bakery, I'll never forget that. Ever."

Sarah couldn't look up again. Despite Ginny's kind and forgiving words, she couldn't get past the thought that she'd failed. But again—why did she feel such responsibility for Ginny's dreams?

Unless ... What if it weren't really Ginny's dreams she was worried about? Was she doing all of this, feeling all of this, because she knew her own dreams would never come true—and solving Ginny's problems had become a fair substitute?

Had she done all of this for herself? That's not what she'd meant to do.

Sarah's hand trembled and she feared dropping the ornament. Once again, she tried to shove it into Ginny's hands.

Her sister's fingers wrapped around Sarah's, but she refused to take the ornament. "How about we both do it?"

"OK."

Drawing strength from her sister's confidence, Sarah pushed a hook through the ornament's top loop and closed the bottom. And with each of them holding on, they positioned the ornament at the center of the tree.

Taking a deep breath, Sarah slid her arm around Ginny's waist and laid her head on her shoulder as Bing Crosby crooned about a white Christmas.

That's when Sarah noticed it—sometime during the last hour, the rain had stopped. Moonlight peeked through the frosty window and illuminated the tree.

Together, they had made something beautiful.

CHAPTER 9

Was she completely out of her depth here?

Sarah clasped the plastic-wrapped plate harder as she stared through the front windows of the Village Pub. It didn't appear as crowded as usual, given the late afternoon hour on a weekday, but things would probably pick up in the next hour or two. It was now or never.

What would Michael think of her traipsing in there and giving him a tray of baked goods? That wasn't something that friends did for each other, was it? Would she be declaring too much with the gesture?

It had all seemed so logical an hour ago. She wanted to thank him for last Sunday's trip to the gardens and for his supportive presence at the parish council meeting three nights ago. What better way to do that than a dessert—one that Ginny had assured her was his favorite?

No sense standing out here in the cold, especially since snow was in the forecast sometime this week. Not even the parka hugging her torso or the cap she wore on her head kept the chill out today.

Or maybe that was the nerves talking.

When Sarah pushed open the door to the restaurant, an assortment of aromas embraced her, warm and welcoming. A fire roared in a hearth nearby.

"Welcome to the Village Pub." The hostess eyed the brownies in Sarah's hands. "Will you be dining with us today?"

"No, I was hoping to …" Deep breath. "Is Michael Hammett here?"

"Let me fetch him for you."

"Thank you."

After a minute or two, the hostess returned with Michael in tow. He wore a black apron over his jeans and sweater. How did an apron manage to look so manly when tied around his trim waist?

When he saw Sarah, the way his face lit up did something to her insides. *Friends, friends. We're just friends.*

"Hey, Sarah."

"Sorry to interrupt you at work." She held out the platter. "I just wanted to bring you these as a thank you."

He untied the apron and eyed the hostess, who was not-so-surreptitiously listening while pretending to study something on the podium. Reaching for the plate, his hand landed on Sarah's wrist. "Take a walk with me?"

"Oh. Sure." Ginny was in another town nearby with Sophia picking out some last-minute serving ware, so Sarah didn't need to be home at any particular time tonight. "I'm all yours."

The moment the words left her lips, her cheeks burned.

Michael's grin was his only reply as he removed the apron, deposited it on a nearby coat rack, slipped on a light-brown jacket and red-and-gray scarf, and led the way outside. He took the platter from her and peeled one corner of the plastic up to peek inside. "Brownies? Did Ginny make them?"

"No, I did." At his look of surprise, she scoffed playfully. "You didn't think she's the only one in the family who can bake? Though, admittedly, she may have loaned me her recipe."

"Excellent." He kept hold of the brownies with one hand and reached for her with the other.

Nearly without thinking, she slipped her hand inside his, and they took off down a path along the harbor. Different than the one they'd taken a few weeks ago, this path wound upward and out of town. "Where are we going?"

He pointed. "The lighthouse."

During her time here she'd noticed the white structure, which overlooked Port Willis like a stately reminder of time gone by. It was only a mile outside of the village, but between readying the bakery and keeping tabs on New Dawn, she hadn't found the time to visit.

"So, what are you thanking me for?"

The brisk air kept them walking at a quick pace instead of strolling leisurely like her heart wished they could. She wanted to enjoy every moment of her hand resting in his, of being near to this man who made her feel things she hadn't felt in a long time. Or ever, really.

But it was probably just the magic of being out from under her parents' thumbs, the gorgeous setting, the time of year—all combined to create the perfect scenario for romance.

Put her and Michael in another time and place, and he certainly wouldn't have this honeyed grip on her heart. Right?

"Sarah?"

"Sorry." On the horizon, clouds gathered and progressed toward them. "You have been really sweet while I've been here—distracting me when I needed it and helping me to get out of my head. And you've helped me try to solve a few problems too. I really appreciate it. So I wanted to thank you for being … such a good friend." She nearly choked on the last word.

Michael didn't speak for several moments that felt like much more. What was he thinking? "Of course." His cheeriness seemed forced, but perhaps she was reading too much into it.

Refusing to look at him, she swept her attention toward the

landscape and gasped. Grassy bluffs dropped off into rocky cliffs, and the ocean below disappeared and became white foam as it crashed against them. A little farther up the path stood the white lighthouse with a bright red door. It was weathered but something about the history behind it sent shivers down her spine.

Or maybe that was the cold in the air thanks to the decreasing temperature and the clouds rolling in.

"Gorgeous."

"You think *this* is gorgeous? Come on." Once again, Michael tugged her gently away into the lighthouse. They climbed the old stone steps and emerged into a room that boasted a whole wall of windows.

Letting go of Michael's hand, Sarah put her nose nearly to the glass. Below, the entire ocean spread before them, and Port Willis was but a small blip on the horizon down the shore. "I've never seen anything like this, not even from my office back home."

Michael set the plate of brownies on the ground and fished out two, handing her one. "You work in a skyrise, don't you?"

She took the fudgy treat in hand, pulled a crumbly piece off the corner, and plopped it into her mouth. Mmm. "Yes, and the view is spectacular, especially when the sun is shining. But this ... it's beautiful even when the clouds obscure the sun, you know?" After some thoughtful chewing, she turned to face him. "And besides, the view at my office is kind of tainted, knowing that I'm staring out from a prison of sorts."

"A prison?" He moved closer, the warmth radiating from his body.

"My job. I hate it." She finished the brownie then brushed her fingertips together. "My father is grooming me to be the CEO, and I just don't want it. But what Father wants, he gets."

Michael's brow furrowed. "Why is that? Why don't you just tell him you'd rather do something else?"

She laughed and the caustic noise grated against the silence. Outside, waves pounded the glass. Sarah wanted to pound back. "I know I'll lose one way or another."

"What do you mean?"

"I mean ..." It was pointless to drudge up the past, wasn't it? But why not? What could it hurt to say the words? If she didn't, they might shred her from the inside out. "To my father, obedience equals love. And despite how awful he and my mom are, I love them. I'm afraid if I go against what they want for my life, what happened to Ginny will happen to me. I'll lose my family."

She felt rather than saw him lean in. "Why do you think that will happen?" He closed the small gap between them, throwing his arm across her shoulders. His clothes smelled like the restaurant—roasted meats, spices, freshly baked bread.

Comfort.

Giving in to the temptation she'd fought for so long, she placed her arms around him and snuggled into his embrace. He moved his face closer, his cheek against her forehead.

"Why? Because it's happened before. When I was thirteen, a girl in my class invited me to a lock-in with her youth group. I liked the girl—she was sweet and real, you know?—but my parents said no." Clearly, her status as a scholarship student placed her beneath the Bentleys.

With her right hand, Sarah ran her finger up and down the zipper line of Michael's coat. Despite the layers of fabric between them, his heartbeat permeated to match hers.

"I was so tired of being ruled by them, so I decided to go anyway. My parents had a charity event that night, and I told the chauffeur that I was allowed to go. Halfway through the lock-in—at midnight, if you can believe it—the chauffeur showed up. Poor Alfred. He said he was sorry then led me back to the car, where my father sat in the back seat." Sarah sighed. "He didn't say a word to me that night or for the next month."

"That's horrible. You were only a kid."

"It's just how he is. Even now, twenty years later, he has me right where he wants me."

Like a fish on a hook. And no amount of wriggling did any good.

Her breathing hitched. Michael's lips feathered a kiss across her temple—a show of support.

And maybe ... more?

Embracing his encouragement, Sarah swallowed past the lump in her throat. "Remember the nonprofit I told you about? That's the job I really love. I founded it with a close friend of mine, and together we have helped hundreds of women out of bad situations. That's the work that feeds my soul."

"Why not just tell your dad?"

"Oh, he knows." She told him about the funding situation and the deal she had to make for the funding to stay in place.

Braving a glance upward, Sarah found Michael's face mere inches away. The compassion in his eyes was a punch in her gut, his companionship too much. All of it was melting her resolve to keep him solidly in the friend zone.

Sarah rushed on. "I mean, he's so controlling that he even thinks he can choose who I date. Just before I came here, there was this guy ..."

Michael's eyebrows lifted.

Why had she brought up Warren? "Never mind. The point is, for the first time, I feel almost like I could leave. Like Ginny did."

"Yeah?"

Sarah nodded. "But I know if I do, not only will I lose his love, but all of those women that New Dawn helps will have no one to fight for them. Either way, I lose something I desperately want."

"I can't imagine you would stop fighting just because you came up against some bumps in the road." His gentle voice matched the softness of his hand as he raised it to stroke Sarah's cheek. "And I'm so sorry that your father uses the word *love* to try to control you. But Sarah, you have another dad who is completely the opposite."

Another dad? Oh. "I … I used to believe that, once upon a time."

"What happened?"

"I was weak." She glanced down but he nudged her chin up with a finger. The constancy of Michael's gaze cracked any defenses that might have still been standing in her heart.

Her lips trembled. "After they didn't let me go to the lock-in, I became angry and defiant for the first—and only—time in my life." Until a few weeks ago, anyway. "I started sneaking off to attend youth group with Rachel, and I actually became a Christian. But I let my parents talk me out of it. And then I started to embrace their way of doing things because it was easier than fighting them. But now, I wonder if …"

If God could ever love me again.

He tilted his head. "Come on. I want to show you something." He pulled away from her, but only so he could lead her through a door behind them, one worn around the edges.

"Are we supposed to go in here?" It was probably closed for a reason.

"It's fine. Just an area most don't know about."

The door shut, leaving the space dark except for the light coming through a tiny window. In the middle of the room, a staircase led up to another level. That was unexpected. But now that she thought about it, there was an outdoor catwalk ringing the top of the lighthouse, wasn't there?

They took the stairs into a small lantern room. Up here they were completely surrounded by 360 degrees of glass. In the very center of the room sat a cracked lens, the glass encircling it caked with smudges. Clearly the lighthouse had been out of commission for a long time. One of the outer glass panels swung out, allowing access to the catwalk. Sarah took tentative steps out onto the metal banister and gripped the railing.

Oh wow. Everything was clearer, crisper, more vibrant and beautiful up here. She'd thought the view amazing before, but this …

If she hadn't stepped out, she'd never have known what she was missing.

Sarah laughed and closed her eyes, allowing the moment to sweep over her. The ocean bellowed, showcasing its sheer power yet calling to her just the same.

She was in the middle of the coming storm but somehow also cradled in an invisible hand.

"It's majestic and enthralling and …" She turned to Michael and snagged his hand, tears stinging her eyes. And though her heart raced within her at the contact, right now she wasn't thinking about romance—even though she was more drawn to him than she'd ever been before.

Right now, she was thinking about another kind of love entirely. One that, she saw with new eyes, had been pursuing her throughout her entire life.

As if understanding her thoughts, Michael leaned in, pressing his forehead to hers. "Sarah, real love isn't selfish." Despite the wind and the waves, she heard him down to her toes. "'Love doesn't force itself on others, isn't always 'me first,' doesn't fly off the handle, doesn't keep score of others' sins, doesn't revel when others grovel, takes pleasure in the flowering of truth, puts up with anything, trusts God always, always looks for the best, never looks back, but keeps going to the end.'"

Michael was speaking but they were words she'd read a long time ago in a book written by a father who loved her. The truth of them, like the wind, spun all around her, inviting her to dance.

So, she finally did.

CHAPTER 10

She'd made a decision—one she prayed she wouldn't come to regret.

Leaning on the pillows propped against the headboard behind her, Sarah's thumb hovered over her father's name in her phone's contact list.

Laughter fluttered down the hallway. It was five days before Christmas—three until the bakery was supposed to open—and Sophia was keeping Ginny company as she made a few last-minute tweaks to the recipes she anticipated being most popular. Her sister's optimism amazed Sarah, especially given that they still had no plan to have the ordinance changed before opening day. But Ginny trusted God to come through if it were meant to be, so Sarah was trying to follow her lead.

Sarah's heart beat erratic thumps against her chest. She longed to join the women in the kitchen, but first she needed to call Father. Gathering her courage, she dialed.

The phone rang three times before he answered. "Nice to finally hear from you, Sarah." His words dripped with condescension.

"Hey, Dad." Yes, Dad—not Father.

She was taking back the authority he had over her life.

"I'm looking forward to seeing you this week." In the background, the click of keys sounded. It was Sunday evening in England, so sometime in the early afternoon in Boston. He must be at work, as usual. "Your mother has outdone herself for this year's Christmas Eve soiree. It will be the talk of the town, I'm sure."

Here went nothing. "Actually, that's what I was calling about." A pause while she swallowed. "I am not going to be able to make it back after all. Ginny's bakery is set to open, but there have been some difficulties—"

"What kind of difficulties?" Had she imagined it or did he actually sound concerned? "And what does that have to do with you keeping your word?"

Or not.

OK, so staying longer wasn't just about Ginny. It was about Sarah too. She had no desire to return yet. There was so much left to explore here. With Ginny. And yes, with Michael. In the three days since she and Michael had visited the lighthouse, they'd been together almost nonstop in the evenings. Things between them had stayed friendly, but something new hovered there. Something that Sarah longed to explore despite all the odds stacked against them when it came to having any sort of romantic relationship.

Not that she was going to tell Father—er, Dad—any of that. Sarah pulled herself upright. He didn't hold power over her anymore. She was an adult, and she was his daughter too. Dad needed to respect her. But if she never stood up for herself and did things her own way, he never would.

And if he decided to follow through on his threat and pull funding from New Dawn, then Melissa was right. They'd find a way to keep it going.

"I realize that you might be disappointed, but we can celebrate together when I return."

"What about Warren?"

Poor Warren. He'd gotten in the middle of all this, and that wasn't his fault. "I called him yesterday and let him know that I needed to cancel our date." He'd been so understanding and sweet, albeit concerned. She'd tried to let him down gently by explaining that she needed more time in England and that when she returned, she'd be happy to meet up as friends. Emphasis on "friends."

He had been quiet afterward, but she'd expected that.

Her father harrumphed. "I don't like this one bit, Sarah. It sounds as if your sister has been a poor influence on you."

"Don't blame Ginny for this, Dad. I have my own mind, and I'm finally using it." Well, that had come out a bit harsh. She blinked slowly as she focused on softening her tone. "I love you and will miss seeing you for the holidays. Please let Mom know that I'll buy her a fabulous gift while I'm here."

"I'll tell her you won't be at her party, and it will crush her."

She eased out a breath through her teeth. "Well, I'd better go. I'll call you guys on Christmas."

"Just when do you plan to be home? I won't be able to give you vacation time off work indefinitely, you know."

"I'll be back in the office on January 2. I called to make sure Thomas can cover for me the extra week. Nothing ever happens between Christmas and New Year's anyway."

And with that, the phone went dead. "Real mature, Dad." Sarah sighed.

Oh well. Her part was done and she hadn't felt this free in a long time. Hopping off the bed, she set her phone onto the side table and strolled down the hallway toward the kitchen.

Sophia sat on the counter-height stool while Ginny glazed cinnamon buns. They stopped their conversation and focused on Sarah, expectation heavy in their eyes.

"Well?" Ginny licked the spatula and set it in the kitchen sink. "How did it go?"

She'd asked her sister and Sophia to pray while she'd called Dad. "About as well as could be expected. But I'm still standing, right?" She walked over to the pan in front of Ginny, pulled a large sliver off the corner bun, and shoved it into her mouth. Light and decadent and just what the doctor ordered.

"No fair," Sophia said. "My baby has been dying for one of those buns since they came out of the oven. Hand one over before I go all mama bear on you both."

They laughed and Ginny took out some plates and dished a bun onto each. Then they gathered at the small table by the window to relax. A soft snow had started falling earlier today and was supposed to continue off and on until Christmas. Apparently it was rare to get it this early in Cornwall, but some said that last year's weather had started a new trend.

"So. Inquiring minds want to know." Sophia slid a fork into her roll, slicing it down the middle. "What's going on with you and a certain local photographer?"

"Oh yes, inquiring minds *do* want to know that." Ginny flashed Sarah a pointed look and saucy smile as she twirled her fork in the air.

So this was what an ambush felt like. Sarah stabbed her roll. "Nothing is going on." That didn't mean she had no interest … but did Michael? He'd flirted, sure, and he'd been an amazing friend. But he hadn't said anything so far that had led her to believe he wanted any sort of romantic relationship with her.

And that probably made him the smarter of the two, given that her life was in Boston and his was here.

At Sophia's snort, Ginny laughed. Then they all dissolved into giggles. What were they, middle schoolers?

But she had to admit it felt good to laugh. Things had been far too tense as of late, and Sarah had allowed circumstances to shadow her joy and zest for life, for the things she cared about. That was something else she'd discovered during the last several days in spending time with Michael. He had this infectious happiness, this optimism, despite his struggles.

He'd confided to her that he was expected to go into the family business but that he'd much rather pursue his photography instead. And while his parents weren't anything like hers, a sense of family obligation pulled him to stay in Port Willis.

Even still, he remained positive about the future.

"Just know we don't believe you one bit. And we've both been exactly where you are." All teasing aside, Sophia watched her with knowing eyes lit with compassion.

Ginny nodded. "And also know that you two are about as cute as cherry pie. Oh, or cupcake ice cream cones. And of course, my personal favorite, chocolate-glazed donut cookies."

Sarah rolled her eyes. "I believe the title of World's Cutest Couple goes to you and Steven."

A blush crept across Ginny's cheeks. "And to think I almost missed it."

What if Sarah left for Boston and never told Michael how she felt about him? Would she regret it forever? The idea equally terrified and electrified her insides. She pushed the remainder of her roll around her plate, sticky cinnamon filling trailing behind.

Wow, OK, she really needed to shift her thoughts away from romance. Sarah cleared her throat. "Has anyone heard anything else from Rebecca Trengrouse?" The woman had been a veritable ghost since the council meeting. Of course, it wasn't like Sarah was frequenting Trengrouse Bakery much these days, but it was strange to have not seen her around town either.

The change in subject seemed to catch Ginny off guard. Her shoulders drooped. "Not a word. I tried to stop by a few days ago, but the bakery had shut down early. When Mr. Trengrouse ran things, he stayed open until 5:00 p.m. sharp every day. But I guess it *is* right before the holidays. Maybe Rebecca wants to spend some time with him, especially if he's as sick as she seems to imply."

Something niggled at the back of Sarah's mind. "Haven't you seen him recently?"

"No one has. Not that I know of, anyway." Ginny set down her fork and leaned back in her seat.

"You're right." Sophia rubbed her stomach, eyes squinting in concentration. "I haven't seen him in a long time. He hasn't been at church for more than a month. I saw him just before Thanksgiving. Remember, he brought all those pastries for the baskets we made up for the less fortunate? But that's the last time from what I can recall."

An idea sparked but Sarah needed more information before it could fully ignite. "Are he and his daughter close?"

Sophia stood, gathering up the ladies' plates. "I'm not sure. Gin? You've lived here longer than me."

"I don't know much about her, but Steven said Mr. Trengrouse was always a bit gruff around the edges. Apparently he had pretty high expectations for Rebecca and her younger brother." Ginny joined Sophia at the sink and took one of the plates from her friend's hand, flicked on the faucet, and ran the dish under the water. "But ever since his wife died a few years ago, he's really softened up."

Hmmm. So maybe the plan forming in Sarah's brain wouldn't work. Then again, it might.

And she wasn't above a Hail Mary right about now, especially for Ginny's sake.

Sarah stood. "Be right back." She headed for her room, grabbed her phone, and shot up a prayer as she composed a text to Michael.

Sarah: *You up for a rescue mission tomorrow?*

Michael: *Sure. I'm off work at four. Who are we rescuing?*

Sarah: *Not who. What. And the answer is Ginny's bakery.*

Michael: *I'm in.*

Sarah sent him a thumbs up emoji, closed her messages, and pushed away any lingering romantic thoughts. Whatever feelings she had for Michael were nothing compared to the adrenaline coursing through her veins.

Tomorrow, she would save her sister's bakery.

CHAPTER 11

"Do you think this will work?" Sarah studied the front of the quaint stone cottage situated against a hillside overlooking Port Willis. Turning, she could see the harbor, the shops, the week-of-Christmas crowds bustling about. Up here, out of the main part of town, the stress had the potential to melt away.

How ironic then, that hers was at an all-time high.

This was her last shot at helping Ginny open her bakery on time.

Michael nudged open the wooden gate surrounding the property and beckoned for her to go ahead of him. "I'm not sure but we have to try. I can't believe we didn't think of it sooner."

"Same here." She stepped through, her boots crunching some dead fallen leaves from the tree in the front yard.

Though the sun had shown almost all day, sporadic cloud cover that threatened more snow dimmed the last vestiges of sunlight. None of what had fallen so far had stuck, but that didn't make it any less magical. Sarah had tried to force herself to enjoy the peaceful flutter, but her head—and her heart—had been so full of other thoughts.

They arrived at the front door, and Sarah's fingers tingled. "Here goes nothing."

She knocked.

The door opened quicker than she expected, almost as if the house's occupant had been sitting by the front window in anticipation of visitors. Sarah squinted to see into the dimly lit home, but finally her eyes focused on a stooped man in his seventies with a white beard and round eyeglasses perched on the end of his nose.

"Mr. Trengrouse?"

"Yes?" He took another step outside, stopping under the light cast by a wrought-iron lamp on the other side of the gate.

"Hi, I'm Sarah Bentley and this is Michael Ham—"

"I know Michael. How are you?"

Michael cleared his throat. "I'm good, sir. It's been some time since I've seen you."

"Not that long. Wasn't it just last week that you stole a peppermint stick from my counter?" Though his words could be interpreted in several different ways, his tone left his meaning clear. The lazy smile that spread across his face also clarified his teasing.

With a laugh, Michael shook Mr. Trengrouse's hand. "Not last week but perhaps last month." His expression grew more serious. "How are you, Mr. Trengrouse?"

The older man waved a hand. "I'm fine, fine. I've had a wet cough and something about walking pneumonia, but you know nothing will keep me down long." He turned to Sarah. "I've heard tale that you're Ginny Rose's sister."

"Yes, sir." His hawkish eyes pierced her—as if they could discern more than he was saying. She gulped. "And that's actually what we've come to talk with you about. My sister. And her bakery."

"Ah, the opening is rather soon, is it not? I'm trying to convince Rebecca to let me go, but she keeps insisting my doctor wouldn't be on board with me getting out just yet." A warm smile brightened his face. "You know daughters. Much too overprotective." A cough fell from his drooping lips, enveloping his body in fits for a few moments. "Pardon me."

Michael exchanged a glance with Sarah. They'd agreed that he should do most of the talking since he had a relationship with the man—or, at the very least, wasn't a complete stranger. "Mr. Trengrouse, would you mind if we come inside for a moment?"

The man's scrutinizing gaze fell on Michael. "I suppose that's all right. Come along."

Sarah and Michael followed Mr. Trengrouse to a green couch that had seen better days. The house smelled of cinnamon and flour. Did Mr. Trengrouse still bake? How would that be, to no longer be able to do the thing you loved? Although if he'd been honest with Ginny, he seemed to be looking forward to retirement.

Michael assisted the older man in lowering himself into a worn chair boasting an indent of its favorite recipient then joined Sarah on the couch.

"Now, what is all this seriousness about? It's almost Christmas, you know." Mr. Trengrouse folded his hands over his paunch of a stomach and leaned back against the overstuffed seat.

Sarah bit the inside of her cheek. What a nice Christmas present for Ginny this would be if she and Michael could pull it off.

Even though they'd discussed him taking the lead, one glance at Michael indicated he was waiting on her. His hand found Sarah's fingers, tucked them inside—a reminder that he was here, whatever she needed.

Sarah took a deep breath. "Sir, my sister's bakery isn't going to open."

The man's wry gray eyebrows launched up. "Whatever do you mean?"

"The parish council that oversees Port Willis won't allow it. Because of your daughter." Sarah launched into an explanation of the situation, trying to keep her tone from wandering into accusation and staying focused on the facts. That part was more difficult than she'd thought.

As Mr. Trengrouse listened, his face and shoulders sagged. "You'll have to forgive Rebecca. She's a good girl and she means well, but ever since her mother died ..." His eyes wandered to the fireplace mantel where a portrait of his family hung. "She couldn't wait to get out of Port Willis when she turned eighteen, so I didn't expect her to want the bakery when I retired. Her brother certainly doesn't. But now that Rebecca is back, I can see she's afraid of losing it. Perhaps she's holding on out of fear."

While Sarah couldn't relate to wanting any part of her family's inheritance, she most certainly understood allowing fear to run one's life and making decisions because of it. "We have no problem at all with her continuing to run your bakery. I know for a fact that Ginny purposefully is planning a menu that doesn't conflict with any of your most popular items out of respect for you both." She leaned forward, gripping Michael's hand tighter than she'd intended. "But sir, do you think that you could talk Rebecca out of having this ordinance enforced? There is still time to turn it around if we work quickly."

Brow furrowed, Mr. Trengrouse flicked the edge of his nose with his thumb. After a few moments of contemplation, he nodded. "Yes, of course. Ginny is far too talented and has put too much into this to allow her to go under." He straightened as if forcing the resolve through his whole body. "I will talk with Rebecca when she returns home tonight. And if she protests, I will contact the council myself and sign whatever document needed to allow this ordinance to be dismissed."

"Really?"

At Sarah's jubilant response, Michael threw his arm around her shoulders and squeezed. "Thank you, sir. We appreciate this so much."

We. That had a nice ring to it.

With a kiss to his weathered cheek, Sarah thanked Mr. Trengrouse and followed Michael out the door, out the gate, and down the path to the edge of the nearest bluff heading back into town. Snow had begun to fall once more, creating a beautiful mosaic of white against the darkening sky, with lights from the villages twinkling below and dim moonlight falling from above.

Before they could go any farther, she stopped and launched herself into Michael's arms. "We did it!"

His arms came around her, hugging her and lifting Sarah off her feet. "*You* did it. And were quite brilliant, I may add." He set her down and pulled back to look at her.

The heat from his gaze nearly warmed her enough to forget about the snowflakes falling on their lashes and cheeks. Her toes curled. "Thank you all the same for being here."

"Always." He moved his hand from her waist, and it lingered near her face, his fingers skimming her cheek as if he didn't know what to do with them—what to do with this moment stretching between them, one instant yet a thousand just the same.

But Sarah knew. Even as Michael's hand dropped back to her waist, she summoned her courage. "So, I've been meaning to tell you. I'm not leaving on Wednesday night."

"You're not?"

She shook her head. "I'm staying for another week."

"That's great." His words fell flat—and so did her heart. Did he not want her to stay? Had she misinterpreted things?

But whatever the case, she needed to tell him how she felt, or she'd always regret it. No, she didn't know how things would ever work between them or if they ever would, but she was free of her father now.

She finally had the luxury of finding out for herself.

With trembling fingers, Sarah lightly cupped Michael's cheeks. He didn't take his eyes from hers, but even in the dim light, his question burned.

She'd answer it as best she could. "I want more time with you, plain and simple." Then she rose on her heeled boots and captured his mouth with hers.

For a moment, he stood frozen. But then his hands tightened around her, pulling Sarah closer as his lips explored hers, first a gentle touch then with fervent emotion. Sarah melted against him, into him, as if she'd always belonged there.

Maybe she had.

At long last, the kiss ended. Sarah sighed as she snuggled against him and looked out over the ocean. Snow wet her hair, and a tiny shiver ran up her spine—but if it were weather or kiss induced, who could tell?

"In case it wasn't clear, I want more time with you as well." Michael's voice rumbled in his chest.

They both laughed and she tapped him on the arm with the back of her hand. He snatched it and pulled off her glove. Then he kissed the tip of each finger slowly, lighting a fire in Sarah's toes until she couldn't do anything but turn and kiss him again.

Finally, he squeezed her waist. "I think we'd better get you back to your sister so you can tell her the great news."

"About this?" Sarah moved a finger back and forth between them, grinning.

"What else would I be talking about?"

Joining hands, they meandered back into the heart of town, chatting about plans for the next week. "I'd love for you to join us for supper on Christmas Day."

She'd met his parents, sister, brother-in-law, and niece in passing, but a holiday together? Wow. "Um, OK. If you're sure."

"I am."

All right, then.

As they drew closer to Ginny's place, the snow stopped. A light was on in the kitchen. Huh. Ginny was supposed to be at the bakery until late tonight. Maybe her plans had changed.

Sarah turned to Michael and hooked her arms around his neck. "I don't want to go inside. But I promised Melissa I'd do a few things online tonight."

"And I'd better get started on my Christmas shopping."

She shook her head. "Figures."

"I'm sure you've had yours done for a long time." He pressed his forehead against hers, his grin teasing.

"November, to be exact." Of course, now she needed to shop for one person she hadn't anticipated …

Nothing about this had been expected.

"That's adorable." Michael leaned in and brushed his lips against hers. The kiss ended far too soon.

She was just about to pull him back in for another when the door opened behind them, flooding the spot where they stood with light. Turning, she blinked against the glare to find a figure standing in the doorway.

"Sarah?"

Her hands fell from Michael's shoulders as she squinted. "Warren?"

CHAPTER 12

"Hi, Sarah."

It took her brain a few moments to catch up with her eyes. Warren Kensington stood outside Ginny's door, hands crossed over his gray cashmere sweater, a strange look shadowing his face. "What are you doing here?"

Warren shifted from one foot to another. "I came to see you."

Obviously. But why? She'd tried to be clear on the phone about their status as just friends.

Michael cleared his throat and, with one arm still tucked firmly around Sarah's waist, extended his free hand toward Warren. "Michael Hammett. Pleasure to meet you."

Eyeing the placement of Michael's other arm, Warren shook his hand. "Warren Kensington. Sarah's ... friend from Boston."

The men lowered their hands and turned toward Sarah. "Why don't we get out of this cold?" She stepped forward and out of Michael's embrace, but as she crossed the home's threshold, Warren put out his hand to block Michael.

"Hey, man, I'd love to chat with Sarah alone for a minute if you don't mind?"

Goodness. She'd never known Warren to be this rude. But it

must have been a surprise for him to find her embracing some other guy less than a month after they'd gone on their perfectly pleasant date, so she supposed she'd give him a pass, especially if he'd witnessed their kiss.

The firm line of Michael's lips drooped, and his gaze found hers. "What would you like, Sarah?"

Just the fact he asked made her want to kiss him again. But it was probably easier to deal with the Warren situation—to get to the heart of why he was here—if it were just the two of them. "I'll call you, OK? Soon."

It seemed like the logical choice, but when she saw the way his jaw tightened, the fake smile he forced, it seemed her brain had perhaps led her astray. "Sure. Yeah. I'll see you." And without another word, he turned and walked away into the darkness.

She wanted to rush after him, explain her thoughts, her reasons for wanting to be alone with Warren. But she'd do that later.

Warren shut the door and tapped the doorknob a few times before rotating toward Sarah. He cocked his head. "Sorry about that. I know I was impolite. It's just ... I took a few red eyes to get here and haven't slept much. And well, I ..."

Now that she studied him, his eyes did look a bit bloodshot, his hair more tousled than usual. Poor man. She approached him and squeezed his forearm. "It's fine." A pause weighted the space between them. "How are you?"

As if waiting for an invitation, Warren leaned into a hug, and his mandarin orange, black pepper, and lavender cologne enveloped her. It was a pleasant scent—maybe even an enjoyable one—but it didn't draw her in like it might have once.

Warren held on, perhaps for a moment too long, but finally released her. "So, you're probably wondering why I'm here."

"I'm guessing you're not just in the neighborhood." She attempted a weak laugh.

He didn't even crack a smile. "Not exactly. Can we sit?" He gestured toward the couch, and they headed that way. "I hope you don't mind that your sister let me in. She had to run back to the bakery but said I was welcome to wait for you here."

Both sank onto the couch, and Sarah turned her body slightly to face him before realizing too late that this position left their knees touching. Warren placed his left arm along the back of the couch and reached his other toward her hands, which she'd folded in her lap. His serious eyes studied her for a minute before he spoke. "I'm just going to come out and say it, if it isn't obvious. I like you, Sarah. A lot. More than anyone I've ever dated. You're intelligent, caring, and passionate. And I didn't like the way we left things on the phone the other night."

His Adam's apple slid up and down his throat.

Her stomach constricted at the sight. "Warren—"

"Let me finish, please." At her nod, he continued. "I know you think I only pursued you because of your father's urging, and that may have been what prompted me at first—but only because I assumed you'd never date someone like me."

"Are you kidding? You're the kind one, Warren, and that's a rarity. I'm sorry I let my family stuff get in between us. That wasn't fair to you."

"No, I get it." With his free hand, he played with a piece of Sarah's hair as he spoke. Though a bit beyond friendly, the gesture didn't freak her out. Something about Warren just put her at ease, even if her veins didn't catch fire with him near. "I guess I just wanted to let you know I'm still here. And to make some sort of grand gesture or something. Maybe that was idiotic of me." A pause. "Or maybe I'm too late."

So he *had* seen the kiss she'd shared with Michael. "That's sweet of you, Warren." And if she'd never met Michael, then maybe she and Warren could go back home and see where things led—see if this comfort, this friendship, could develop into stronger, more passionate feelings.

But she *had* met Michael, and now she'd compare everyone to him.

"As for being too late ..." She squeezed his hand again. "I'm sorry. I didn't mean to hurt you."

He tacked on a sad smile. "I understand." He extricated his hands with a gentle pull then placed them into his lap. "Guess I'd better get out of your hair."

"Don't be silly. Stay. Cornwall is beautiful this time of year." Yes, that would make things a bit awkward, but he'd come all this way.

His look told her exactly what he thought of that plan. "I'll stay the night but head out tomorrow." He stood and she followed suit. "Oh, that reminds me." He picked up his jacket, which he'd draped over the arm of the couch, and dug in the pocket, producing a sealed envelope. "This is for you."

"You wrote me a letter?"

"No. Your father did. I promised I'd deliver it to you."

"He knew you were coming?" At Warren's glance, she held up her hand. "Who am I kidding? Of course he did."

Warren threw on his jacket, leaned in, and kissed her cheek. "If you happen to change your mind, I'll be at the B&B around the corner."

She hugged him and he left. Then she snagged a kitchen knife, cut open the envelope flap, and sank onto a counter stool to read the letter, which, of course, was typed on her father's official letterhead.

Sarah,

Doubtless by now you will have seen Warren and heard him out. I hope you give him a chance. Whatever you may think of me, I do want you to be happy, and I feel he is the right sort of man to do that. However, if you see things differently, then perhaps we can discuss some alternative solutions to encourage the merger with his father's company.

I'm sorry that you seem to feel the best way to spend Christmas is away from your mother and me—and that it's likely my own fault. I pushed you with all my expectations. I never meant to be overbearing. I merely see greatness in you. You have the fortitude and commitment your siblings lack, and I trust no one more than you to run my company when I am gone.

That being said, this experiment of yours—running away to England, just as Virginia did, manipulating me to get what you want —doesn't sit well with me. I do not appreciate my loyalty and love being tested in this way.

You have a choice, and the ball, so to speak, is in your court, Sarah. Come home for Christmas and all will be forgiven.

Father

PS: I recently spoke with a good friend of mine, Jeff Gentry, and he's informed me that your charity is representing his wife in a nasty case that spreads all sorts of malicious rumors about him. As your main donor, I insist that you look more closely into this case. I'm sure we can all come to some sort of agreement that will be best for everyone involved. I'd hate to have to pull my funding, but I cannot have my name tied to anything untoward. You understand, I'm sure, my dear.

Sarah's hand trembled as she crushed the paper into a ball. A sob rose from deep in her chest. So this is what it had come to. Father was never going to let her have her own life. Deep down she'd always known it, even though she'd hoped that standing up for herself would change things.

But it didn't matter how good of a daughter she was, how much she loved him, how much she sacrificed.

He would always win.

Because there was no way she could stay in Cornwall, wiling away the week with Michael, now that Father had threatened New Dawn. She knew without a doubt that if she didn't get back there and fight him on the Jeff Gentry issue, New Dawn would be no more. Not only would he pull his funding, he'd find a way to drive it into the ground, into dust.

All of this—Cornwall, Michael, her time with Ginny—had been a lovely Christmas dream. Nothing more.

After the opening of Ginny's bakery, Sarah would return to her role of dutiful daughter. Although this time, she wouldn't sacrifice everything. Not her faith. And not New Dawn. She'd fight for Elise Gentry, no matter what her father said.

Where she worked and who she dated, well, those weren't as important as making sure that her life's work wasn't overturned, that others were protected. Her father might never love or respect Sarah the way she'd hoped he would, but by committing her life to serving others, at least one Father would be proud.

CHAPTER 13

Making a decision one day and following through the next had never been so difficult.

Sarah braced herself against the wind blowing upward from the harbor as she made her way down High Street. The bright, cloudless sky disguised the bitter cold that only showed itself when she huffed and her breath became visible.

The weather that, just yesterday, felt magical mocked her today.

She'd already informed her sister about her change in plans. Sarah had even texted Warren and let him know she'd be flying back tomorrow night. It was only fair, since he had come all this way to see her.

But now she needed to tell Michael.

Her legs threatened to give out on her after a full night of pacing. At four-something in the morning, Ginny had finally interrupted her brooding, and the two had talked at length. But despite Ginny's attempts to bolster Sarah and encourage her to live her own life, Sarah knew that the only way to move forward was to move backward.

Which, of course, had led to more pacing. Because how discouraging was *that*?

As she made her way to meet Michael in their spot on the grassy bluff above the harbor, Sarah was so lost in thought that she nearly missed someone calling her name.

She halted and turned her head. Trengrouse Bakery stood just across the way. And there was Rebecca Trengrouse, waving at her and shouting for her to stop.

Did the woman want to chew her out for meddling by talking with her father yesterday? Oh, who cared anymore? Let her come. Sarah waited while Rebecca crossed the street, her arms pumping before wrapping tightly around her chest as she approached. "Thanks for stopping."

"It seemed important." Sarah eyed her. The woman must be freezing without a jacket on. "Do you want to go inside?"

"This won't take long."

Here we go. "All right."

Instead of straightening to her full height in true Rebecca fashion, her shoulders drooped under Sarah's scrutiny. "I just wanted to let you know that, as per my father's wishes, I've spoken with the parish council and agreed to bypass the ordinance. Your sister can open her bakery as planned."

Sarah bit her cheek to keep from saying what she really thought of Rebecca's "generosity." The important thing was Ginny's dream could continue forward as planned. "Great." She paused, forcing the next words from her mouth. "Thank you."

Rebecca's feet shuffled against the cobblestone, and she stared at the ground.

Sarah quirked an eyebrow. "Was there something else?"

"It's just ..." Rebecca bounced on the balls of her feet. "I'm sorry, all right? I got a bit overzealous and, well, I guess that I just thought if I kept the family business going, maybe things would change. Maybe I'd finally have a good relationship with my father.

Maybe I'd finally … be happy." She blew a blond strand of hair out of her eyes. "Sorry, I don't know why I'm telling you all this. The point is, I was wrong and I'm sorry for the trouble I've caused."

For the first time since meeting her, Sarah didn't completely despise Rebecca Trengrouse. Like Michael had suggested, perhaps she and Rebecca were more alike than Sarah cared to admit. Still … "You should tell that to Ginny, not me."

The woman nodded. "I will." She turned and headed back to the bakery.

Mr. Trengrouse had come through, and Sarah would indeed be leaving Ginny with her bakery intact. Even if her own dreams had fallen to pieces around her, at least she'd managed to do something right while in Cornwall.

Heaving a sigh—of relief, of trepidation?—Sarah turned and continued her march toward the harbor. Calm waters lapped inside the quay, but beyond it the wind skimmed the top of the sea. She climbed the path to the cliff overlooking the waters and found Michael standing near the edge, embracing the breeze.

Whatever came after this, she'd try to shove it from her memory. *This* is how she'd choose to remember him.

A few pieces of gravel tumbled down the path as she walked, alerting him to her presence, and the smile on his face as he turned toward her stabbed her insides.

"Hey there, gorgeous." In seconds, he was hugging her and leaning down for a kiss. How natural it felt.

And Sarah, God help her, let Michael hold her. If this was going to be the end, she needed to soak up all the warmth from their last moments together.

Don't cry, don't cry. Don't ruin this.

But she couldn't fake her emotions anymore, and soon, tears came faster than she could swipe them away.

Michael pulled back, hands on her upper arms, a look of alarm replacing the smile. "What's wrong, love?"

"Everything." A fresh torrent of tears sprang from her eyes.

He held her again, not saying anything. Eventually, he led her to a huge blanket he'd laid on the ground. They sat down and wrapped it up and over their shoulders and backs, enclosing it around them, cocooning their warmth.

How pathetic she was—about to end things with him yet accepting the comfort he gave. She had to tell him so he'd stop being so wonderful.

Sarah finally removed her head from his shoulder and sat up, using the blanket to dry her eyes. Clearing her throat, she chanced a look at Michael.

The space between his brows had narrowed, and his eyes questioned her. "You're leaving tomorrow, aren't you?"

How did he … "Y-yes." The word croaked in her throat. "After Ginny's opening. As originally planned."

"Was it something I did?"

"No!" She fumbled under the blanket until she found his hand. "You were perfect. It was all … perfect. Just not meant to be."

He looked like he wanted to ask why, but instead he turned and gazed at the horizon. Wasn't he going to fight her on this? Scream at her? She surely deserved it for jerking him around.

But as they sat there holding hands and watching the ocean beat the rocks in the distance, realization settled upon her. He was doing the one thing no other man in her life had ever done for her.

He was accepting her decision.

Which made this the best and the worst moment of her life.

CHAPTER 14

How was she ever going to go home after this?

Sarah stopped moving for just a moment to catch her breath. Her feet and lower back ached from a full morning and afternoon of constant movement, but every step had been worth it. Sarah's eyes roamed Ginny's bakery from her place in the corner. All day customers had streamed in and out. At times, like now, there was a line out the door and every seat was filled.

Customers still padded in, shaking off loose snow from their boots onto Ginny's welcome mat. The weather had finally caught up with Sarah's emotions, painting the sky a dark gray.

William, Sophia, and Steven took turns behind the registry—though both men made sure Sophia didn't stand for too long—while Ginny and Sarah restocked the shelves and greeted guests. Two of Sophia's employees manned the bookstore so Sophia could be here for Ginny's big day.

Sarah watched as her sister patted a vaguely familiar elderly man's arm and laughed with him. Who was he? The man grabbed his cane from the table where he'd sat to eat his baked good. Ah, yes. He was the older gentleman from Trengrouse Bakery, the one Rebecca Trengrouse had treated so terribly.

Good you for, Gin.

As if she'd heard Sarah's thoughts, Ginny looked up at her and grinned. She said goodbye to the man and walked toward Sarah. "I still can't believe these people gave up some of their day to be here and encourage me."

Sarah slipped her arm around Ginny's back as they watched the crowd eating and enjoying. Classic rock music played on low in the background. The door between the bakery and the bookstore stood wide open, and guests trickled back and forth exactly as Gin and Sophia had intended. "They're not just here to encourage you, though I do think many of them love you very much." The words caught in Sarah's throat. Goodness, she had been emotional the last few days. "But you've opened an amazing bakery, with delicious treats that are going to become fast favorites. You'd better start hiring some employees to help out, you know."

"I plan to, once I know the sales volume can support it." Ginny chewed her bottom lip. "Sarah, I understand why you're leaving, but I wish ..."

"I know." Sarah laid her head against Ginny's. "I'm so extremely proud of you, little sis."

"And I'm proud of you."

She shouldn't be, but Sarah wouldn't ruin a perfectly good moment by saying so. "Don't think that just because I'm leaving that it'll be years before you see me again. I have plans to visit this summer." She hoped by then that she and Father would have worked out whatever was between them so she could take off the time without feeling guilty.

"I'm going to hold you to that."

"You'd better." Who knew what would happen by then? Between her and Father ... or her and Warren. Her gaze swiveled to the corner of the bakery. Warren had been stationed there for most of the day, welcoming newcomers and handing out menus Steven had designed.

When Sarah had decided to leave, Warren had kept his original travel plans. He'd claimed it was easier than rescheduling, but Sarah couldn't help but wonder if the real reason was so he could spend an extra day with her. Instead of trying to persuade her to reconsider dating him or sightseeing together, he'd rolled up his Gucci sleeves and helped her and Ginny put the finishing touches on the bakery last night.

Even Sarah had to admit that she'd been surprised. Most senior-level executives weren't willing to dirty their hands—literally speaking, at least.

"He's not a bad guy, you know."

Sarah started. Ginny had caught her staring at Warren. "I never said he was." He just wasn't Michael. But Michael wasn't in the picture anymore. He hadn't even stopped by yet today. Maybe he was just working.

Or maybe she'd broken his heart.

All she knew was her own would never be the same.

"Just make sure you don't settle. That's not fair to anyone."

"I know, Gin." And she did.

"I'd better get back to it." Ginny hugged Sarah and flitted off to work the register for a while. Side by side, she and Steven made quite the team.

As Sarah bussed a few newly emptied tables—sometimes scrubbing much harder than necessary—the hairs on the back of her neck prickled and she glanced up.

Michael stood in the doorway, his gaze on her mournful. He tugged the beanie from his head and ran a hand through his curls. Then, as if ripping Velcro, he maneuvered his eyes toward the register, plastered a smile on his face, and headed toward Ginny, shouting his congratulations.

Sarah turned back to the table and pushed the wet rag in her hand across the table so hard that her upper arm vibrated.

A few minutes later, the music quieted. "Excuse me, everyone?" Ginny's voice filled the room from where she stood in front of the register. All eyes, including Sarah's, turned to face her sister.

"I just wanted to say thank you so much for all of your support today." Ginny's lips quivered as she took the time to look at each person, lingering longer on William, Sophia, Sarah, and—of course—Steven, who stood off to the side only feet away from her. "There was a time when I didn't know where I belonged. When I let everyone else tell me my worth and allowed others to define me. This bakery is a culmination of so many things for me, but ultimately, it's a homecoming. It's like the perfect marriage of cinnamon rolls and icing. Of spaghetti sauce and noodles. Of … well, you understand."

The crowd laughed but Sarah worked to keep tears from spilling down her cheeks.

Ginny took the few steps toward Steven and held out her hand. "I couldn't have done it without each and every one of you, but most especially this man right here. He's been incredibly supportive through all of the ups and downs." Then she got down on one knee. "And speaking of marriage …"

Now a quick gasp and several *ahhhs* flew from all directions. Was Ginny doing what they all thought she was doing?

But before she could say another word, Steven lowered himself to the ground as well, so they were once again face-to-face. "What do you think you're doing?"

"Asking you to marry me, silly."

Steven snorted as he reached into the back pocket of his jeans and pulled something from it. When he opened his palm, a diamond ring winked under the bakery's lights.

Ginny put her hands to her mouth and her eyes widened. "What's that for?"

"Before you jumped the gun, I was planning to ask you the same question tonight." He slid the ring onto Ginny's trembling finger. "So, Ginny Rose, will you make me the happiest man alive and marry me?"

"Yes!" Ginny threw her arms around Steven's neck and kissed him.

Oh, Gin.

Now Sarah really was crying. The bell above the bakery's door jingled and she turned to see Michael's retreating back.

Beside the door, Warren stood taking in the scene. He caught her eye and smiled.

Sarah swung her gaze back to the happy couple and brushed the tears from her cheeks as she moved forward to congratulate them.

As horrible as the goodbyes had been, it was the hellos Sarah dreaded most. She shuddered as she imagined the look of satisfaction on Father's face when he saw her walk into the Christmas Eve party tomorrow night.

"Are you cold?" Warren unwound his scarf as they waited in line at Cornwall Airport Newquay to check their bags.

"I'm fine, thanks." In fact, it was actually rather hot inside the airport, probably from the combined body heat of all these people pressed together—a phenomenon for such a tiny place.

Sarah flicked her passport back and forth against her palm. Could this line be any slower? "I'll bet you're wishing you'd left earlier." Two days before Christmas certainly wasn't the best day to travel.

"I'm right where I want to be."

Oh, how she wished she could force herself to feel weak in the knees at his sweet statement. "Warren—"

"Sarah Bentley, is that you, my dear?"

She turned at the kind voice to find Mavis Lincoln looking at her. "Hi, Mrs. Lincoln. What are you doing here?"

The woman didn't have any suitcases with her, just a small purse slung across her shoulder. Funny. Sarah had pictured the owner of an antique shop carrying something oversized and vintage. "I was just making my way back to the waiting area when I saw you. I'm here for my nephew and his wife. Their flight was supposed to come in last night but got bumped to this evening."

"Oliver and Joy, right?" At Mavis's nod, Sarah turned to Warren and made introductions. "We're headed home in time for my parents' Christmas party tomorrow night."

Mavis eyed Warren, a smile at odds with the crease of curiosity on her forehead. "I am glad you were able to stay for your sister's opening. I stopped in first thing, and I know it's going to be a raving success. I'm only sorry Joy and Oliver won't make it."

Warren and Sarah advanced in the line. Mavis took a step to follow them but winced at the movement.

That's right, she had gout. Why had her family sent her to the airport to fetch her nephew? Sarah glanced at Warren. "Would you mind getting my suitcase checked in?"

"Not at all."

"Thanks." Sarah slipped under the rope dividing the lines, and took Mrs. Lincoln's elbow. "May I sit with you for a few minutes?"

"That would be lovely." The woman shuffled toward a bank of chairs in the main terminal area with Sarah beside her in case she needed assistance. They wound their way across the crowded floor until arriving at a pair of empty seats.

Mavis grunted as she lowered herself. The woman's cheeks appeared flushed. "Thank you, dear."

Sarah sat between her and a teenage boy glued to his phone. "Of course."

Grasping Sarah's hand in her knobby red one, Mavis tilted her head. "Now, just who is that handsome young man to you?"

"Warren? Oh. He's … complicated." Sarah looked away. The windows facing the tarmac were smudged from the cold. A child stood there next to his mother, pointing and exclaiming about the planes and their lights in the dark.

"Complicated is right. From what I saw, I thought one of our locals had perhaps caught your eye."

Michael. Even just thinking his name pricked Sarah's eyes with hot tears. "Perhaps one did. But he's not the practical choice."

"What does practicality have to do with love?"

Sarah whipped her gaze back toward Mavis. The temperature in the overly warm room seemed to drop. "If you're my father? Everything."

"And are you your father?" The tip of Mavis's nose shone.

"No. But he wants me to be. Or, at least, to obey him. In his eyes, that's the only time I'm useful." Sarah sighed, rubbing her temple with her free hand. "It's a long story, but suffice it to say, I've given up trying to please him. The only one I'm interested in pleasing now is God. So I'm going back, leaving all this, leaving a good man, to keep fighting the good fight."

Mavis was quiet for a moment as she studied Sarah. "Usefulness is quite an interesting subject and one I'm well acquainted with. One I've struggled with too, I must admit."

Really? "In what way?"

"The world at large would paint me as useless because of my malady. I cannot run my own shop without help anymore. I have trouble finishing duties without aching for days. And to pick up my nephew and his wife from the airport, I have to argue for an hour for anyone to believe I'm up to the task."

Didn't this woman know how amazing she was? "And yet, you find time to encourage everyone you come in contact with.

You pray for them." Or so Ginny and Sophia had told her. "*That* is not useless."

"But what is useful about loving others well if it doesn't produce results?"

"What results matter more than making someone feel loved or loving in return?"

"What results indeed?" A twinkle lit in Mavis's eyes, reflecting the lights overhead.

Ah … "I think I understand what you're saying. But I've told you, I've already given up on trying to make my dad love me."

"But what about God? You say you want to please him—and that is good. Very good. But do you know the thing that pleases him most? Not all the things you do for him or do in his name but *sitting* with him. Enjoying his presence. Loving him. Talking to him."

Mavis squeezed Sarah's hands. "My dear, you do not need to do anything to make God love you more. He already loves you as much as he possibly can simply because he made you and you are his daughter. And as such, he wants you to enjoy the good things he gives you. Good things, perhaps, like the love of a good man."

Now Mavis had done it. The tears threatening to fall whooshed down Sarah's cheeks. She couldn't remember the last time she'd cried so much in one week. "But why? Why would he love me like that after how I've disappointed him? All the times I turned away when I should have run to him? All the times I behaved in a shameful way that wasn't what he would want for me?"

"Why?" Mavis cupped Sarah's chin as a grandmother might. "Because he's a good father. He's a good God. And his sacrifice is enough to cover all of our imperfections."

Sarah couldn't help it. She leaned forward and hugged Mavis, whose sugar and flour scent brought scenes from Ginny's bakery to mind. "I don't know what to do."

Mavis feathered a kiss across Sarah's temple where a headache had started forming moments before. "You don't but he does. Seek God's wisdom. And in the meantime, stop concerning yourself with what everyone else would have you do, even yourself."

CHAPTER 15

"The final flight to London Heathrow tonight will begin boarding in one-half hour." Despite the late time, the gate agent's peppy voice flowed from the speakers through the departure lounge.

All around them, people gathered in seats, on the floor, against the walls, some sleeping, some watching movies on their devices. Her soon-to-be-fellow passengers snagged last-minute coffee and cocoa from the small cafe and packaged snacks from the gift shop. A mom across the room fed tiny cheese crackers to her messy-mouthed toddler while a baby slept in the stroller next to her. Down the row of chairs, a woman spoke into her phone in a language that sounded Slavic in nature. Someone nearby smelled as if they hadn't worn deodorant in years.

"Do you need anything else before we board?" Warren set his iPad on his lap. He'd spent the last hour working while Sarah had pretended to read her own emails. Melissa had sent a slew in the last few days, and Sarah needed to catch up. But not even New Dawn work could distract her from the fraying edges of her heart.

"I'm good. Thanks." Sarah diverted her attention to her phone.

"Sarah."

"Hmmm?" When she peeked back up at him, he wore a grim expression.

The iPad was shoved into his laptop bag, and he crossed his arms over his chest. "I know you don't have to tell me this, but I've been wondering about something. What was in that letter your dad asked me to deliver to you?"

"Oh, that. Nothing." She shrugged and once again looked at her email, swiping her screen for good measure.

But her efforts to make it seem as if she were busy proved fruitless. With a light touch, Warren tugged the phone from her hand and set it inside her purse.

She sighed and twisted her studded earring. "He pulled out all his tricks to try to get me to come home."

"Like ..."

She pursed her lips. After all, as nice as Warren was, he was part of the Boston business community, part of her parents' world. And as her mother had frequently reminded her as a child, *family laundry should never be aired in front of others.*

"Oh, come on, Sarah. Forgive me for saying so but everyone knows your dad is a bully."

Her eyes widened of their own accord before she could control them. "But he seems to have so many friends."

"Ever heard the term 'frenemies?' It's childish, I know, but it seems to suit." He tilted his head. "People aren't dumb. They hold your father close enough to benefit from his acquaintance, but no one really trusts him."

"But your father is thinking of going into business with him."

"Yes, but as you may remember, when it comes to business, my father is also someone who does what is best for himself."

"So ..." She gestured between the two of them. "You and I dating or not dating ..."

"Won't affect his decision to merge companies with your father's in any way."

Sarah slumped in her chair, her shoulders lightened. "I'm so glad to hear that."

"I'm sorry that you felt pressured to date me at all."

She straightened at the hurt pervading his words. "No, Warren, that's not it. I've told you I think you're wonderful."

"I know. But someone else has captured your heart."

"Yes."

"Yet here you are."

"Yes." Her nose tingled. Oh goodness. No more tears. She couldn't take it.

"So"—Warren leaned closer—"what exactly was in that letter?"

Rubbing her eyes, Sarah considered his request. Oh, forget what Mother always said. The fact was, Sarah trusted Warren. He was a friend, and even though she'd hurt him, she prayed they could remain so. Goodness knew she'd need friends when heading back to the wolves. She leaned over, snagged an envelope from her bag, lifted the crumpled paper from inside, and shoved it into Warren's hands. "Read it for yourself."

"Are you sure?"

"Yes."

While he read, she watched as his face turned steadily redder. The paper lowered from his hands in slow unease. "I hope you'll forgive me for what I'm about to do." He stood, walked to the trash can, and tossed the letter inside.

A staccato laugh pulsed from her throat. "Why did you do that?"

Warren sat again. "That's where it belonged." Tapping the metal arm of his seat, Warren studied her. "Sarah, I've already told you that people in our circles think of your dad as a bully. But I would be remiss if I didn't tell you what they think of you."

"Oh, I don't—"

"You need to know this. Despite that you're George Bentley's daughter, you are well respected. And do you know why?"

"Because I work hard?"

"That's important, sure, but we all work hard." Warren's fingers stilled. "People like dealing with you. You're honest and trustworthy and impress people just because you're you. You don't have to be or do anything else. Being Sarah Bentley is enough."

Was that really true—for people and for God?

Yes. The answer resonated deeply in her soul.

But where did that leave her? More self-assured, maybe, but how did she move forward differently? Changed?

Mavis's words from earlier this evening flew back to her mind: *"Seek out God's wisdom. And in the meantime, stop concerning yourself with what everyone else would have you do, even yourself."*

OK then.

She squeezed Warren's hand. "Thank you."

"You're welcome. And one more thing."

Sarah arched an eyebrow. "What?"

"Like your father, I know Jeff Gentry. He's a terrible man, and I'm not surprised that he may be abusing his wife." He sat up straighter. "I want to support your work at New Dawn. And I'm confident my father will too. His father was abusive to my grandmother, and my dad despises men who aren't kind to their significant others."

"What? Seriously?" Sarah's heart pounded as her brain processed the words he was saying.

"Yes, seriously. And I'm sure we can find many others to donate to such a worthy cause. In fact, I'd love to host a charity ball in New Dawn's honor to raise funds."

And here came the waterworks once more. "Warren Kensington, you are amazing."

A smile flashed across his face. "So I've been told."

"But for real. Thank you." She gave him a hug. "Whoever you end up with will be a lucky woman indeed."

He squeezed her shoulders and then let her go. For a moment, he studied her. "So, what are you going to do now?"

She glanced at the clock behind the gate agent's desk. Only ten minutes until the flight was supposed to board—ten minutes to make a decision that would change her life forever.

But it only took ten seconds.

She reached into her bag, pulled out a notebook, wrote the words "I quit," and ripped the page from the binding. Then she folded the paper and handed it to Warren. "Give this to my dad, will you?"

"Absolutely."

"And would you mind collecting my suitcase in Boston and holding onto it until I get home?"

"Of course not."

"Thanks." Sarah pecked Warren on the cheek. "Merry Christmas, Warren."

"Merry Christmas, Sarah."

Sarah stood, gathered her bags, and raced for the exit.

CHAPTER 16

Today had been magical. Sarah only prayed that this evening would be as well.

From her spot inside the lighthouse, she had watched the sky move from a golden mist to a black velvet blanket sprinkled with stardust. At Ginny's enthusiastic insistence, Steven had helped Sarah lug all the things she'd need for tonight here, a mile outside of the village, on Christmas Eve. She'd given her future brother-in-law a hug and he'd shrugged. He was, he'd said, glad she'd be with them for Christmas after all.

Sarah sat on a cozy quilt, a basket of Ginny's goodies opened and a portable heater going nearby. From her spot next to the windows, the ocean looked like a painting, one that moved and crashed and frolicked. She'd brought a plastic lantern, but the moon's rays spilled inside, providing all the light necessary.

It was perfect.

All that she needed now? Her date.

Sarah picked up her phone once more and woke up the screen. Bright white font flashed that it was 6:08 p.m. He should have been here by now. Maybe he wasn't coming. Still, eight minutes late wasn't really late, was it? Especially when she didn't know for sure that he was free.

He hadn't responded to her texts, after all.

And she'd sent several. In fact, today had been as much about self-reflection as preparing for this date, this chance to woo back Michael and apologize for how she'd treated him. She'd conquered the trepidation of driving on the wrong side of the road and borrowed Ginny's car to go to the gardens where Michael had taken her a week and a half ago. All by herself, she'd snapped photo after photo of the gorgeous greenery.

Sure, the photos were on her phone and not Michael's fancy camera.

But she'd remembered what he'd said that day: *"They're yours, and that makes them perfect. Don't let anyone ever tell you any differently."*

And she wouldn't. Not anymore.

After that she'd gotten back into the car, turned on the heater to warm her numb fingers, and sent him a few of her favorites. No caption. She figured he'd just understand her in that way that he seemed to have.

Next, Sarah had made her way back to Port Willis and visited all the spots of significance to the two of them—the spot on the bluffs above the harbor, Ginny's kitchen, and, of course, the hills outside of Mr. Trengrouse's cottage where she'd first kissed him. Then she'd texted a photo of each one to him.

And at last, she'd sent him a photo from the lighthouse an hour ago, finally attaching a caption: *Would you meet me here, in the place where my heart became yours? I'm waiting.*

Sarah checked her phone again, but the only texts were from her father. She didn't bother to read them, just deleted each one as it came through. Yes, she'd have to deal with him eventually, but he wasn't ruining tonight for her.

And even if Michael didn't show up, she'd be OK. After all,

she was loved by the Most High, and nothing would ever change that.

Still … she really hoped he'd come.

"Sarah?"

Her neck swiveled toward the stairs where Michael stood, a bewildered look on his face. Dressed in only a sweater and jeans —no gloves covered his reddened fingers, and no coat protected him from the wind—he didn't seem to be anything but unsure, shocked to see her. Wasn't he freezing?

"Hi." Though she longed to throw herself into his arms, she couldn't. Every muscle in her body stiffened from where she sat on the blanket.

"Are you really still here?" Michael took one step toward her then stopped, blinking at a quick pace as if to confirm what was in front of him.

"I am." She lifted her hand toward him. "Join me so I can explain?"

And then he was there, lowering himself to his knees in front of her, his eyes scanning her, drinking her in.

He lifted his hand to her face, and she flinched at his icy touch.

"Sorry."

As he started to pull away, she snatched his fingers between her own and blew into them, her eyes never leaving his. Then, she put his hand back on her cheek and turned her lips into his palm, kissing it. The tips of his fingers dug with a light touch into the roots of her hair near her ear.

Sarah cleared her throat. "No, I'm sorry. I left without explanation. Michael, I was scared, and I'll admit I still am. But I know now, without a doubt, that you were right that day. Real love isn't selfish."

She bit her lip, praying she could remember the words she'd read earlier, the ones she'd been committing to memory all day long. "'And more than that, we don't yet see things clearly. We're squinting in a fog, peering through a mist. But it won't be long before the weather clears and the sun shines brightly! We'll see it all then, see it all as clearly as God sees us, knowing him directly just as he knows us! But for right now, until that completeness, we have three things to do to lead us toward that consummation: Trust steadily in God, hope unswervingly, love extravagantly. And the best of the three is love.'"

"That's one of my favorite passages of Scripture."

"Mine too. Because it speaks just perfectly to where I am right now. The truth is, Michael, I *don't* know exactly how to reconcile this thing between us and my love for my ministry back home. But I don't have to. I just have to keep trusting in the love of my heavenly father, hoping for amazing things … and loving with everything I have."

She paused then took a deep breath. "And I do. I love you." Would he think her crazy for saying it? Yes, they'd known each other such a short time, but—

"I love you too, Sarah Bentley. Most extravagantly." The pad of his thumb traced a line down the side of her face until he reached her lips.

"Oh?" The word released from her lungs, a happy sigh, and she angled her face upward.

"Yes, oh." His face split into a smile as he chuckled. "And as for what comes next, I've got a lot of vacation time saved. Perks of working for your parents." He winked. "I think a long visit to Boston may be in order."

"Oh?"

"Is that all you can say?"

Her hands came up and around his neck, resting there as she played with the curls at the base of his neck. "No. There's one more thing I'd like to say to you."

He moved in closer, so only their noses touched. Beyond the glass, she could hear the distant roar of the ocean, as if it approved. "And what's that?"

"What did you think of my photos?"

His guffaw shook them both, and he pulled back ever so slightly. "That's not what I thought you were going to say. But since you asked, I thought they were brilliant. I suppose I'm a bit biased, though."

"Hmmm." A lazy grin spread across her lips. "I find I'm quite all right with that. Now." She tilted her head. "Would you please kiss me already?"

"I thought you'd never ask."

And he complied with her request most thoroughly.

LIKE A SILVER BELL

A PORT WILLIS ROMANCE

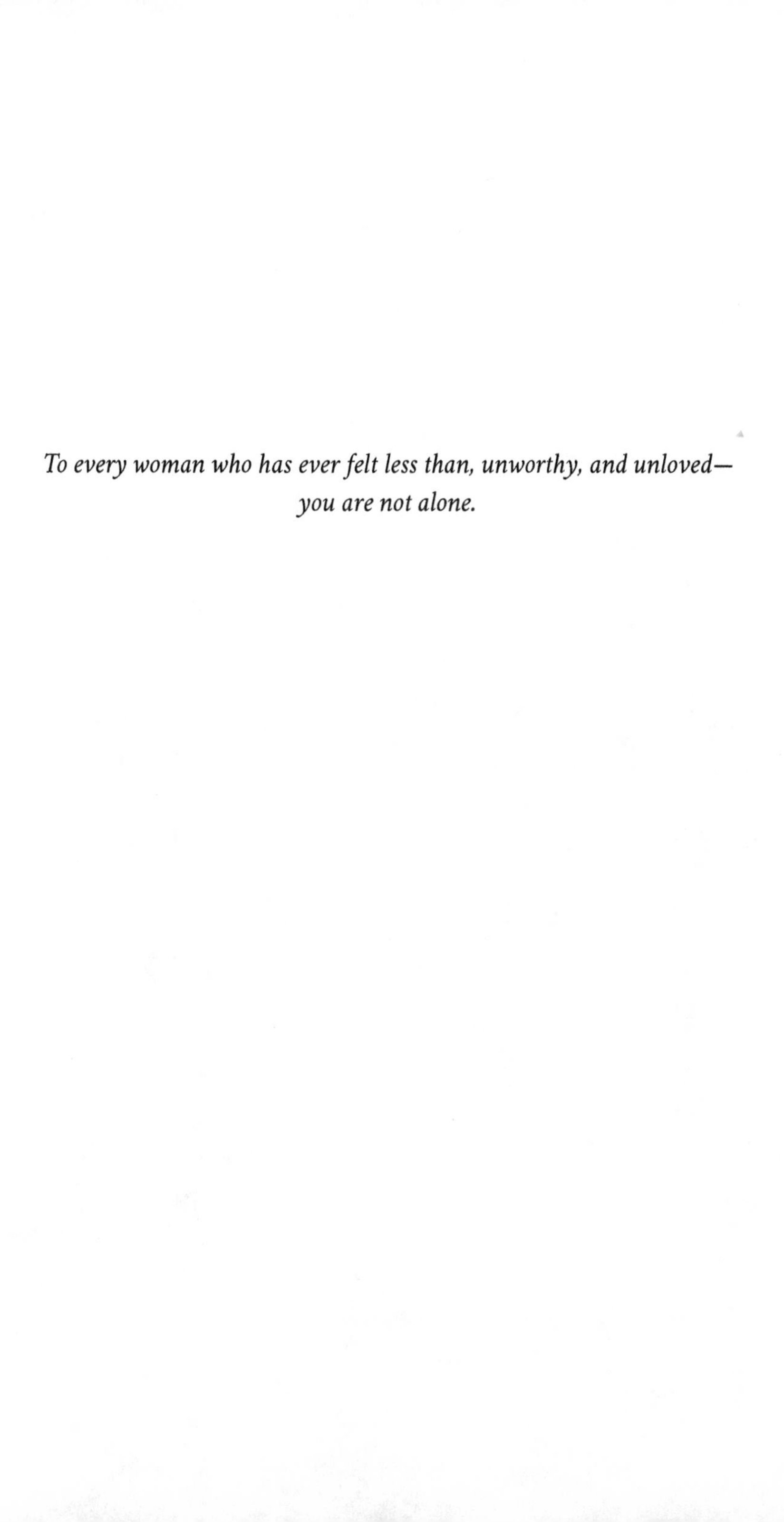

To every woman who has ever felt less than, unworthy, and unloved—
you are not alone.

CHAPTER 1

Some said the devil was in the details.

But to Kara Elise Gentry, the details were the only thing that kept her sane—that kept her from thinking about the actual devil she had to face later tonight.

Kara clicked on her computer screen to bring up the flight schedule for tomorrow and breathed a sigh of relief that she and her traveling companions hadn't been unknowingly bumped to a later flight. With the time change from Boston to England, they were already losing five hours that could be used to work on the fundraiser. And with eleven hours of travel—

"Knock knock." Sarah Bentley-Hammett stuck her head into Kara's doorway. Today, the stylish CEO of New Dawn Women's Council—a nonprofit that provided free legal counsel to survivors of domestic violence during divorce and custody proceedings—wore low-slung heels and a blue dress that hugged her slightly rounded belly. Her red hair was pulled back in a loose bun at the nape of her neck. "You heading out soon?"

Kara pressed her hands down her green blouse, smoothing out an imaginary wrinkle. "Yes, I was just finishing up some last-minute prep for our trip."

A smile quirked her boss's lips. "Have I told you lately how amazing you are?"

Because there wasn't room in Kara's tiny office for more than a desk, chair, and filing cabinet, Sarah leaned against the doorway. But what the office lacked in size it made up for with an amazing view of downtown Boston out Kara's window that, at the moment, showcased the darkening sky and swirling snow of a December late afternoon.

Blushing, Kara pushed a strand of brown hair behind her ear. "Thank you." After a decade of being berated by Jeff, it was still difficult to accept compliments, but Kara's therapist reminded her often how important it was to try. Just try. "While I have you, can I get your thoughts on the final dinner menu for the ball?"

The upcoming fundraiser, which was the official launching point of New Dawn's London branch, consisted of a three-night stay at a historic manor in Cornwall and would culminate in a winter ball. Sarah—who was still a born-and-bred member of Boston elite despite her marriage to a middle-class British photographer—and a few of her friends had leveraged their overseas contacts, and the fundraiser had sold out in days.

Now, it was up to Kara, New Dawn's special events coordinator, to make the whole affair a raging success.

Sarah swiped her hand through the air. "You don't need my input, Kara. How many fundraisers and charity events have you put together over the years? You've got this."

It was true. In her former role as the wife of Jeff Gentry, the CEO of Gentry Pharmaceuticals and all-around Boston golden boy, she'd hosted her fair share of events.

But it didn't matter how many events she had under her belt. This one mattered more than all of them combined, because she simply couldn't fail New Dawn. She *wouldn't*. The organization —and Sarah and Melissa, the wonderful ladies in charge—had not only rescued Kara from her ex-husband's clutches three years ago, but they'd also been kind enough to give her a job afterward. A job she'd so desperately needed.

Sure, Jeff had been forced to pay alimony in the divorce, but Kara refused to touch any of that man's money ever again. Every penny she received from him automatically went into Rose's college account.

Kara would prove to him—to everyone—that she could stand on her own two feet. It was what she should have been doing all along, really. If only she'd listened to her mother all of those years ago …

"I just want everything to go well." Kara fidgeted in her chair, her eyes flitting to the clock above the door. Time to go. "Never mind. The menu is fine, I'm sure." Well, not *sure,* but she didn't want to give her boss any reason to doubt her efforts.

"I sneaked a peek earlier, and it's not just fine. It sounds divine. Baby boy and I are more than excited to try the spiced Victoria sponge cake." Laugh lines creased the corners of Sarah's bright blue eyes. "Not that I need any more desserts. My belly is already humongous."

"It is not." Kara shut the lid of her laptop, unplugged it, and shoved it into her bag. "It's adorable." Sarah was five months along but looked more like two. "I wish I'd been that cute when I was pregnant with Rose."

Instead, Jeff had made sure Kara knew what a fat cow she'd become. At least he'd held off on hitting her for those nine months, though. Hadn't wanted to damage his "heir," after all.

Stop thinking about him. Kara hated that even now, there were times he and his words still got a hold of her. It had taken several years of therapy to become the functioning adult she was today, and she would not give him any more power than he'd already wielded in their seven-year marriage.

She and Sarah chatted for a few more minutes about the details of tomorrow, then Kara waved goodbye and started the forty-five-minute trek toward home. And despite the Christmas music she cranked in her twelve-year-old Corolla—a far cry from the brand-new Porsche she used to drive—she couldn't stop her mind from wandering to the task ahead of her.

The one that always made her sick to her stomach.

Maybe she'd get lucky and Jeff's housekeeper would answer the door instead. But probably not. Jeff knew how his presence grated on Kara. Even though he didn't control her like he once had, he still derived sick pleasure from her pain.

And nothing was going to be more painful than dropping Rose off for ten days with the monster who had made Kara's last ten years a living nightmare.

But rules were rules, and the judge had been clear—Kara had custody during the week, Jeff got Rose every other weekend, and the holidays were split fifty-fifty. Because Kara was going to be out of town for work, Jeff had agreed to take his holiday time with their daughter from December tenth through the twentieth, and then again for a few days at New Year's.

If only the judge had believed Kara about the abuse, she might have Rose full-time. But Kara's one comfort was that Jeff had never lifted a finger to harm his daughter. For all of his faults, he really did seem to love her—or at least, recognize that she was something special. And Kara made sure to take Rose to counseling regularly, on high alert for any abuse that might be occurring.

When Kara pulled into the driveway of Cindy and Travis's tiny three-bedroom craftsman, she inhaled deeply, determined her daughter would not sense her tension. Easing from the car, she tugged her coat closed to protect herself from the light snow flurries as she rushed to the front door.

"Hello," she called as she entered the place she and Rose had called home for the past three years. The vintage-decorated Christmas tree in the corner of the living room added a warm glow to the house, as did the tantalizing smell of cookies.

Kara hung her coat and purse on the entry-way rack and

headed for the kitchen, where two voices sang along to "Rudolph the Red-Nosed Reindeer."

She stopped at the sight of her older sister and seven-year-old Rose belting into used egg beaters, their holiday spirit in full swing. Rose's wispy blonde hair was pulled back into a messy ponytail, and flour dusted the navy blue jumper and red long-sleeved polo she'd worn to school this morning. Jeff still insisted on her enrollment at the same prep school he'd attended as a child, and even though it now took her an extra thirty minutes to drive there every day—in the opposite direction from work—Kara had agreed.

Whenever possible, she tried not to violate the judge's custody order for "no unreasonable request" to be denied. Besides, the choice of school was not a hill she was willing to die on, especially when it was a good school and Jeff paid for it.

Rose's eyes widened when she caught sight of Kara. "Mommy!" She hopped down from her stool at the counter and raced to Kara, flinging herself into her arms. Kara leaned down and breathed in the warm scent of her daughter's skin—crayons and cinnamon.

"Hi, sweet pea." Kara pulled back and smoothed some flour off of Rose's smiling cheeks. "Smells delicious in here."

"Aunt Cindy said we should make some cookies for you to take to England." Rose's smile faltered for a minute as she tilted her head. "Do you really have to go?"

They'd been over this a thousand times already. As much as Kara loved the idea of a trip overseas in theory, it would hardly be all fun and games. "I'm afraid I do."

"Why can't I come?"

Kara caught Cindy's eye before her sister swiveled to place a cookie sheet in the oven and set the timer. Then she looked back at Rose. "I wish I could take you, but I'll be working the whole time. Plus, you've got another week of school, silly." She swallowed hard and forced a smile. "And your daddy is looking forward to spending time with you."

Rose's face brightened as she turned and skipped back to the counter, remounting her stool. "Maybe he'll take me to the movies. Regina doesn't like the movies, but I love them. So maybe."

Regina, Jeff's twenty-something girlfriend, didn't like a lot of things—including children, from what Kara could tell. More than once, Rose had come home telling Kara about something cruel the woman had said in passing. Thankfully, her daughter didn't seem to understand the slights.

Kara had complained to Jeff, but he'd only said she was exaggerating ... and was she sure she wasn't jealous?

Striding to the counter, Kara shook out her hands. "Give me something to do. Got any cookie dough that needs pounding?"

Cindy's eyebrows lifted behind her wire-rimmed glasses as she slid a tray of cookies in front of Rose. "Not at the moment, but you can decorate these with Rose if you'd like."

"Perfect."

For the next half hour, Kara and her daughter sang along with silly Christmas songs and iced cookies, licking the red and green frosting from their fingers while Cindy stuck a casserole in the oven for dinner.

When a slew of messy treats dotted the counter and the smell of baked cheese and chicken filled the air, Kara glanced at the clock and held back a sigh. "Almost time to go, sweet pea. Is everything packed that you want to take to Daddy's?"

"Oh! There are a few things I forgot."

"Why don't you clean up and get those into your suitcase, okay? Then we'll eat a quick dinner and get going."

"Okay!" Rose hopped down and raced out of the kitchen.

"It's going to be so quiet around here with her at Jeff's and you gone." Cindy used a thick chef's knife to slice a tomato for the side salad. She was still dressed in simple slacks, a cozy sweater, and flats, her gray-streaked brown hair pulled back into a low ponytail—the perfect attire for an elementary school librarian.

Kara made her way to the sink and squirted soap in her hands, lathering it up until she could see her reflection in a few of the bubbles. "It'll be a welcome respite, I'm sure. When do Sam and Charlie get here?" Cindy was nine years older than Kara's thirty-eight years, and her two sons were currently away at college.

"Next Thursday." The sound of the knife hitting the cutting board filled the modest kitchen. "It'll be nice to have us all together under one roof."

"I still feel bad for stealing their rooms." Kara washed the bubbles off her hands and down the drain, then dried off with the dish towel hanging from the oven handle. "Hopefully we'll be out of your hair soon. I've almost got the down payment for a house saved."

Okay, fine. She technically had enough as of last week. But saving even more couldn't be a bad thing, could it?

Her sister looked up, her gaze narrowed. "You are not in my hair."

"I know, I know."

"But ..."

Here it came. The big sister tone that Kara was oh so familiar with. But she couldn't blame Cindy.

"I do think it will be a good step toward recovery for you, to get your own place. In fact"—*thwap, thwap,* went the knife—"I forwarded you a few listings I found around here. They look really cute and affordable."

"I'll take a look when I get back from England." Kara tried to infuse enthusiasm into her voice. She *did* want to move out. Truly.

But what if ...

"I know you're worried about the nightmares scaring Rose, but you don't have them as frequently now."

Kara leaned against the counter. "You're right. Still ..."

Cindy set down the knife and approached Kara, pulling her into a swift hug. "You know you'll always have a place here with me. I'm sorry if I'm being pushy. Just think about it, all right? For you. For Rose."

"I already told you that I'm going to do it." Because Kara would do anything to provide the most stable existence possible for her daughter. If only she could get past the paralyzing fear of being on her own. What if she failed her daughter ... and herself ... again? "It's just taking me a little longer than I'd hoped."

"I know, Sis." A pause. "Hey, so, how are you feeling about your trip? I know you'll be working, but I hope you at least try to enjoy your time overseas." Letting go, Cindy went back to her cutting board and placed the tomato into a bowl. "It'll be like a vacation. I mean, you'll be staying at a mansion, for goodness' sake."

Kara wandered to the counter and plucked out a juicy square of tomato. "Right. A vacation. What's that again?" She popped the piece into her mouth and chewed. Sweetness exploded on her tongue. Mmm. It was nice for food to have flavor again. She'd spent so much of her life in recent years fearful, depressed, that it had been hard to take pleasure in even the smallest things.

But she was making strides forward. Just not as quickly as she'd sometimes like.

Cindy hip bumped her sister out of the way and grabbed plates from the cupboard. "You should find out. Too bad you can't stay longer."

"There's no way I'm missing Christmas with Rose."

"Of course not." Cindy's mouth moved side to side as she snagged the stack of plates and placed them on the placemats at the eat-in table. "I just wish there was a way to get her to England once her time with Jeff is over."

Kara plucked a handful of cutlery from the silverware drawer and brought them to the table. "I'd never let her fly alone." But the idea of getting away for Christmas did sound lovely.

"I don't blame you." Without asking, Cindy took a few of the forks out of Kara's hands and placed them next to the plates. Once a big sister, always a big sister. "So ..." She glanced up at Kara, eyebrow lifted.

"So, what?

"Will there be any handsome, single men at this event—in particular, the ball?"

"Stop." Kara snatched a dish towel off the counter and flicked it at Cindy, who laughed and dodged out of the way. "I'm going there to work, not to fall in love."

"Eh, semantics." Cindy snapped her fingers. "What about that one man I met at the Christmas function last year? Winston something?"

"Warren? Warren Kensington?"

"Yes! Him. Will he be there? He's a cutie. Is he single?"

Kara's cheeks burned at the mention of the president of New Dawn's board of directors—because yes, she couldn't deny the guy was handsome with his broad shoulders, perfectly styled brown hair, and thick-framed glasses that reflected kind eyes behind them.

Or what seemed like kind eyes.

But Jeff's had seemed kind to her too, once upon a time.

She shook her head. "No."

"No, he won't be there? Or no, he's not cute? Or no, he's not single?" Cindy wagged her eyebrows as she set three wine glasses on the table, along with a milk cup for Rose.

"That's not—" Kara rolled her eyes and marched forward to grab the wine off the counter before Cindy could. She uncorked the bottle like a pro and began filling the glasses with the Chenin Blanc. "Yes, he will be there. The international board is taking the opportunity to have a meeting. And fine, he's attractive. I don't know if he's single, but I haven't heard of him dating anyone." She took a deep breath. "But Cin, he's also rich."

Cindy placed her hand over her mouth and gasped—in an extremely exaggerated way that Kara did not appreciate. "No! Not that! Oh, cross him off the potential husband list right away then."

Pressing her lips together, Kara concentrated on not spilling a drop of the wine. "Even if I was going to let a new man into my life—and that's a big *if*—it wouldn't be a wealthy man. You know as well as I do what Tom did to Mom. I thought she was making it all up for attention. Or exaggerating at the very least."

"You can't trust a rich man, Kara. They'll take all your dreams and crush them. You've got to make sure you can stand on your own two feet."

And Kara had said the most horrific things in reply.

Now it was too late to apologize—her mother had died in a car accident a few years after their argument. "And then I went and did the very opposite of what she said. I married Jeff, a man ten times worse than Tom."

Ten times richer, too.

Not only had Jeff been abusive scum, but he was a liar to boot. All those nights he was gone, and she'd trusted that he was at work like he said ... but then, when she'd started to wonder and asked him, he'd replied with his classic line: *"It's nothing you need to worry about."* Then he'd hit her for questioning his loyalty, even though her instincts had been correct.

Regina—and others like her—had been the real reason Jeff hadn't been warming his side of the bed.

"Kara."

She turned away from her sister and recorked the bottle. "I know what you're going to say, but it's no use. I'm not interested in dating again, anyway. I have Rose to consider. I can't afford to …" Oh no, she was *not* going to cry over this. Again.

Would it be nice to have a co-parent? Yes, oh yes. But only if he was a good man, one who would look past her scars and see someone worth loving.

As far as she was concerned, a man like that couldn't possibly exist.

Definitely not someone like Warren Kensington, a premiere member of the East Coast Elite. Just because she'd never seen him *act* entitled didn't mean he wasn't, deep down.

Cindy snagged her elbow and turned Kara gently toward her again. "Sis, I know you've walked a hard road. I've watched you take step after difficult step toward a brighter future. You are the bravest person I know." Her eyes radiated concern and unconditional love. "But you have to start trusting again."

"I do. I trust you." Kara wouldn't have survived the last few years without her sister, and she owed her everything. "And I trust Sarah and Melissa."

"That's not what I meant." Cindy tilted her head. "Someday, you're going to have to learn to trust men again."

Kara's eyes burned, and frowning, she bit the inside of her cheek. "Maybe."

But probably not. Because unless she could guarantee that she would never be lied to, betrayed—abused—again, she wouldn't allow a man into their lives.

And life just didn't come with those kinds of guarantees.

CHAPTER 2

The next hour flew by until Kara loaded Rose and her stuff up into her car and started toward Jeff's historic home in Beacon Hill—the home where Kara had once lived in the lap of luxury.

But luxury was only skin deep, a fact of which she was now all too aware.

Rose chattered from the back seat, and Kara did her best to engage with her daughter—to keep her mind off of the reality of what she was about to do.

Maybe she'd been wrong. Maybe she *could* take Rose with her. Perhaps she could hire a sitter during the day while she worked. Rose would surely love to see the tiny Cornish village of Port Willis, all lit up for Christmas. And the gardens at the manor where they were holding the fundraiser were supposed to be some of the finest in the whole country. Rose could look at flowers for hours on end …

But no. Jeff would never allow it. And there would be too many details to work out in too short a time. Kara would just have to live with her decision and pray she'd made the right one.

Not that praying had done her much good over the years. Every time Jeff had lifted a fist, Kara would pray for him to stop.

He never had.

That's when Kara had known—she was the only one who could get herself out of the mess she'd somehow found herself in. Yes, others had been willing to help, but she'd had to be the one to take that first step toward being a survivor and not a victim.

And every day afterward, she had to keep stepping. Keep trudging.

For Rose.

Kara gripped the steering wheel harder and refocused on what her daughter was saying—something about the project she'd made in art class.

All too soon, they arrived at their destination.

As Kara and Rose got out of the car, Kara couldn't help the pinch in her chest that came every time she took in the beautiful home where she'd lived during her marriage to Jeff. The brick exterior had been restored, as had much of the inside, and there was a wide portico with columns flanking the doorway. An endless number of windows gave off a feeling of grandeur, of openness to passersby.

In reality, the place had been a prison.

Thankfully, Rose didn't seem to agree. She skipped right up the walkway and rang the doorbell. Even from out here, Kara could hear the ominous sound vibrating throughout the high-ceilinged entry. The wind whipped at the bottom of the black coat she'd found a few winters ago at Goodwill. It wasn't Gucci, but it kept her warmer than many coats she'd had as a child in a single-parent home—before her stepdad had swept into their lives and dropped them into a shiny new world.

Her spine stiffened as the large oak door creaked open slowly, every second adding to her rising anxiety.

Jeff stood on the other side. Her ex-husband still looked

every inch the tall, chiseled forty-five-year-old man who commanded boardrooms and charmed everyone.

And he was still the man who haunted her nightmares.

"Daddy!" Rose flew into his arms, and Jeff took his eyes off of Kara for a moment to hug and kiss their daughter.

He pulled away and patted her cheek. "Doris has some cake waiting for you in the kitchen. Go put your things in your room first while I talk to your mom."

"Okay." Rose turned to Kara and gave her another hug that twisted Kara's gut. "See you soon, Mommy!" Then she skipped away down the hallway toward the staircase that led to her bedroom upstairs.

An awkward silence followed.

"So." Oh, wonderful. Of course her voice would choose this moment to crack. She didn't want Jeff to think his presence still had an effect on her whatsoever—even though it did. She cleared her throat. "I'll pick her up Monday the twentieth at seven in the evening as discussed."

"Hello, Elise." Jeff stuck his hands into the pockets of his slacks and leaned against his doorway, his figure backlit with the brilliance of the chandelier that they'd chosen together in the foyer. "It's nice to see you too."

She bit the inside of her cheek. "I've told you, it's Kara now. Again." She'd only gone by her middle name in the first place because Jeff liked it better. Said it sounded more distinguished, a better fit for the wife of a CEO. But she'd never felt like Elise. Elise was her great-aunt namesake who smelled like a strange mixture of fresh-cut grass and peppermint.

Returning to "Kara" had been her first step toward throwing off the proverbial shackles Jeff had placed around her wrists.

"Of course." Running his hand through his full head of black hair, Jeff flashed her that wolf-like grin she had once-upon-a-time found so irresistible. "Listen, about the twentieth …"

Something about his tone caused a jolt to her nervous system. "What?" Kara burrowed deeper into her coat.

"Forgive me. You look cold. Would you like to come in?" He stepped back and gestured toward the tiled entryway, where a sunburst pattern decorated the flooring. "Regina's not here right now. We could get drinks in my office. Catch up." He paused. "Revel in each other's company like old times."

Then he had the audacity to wink.

Kara had never been violent a day in her life, and yet, right now—with his dirty insinuations—she had the strongest urge to punch her ex in the teeth. But knowing him, he was baiting her. And he'd take her to court for violence so quick, that she'd lose her custody of Rose completely.

The idea of *her* losing custody for hitting *him* was quite ironic. And yet, that was her life.

"Thanks for that *oh-so-tempting* offer, but no." She straightened her back and dropped her arms, proving to him that she didn't need his warmth. Not anymore. "Now, what about the twentieth?"

The pungent smell of his sandalwood cologne wafted between them, and triggered the strong desire to flee. But she stood her ground.

"Regina has her heart set on taking a cruise for Christmas. It leaves on December nineteenth and returns on the twenty-ninth."

"Oh." Was that all? "I'm sure Cindy would be happy to watch Rose for the last few days of my trip."

"That's not what I'm saying." Jeff raised his strong, dark brow. "I want to take Rose with us."

"But—"

"I don't think it's terribly *unreasonable* for her to spend a memorable cruise with me during the holidays, do you? In exchange, she can be with you for New Year's and the next big holiday when I'm supposed to have her. Sound good?"

Unreasonable. There was that word again—the one the judge had used to set a precedent. The constant threat to their somewhat amicable custody arrangement. The one Jeff liked to throw in her face far too often.

But to take away Christmas with her girl? It was going too far. "No."

He tilted his head. "Come on, Elise. I mean, *Kara.*" Anyone else hearing the words probably wouldn't notice the sarcastic undertones, but Kara certainly did. "Rose would love it. And it wouldn't be the same without her there."

"Can't you do it a different time?"

Anytime but Christmas. Christmas wasn't like other holidays. It was ... different. Special.

Despite so many years with nothing under the tree, Kara's mother had made sure that Christmas was always memorable for her and Cindy. Window shopping in the snow, a fifty-cent hot chocolate at Bernadette's Diner, a large candy cane stick that lasted for weeks, watching *Miracle on 34th Street* on the tattered couch in their mobile home—it had been magical.

Because they'd been *together.*

"I'm afraid this is a once-in-a-lifetime cruise. I won't bore you with the details, but suffice it to say that it's very exclusive and very expensive. I know you're not used to that anymore, but I won't deny Rose just because you choose to dress like you live in a halfway house."

Kara's fingers curled at the patronization dripping from Jeff's words.

"Besides, this way you can stay in England even longer than planned and get an actual vacation out of it. I imagine England is quite enchanting at Christmastime."

It probably was—but not without Rose. Her daughter was the only thing in the world that mattered. Everything Kara did, she did for Rose.

That's why she was going overseas before Christmas in the

first place—because work required it, and work meant a paycheck, and a paycheck meant their own home, and their own home meant stability.

Maybe she could sweet-talk him. The idea made her shudder, but she had to try. Kara put on a quiet, submissive tone. "Jeff …"

"I hate to do this, El—Kara—but I've got the judge on speed dial." He pulled out his phone and waved it in the air. "Maybe we should see what *he* thinks of your refusal. Whether he thinks it's reasonable."

Kara took a step backward, nearly stumbling off the porch stoop. How did he—? But of course he had the judge's number. *Of course* he was buddy-buddy with the guy. Probably played golf with him too. Maybe even had slipped him a bribe at some point.

It was the way of rich men to protect each other from every bad thing they deserved.

And Kara was just a mom trying to fight for her daughter. All she had was love and the backing of a few well-meaning family members and friends.

But none of those people was strong enough to win the war with Jeff completely. Sarah and her business partner, Melissa, had already fought hard to get Kara the current arrangement.

The last thing Kara wanted to do was bow to Jeff and his whims. But what choice did she have? One wrong maneuver and she just might lose Rose forever—New Dawn or no New Dawn.

She gave a clipped nod. "Fine. Take your cruise. But she calls me frequently. And I will get her on the thirtieth and not a day later."

"Of course, of course." Grinning, Jeff shoved his phone back into his pocket. "Thank you for being so accommodating."

As if I have a choice.

"Let me tell Rose what's going on."

"Ah, ah, ah." Jeff tsked. "This is my time now. I'll inform Rose about the change of plans."

She knew better than to argue or plead. But she wouldn't have him thinking she was a wilting flower. Not anymore. Kara narrowed her eyes. "You'd better not spin it as me abandoning her for work."

"I hadn't thought of that …" Jeff rubbed his chin, grinning.

Holding back a growl, she longed to say just the right thing to put him in his place. But nothing would because he belonged in—

Calm down, Kara. This is what he wants. You, angry. He's trying to control your emotions again.

"I'll be calling your phone to speak with her tomorrow. She'd better be available." Kara turned on her heel and walked away from him, fighting the falling tears at the prospect of Christmas without her baby.

What a dreary holiday this was turning out to be. And yet, somehow, she had to make it magical for a hundred-plus donors who were about to travel to Port Willis expecting a grand time.

Okay, then. Kara stomped through the snow, each step more determined than the last.

She would throw every ounce of energy into doing what she did best—organizing, planning, and making sure everyone else was happy.

CHAPTER 3

Jeff might be a lying, abusive jerk, but he was right about one thing—England *was* enchanting at Christmastime.

Kara turned slowly, taking it all in. From her spot, where the Port Willis harbor met the end of High Street, she could see a good chunk of the Cornish village. Dinghies and other small fishing craft bobbed in the waves that were gentled by the rocky quay extending parallel to the land. Adorable wooden storefronts painted in a variety of pastels lined the cobblestone street, piping smoke into Sunday's early evening sky.

She, Sarah, and Sarah's husband, Michael—New Dawn's photographer—had only been in town a few hours, after their long trek had landed them finally at Cornwall Airport Newquay. There, Sarah's in-laws had picked them up and dropped Kara's luggage by Rebecca's, an adorable bed and breakfast taking up residence next to a charming bookstore and bakery combo.

That was the whole town—adorable. And so different from the hustle and bustle and smog of Boston.

Kara couldn't wait to see the manor where the fundraiser

would take place. It was several miles outside of town, but if it was anything like the village itself, the pictures wouldn't do it justice.

After the stop at the B&B, Michael's parents had insisted Kara join them for a late lunch at their restaurant, the Village Pub, where she'd had her fill of delicious roasted chicken stew and homemade bread. Sarah's younger sister and brother-in-law, Ginny and Steven Applegate, had joined them, as had Michael's sister and her young family.

It had been a loud, raucous affair, but Kara was glad for some quiet just now.

Though she'd hated to admit how tired she was—lack of sleep plus jet lag would do that to a person—the fact that Kara had nearly fallen asleep in her meal had been a fairly good indicator. A walk would be just what she needed to unwind from the lengthy travel and keep her awake until evening.

She started the jaunt back toward the bed and breakfast, anxious to change into loungewear and curl up with a mug of hot chocolate and a good book. Most of the shops—from an antique store to a grocer to a few restaurants—appeared to be closed. Sarah had mentioned something about Sundays being big family days here. The thought pierced Kara's chest. Her own family was so far away.

Reaching into her purse, she pulled out her phone and dialed Jeff's number for the first of her daily chats with Rose. The phone rang and rang before rolling over to voicemail, and her chest tightened even more. Jeff had better not try to keep Rose from talking with her. They'd agreed.

Not that he kept his word all that often. But still. Kara would go full mama bear on him if he tried to withhold her daughter.

She left Rose a quick, peppy voicemail asking her to call back soon and hung up just as she passed a small park that sat on the bluffs overlooking the ocean. "Wow."

Her feet tugged her forward. On one end of the park was a

small playground where a handful of children played. Kara listened to the sound of young laughter, wishing Rose's was among them. What was her daughter doing right now? Was Jeff taking good care of her, or was she hanging out in her room or on the iPad he'd insisted on getting for her even though Kara disapproved?

Shaking free of the thoughts, Kara moved toward a gazebo at the opposite end of the park. Beside it stood a Christmas tree that must have been fifteen or maybe even twenty feet tall. It was decorated with red and silver bulbs and strand after strand of darkened lights. The gazebo roof had also been strung with lights. She imagined it all lit up against the sky—gorgeous, especially if the stars shone out here with any amount of brightness. The clouds would need to clear away first, though.

A sudden gust of wind whipped Kara's hair back from her face and she hurried toward the gazebo, where a ring of wooden benches would allow her to sit in shelter and enjoy the scenery.

She didn't notice someone already sat there until she was nearly inside.

Him.

Kara halted. Oh no. She could almost hear Cindy cackling with glee from across the pond.

But maybe if she backed away slowly, he wouldn't notice her.

No such luck.

The man glanced up from his phone and blinked a few times. "Kara?"

"H-hi, Warren." She swallowed, her throat suddenly dry. "Good to see you."

Warren tucked away his phone and stood. "You too." He wore jeans that likely cost more than she made in a month, a fashionable black trench coat—probably Burberry—and a purple woven scarf that looked both stylish and functional.

Though Kara wasn't petite by any means, his solid presence made her feel short. "Did you just get into town?"

She straightened her spine, hoping to appear taller than she was. Not that it mattered what he thought. "Yes, a few hours ago. I'm staying at a bed and breakfast not far from here and thought a walk sounded nice."

Sarah and Michael were bunking with Ginny and Steven, who had also invited Kara along—but she preferred to have her own place to retreat to. Plus, she'd be in and out so much with preparing for the fundraiser and didn't want to disturb anyone.

"Rebecca's? Me too." A smile lit Warren's face. Though he was normally clean-shaven, today a dusting of dark stubble covered his sculpted jaw, lending him a rather rugged appeal.

And why exactly are you noticing that?

Kara bit the inside of her cheek. "Small world."

He chuckled. "Not as small as you'd think. I'm pretty sure this town only has a few places to stay."

"Right." Taking a step backward, Kara forced a smile. "Well, I'd better be getting back there. Work is calling my name."

"I'll join you if you don't mind. I've got hundreds of emails to comb through myself." In addition to heading up New Dawn's board, he was in charge of the Boston branch of his family's New York-based corporation, which specialized in everything from technology to pharmaceuticals.

Warren stepped forward, and Kara caught a whiff of mandarin orange, black pepper, and lavender. It sent a shiver through her.

Goodness. For the scent of mere cologne to have such an effect on her, she really *was* tired—either that or Cindy's words from two days ago had unfortunately embedded themselves in her brain.

Well, her brain had better get the memo that her heart was trying to send it.

No romance.

Especially not with him.

"Sure. I guess if we're both headed that way." It wasn't as if walking with him signified anything. Besides, he was on the board of directors, which kind of indirectly meant he was one of her bosses, right? She should be polite to her boss.

Kara headed back toward the street.

Following along, Warren inhaled a deep breath and stuck his hands inside the pockets of his coat. "It's nice to be back here."

"You've been to Port Willis before?"

"Once. Three years ago." He glanced at her. "It was actually on that trip that I decided to become part of what New Dawn was doing."

Three years ... right about the time she'd decided to leave Jeff.

"Has the town changed much?" Because the last three years had changed everything for her.

"Not really. I think that's what I love about this place—so classically charming, like something out of a painting or kids' storybook. It's why I suggested we hold the fundraiser here instead of London."

As they crossed the street, an old metal lamppost flickered on. Dusk had arrived.

Kara lifted an eyebrow. "That was your idea?" To be honest, when she'd first heard it, she'd thought it a bit of a risk. "How did you know donors would want to travel down here so close to the holidays?" Most of them were not only busy but also lived in London, a four- or five-hour drive from Cornwall.

He shrugged. "I just thought about my ideal holiday and figured others might feel the same way."

Well, that was a mysterious answer. "What's your ideal holiday?" She really didn't want to ask such personal details of him, but it would be good to understand the mindset of the guests who would be attending the fundraiser. After all, if their expectations weren't met, she wouldn't have done her job.

And they wouldn't be likely to donate again.

"Oh, nothing fancy—though I know the ball will be a hit." Warren stepped off the sidewalk onto the street so a family with a stroller could pass. He smiled and nodded a greeting at them before refocusing on Kara. "Mostly, just time away from the craziness of work, a place where I can breathe, where normal life seems a world away."

"You can't get much farther from the norm than here, I suppose." She followed him as he continued around a bend in the road. The bed and breakfast loomed in the distance. "What about planned activities? I have some options for people—daytime sightseeing, tours about the estate grounds, and some nighttime activities in town and at the manor—but I thought most might want to plan their own excursions." She hoped she was right in that regard.

"That sounds great. Our lives are so over-planned already, our calendars so crowded, that I think guests might appreciate some downtime." He chuckled. "Although some might not know what to do with themselves."

"True." She tilted her head, curious about something. "Pardon me for asking, but is that why you're here so much earlier than the other board members?" As far as she knew, they weren't set to arrive until the day before the other donor guests did on Thursday.

Warren nodded. "Sarah invited me to come out early and spend some time with them." He reached for the handle of Rebecca's front door. "Over the last several years, I've become closer with her and Michael than my own family."

Huh. And why was that?

But no. She closed her lips before she could ask the question. She didn't need to know anything more than necessary about this man—however pleasant he was being in this moment.

As he opened the door, a rush of warm air met Kara's cheeks. She inhaled the lovely scent of spiced cake and apple cider, which sat on the sidebar of the smallish dining room to the right of the entryway. A petite woman with dirty blonde hair stood behind a wooden desk—Rebecca Trengrouse, the owner. She gave a gruff wave to Kara and Warren before turning back to her computer screen.

It had been a while since Kara had stayed at a bed and breakfast—the last one had been in the Poconos for her and Jeff's third anniversary—and the first time she'd been at one by herself. But one glance at the cozy living room warmed by a stone fireplace that was flanked by bookcases and an undecorated Christmas tree, and Kara knew she'd found a home away from home.

She'd stay here every night of her trip if she could, but she needed to be on hand at the estate come Thursday and until she flew out next Sunday. Unless she decided to stay longer, like Cindy had suggested when Kara had told her about the change of Christmas plans. Hmm.

Either way, for now, she'd enjoy the peace. The quiet. The warmth.

Kara let loose a contented sigh.

"It's quite charming, isn't it?"

Her hand flew to her chest. Right. Warren was still with her, wasn't he?

"Yes." She grimaced at the sudden coolness in her voice. "I guess I'll see you around."

"It'll be hard not to. I think we're the only guests staying here this week."

Her breathing ratcheted up a notch. "What?"

That couldn't be right. Surely more would be coming in at some point. She'd have to check with Rebecca. Otherwise, how was she supposed to avoid Warren? Kara already didn't like her body's response to him. And with the absence of Rose and the stress of pulling off this event, her mind was in a fragile place.

She could not afford any distractions—even one so handsome as Warren Kensington.

As quick as St. Nick in that Christmas Eve poem her mom had read to her and Cindy as kids, the peace Kara had sensed in this place flew out the charming little B&B window.

CHAPTER 4

She'd slept surprisingly well. No nightmares as far as she could remember.

Hopefully today's mission—running through details with the fundraiser venue's events coordinator—wouldn't be a nightmare either.

Kara's stomach rumbled as she made her way down the stairs to breakfast. The aroma of sausages drifted up the staircase from the dining room, where she found Rebecca reading a newspaper and eating breakfast at the twelve-person oak table.

The woman, who must have been about Kara's age, glanced up and set her paper aside. "Morning." Her voice wasn't exactly chipper, but not unfriendly either.

"Good morning." Kara glanced between Rebecca and the covered dishes on the sidebar. She didn't see any coffee—and that was a necessity. "Could you please direct me to wherever the drinks are?"

"I've only got tea, juice, and water." The owner fluttered her hand. "If you're looking for that dark, terrible drink that you Americans enjoy, you'll have to go a few doors down to Ginny's bakery. I refuse to make it." Rebecca made a face. "Can't stand the stuff or the smell."

Kara didn't know what to make of this B&B owner who wouldn't cater to her guests, but something about the small woman's chin tilted in challenge—as if she was used to the whole world being against her, used to having to fight for what she wanted—instantly made her feel like a kindred spirit.

She smiled. "Tea is fine, then."

Standing, Rebecca grunted her approval. "Earl Grey or English breakfast?"

"Surprise me."

After staring at Kara for a moment, she nodded and flounced from the room. Kara took the opportunity to surreptitiously glance about the room. No Warren in sight. Perhaps he'd already left for the day, or maybe he was using this opportunity to sleep in. Whatever the case, hopefully she could make it through breakfast without a forced interaction.

Not very professional of her, but there it was.

She walked to the sidebar and lifted the lid off the first platter to reveal sausage links and scrambled eggs. After placing a spoonful of eggs and two links on a china plate, she moved onto the bowl of pears and snatched one out, ignoring the stack of delicious-looking pastries before heading back to the table. Experience told her that her dress for the ball wouldn't fit if she overindulged in the days leading up to the event.

Just then, Rebecca returned carrying a steaming cup of tea on a saucer. She plopped it in front of Kara and pushed a small creamer toward her. "It's best with a spot of milk."

"Thank you." Kara lifted the porcelain container and poured in a dash of the liquid, stirring it with the tiny spoon set on the saucer. "How long have you owned this bed and breakfast?"

Picking up her fork, Rebecca pushed the remainder of her eggs around her plate. "Two years now. My dad owned the bakery in town—Trengrouse Bakery, not the one Ginny runs—

since before I was born, but he closed up shop after Ginny opened hers. He was ready to retire, you see." She stabbed the eggs. "It took time to make peace with that, but now Ginny and I get on just fine. Not sure her sister holds much affection for me, though."

"Sarah?" Kara's boss could be tough if she needed to be, but she was all softness and goodness as far as Kara could tell. Maybe that was a story for another time, though. She took a sip of her tea, and hummed in pleasure at the notes of bergamot.

"Yep." Rebecca finally took a bite of her eggs. "Anyway, Dad was kind enough to give me my share of the proceeds as a sort of inheritance, so I bought this place. Used to be Loretta's, but Loretta wanted to retire, so I took it off her hands for a steal." She pointed to the doily-laced tablecloth. "Not exactly my style, but I don't have the funds to change out the decor just yet. Guests seem to like it all right, though, so no matter."

Kara lifted a sausage to her lips. "It's a lovely place, that's for sure. I can't wait to sit in that armchair over there and read by the fireplace." If she had any time to do so. She bit into the sausage and chewed, sighing at the burst of spicy flavor in her mouth.

"You won't have much competition for it. I have a whole party that's coming in this weekend—just in time for the forecasted snow—but no one during the week." Rebecca studied her like a mom watching a child for a reaction. "So it's just you and Tall, Dark, and Handsome for the next several days."

Focusing all her attention on her breakfast, Kara felt her cheeks go hot. So Warren had been correct. Well, that didn't matter. With how busy she was going to be, she'd hardly see him.

As if sensing her need for a change in subject—stat—the B&B's front door opened and in breezed a woman even shorter than Rebecca.

With blonde hair that came to her shoulders, a bright orange puffy coat, and dangling neon green earrings, Joy Lincoln was a walking ad for confidence. "Hello!"

"Joy!" Smiling, Kara rose to greet her friend, whom she'd met only once in person but many times over video chat. "So good to see you again."

Joy yanked her into an enthusiastic hug. "Same to you." The forty-six-year-old had way more energy than most twenty-somethings Kara knew. She released Kara. "I'm so excited to show you Pendolphin House."

Joy, an American who had married a Brit she'd met while at a friend's wedding in Port Willis four years ago, was a women's therapist living in London. She believed in New Dawn's mission so much that she'd donated hours of her time to make the launch of the new branch a success. In fact, she'd been the one to scout the perfect location for the fundraiser and meet with vendors that Kara had chosen from afar.

Together, they'd make this fundraiser a success.

"And I can't wait to see it." Kara took a final sip of her tea. "Thank you for the lovely breakfast, Rebecca, but I've got to scoot. Should I take my dishes to the kitchen?"

Rebecca eyed Joy warily, but waved her hand at Kara. "No need. Go enjoy yourself."

Joy glanced at Kara, clear mirth in her eyes and a twitch at her lips. "I'll go keep the car warm while you get your things."

"Thanks." Kara ran upstairs, threw on her jacket, and grabbed her purse from the adorable nightstand. She tossed on a black beanie for good measure. It didn't snow often or all that much in Cornwall, but her weather app had shown a dip in temperature for today.

Snatching her gloves, she turned and cruised out of her room—and right into a solid chest.

"Whoa." Strong arms held her steady, and the most glorious whiff of fresh, manly shampoo surrounded her. "Sorry. You all right?"

She jerked away from Warren, who very obviously had just come from the still-steamy bathroom across the hall. His normally gelled hair was damp, making it appear longer than normal, and he wore a simple white T-shirt and sweatpants. She would have expected him to wear slippers, but no—his feet were bare.

Something about seeing him so casual did things to her insides. Things she didn't like.

"Kara? Are you okay?" Warren's voice indicated his clear concern.

And now she was staring. "Oh. Yeah. I'm fine. Sorry for nearly running you down."

"No worries." He chuckled and ran a hand through his hair. She tried to ignore the way his bicep bulged with the motion. "Where are you off to in such a hurry this morning? Trying to beat me to the coffee?"

At that, she couldn't help but smile. This man, who was used to everyone catering to his every whim, was about to get the shock of his life. Kara leaned in like she had a secret. "Rebecca doesn't believe in coffee."

"What?"

She giggled—giggled!—at the incredulous look on his face. But it was too funny to suppress her laughter. "She said we had to go to Ginny's bakery if we want any."

"I guess you know where I'll be all day then."

Her nose scrunched. He hadn't reacted in the way she'd expected. If he'd been Jeff or anyone in his inner circle, Warren would have marched down the stairs and demanded Rebecca make him a batch of coffee on the double—because he was the guest, and the guest was always right. Always entitled. They were the ones with the money, after all.

But instead, he'd rolled with the punches and accepted Rebecca's little quirk—and hadn't even gotten upset about it.

What was Kara supposed to make of that?

Nothing. It doesn't matter. He doesn't mean anything to you, remember?

Right. Right!

"Okay, well, I've gotta go. I need to check out the venue and all that."

"That sounds much more fun than my activities for the day. I'm tempted to tag along."

"No!" She was already having trouble reminding herself that he wasn't someone she wanted to get close to. If she were forced to spend the whole day with him, it would be even harder. And she needed to focus today.

But oh man, if the crinkled corners of his eyes and frown were any indication, her outburst had clearly hurt his feelings. And he hadn't done anything to deserve that.

"Um, that is, you'd be bored. We've got a thousand details to still work out, and I know you're working today. And you have lunch with Sarah and Michael, right?" Hadn't he mentioned something about that? No? Maybe? "Anyway, I'd hate to keep you from … whatever. Okay, bye."

She scrambled away before he could answer, mentally kicking herself for how she'd sounded.

Desperate.

Unconfident.

Weak.

Kara shook out her hands as she walked down the stairs and out the front door, calling goodbye to Rebecca and receiving another grunt in reply. Joy was waiting in a cute yellow Smart car and didn't look intimidated in the least to be driving on the "wrong" side of the road. Guess she'd had lots of practice over the last several years.

Climbing inside, Kara set her purse at her feet and buckled herself in. "This is cozy."

Joy lovingly pet the dashboard. "I love Rascal here."

"Rascal?" Kara couldn't help the laugh that exited her mouth as Joy pulled out of their spot and onto High Street. The Monday morning traffic was heavier than yesterday, but nothing compared with Boston.

"Yes, Rascal. Named after the beloved dog that brought Oliver and me together." Joy smiled as if lost in thought.

"Oh, I'm so sorry. When did he pass away?"

"Pass away?" Joy arched an eyebrow, then seemed to realize Kara's assumption. "Oh, he's still very much kicking. In fact, he rules the roost in our home. We've adopted five others since and he acts like a mama to them all."

"You have six dogs?" Kara settled into her seat and watched the scenery change out her window as they left Port Willis behind and headed for the open road. Dark clouds gathered on the horizon. Apparently they were in for a storm later today.

"Yes, and I'd get more if we had the space." Joy sighed. "I've tried convincing Oliver to move from our London flat to the country, but it's just not practical with our work situations. Maybe someday."

Oliver owned an accounting firm in the city, and Joy had started working part-time at a shelter for battered women. They'd moved to London full-time a year ago after Joy's mom had passed away from Alzheimer's. Her dad had decided to stay in Florida, except in the hot summers when he visited them for three or four months at a time.

The trees outside Kara's window swayed in the breeze and the countryside bluffs rolled past. Sheep grazed in a far-off meadow. If Rose had been here, she'd have begged to stop and pet them. Not that Kara would have allowed it—weren't sheep notoriously filthy?—but the thought made her miss her daughter something fierce. She'd never gotten ahold of Jeff last night and would have to find time tonight after Rose was done with school to call. Hopefully this time, he'd answer.

"We're actually about to enter Pendolphin land." Joy turned off the main road and pointed to a stone arch extending over the smaller road they were now on. "You probably remember this from the website, but it's one hundred acres and our guests will have access to the whole place, including the surrounding land."

"It's so beautiful." Trees and seasonal flowers dotted the green landscape. Kara remembered from the map that the estate backed a gorgeous cliffside view of the Atlantic. "Hopefully the snow doesn't keep them from enjoying the outdoors."

"Eh, the snow is usually just a dusting." Joy tapped the steering wheel to an imaginary tune. "Not like the year Sophia got married, and Oliver and I were trapped in London together overnight in a freak snowstorm."

Whoa. "That sounds like quite a story."

Joy's tinkling laughter filled the vehicle. "Not as scandalous as it sounds, but yes. Quite a story indeed." She squinted ahead. "Look. There's the house."

Kara inhaled a sharp breath that got caught in her lungs at the sight before her. A three-story house that rivaled Pemberley in the *Pride & Prejudice* movies sat at the end of a long drive. Its facade was made of gray stone and colonnaded wings of brick, with an array of windows that must let in a lot of whatever light the country sun might afford. At least a half dozen chimneys topped the manor, showcasing the sheer volume of rooms that were visible just from the front. A series of stone steps descended from the large entryway into a graded walkway that led to the lush gardens.

"It's perfect."

"Isn't it?" Joy guided the car up the driveway and parked in a small lot off the side. "And I know you've talked with her a few times, but the coordinator, Meg, is wonderful. She's more than willing to answer any of our questions, and she's been very on the ball with everything I've asked of her so far."

Kara climbed from the vehicle. The air felt somehow crisper

out here—probably something about the countryside. "She seems to be really accommodating and organized."

A few minutes later, when she met Meg for the first time in person, Kara found her first impression to be true. The woman gave them a tour of the house and grounds—all beautiful—and after that was complete, Meg handed Kara a copy of the detailed plan for the upcoming weekend.

Everything seemed to be perfectly in place. All signs pointed to the fact that Kara could relax a bit. That the fundraiser was going to go off without a hitch.

She was tempted to wonder what could go wrong. But that was a question no events coordinator should ever ask.

Besides, in her experience, it was just when life seemed grandest that it turned and slapped a person in the face.

❄

Kara probably should go to bed.

But the licking flames of the fire in the hearth were mesmerizing, especially when combined with the Christmas music lilting across the airwaves from Rebecca's radio up front. Add to that the hot cocoa in the mug currently clutched between Kara's hands, and her life was a gorgeous, pine-scented Christmas commercial.

And yet, she still couldn't fully relax.

Because despite the hours she'd spent this afternoon and evening poring over Meg's binder and finding no discrepancies with her well-crafted plan, Kara couldn't seem to quiet that pesky ball of worry in the pit of her stomach. Ultimately, if anything went wrong with this fundraiser event, it wouldn't be Meg's reputation and career on the line. It would be Kara's.

Not that Sarah would fire her, but Kara would never forgive herself if the fundraiser flopped.

Tomorrow, she'd head back to Pendolphin House to lead the

decoration efforts. But tonight, there was nothing more to be done. She glanced at the clock—eight nineteen. Too late to do anything in town, since most of the shops closed before dinner this time of year. And much as she loved reading, her nerves were too shot to concentrate on anything.

Kara stood, stretched her back, and walked toward the front desk. Maybe talking to Rebecca would ease her tension. The woman had the uncanny ability to make her laugh.

But she wasn't at reception. Perhaps the kitchen …

As Kara swung through the door, she pulled up short at the sight of Rebecca and Warren rolling cookie dough. Warren's cheeks wore a five o'clock shadow and a few dots of flour, and he listened intently while Rebecca bossed him around. The innkeeper rolled her eyes at something Warren said, and he laughed despite her unsmiling demeanor.

This certainly wasn't a sight Kara had expected to see. First, a man like Warren baking, but also, the two of them … together. Could it be their host held some affection for the handsome VP?

Something twisted in Kara's gut at the thought.

Which was ridiculous. Surely Warren had women all over the globe constantly throwing themselves at him. Why should Kara care?

I don't.

Whatever was going on here though, she wasn't going to interrupt. Slowly, she backed out of the kitchen.

But just before she'd fully exited, Rebecca looked up. "Oh good. Are you done working?"

Warren's gaze connected with Kara's, and she hated the way her body responded to the pools of chocolate in his eyes—flushing warm and tingling all over.

She cleared her throat. "Yep. About to head to bed. Just wanted to say good night."

Rebecca shook her head. "Nope, you can't yet." She left her dough on the counter, turned to wash her hands in the sink, and dried them on her apron before turning back to Warren and blinking. "Well, come on. I need your help. Both of you." Then she sprung from the room.

Warren just stood there for a moment, hands still sunk into the dough. "She sure is ... spirited."

"That's one word for it."

A smile touched the corners of his lips. "I guess we should follow her, huh?" He released the dough and cleaned off his hands.

Kara shrugged. "I suppose so."

Warren stepped toward her, but halted—almost like he'd thought better of crowding her. "Sorry." Then he gestured toward the door. "After you."

They left the kitchen, Warren behind her but not close. Why had he apologized? Was he just being thoughtful? Perhaps, given her past, he thought she'd be jumpy around men. And maybe at times she was. But while something about him set her on edge, it wasn't fear—not fear that he'd hurt her, anyway.

She hadn't felt zings of attraction like this since ... well, since Jeff.

And *that's* what scared her.

When they emerged in the living room, Rebecca was nowhere to be found. "Hello?" Kara called.

"In here!" The muffled voice seemed to be coming from a hall closet sitting ajar on the other side of the room.

Kara and Warren made their way over and found Rebecca tugging on a large box, huffing like she had a house to blow down. The woman threw her hands on her hips. "Don't just stand there. Help me!"

Together, the three of them lifted the box and set it down beside the Christmas tree as directed by Rebecca.

"What's inside?" Warren asked, massaging his chin.

Rebecca tugged a box cutter from the back pocket of her jeans like it was the most natural tool to carry around. "Your project for the evening." She sliced the tape and opened the box to reveal holiday ornaments of all shapes and sizes—from dainty bells and lace-encrusted balls to sparkling figurines and vintage-looking candy canes.

Kara pulled loose a tiny snow globe ornament with a bit of snow and a tree tucked inside a clear round shell. "What do you mean, our project?"

"For every group that comes to stay here, I un-decorate the tree and allow them to re-decorate it. It's a tradition Loretta started. And, I don't know, I liked the idea of a fresh start every week." She stared at Kara, her nose scrunched. Then she glanced at Warren, before returning her gaze to Kara. "Well, go on, then. Have at it."

Wait. Suddenly the fire felt warmer than before. "Aren't you going to help?"

"I've got cookies to bake. Besides, it's a tradition for the guests to enjoy. And since you two are my only guests at the moment ..."

Kara felt Warren's eyes on her but couldn't bring herself to look. A few run-ins, that was one thing. But an entire evening, just the two of them, decorating the tree like they were in some cozy Hallmark movie?

Just ... no. "Um, like I said, I was headed for bed."

Rebecca's eyes narrowed. "Fine, I'll make you coffee if you insist. But only so you can stay awake. Tomorrow, we return to tea and only tea." Her petite frame charged from the room once again. Did the woman ever slow down? She was like a train going full steam ahead at all times.

And right now, though she'd left the room, she was steam-rolling Kara.

She leaned against the back of one of the winged chairs, digging her fingers into the *fleur-de-lis*-patterned fabric. How was she going to get out of this without being rude? "Warren ..."

"It's okay." His voice was gentle as he knelt beside the box and began pulling ornaments from inside, arranging them along the stone base that stuck out from the fireplace. "I can do it myself."

There was something dejected in his tone—almost disappointed. No, that couldn't be right. Why would he care if she helped or not?

But before she could really examine his reaction further, her attention snagged on one of the ornaments he'd unearthed. Her breath caught and she surged forward. Kneeling beside Warren, she picked up the ornament and cradled it in her fingers. The tiny glass figurine depicted Santa on a rocking horse.

Her hands shook.

"Everything okay?"

"What?" She glanced up at him, blinked, then looked away again. "Oh, yeah. It's just … I got Rose this exact ornament for her first Christmas. It … it broke."

Or rather, two years later, while decorating their tree as a family—the one and only time they'd done so—Kara had said something careless and Jeff had thrown it at her face. It had fallen and shattered on their wooden floors. Then he'd made her walk barefoot across the broken glass to get the broom and clean it up.

Her heart ratcheted up at the memory.

"You must miss her a lot."

Warren's soft voice contrasted sharply with the remembrance, but it was enough to tug Kara away from that time. Enough to make her want to remake her memory of this ornament into something pleasant.

Surely she could spend one evening making a tree beautiful, even if it meant enduring an hour or two alone with Warren. It beat going back to her room and facing the quiet, which—after that terrifying flashback—was sure to be filled with screams of her past.

So, Kara stood, walked to the tree, and placed the Santa

ornament on one of the branches. "I do miss her. Because of the time difference, finding the right time to connect the last few days has been difficult." In fact, she'd only managed to catch a five-minute call with Rose today because of homework and dinner plans that Jeff had made with his parents.

"What do you miss most?" Warren snagged a few ornaments and moved past Kara to hang them, unaware of how his casual question had stilled Kara in her tracks.

To be honest, every instinct in her body yelled at her to run up the stairs and not come back down until Warren Kensington was nowhere in sight.

But why? He'd only asked a simple question—one that actually showed he cared. That he was interested in her life, even if he was just making simple conversation for conversation's sake.

Was she so screwed up now that she was suspicious of every man's motives in asking about her life?

Or was it more?

Kara forced herself to take up another few ornaments and arrange them on the other side of the tree from where Warren stood fluffing a few branches. Inhaling a breath, she answered his question. "Everything. Her little girl smell. Her smile that can melt the heart of the Scroogiest Grinch. The sweet way she takes my cheeks between her hands and reminds me it's going to be okay."

She paused with an ornament mid-air, nearly choking on the last words as the memories surged fast and sure. "She's had to do that a lot over the last three years." Kara blinked away a few tears. Ugh. Why had she said that? The last thing she wanted to do was talk with Warren about what she'd been through.

All he needed to know was that she was capable of doing the job that the board—and Sarah—had hired her to do. So far, she'd proven her worth. That was all that mattered.

And yet, when the silence grew between them to an uncomfortable degree, she lifted her head to find him watching her. "I'm sorry, Kara."

She shrugged a shoulder. "It's fine. In the past. We're all good now." Turning, she swiped at her eyes before grabbing yet another ornament. "What about you? What are you missing this Christmas?"

Please, please, please let him take the hint. *Move on.*

After a moment, Warren ran a hand through his hair and studied the tree, frowning as he repositioned a few ornaments. "If I were a good son, I'd say my parents."

"I'm sure you're a good son." Shoot. Had that sounded flirty? Kara rushed on. "I mean, you're generally a good person, so ..." Ugh, no. That was worse.

But it was true. Right?

Or was she just being fooled by a handsome face and rich exterior once more?

Then again, had Jeff ever been this ... relaxed? This mellow? This easy to talk to? They'd only ever decorated the tree together the one time, and it was because Kara had begged.

No, looking back, all of her dates with Jeff revolved around public events—chances to show her off as a trophy of sorts. Expensive dinners out. The opera. Fundraisers that started at one thousand dollars a plate. They had never been the couple who sat on the couch after work watching television and eating takeout. He'd been too busy. Too self-absorbed to really see her and what she wanted.

And not that she was perfect, but Kara didn't care about fancy dates. She had just wanted to be with him.

Warren seemed different.

Not that this was a date. And besides, what seemed to be and what were ... those could be two very different things.

Still, when Warren's lips curved into a smile at her compliment, she felt a zip of pleasure all the way to her toes. "Thanks for that, but my parents would probably disagree with you. I never quite seem to live up to their expectations for me."

How could he not? On the outside at least, Warren Kensington was handsome, philanthropic, successful—the whole package. "In what way?"

He rooted inside the box a bit, causing a few ornaments to clink together. "I'm thirty-seven and not married yet, for one." Finally, his hand emerged with a set of stocking ornaments that looked about as old as him. The red fabric was delicately stitched with white and gold threading that read Merry Christmas. Warren ran his finger over the words. "My younger sister fulfilled her duty to the family five years ago, but I've yet to produce an heir to the Kensington name."

"An heir." Kara rolled her eyes. "What is it with rich families and their obsession with carrying on the family name? Jeff was so insistent on having a boy for that very reason. It's not like you're royalty."

Too late, she realized her mistake. Kara covered her mouth with a hand. "Oh, I'm sorry." She shouldn't have criticized Warren's family or social sphere.

Warren stepped closer and Kara couldn't help it—she flinched. Because after a remark like that, Jeff would have backhanded her to next Sunday.

"Hey." The tender word reached out, feathering Kara's cheeks.

When she peeked at Warren, he was close. Still giving her space, but not quite as much as before. She bit her lip. "I shouldn't have said that."

His eyes crinkled at the corners. "Why not? I happen to agree with you."

Her chest loosened. "Really?"

A nod. "I only wish my parents did too. Then maybe they'd lay off their search for my future wife and let me live my life in peace."

She shouldn't ask—it was absolutely none of her business—but Kara couldn't help herself. "So … you don't want to get married?"

He studied her, his gaze skimming her cheeks before meeting her own. "Actually, I'd love nothing more than to have a family to come home to at night. Kids to wrestle with, to read to at bedtime." Warren adjusted an ornament that wasn't crooked. "A wife to partner with. One who wants me for more than …" He paused.

"More than what?"

"Ah, never mind." Shrugging, he gave her a wry smile. "I just haven't found someone worth giving my everything to yet … no one who's willing to give hers in return, anyway."

CHAPTER 5

Had Kara ever known the meaning of the word "tired" before today?

She stepped into Once Upon a Time Bakery and allowed her exhausted muscles to thaw in the heated room filled with patrons. The light of the day had faded a few hours ago, and with the disappearance of the sun had come an unexpected chill. Snow was in the forecast this weekend, but thankfully not until after tomorrow, when her guests would begin arriving.

This was only her second time inside the small bakery, since she'd stopped by once yesterday morning to grab a box of cookies before heading out to Pendolphin House with Joy and Sarah for a day of decorating. Funnily enough, the bakery—with modern yellow-accented decor arranged behind the long counter, large metal whisks that had been made into light fixtures, and gray-and-white, diamond-patterned tile—wasn't exactly Kara's style, but something about the place instantly felt like a piece of home.

That very well could be due to the owner. Sarah's sister, Ginny, had lived in England for nearly a decade but was still American at heart.

"Kara! Welcome back." Ginny waved from behind the cash register, a wide grin on her face as she gestured Kara closer.

Kara should have expected that in a town as small as this, she couldn't simply stop in to grab a late-night coffee without being noticed. Too bad, because all she wanted to do at the moment was snag a hot bath at the B&B and hunker down in her pajamas next to the window in her bedroom—after all, it had been another brutal day of working through details at Pendolphin House.

The rest of the board had arrived a day earlier than the paying guests, and many of them had had questions for Kara. So, she'd spent a large part of her day sequestered in the Pendolphin boardroom outlining not only her plan for this weekend's fundraiser, but also upcoming fundraisers and donor relations efforts that would garner even more donations next year.

And the whole time, she'd tried to ignore the stupid way her heart had skipped a beat every time she'd caught Warren's eye. His words two evenings ago still made the rounds in her head anytime she had two seconds alone: *"I just haven't found someone worth giving my everything to yet ... no one who's willing to give hers in return, anyway."*

Oy. Exhausted was an understatement. But coffee could help with that, so instead of retreating, Kara worked up a smile. "Hey, Ginny. How are things here?"

"Booming, as you can see." Ginny bounced on her toes, her long brown ponytail springing with her movement. "It's as wonderful as chocolate and peanut butter blended together."

Kara couldn't help but laugh. She and Sarah may be sisters, but Ginny's youthful exuberance was quite different than Sarah's more stoic nature. "That is quite wonderful, I must say."

"Isn't it, though?" Ginny cocked her head and tugged on the long sleeves of her Beatles T-shirt. "I still can't believe my life sometimes. I've got my dream job, working next door to my best friend."

Ah yes, Rosebud Books was next to the bakery—in fact, a door between them allowed customers to flow more easily from one business to the other—and the owner was Sophia Rose, who was married to William. They had an almost-three-year-old named Emily and a four-month-old son, Edward. Kara had met them all yesterday when she'd snuck over and spent an hour perusing the bookstore's offerings.

Ginny continued. "And then, I got a second chance at love despite a rocky divorce. Now, Steven and I are in the process of adopting a little girl from London." She sighed, contentment written all over her face. "God has been really good to me."

Something in Kara's heart leaped at hearing Ginny's story—from the pit of devastation to this.

Could that ever be her?

But Ginny had credited God with her happiness. No offense to her, but Kara had to learn to stand on her own, and that meant depending on no one else—especially someone who hadn't answered her prayers in the past.

"Sorry, you didn't come here to hear how great my life is." The bakery owner chuckled. "What can I get for you tonight?"

"Just an americano, please."

Ginny took Kara's payment, then saluted. "Feel free to take a seat. My sister's tucked away in the corner if you need someone to sit with. I'll bring your coffee over when it's ready." Before Kara had a chance to thank her, the brunette turned on her heel and headed for the gleaming espresso machine.

Sarah was here? Kara turned and studied the crowded bakery. Sure enough, there sat her boss behind her laptop, a half-eaten blueberry scone and a teal mug on the table beside her. Kara made her way over. "Still burning the midnight oil?"

Sarah peeked up, smiled. "Always." She shut her laptop, moved it aside, and gestured to the seat across the booth. "Join me?"

"I don't want to interrupt. Just stopped in for a coffee." Kara rubbed the back of her neck where she'd had a crick since waking up this morning.

"You aren't interrupting, but I completely understand if you'd rather head straight back to your room." Sarah tilted her head. "I'd love to hear how your day went if you can spare a few minutes, though."

"Of course." Kara slid into the booth, the coolness of which seeped through her skinny jeans. "Today was great. As you saw yesterday, Meg has everything well in hand. I spent most of my time with the board." She updated Sarah on the details of the day. By the time she was finished, Ginny had dropped off her americano in a ceramic mug.

Oops. She'd forgotten to get it to go. Oh well. Sarah didn't look overly eager to get back to her work. "What about you? How was your day?" She lifted the mug to her lips and sipped. The sweet and bitter combination of the beans and milk toasted her insides.

Sarah gnawed at her bottom lip. "I'm helping Melissa with a tricky case that reminds me a lot of yours." She cocked her head. "Is that okay to tell you? I don't want to make things harder for you. I imagine it's already an emotional time of year."

The concern in her boss's eyes nearly undid Kara, and she gripped the mug with both hands, staring into the dark brew. Yes, December did not bring with it the most pleasant of memories.

There was the fear, of course—once she'd made the decision to leave Jeff, she'd waited until he was out of town and called her sister to come to help her pack and get out of the house.

But then had come the uncertainty, the doubt over whether she'd even done the right thing.

The worry over whether she'd lose Rose.

That's when the nightmares had started.

Sure, over the last few years, they'd tapered off some, but she still woke with fairly regular frequency drenched in sweat, her heart running a marathon, wondering if she'd screamed out loud the same way she'd been screaming in her dream.

Kara cleared her throat. "I'm fine. Sorry you're dealing with such a hard case."

"I just wish I could do more, you know?"

"More? Sarah, you've dedicated your whole life to helping women like me get out of bad situations." She'd *saved* Kara. "What more could you possibly do?"

Sharp, loud laughter rose from the table next to them—two older women having a grand old time, from the sound of it.

Sarah waited until they quieted to say anything. "It just never feels like enough."

Behind Kara, the bell over the door jangled. At the noise, Sarah glanced up and her frown quickly turned into a grin. She waved. "Michael! Warren!"

Warren was here? Kara couldn't help but sink a little lower into her seat as she white-knuckled her mug.

Sarah noticed the movement and narrowed her gaze. "What's wrong?"

"Nothing." Kara inwardly groaned at the crack in her voice. *Please don't ask again.*

But Sarah was a lawyer—she didn't let stuff go. The woman placed her elbows on the table and leaned forward, lowering her voice. "Is something going on between you and Warren?"

"What? No!" Kara peeked around the corner of the booth. Michael, whose unruly brown curls were stuck underneath a beanie, and Warren were chatting with Ginny at the counter. Kara had a minute, maybe two, before they made their way over here. What excuse could she give for leaving when they did?

Being tired was always a good reason—and true. The problem was, if she said she needed to go, Warren might try to be chivalrous and escort her home. Then there would be an awkward few moments of being alone with him—moments she'd need to fill with conversation.

And for some reason, conversation with Warren tended to get serious quickly. Could she really afford another evening of delving into matters of the heart with him?

Sarah studied her, one eyebrow raised. "I dated Warren once upon a time, you know."

Kara's mouth fell open. That was definitely not what she'd expected to hear. "What? When? Why?"

"Colonel Mustard in the library with the wrench." Sarah's lips twisted into a wry grin. "Sorry, it just suddenly felt like we were playing Clue."

Kara allowed herself a laugh. "Ha ha."

"Anyway, Warren and I went out on a few dates three years ago. He even followed me out here when I came for a visit to make amends with Ginny. A grand gesture of sorts."

Oh, right. The month-long trip Sarah had taken just after Kara had left Jeff. She nodded. "What happened?"

"Michael did." Now Sarah looked past Kara, presumably at her husband, who must still be ordering something and talking with his sister-in-law. "Once we met, my heart belonged to him, no matter how good of a guy Warren was."

She paused, returning her focus to Kara. "And he *is* a good guy, Kara. I'd trust him with my life. In fact ..." Sarah shook her head. "Suffice it to say that New Dawn wouldn't have survived without him. He's one of the good ones. So, if you were ever interested—"

"I'm not." Kara swigged her coffee, the liquid—and the lie—burning a trail down her throat.

"Okay, okay. I get it. You've been hurt. Majorly. No one would blame you for not trusting easily again." Her boss reached out, patted Kara's hand. "But I'm just saying. If—hopefully when—you decide you are ready to get back out there, you can't do better than Warren Kensington."

Before Kara could respond, the man himself—and Michael, a gregarious smile on his face—sauntered up, mugs in hand. They both greeted the women warmly and asked if they could join them.

Sarah glanced at Kara. "Did you still need to get home?"

Bless her. She was giving Kara an easy out.

But something about their conversation niggled, making Kara not quite as anxious to retreat to her lonely room. She may have trouble trusting men, but she trusted Sarah more than anyone in her life, save her sister. And if Sarah said Warren was a good guy …

Besides, staying didn't mean Kara was opening her heart to a relationship. Staying merely meant she was open to good conversations with friends.

Old friends … and new ones too.

She chewed the inside of her cheek before shaking her head. "I can stay for a bit." Then she slid over, finally peeking up at Warren. "Sit if you'd like."

And his responding smile was like coming out of the cold and into a cozy, heated room with a fire crackling in the corner.

Kara only prayed that she wouldn't get burned.

CHAPTER 6

The first guest could arrive at any moment.

Kara paced the entryway of Pendolphin House, which served as a foyer of sorts. A large registration desk sat in front of a paneled wall, nestled between two sweeping staircases that led to the second and third stories of the manor. Thick brocade rugs in deep maroons and golds adorned the wood floors and lent a certain luxury to the place. Everywhere Kara looked, there seemed to be some nook or cranny that held a treasure from the past—portraits of men and women long gone, vases with flowers frozen in time, old wing-backed chairs with faded fabric.

The guest rooms were equally as elegant, with beds that featured rosewood canopy beds and matching bedside tables, dressing tables with curved mirrors, and chests of drawers. Even Kara's room—a tiny space tucked away in the servants' quarters—was adorable with its pale green floral-patterned wallpaper and lacy coverlet. Of course, she'd been sad to leave Rebecca's behind, but it made much more sense for her to stay here in case one of the guests needed something that she could help with. Besides, she'd get to return to Rebecca's after the fundraiser ended, now that she'd decided to stay through Christmas. Last night, Sarah and company had convinced her.

And her decision had absolutely nothing to do with the fact Warren was also staying on through Christmas.

Nothing.

"Ma'am, I really do have this handled if you want to relax." Gwen, a twenty-something who worked for Meg at Pendolphin House, arched a thinly plucked eyebrow Kara's direction—specifically, at the way her heels were probably wearing a path in the old floorboards.

Kara withheld a sigh and smiled instead. "Of course you do." After all, Meg seemed confident in Gwen's abilities to get everyone checked in just fine, and the woman hadn't let Kara down yet. "I'm just here to help if you need me."

She hoped her presence would lend even more credence to New Dawn's cause. Donors liked to feel welcomed, special. And this wasn't just some five-course fundraising dinner they'd committed themselves to. No, this was an entire weekend. It was imperative that these guests be wooed and kept—that they loved the experience so much they told all of their friends about it and encouraged them to become donors too.

A lot more was riding on this than Gwen knew, so Kara would stay right here, thank you very much.

The rumble of a car engine emanated from outside. Someone was here. Kara's insides tightened as she stopped her pacing, hurried to the staircase, and tried to stand casually next to it. There went the lift in Gwen's eyebrow again as she no doubt had some thought about crazy Americans. Before Kara could think of something to say to lighten the mood between them, the large dark front door swung open.

Showtime.

In walked Warren, looking somewhat windswept as he rolled a small suitcase behind him and slid off his overcoat. He caught sight of her and flashed her a dimpled grin. "Afternoon."

"Hi." Kara's stupid voice chose that moment to squeak as if she were in junior high.

But honestly. A man really had no right looking that handsome.

What? No, no, no. Kara's cheeks burned at the thought—but maybe it was natural, this attraction. After all, he was a good guy. Sarah's ringing endorsement and everything Kara had witnessed said as much.

And that goodness made him all the more attractive.

Even now, as he checked into his room, he treated Gwen with the utmost respect—friendly but not flirtatious.

And last night, they'd spent a few hours chatting with Sarah and Michael about everything from work and New Dawn to their favorite vacation spots to kids. Warren had entertained them with stories of his nephew and niece and his escapades in changing a diaper for the first time when babysitting last year.

But she didn't have time to think any more warm—and slightly uncomfortable—thoughts about Warren, because another couple swooped in while Gwen was helping him. Kara moved forward to assist the woman with her bag. Didn't they have a bellhop here? She thought she'd seen one, but he didn't seem to be at his station. "Let me get that."

"Oh, thank you, dear." The woman appeared to be in her sixties or seventies, her refined white hair perfectly styled and coiffed. From her head to her Louboutin-ed toes, she oozed money. "The traffic from London was simply atrocious, and on a Thursday, no less. But we are here now and oh so happy to have a weekend away."

The man standing beside her didn't reply to his wife's chatter—just frowned and wiggled his gray mustache. Then, "How long does it take to get checked in around here?" His impatient British accent filled the space despite the high ceiling.

Out of the corner of her eye, Kara saw Gwen stiffen. Thankfully, though, Meg had trained her employee well because she didn't lash out or say anything, really. She simply kept helping Warren, detailing the week's events and where to find the manor's restaurant.

Hopefully Kara could smooth any ruffled feathers before the grumbling got worse. She surged forward, hand outstretched. "I'm Kara Gentry, the special events coordinator for New Dawn."

The man stared at her hand for a moment before shaking it. "What's New Dawn?"

His wife rolled her eyes. "It's the charity we're here to support, you oaf."

"I thought you dragged me out here to celebrate our anniversary."

"I'm not sure it's worth celebrating after all." The woman turned her nose in the air.

Well, this was devolving quickly. Kara cleared her throat. "I'm sorry, I didn't catch your names."

"Robert and Bobbi Clyde, dear." The woman shot her husband a "be nice" glare before taking Kara's hand between her own. Her skin was cold, her fingers adorned with several rings, including a monstrosity that had to be at least three carats.

Despite the man's poor behavior, these were exactly the sort of people Kara needed here. They had deep pockets and were willing to give some of their money to charity. But his mannerisms—the superiority, the rudeness—reminded Kara of why she was glad to no longer be part of the upper echelons of society, at least in her personal life.

And Warren … well, this was his world.

Which was one big reason to stop the line of thinking that might lead her to consider him as anything other than the president of her workplace's board of directors. And, fine, maybe as a friend.

She could do friendship, right?

Kara snuck a glance at him as he grabbed his room key from

Gwen and turned her way, the gleam of his glasses catching the light and his chiseled jaw looking as rock-solid as ever.

Friends. Right.

Maybe?

He approached. "Did I hear you say you're the Clydes?"

The man seemed to puff out his chest a bit. "Depends. Who's asking?"

"Warren Kensington, sir."

Robert harrumphed. "I believe your father and I went to school together." But there seemed to be a crack in his defenses. Unbelievable, the connections that a Bostonian had across the pond—all because they belonged to the same social class.

"They did. He has told me many a story of your antics together. And how smart you are."

"Yes, well." Robert finally took Warren's hand and pumped it up and down.

Warren turned to Bobbi, reaching for her hand and kissing it. "It's a pleasure to finally meet you, ma'am."

She giggled. "Oh, the pleasure is all ours."

"Indeed." Stroking his mustache, Robert nodded. "We should chat more. I'd love to hear what your father has been up to these days."

Kara had been all but forgotten—probably as it should be. She took a few steps back. Another couple had walked in the front door and were headed for the registration desk, anyway.

Warren continued. "Let's get you both checked in and situated, and then I'd love to talk." He glanced at Kara. "Kara, won't you join us? I'm sure the Clydes would love to hear all about New Dawn and how their contributions have helped countless women in horrific circumstances."

The sincerity in his tone, the light in his eyes, the smile on his lips … he was helping her do what she couldn't on her own. And while she hated that she needed an "in" in the first place, she also couldn't help smiling in return, expressing her gratitude with a mouthed "thank you" when the Clydes weren't looking.

And then, Warren winked at her—and her knees felt like those of a baby giraffe, just born, not knowing how it had gotten there.

Friends, Kara. Just friends.

Oh, goodness. She was in trouble.

The Clydes smiled and agreed to Warren's proposition, so he helped them get checked in while Kara greeted the fresh influx of guests. Gwen was swamped but handling it like a pro, so Kara wandered to the expansive kitchen and prepped some Earl Grey tea, which she placed on an adorable platter along with some "biscuits"—also known as cookies in the United States.

Then she made her way to the lobby-slash-library, where Warren sat with the Clydes. Kara set the tea tray onto the coffee table and placed a hand against her chest as she took in the sights around her. How had she missed the grandeur of this room on her tour? She must have been so caught up in the details of the event that she hadn't noticed the painted teal walls, the sparkling chandelier overhead, the cozy-looking settees and couches and chairs, the adorably Victorian fireplace—and the rows and rows of dusty old books.

The *Beauty and the Beast*-loving girl in her—who had envied Belle her library—wanted to squeal.

Of course, Kara was much too distinguished for that, so she tamped down her inner enthusiasm and turned to the guests with a smile as she lowered herself into a chair beside Warren. "I brought some tea to warm you up. It's getting chilly outside."

"Thank you, dear. How thoughtful." Bobbi's smile was genuine enough, despite her grumpy husband. Although, actually, the lines of the man's face had seemed to ease here among the books. Perhaps he was merely uncomfortable in new places, in crowds, in awkward social situations.

She could at least give him the benefit of the doubt. Not

everyone was like Jeff, after all—Warren least of all. He proved that much when he leaned forward and helped pour the tea. Their hands brushed and Kara sucked in a sharp breath at the contact, but Warren didn't seem to notice. He just kept chatting up the Clydes, keeping their conversation light, airy, comfortable.

He seemed to have that happy knack with everyone, didn't he? But it wasn't smarmy or slick, like Jeff, who was always looking to gain an advantage in the conversation. Warren seemed genuinely interested in others and their lives.

It was a welcome—albeit confusing—quality to observe in someone.

"Kara, I've told the Clydes a little about New Dawn, but I think you could probably do it more justice."

The warm look in her new friend's eyes once more stole her breath and made her mouth go dry, but she pushed past the discomfort. For the next half hour, she detailed the work they did at New Dawn—even hinting at her own story. Mr. Clyde remained quite silent, while his wife murmured and hmmed at several points.

When Kara sat back in her chair and took a sip of her tepid tea, Mr. Clyde finally spoke. "Well, young lady, I must confess that you've moved the heart of this old codger. I'd like nothing more than to give an extra donation to your worthy cause."

And when he named the amount, Kara nearly fell out of her chair. "Sir, you have no idea how many women you will be helping." Tears stung the backs of her eyes. "Thank you."

"Now, now." Robert stood. "Bobbi, my old bones need a rest in our room. Are you coming?"

His wife stood and patted his arm. "You old coot. Of course I am." Then they shuffled out of the room.

Kara shook her head as she watched them go. "That was … incredible." Biting her lip, she glanced at Warren. "Thank you."

"Hey." He held up his hands. "That was all you. You convinced them to donate."

"You got my foot in the door."

"We make a good team, then." He cocked his head, pausing, as if he wanted to say more.

Kara's heart picked up. Did she want to hear it? She glanced away, toward the fireplace, which was void of fire. Cold.

Thankfully, before she was forced to make a decision for better or worse, Gwen swept into the room. "Ms. Gentry, we have a problem, and I can't get ahold of Meg." The woman's voice was tight, unsure for the first time since Kara had met her.

"Call me Kara. And breathe, Gwen." Kara jumped up and met her halfway, snagging her hand and squeezing. "What's going on?"

"The Chestertons showed up wanting an extra room for their friends—the Galbraiths, I believe. They were sure we could accommodate them despite not having a reservation." Gwen leaned in. "But when I tried explaining that all the guest rooms are taken, you'd have thought I'd murdered their best friend. The looks I got ..."

Kara's stomach twisted. The Chestertons were huge donors —one of their first supporting families for the London office. They couldn't afford to upset them. She pushed her fingers against her temples and paced. "Think, think." There had to be a solution.

Was it just her, or had the heater kicked on? Her silk blouse clung to her back, which was beginning to sweat.

"Might I make a suggestion?"

She halted and looked at Warren, who was now standing. "You've already rescued me once today." Which she hated in a way—what must he think of her ability to do this job?

But he just ribbed her slightly with his elbow and smiled. Then he faced Gwen. "Are there any other rooms in the servants' quarters?"

"Yes ..." Gwen's hesitation was clear.

And for good reason. Kara shook her head. "We cannot put the Chestertons' friends in an attic bedroom. For one thing, a double bed is much too small for a couple. And there's a fireplace, but it's still a bit on the chilly side up there."

"That's true. And the furnishings are more plain since we don't regularly rent those rooms out," Gwen added. "It's just the staff who uses them."

Warren chuckled. "I wasn't proposing we stick the Galbraiths up there. If it's the Galbraiths I know, that would never work. Let's just say they're used to the finer things." His eyebrows waggled as he touched the side of his nose.

"Then what *are* you saying?" Kara asked.

"Give them my room and I'll stay in the attic. Simple as that."

"Warren ..." She frowned. "We couldn't ask you to do that."

He shrugged. "You're not asking. I'm volunteering. I don't need much. Just somewhere to lay my head and plug in my electronics."

One thing was certain—Jeff would *never* offer to give up his room for the good of the charity or someone else.

No, make that two things. Kara was also certain that she shouldn't be comparing Jeff and Warren. That would mean she was looking at Warren as more than a friend.

As a ... possibility. For more.

And well, that might just spell disaster. She'd trusted a rich man before, and her heart had been broken. Even if Warren and Jeff were different—she could now admit that Warren was not someone who was likely to abuse her—how did she know that he wouldn't betray her trust in some other way?

No, remaining single was just ... better. Easier.

But as she followed Gwen out of the room to sort out the mess up front, Kara couldn't help but wonder if her definition of "easy" would someday bring her heartache of a different kind.

One minute, Kara was back there—in *his* house.

Cowering in the corner.

Begging him to stop.

Pleading with him to return to the man she'd fallen in love with.

The next, she was jolting upright in bed, her hair clinging to the back of her neck, a scream reverberating through the still night.

Kara's heart clattered around in her chest. Would these nightmares ever go away? It was something she and her therapist were slowly working on, but there were no easy answers.

A knock on her door nearly had her crying out again. "Kara?" It was just one word, but she couldn't miss the care in Warren's voice. Now that his room was next to hers, she must have woken him with her screaming. Thankfully, they were the only two staying on this floor of the house. She prayed that meant no one else had been disturbed.

Kara climbed from her bed, wincing when her bare feet touched the cold floor. She pulled her sweatshirt on over her pajamas—a PTA T-shirt and pale pink lounge pants—before pattering to the door.

Warren stood there in the same white shirt and sweatpants she'd seen him in the other morning at Rebecca's. The moonlight streaming through one of the upper-floor hallway windows revealed that he was squinting at her. "Hey." Despite his lack of eyewear, he peeked into her room, scanning it as if looking for intruders. "You okay?" His voice was on the breathless side.

"I'm fine." Kara snagged a strand of hair and tugged on it, smoothing it with her thumb and forefinger. No doubt she looked less than gorgeous with her tangled mane, smudged mascara she'd forgotten to remove last night, and baggy clothing. Jeff had joked more than once that he didn't recognize her in the morning before she put on her face. "Sorry to wake you up. Just a nightmare."

Warren's jaw flexed at her answer. Sticking his hands into the pockets of his sweatpants, he leaned against the door frame. "Do you get those often?"

To admit her weakness or not? That was the question. But there had always been something mystical about nighttime—for some reason, it was easier to talk about things. Easier to be vulnerable.

Easier to forget that, in the light of day, a person had to live with the consequences of opening up.

Still, despite her better judgment, Kara found herself wanting to answer him honestly. "More than I'd like."

He waited for a few beats before saying more. "I don't know about you, but I'm fully awake now. How about some hot chocolate or tea to calm our nerves?"

Clearly Warren was just being kind, but he was right—there was no going back to sleep right now. And a hot drink did sound tempting …

So did spending time with Warren.

But what about the resolution she'd made earlier this evening to stay single?

He's not asking you to marry him, silly. Just to get something to drink.

Right. She was thirty-eight years old. A mom. Not some young ingenue obsessed with the idea of love. She could have a drink—and a non-alcoholic one, at that—with a man without losing her self-control. "Hot chocolate sounds nice. Thanks."

"Let me just go get my glasses. Be right back."

"I'll meet you in the kitchen."

"No, no. You've worked hard all day. Let me get the drinks, then I'll bring them to the library. Deal?"

Kara bit her bottom lip to hide her smile. "All right." Even though she definitely didn't need it, it felt nice to have someone take care of her. As he strode down the hall toward his room, Kara grabbed her room key and headed for the stairs.

The rest of the guests were tucked away in their rooms, likely sleeping hard after a day of travel, a delicious buffet dinner served in the dining room, and an evening of cocktails and cards in the drawing room. As Kara had made the rounds, it'd seemed like many people already knew each other—again, not surprising given their status and the fact most of them lived in London. Some, however, hailed from Scotland, Ireland, and Wales, and one couple had come all the way from Paris. The conversation had been lively and friendly, and many of those in attendance took the time to talk with Kara about their passion for New Dawn's mission—a conversation led primarily by Bobbi Clyde.

Now, the library was quiet and dark as Kara entered. Instead of illuminating the chandelier, she allowed the moon and the hall light to be enough as she made her way to the fireplace she'd admired earlier. Feeling along the wall, she found the switch and flipped it to ignite the gas fire. Pendolphin House may appear to be a complete step back in time, but thankfully it had been upgraded in a few ways.

Kara settled into one of the chairs facing the fire and breathed in the scent of old books all around her, allowing the hidden words in the stories to penetrate her spirit, to bolster her.

There were times that she felt she'd moved past what Jeff had done to her. Other times—like right now—she wondered if she'd always be a little bit broken.

And no man could ever want someone like that. Especially a man like Warren Kensington, a guy with the world at his fingertips. Someone who could have any woman he desired.

Not that it mattered. They were friends. And the comfort

and hot chocolate? He was just being sweet to her. Didn't mean he was sweet *on* her.

"Here we go." The man in question emerged from behind Kara, two mugs in hand. Gently, he set one on the side table between their chairs, then lowered himself into the other wingback without spilling a drop.

"Thanks." Taking the offered mug, she sipped—and nearly groaned with delight. "This is wonderful."

"You like it?"

"Who wouldn't?" The liquid chocolate was like a gorgeous warm river of silk flowing down her throat. "Did you make this or was the baker in the kitchen?" She'd heard that the woman who made the pastries and bread for the house kept early hours, so perhaps that explained the total divinity in her mug.

Warren cleared his throat. "I did. It was my grandmother's recipe, and luckily the kitchen had everything I needed."

"You keep surprising me." Her words came out low and throaty, which was not her intention. But they were true.

Warren's eyebrows arched over his glasses. "Really? How so?" A chunk of his hair—normally so styled and in place—stuck out behind his ear.

Kara's hand itched to tamp it down, but she held fast to the handle of her mug instead. "I don't know. Most guys who can afford a cook are happy to let the staff handle all food preparation. Why do for yourself what you can pay someone else to do? That's always been Jeff's motto, anyway." She shrugged and sipped her drink again.

"No offense, Kara, but I hope you know that I'm nothing like your good-for-nothing ex-husband."

Mid-sip, she choked a bit. Her cheeks warm, she glanced up at Warren, who was staring at her so intently, she had to look away. The flames of the fire flicked and undulated in front of her, an unsteady rhythm to their dance. "That's not what I meant."

"It kind of sounds like you did." His gentle tone didn't keep her from feeling the admonishment in his words. No, not admonishment.

Hurt.

But still she couldn't face him. "I just …" Her lip trembled. "I've spent a lot of time in your world, but I never really belonged."

"Why do you say that?"

"Jeff never knew this about me, but I grew up poor. Like, really poor." And why was she telling Warren this? But once she'd started, the story rolled from her lips. "When I was twelve, my mom ended up dating and marrying a man she worked for. He was on the wealthy side—not as rich as Jeff, but well off."

Tom had been a smooth talker. So smooth that Kara had believed him when he'd denied cheating on her mother. Denied calling her terrible names. Denied lying to all of them.

Kara took another drink, remembering how unstable her life had been growing up. How she'd craved safety. Security.

How she'd sought it in all the wrong places.

First, in her stepdad, who had showered her with fatherly affection she'd never had before.

Then, in a man like Jeff Gentry.

Both men had ended up liars. Frauds. Betrayers of the worst kind.

"But Tom abandoned us after our mom died." For whatever reason, after her mother's death, he'd written both Kara and Cindy out of his will, leaving every penny of his money to a son from his first marriage. Thankfully, Cindy had already married Travis, and Kara had started working after college, so they didn't need his money. But the fact he hadn't even thought to provide for them still stung.

Kara cleared her throat. "So it was up to me to forge a new path on my own. No one had to know my true past. I'd risen from 'trailer trash' to the step-daughter of a wealthy man, and I got really good at pretending I belonged. When I met Jeff at a charity event my firm had sent me to, he saw my poise, knew my former association with my stepdad, and just assumed that's who I was. And I didn't contradict him." She huffed out a breath. "I openly lived a lie because I was too afraid to tell people the truth of where I'd come from."

"Not sure I'd call that a lie, per se," Warren said. "People put so much emphasis on class, but what really matters is who you are on the inside."

She blinked, the fire almost blinding in its stark brightness against the dark wisps of night. "You're right, of course. It wasn't necessarily the fact that I had *been* poor, more that I was ashamed of it. I thought it made me less worthy of love, like I had to work ten times harder to be seen, to succeed, to find a man who thought I was special."

There she went again, being a Chatty Cathy. Goodness. What was with her tonight?

Other than her therapist and Cindy, Kara had never said any of this to … anyone. So why Warren? Why now? She swallowed, hard, and gathered the courage to look at him again. "I was so desperate to be loved that I let myself fall for a monster. Not that I knew who he was at first. But six months into our marriage, it was clear that I wasn't the only one who had been hiding a part of myself away."

"I'm sorry, Kara." His lips twisted into a deep frown. "I really can't even imagine what that must have been like. And I'm sorry he hurt you. But look at you. You are here, and you're surviving."

"But I'm not thriving." The truth of it nearly strangled her. "And I want that more than anything."

"You'll get there."

"How can you be so sure?" She scooted forward in her chair, whispering the words, a plea for him to reveal a bit of truth she'd somehow missed.

"Because you're brave. Anyone who has endured what you have and is still standing, still fighting … that's a woman I'm proud to know." He paused. "A woman I'm proud to … be friends with."

Friends. Right.

Kara swiped at invisible tears. She took another swig of the chocolate, now significantly cooled but no less tasty. Time to change the subject. "What about you? How did you get involved with New Dawn?"

Warren rubbed the back of his neck. "I've always had a soft spot for charities that helped battered women and children. My grandfather was a hard man who abused my grandmother."

"Oh, I'm sorry."

He nodded, his lips in a straight line. "She lived with it for a long time and didn't tell her story until he'd died. But she shouldn't have had to live with it at all." When he looked at her, there was something apologetic in his gaze. "None of you should."

She couldn't speak. Could only swallow.

And suddenly she realized they were both leaning across the arms of their chairs. If she came two more inches, if he did, then they'd be in each other's space.

Close enough to kiss.

If she wanted to.

The air between them shifted. Something pulsed and moved and breathed—something Kara hadn't felt in oh so long.

Hope.

Anticipation.

The wonder of what could be.

But those were dangerous for a woman like her—because hope led places she wasn't sure she could ever go again.

Kara cleared her throat and sat back against the opposite arm of her chair, as far away from Warren as she could get without leaving her seat. "That explains your passion for New

Dawn's work, but not how you got involved with them specifically." A pause. "Sarah said something about New Dawn not surviving without you. What did she mean?"

"Oh." He shrugged and placed his mug on the side table. "Sarah's exaggerating. With a determined woman like her in charge, it would have survived with or without me."

"Okay, but still. What made you get involved—and not just as a donor, but the president of the board?"

Shifting in his seat, Warren scraped a hand through his unruly hair. Was he nervous? But why? "You."

Oh. "Me?"

"Or rather, your case. Sarah's father said if she didn't drop it, he would cut off his sizable donation. Apparently Jeff was a good friend of his."

Kara gasped. "What?"

Warren nodded. "Of course, Sarah refused, but she was worried about New Dawn surviving without his purse strings."

"I never meant to cause so much trouble." She'd just been desperate, with nowhere else to turn.

"Kara." He waited until their eyes met again. "You've never been trouble, okay? If anything, you spurred me into action. I'd seen you from afar, admired all you did for the charity events community, and when I heard that your husband was hurting you ..." Warren gripped the side of his chair. "I felt so helpless, Kara. Here was a guy I knew hurting someone—his wife, no less —and there were other men in my circle keeping quiet about it. Rallying around him like a good old boy, determined to 'protect their own.' Frankly, it still makes me sick just thinking about it."

Oh, Warren. "You didn't have to—"

"I did." Even in the dim light, she saw the flash in his eyes. Of determination—and something else. "I may have been born into a wealthy family, but that does not get to dictate the kind of man I am. That day, when I saw Sarah's passion for you, for survivors like you, I knew that I could do something too—even if it was just giving my money. I have plenty of it. Why not use it for something that changes people's lives in a tangible way?"

His words … beautiful.

But Kara had to turn away. Had to get out of here. Now.

Because hope was doing a pesky tap dance on her heart—and Kara had the strongest urge to throw open the doors. She was becoming weaker and weaker to Warren Kensington's charms.

And in this moment, with the moonlight making memories hazy, she couldn't remember exactly why that was a bad thing.

CHAPTER 7

"Excuse me, dear."

Kara turned from her place behind the registration desk to find a regal-looking elderly British woman—maybe in her eighties—next to a younger woman. Mrs. Doyle and her granddaughter, if memory served.

Gwen had run off for a few minutes to the restroom, leaving Kara to direct guests to their Friday evening activities. "Yes? How may I help you?"

The younger woman stepped forward. "We saw in the brochure you provided that tonight there's a Winter Walk in the village." She pushed a strand of auburn hair behind her ear, exposing a diamond earring, a funny contrast with her jeans and leather jacket. "Can you tell us more about that?"

"Of course." Kara had been fielding questions about the walk all day long, so the details came easily to her mind. "The Winter Walk is rather new. Several business owners in town decided it would be a fun way to gather everyone together the weekend before Christmas. They've strung lights all over town and are keeping the shops open later than usual."

"Oh, fabulous. We haven't quite finished our Christmas

shopping, have we, Jayne?" Mrs. Doyle winked at her granddaughter, who bit her lip shyly and shook her head.

Kara smiled. What a lovely pair of women. "You'll also want to stop by the tree lighting ceremony at seven. It will take place in the community park just off Fifth and High Street, and the local bakery is providing free treats and hot cider for everyone."

"Sounds magical." Sighing, the younger woman patted her grandma's hand. "I think we should go, don't you, Gran?"

"I do, if I can stay awake that late." Together, they laughed and shuffled off after thanking Kara.

Ensuring that no one else needed her, Kara turned back to her phone. After a quick chat with Rose—who was supposed to leave for her cruise in two days—she'd been texting with Cindy. Her sister's latest text had left Kara wondering how to best answer it.

Cindy: So, how much of Warren Kensington are you seeing?

Too much.

Was that an answer? Yes, but it would spark all kinds of extra questions that Kara wasn't ready to answer. Biting her lip, she set the phone back down.

The bell on the counter rang and Kara's hand flew to her chest as she swiveled.

Warren stood there, a sheepish grin on his lips. "Didn't mean to startle you."

Kara lowered her hand and straightened her shoulders, praying she looked nonchalant—and not guilty for the previous line of her thoughts. "You didn't."

After their talk last night—this morning?—she'd mostly avoided him today. But Kara couldn't forget the way he'd walked her to her room, leaned against the door frame once more, and whispered good night without a single attempt to kiss her.

She also couldn't forget the sinking in her stomach at the realization that she kind of wished he had tried.

Ugh. Why couldn't she get a grip on her stupid emotions?

Before Warren could answer, several groups of people worked their way toward the front door, chattering loudly. She gave a quick glimpse at the clock. Six already? The day had flown by, but that's what happened when running an event. Thankfully, all the details seemed to be taken care of for tomorrow night's ball—all that she could handle for now, anyway. Tomorrow was another story. Once all the vendors arrived, she and Meg would be busy bees.

Warren placed his elbows on the counter and leaned forward, glimpsing the brochure Kara had distributed to the guests. "So, this Winter Walk ... is it new?"

She nodded. "I heard Ginny wanted to mimic something they do in Nantucket, although on a much smaller scale. I guess she grew up going there a bunch as a kid."

"Oh, yeah. That's actually where our families met. We vacationed there every summer."

Of course they had. Kara couldn't even imagine that kind of childhood. Until Mom had married Tom, Kara's summers had consisted of days watching TV at home or reading in the far corners of the public library alone while her mother and Cindy worked.

But that wasn't Warren's fault. Besides, those summer days had grown Kara's love of books, which had served as an escape during her marriage to Jeff.

Kara shook off the memories and returned her focus to the conversation at hand. "Anyway, Ginny and Sophia started the Winter Walk two years ago hoping it would bring in extra tourists from the surrounding villages and beyond. The restaurants and shops are offering discounts all weekend long and staying open later than usual. Since Joy is such good friends with Sophia, she suggested that we coordinate our fundraiser with the timing of the walk so our guests would have something extra special to do in town."

"That was very smart of you." Warren quirked an eyebrow. "I'm surprised you haven't left yet. The tree lighting begins soon."

"Oh, I'm not going." Or, she hadn't planned to. She'd been positive that she would be up until the wee hours of the morning prepping for the ball. But Meg's supreme efficiency had caught her off guard.

"Really?" Frowning, Warren swept his gaze around the entryway. "Seems to me there's not much left for you to do here."

Was it her imagination, or did it seem like he wanted her to go?

But she shouldn't. Right? Thankfully, she still had one excuse that would keep her from having to make a real decision. "Oh, well, Gwen needs me to help work the desk, so ..."

Of course, the woman chose that moment to round the corner, a huge smile on her face when she saw Warren. "How's my favorite guest doing tonight?"

"I'm fine, Gwen. And you?"

"I'd be better if I could get out of here and join you all at the tree lighting." She gave a sigh. "It sounds so romantic. Speaking of, why haven't the two of you left yet? You're going together, right?"

"What?" Kara choked on the word. Why was everyone—Cindy, Sarah, and now Gwen—trying to push her toward Warren? They were from different worlds, and he could never understand hers.

But a quick peek at him, and all her hot air deflated. It made sense. Warren was a good man. The fact he hadn't tried to kiss her last night—or find other ways to take advantage of her vulnerability—spoke to that. Or perhaps he genuinely wasn't interested in her like that.

Even though there were moments ...

But whatever he felt, she couldn't deny it any longer.

Part of *her* was interested—the part that wasn't terrified he'd end up betraying her too.

And that part was starting to shout louder than the fear.

But it had been so long since she'd dated. Since she'd even considered dating. Although, going to a tree lighting ceremony —where the entire town, and her friends would be—wasn't really considered a date anyway, right? So maybe …

Kara squinted at Warren, who watched her closely. "When are you leaving?"

A huge grin found its way across his lips. "Want a ride?"

"I'd need to change first." Her dress pants and heels would hardly make for a comfortable time walking around town.

"I'll wait here."

"All right." Kara nodded at Gwen, who snuck a wink at her, then walked to the staircase. When she was out of everyone's sight, she hauled booty up the stairs to her room and tore open her suitcase. She didn't have much time to decide, so she went with her instincts—a pair of skinny jeans, knee-high leather boots, and a red sweater with a matching scarf.

As quickly as possible, she reapplied some mascara and lip gloss, then gave her sadly flat hair an upside-down shake and threw on her coat over it all.

There. Done. This wasn't a big deal. Just a tree lighting ceremony. In public. It was completely safe.

Not. A. Big. Deal.

But she couldn't fool herself—her insides were shaking.

Employing a few breathing techniques that her therapist had taught her, Kara looked in the mirror and spoke truths to herself—ones she mostly believed.

Some of the time.

Maybe.

Regardless. "Kara Gentry, you are smart. You are beautiful. You are worthy." Her voice wobbled over each word, but she kept going. "No man can give you the validation you seek.

And you don't need it anyway. Your worth comes from elsewhere."

Satisfied, she punched out a text to Cindy—*Miss you! Let's chat soon.*—and headed back downstairs where Warren sat on his phone in the corner of the entryway.

When he glanced up, his entire face—which had been scrunched in concentration—relaxed. He stuffed his phone into his pocket and stood. "You look great, Kara."

"Thanks. You too." She tried to keep from biting her lip, but wasn't successful. "Ready to go?"

"Let's do it."

They both waved to Gwen and headed out to the parking lot, where Warren walked them to a black SUV. It wasn't anything fancy, just sturdy and well built.

Kind of like Warren.

Oh, goodness. She had it bad.

Like the true gentleman he was, Warren opened Kara's door for her, then rounded the vehicle and climbed in on the other side. He cranked the heat. "It's supposed to snow tonight or tomorrow."

"I know." She held her hands up to the vents, but pulled them back when cool air blew out for the first few seconds. "I've been stalking the weather reports, afraid that the snow will keep people from coming to the ball."

"Oh, are more coming in? I assumed it was just the Pendolphin House guests who were attending." Warren aimed the SUV down the house's long driveway, heading for Port Willis.

"Yes, there are about fifty more donors coming tomorrow, mostly from London. Pendolphin House wasn't large enough to host everyone overnight, so I helped them find lodging in Port Willis and surrounding villages." She shrugged. "I thought it might make it more exclusive if only 'premier donors'—those willing to give the most—could stay at the house."

Warren chuckled as they drove down the empty country

road, a velvety blanket of stars tossed over the sky above them. "For someone who doesn't believe she belongs among the wealthy, you sure seem to understand what motivates them."

Them. Interesting. Warren didn't seem to lump himself into the same category.

"How are you doing?" His tone had turned soft, concerned.

"Um, great. Everything is set for the ball. It'll be a busy day tomorrow, but nothing I can't handle."

"That's wonderful." A pause. "But it's not what I was asking."

She sighed. "I know." He meant after last night—after the nightmare. "I was able to go back to sleep when I returned to my room, so that was huge."

"I'm glad." Now that the vehicle was toasty, he turned the knob down just a tad. "You said you get the nightmares more than you'd like?"

"Yes." She grew quiet, her focus on the lights in the distance —the village of Port Willis, all lit up and ready for a fun night. Her guests were there, likely throwing money around and having a grand old time. How she wished she could be as carefree as all of them.

Not with money, but life in general. If she could only let go of the past the way they let go of their credit cards …

Kara closed her eyes and set her head back against the seat. "The nightmares started after I left Jeff. Over and over, I dream that Rose will be taken away from me. Jeff is always there. Sometimes he's looming larger than life. Sometimes he's just his normal self, but stronger, tougher somehow." A tear slid down her cheek. "But always, he's laughing at me, because he knows."

"What does he know?"

Kara swallowed hard and opened her eyes, studying Warren's profile in the moonlight as he watched the road. "That I'm weak. That I can't do this. Can't support my daughter on my own."

"Kara, you're one of the strongest women I know."

"You must not know very many then." She tried a chuckle, but it came out a croak. "I can't even move out of my sister's house, Warren. We've been there three whole years. I have the money. It's not that. I just can't seem to make myself do it, because I'm worried. Like, what if I pick the wrong house? Or I wake up in the middle of the night with a nightmare, and another adult isn't there to talk me down? What if I scar my daughter for life?"

"Not that those aren't valid fears, but are they really what you're worried about?"

"I don't know. Maybe not. I want more than anything to show the world that I can do this. That I can stand on my own two feet without falling on my face." She was quiet for a few moments. "The only thing I know for sure is that my poor sister deserves to have her life back without the burden of constantly helping me."

Silence reigned between them as they entered the town and Warren navigated the crowded streets. Finally, he found a parking lot at the top of the hill and maneuvered the SUV between two Smart cars. When he placed the car into Park, he unclipped his seatbelt and turned to face her. "Kara, I'm willing to bet that your sister does not think of you as a burden."

"She'd never say that. Wouldn't even think it. But—"

"But nothing." Warren reached across the console and took her hand. "While I think it's noble that you want to prove you can stand on your own two feet, it's not weakness to depend on other people. We aren't meant to do life alone."

Kara stared at their connected hands. His words penetrated her heart, and she wanted nothing more than to lean into the solace he was offering to her. Oh, how she wanted to believe him. To take his hand without worrying about the consequences, the what-ifs.

But in this moment, Fear started shouting again—and she was difficult to ignore.

Kara had never seen the streets of Port Willis so full.

Together, she and Warren climbed from the vehicle and followed the flow of people from the parking lot down the hill toward the park where she had first glimpsed Warren in town. There must be several hundred villagers and tourists alike crammed onto the grassy bluff, waiting for the large tree to be lit.

The night sky was perfect for it—clear and crisp. Kara could see her breath in the air as she and Warren ambled toward the gazebo, where several long tables with red and silver tablecloths boasted an assortment of delectable goodies. Ginny and her husband, Sarah and Michael, and a tall gentleman with glasses and curly blond hair—Sophia's husband, William—served guests from behind the tables.

A separate self-serve drink station had been erected on one side, but before Kara could suggest that they grab a cup of cider, a white-haired woman with a microphone climbed the steps of the gazebo with the assistance of a well-dressed, forty-something man with a beard.

The crowd collectively hushed and turned toward her.

"Welcome to our lovely little village of Port Willis." Speaking with a British lilt, the woman was as merry as an elf. "For those who don't know me, I'm Mavis Lincoln, the owner of the local antique shop just up the road. My handsome escort here is my nephew, Oliver. Sorry, ladies, he's taken."

Oliver—oh, Joy's husband! Kara searched the crowd for her friend, who—despite her short stature—stood out like a red dress at a black-and-white ball in her bright yellow jacket and hot pink pants. Joy blew Oliver a kiss from her spot beside raven-haired Sophia, who was holding her son on her hip and trying to keep young Emily from snatching another cookie from the sweets table.

Kara giggled at the sight. The girl reminded her so much of Rose at that age.

Oh, Rose.

Just twelve more days and she'd get to hold her daughter in her arms again. Safe. Together.

Mavis continued. "Thank you for coming to our third annual Port Willis Winter Walk. We hope you'll stick around town and shop to your heart's content until nine o'clock. But first, let us get this tree lit, shall we?"

The crowd cheered, and Warren stepped closer to Kara. Had he meant to or was it simply the jostling crowd that had caused his sudden proximity? Either way, she didn't hate the way their arms now pressed against each other, leaving her whole body warm despite the cold outside.

Different smells swirled in the air—from chocolate to the coming snow—but more than anything, she became aware of the citrusy notes of Warren's cologne as they wrapped around her.

Behind Mavis, Oliver snagged two black electric cords and held them aloft, just inches apart.

"Ten, nine, eight ..." Mavis chanted.

The crowd joined in on the countdown, including Kara and Warren, who looked at each other and smiled. And then, just before the lights came on, Warren's gloved hand snuck inside Kara's.

But this was different than the way he'd held her hand in the car—all comfort and friendship.

This time, he intertwined their fingers. And despite the layers of fabric between their skin, it was hard to ignore the way his thumb stroked hers.

The group surrounding them oohed and aahed with delight as the tree came alive before their eyes. The explosion of white light matched Kara's insides as the warm glow burst forth.

How had this happened? One minute, she'd been so determined to remain single forever. The next, Warren had taken down her defenses with his sweet ways and to-die-for smile.

And she'd given in.

Was it weakness? Or was it true strength?

"We aren't meant to do life alone."

The thought curled and twisted—and settled—as Kara's eyes took in the splendor before her.

When the cheers died down, Mavis spoke again. "Now, before I release you to shop till you drop, as my American friends would say, please enjoy our local handbell team's rendition of a holiday favorite."

Kara hadn't even noticed, but just to the left of the tree, a group of fifteen or twenty had gathered behind four or five long lined tables. Each person held two bells with more on the table in front of them. On their conductor's signal, they began to play, and the sweet melody of "Silver Bells" lifted over the crowd.

Some audience members quietly dispersed, while others snuggled together and listened to the music twining up, up, up into the air. When the group had finished, Kara reluctantly pulled her hand from Warren's to offer a polite clap. "That was lovely."

"It really was." Warren eyed her for a moment and then tucked his hands into his pockets. Oh no. Had he thought she didn't want to hold his hand anymore? "Want to snag a cider?"

"S-sure." With his absence from her side and the continually dropping temperature, her teeth had started to chatter. She could use a hot drink to warm her up.

Making their way toward the drink station, they joined the line for cider. Kara racked her brain for something to say. "I've never heard a handbell choir before, have you?"

"Actually, I have. My mother is obsessed with them."

"Really?" Kara huffed out a laugh as they moved forward a few inches in line. "Why?"

"She grew up in a small town in Connecticut. I guess bells were a really huge deal there, at the holidays and all year round. The local church on the square rang them at every birth, every death. And of course at Christmas, to symbolize Christ's birth too." Warren kicked at a blade of grass under his boots. "My mom loved them so much that as a teen, she ran around town convincing people to restart the local handbell choir, which had fizzled out years before that."

"Wow." Kara knew Warren's mom from a distance—they'd been on a few charity committees together when Kara had been married to Jeff—and had a hard time picturing her as a carefree young woman who was passionate about handbells, of all things. "Does she still play?"

He shook his head. "Not since my grandpa died. I think a lot of her love for them stemmed from him."

"Why is that?" They'd almost reached the front of the line. Kara could smell the spiced apple drink and couldn't wait to taste it.

A flicker of a smile crossed Warren's lips. "My grandpa was quite a character. Mom told me how he used to carry around a silver bell—all the time, not just at the holidays—and ring it whenever something made him happy."

"Did he ring it a lot?"

"Yeah, I guess he did." Warren coughed. "He died when I was a kid, so I don't remember much about him. In fact, that bell actually sat on our mantel for a long time and I didn't know what it was. But when my mom reminded me of the bell and what it had meant to my grandpa, then I recalled him ringing it. And I asked her if I could have it."

Now at the front of the line, Kara reached for a cup and handed it to Warren. "Did she give it to you?"

"She did." He took the cup from her. "I try to take it with me whenever I travel. Just a little piece of home, you know?"

Grabbing another cup, she held it under the dispenser's spigot and pressed on the handle. Steaming light brown liquid flowed into her cup. "And do you ring it like he did when something makes you happy?" She stepped back to allow Warren access to the dispenser.

He quieted for a moment, filling his cup, the din of the crowd bustling and swirling around them. When his cup was full, he joined her, but didn't take a drink.

Instead, he took her free hand in his and didn't remove his gaze from hers. "I'll admit, I don't always remember to ring the bell."

Her blood thrummed through her veins. The way he was looking at her …

"But if I had it with me right now, I'd be ringing it to the moon and back."

"Warren …" That was all she could say because he—his presence—turned her brain into mush.

"Kara, I don't know how you feel, but I like you. A lot."

Sweet apple cider, kill her now. "I don't …" She trailed off, looked away.

"It's okay if you don't feel the same way." His voice didn't communicate hurt. Instead, it remained strong, but tender. "That won't change how much I like and respect you. But I *will* back off if you don't feel the same way."

Her gaze collided with his once more. "It's not that. I … I do. Like you, that is." Had she really just admitted that to his face? *Oh my*. "I'm just not sure if I'm ready. Jeff …"

"I know." Warren squeezed her hand. "And that's okay too. There's no pressure here. I just wanted you to know where I stand."

From several feet away, someone called to them.

Kara glanced over and saw Sarah and Michael waving them

over to their horde of friends. Quickly, she dropped Warren's hand. It was one thing to consider dating again, but another for others to observe it. That would somehow make it more real. "I'll think about what you said, okay?"

"Take all the time you need. I'm not going anywhere." He angled his head toward the group. "I guess we've got some mingling to do, huh?"

"Let's do it," she said in a teasing voice as she mimicked his enthusiastic reply from earlier this evening.

He laughed and they walked toward Sarah and the rest of the gang. Their "date" may have been over, but who knew what the rest of her trip might hold?

So much of it depended on Kara—on her ability to let go of the past and embrace the possibilities of the future.

But that required trust.

And she just didn't know if she could get there, however much she wanted to.

CHAPTER 8

Everything was perfect.

Kara glanced around Pendolphin House's ballroom, a pure vision of wonder and wintry delight. Shimmery blue curtains hung as backdrops along the walls, and soft snowflakes had been spotlighted on the dance floor. On the far end, near the stage where the musicians would play, three Christmas trees of varying heights had been arranged, iridescent "snow" flocking their branches.

Guests would begin arriving in an hour, where they'd dance for a bit, then join together in the dining room for dinner and a guest speaker—a woman Sarah personally knew who had once been in an abusive relationship but had become one of London's loudest advocates for battered women and children. After that, the evening would continue with dancing until the wee hours of the morning.

Windows lined the upper third of the ballroom walls, showcasing the brilliant nighttime starry jewels in the sky, a full moon, and wisps of clouds that were carrying snowflakes. The snow had begun to fall last night in London, and the storm was making its way to Port Willis as Kara and the others—caterers, florists, musicians, and more—bustled around Pendolphin House preparing for the ball.

Clasping her clipboard, Kara reviewed her checklist one final time. Check, check, check.

It was done. All had gone seamlessly. She could hardly believe it.

It was too good to be true.

"Kara!" Sarah's voice rang out above the squeaks and squawks of the string quartet tuning their instruments on the raised platform in the corner of the massive ballroom. She dodged staff members as she made her way over in a dark green ball gown that hugged her baby bump. Hair curled and swept to the side with a diamond pin, Sarah looked every inch the socialite she'd been raised to be.

"Sarah, you look so beautiful." Kara embraced her boss—who, in the last few days, had become even more a friend. "Has Michael seen you yet? If not, be prepared for him to be speechless."

Sarah laughed as she pulled back from Kara's embrace. "My husband? Speechless? Please." She took in Kara, with her floor-length dress in a deep Christmas red. "And I'm not the only one who looks beautiful. Kara! Wow. Warren isn't going to know what hit him either."

"Oh, well." Kara looked away, biting her lip. It's not as if she and Sarah had even spoken about Warren again after that night in the bakery, but maybe she'd seen the way Kara hadn't wanted to leave his side last night at the tree lighting. She had to admit, if Warren hadn't been here, she might not have taken such care with her appearance tonight. But when Gwen had offered to fix her hair in a lovely updo, she hadn't been able to resist.

She let her fingers glide over the beaded bodice of her dress. "You don't think it's too much?" Kara had planned on a years-old black dress she'd worn to countless functions, but then Cindy had bought her this one. Her sister had been shopping at her favorite consignment shop in Boston when she'd found the off-the-shoulder gown with a tulle skirt that shimmered when it caught the light.

But though Kara had protested the purchase at first, she had to admit ... when paired with a faux-diamond drop necklace and earrings, the dress kind of made her feel like a princess at the ball.

Now all she needed was her Prince Charming.

But was she really ready? She'd told Warren she wasn't sure, but a late-night gab session with her sister when she'd returned last night had bolstered her confidence.

"You will never be able to guarantee anything in this life, Kara. The best you can do is pray, ask for guidance, look for red flags, and dive in. No toe dipping. Dive."

Now, Sarah returned her to reality with a gentle touch to Kara's elbow. "It's definitely not too much." She tucked her bottom lip under her teeth. "So. Not to change the subject, but I have a huge favor to ask."

Her tone of voice made the hair prickle on the back of Kara's neck. "Okay. What's up?"

"I just spoke with our guest speaker, Linda. Turns out, thanks to the weather, she got into a car accident on the way down here." Sarah waved her hands in the air. "Nothing serious, but her tires are flat and she's still a few hours away. We need to find a Plan B for our dinnertime talk."

Kara began to pace. This wasn't good. "We were counting on Linda's talk to bring in extra donations—donations that we desperately need as we open the London branch."

"I know."

"And I didn't have a Plan B for that." For flowers? Appetizers? Musicians? Yes. Those could all be replaced easily. But a guest who could speak to the atrocities that battered women faced every day? One who might move attendees enough to encourage them to open their wallets even more?

What were they going to do?

"I have an idea." Sarah's voice was guarded, hesitant.

And when Kara glanced up at her boss, she knew why. She held up her hands and shook her head. "What? Me?"

"Yes. You."

"Oh no. I … I can't."

Sarah snagged both of Kara's hands, holding them fast. "Kara, I know what I'm asking is a lot. But there's no one better qualified to speak about this than you."

"I …" Kara squeezed Sarah's hands harder than she'd squeezed those of the nurse who had been at her bedside when Rose was born. How could she go on that stage and tell the world what Jeff had done to her? Not even Sarah knew the particulars. Not all of them.

And Warren—he'd never look at her the same way again.

Oh sure, they knew in theory that Jeff had beaten her. Manipulated her.

But if she described the depths of his depravity—and then talked about how long she'd let him treat her like that?

It would be mortifying.

Because even though her therapist had talked her through the shame, it still lurked. And right now, it was choosing to rear its ugly head.

Bearing the shame inside herself was one thing, but to show it off to the world—or at least, a roomful of people who hadn't lived what she had lived? To confess that she'd been a victim because she hadn't been strong enough to stand up for herself the very first time Jeff had smacked her?

But what other choice did they have? New Dawn needed this—needed her to step up.

Kara had always said she'd do anything to further the mission. She'd just never expected this.

Still …

"I'll do it."

"Really? Are you sure?"

No. "Yes, of course. Whatever it takes, right?"

"Well—"

"Excuse me. I've got to go ... think."

Before Sarah could say more, Kara raced down the long wooden ballroom and out into the hallway, down the stairs, and out a side entrance that led to the vast gardens. The chill in the air made her gasp, but that didn't stop her from clomping down the pathway in her heels, following its twists and turns until she ended up next to a large tree near the edge of the bluff.

The dark ocean tumbled and crashed on the rocks below, signifying everything she felt inside.

Her chin trembled and her eyes burned. She tried to hold back the tears—she'd spent way too long on her makeup to let her mascara run—but eventually lost the battle.

Placing a closed fist at her stomach, Kara leaned against the tree and allowed the tears to fall. She cried and cried, losing track of time, the wetness stinging her now freezing cheeks. A guttural moan left her lips, and she was grateful no one was around to see her completely fall apart. Her legs shook and nearly gave way.

But just when she was about to collapse, strong arms came around her waist, supporting her.

And she knew who was holding her even before she turned around and tucked her arms inside the warmth of his black Armani tux jacket.

How had he even found her all the way out here?

"Shh." Warren rubbed circles on her back as she cried. "It's okay. You're not alone, Kara."

That nearly had her crying even harder, but eventually, her body shuddered and the tears stopped. She needed to get back to the ball—back to her job—but Kara allowed herself to enjoy Warren's embrace just a bit longer before pulling back and running her hands down the front of her dress. "I'm sorry."

The clouds above them threatened to dump their quarry at any moment. The smell of snow was imminent.

"You don't have to be sorry." Warren pulled a handkerchief from his pocket and gave it a shake. "May I?"

She must look terrible—all the time she'd taken on her appearance, wasted. Thanks to the partially blocked moon, perhaps Warren couldn't see the disastrous details, but there were lampposts along the pathway and one not too far away that might be giving him a full view of Kara in all her post-cry glory.

Nevertheless, she nodded.

Slowly, as if not to spook her, he lifted the cloth to her face and dabbed first her cheeks, then underneath her eyes. Even in the dim lighting, his intense focus and drawn lips showed that he was a man on a mission.

Finally, he stepped back, tilting his head and lowering the handkerchief. "Beautiful."

At that, Kara couldn't help but snort. "Liar."

But he didn't crack even a smile. Warren closed the distance between them once more, placed one hand around her waist, and raised his other to trace her cheekbones. "I'm not lying. Kara, you are never more beautiful than when you're showing off your true self."

Oh, this man. "How did you find me?"

"I saw Sarah right after you'd left and she pointed me in your direction. She thought she might have upset you."

Kara shook her head. The moonlight cracked through a few clouds, just for a moment, then mostly disappeared again. "*She* didn't upset me so much as her request."

Warren's hand flexed at her waist. "What request?"

Breathing deep, she informed him about Linda being a no-show. "And she wants me to fill in."

"But?" Warren studied her, and for the first time she took in the full effect of him all dressed up for the evening. His tux hugged his shoulders, making them appear even broader than she remembered, and his hair seemed to have a bit of extra wave to it tonight. Gone was the five o'clock shadow he'd sported more than once while here. While she kind of missed it, her fingers itched to run along the now-smooth skin of his jaw.

"Kara?"

Her cheeks warmed. She hadn't meant to stare.

"But I don't have any clue what to say. I've never told my story publicly." Kara sighed. "My therapist and my sister are the only ones who know everything."

"No one is asking you to give every detail." He tucked an errant hair behind her ear, his touch so sweet, so gentle, that she leaned into it. "And if you don't feel comfortable, then we will think of something else. It's not up to you alone to save the organization. We're a team."

That was true. There had to be other options—what, she didn't know, but surely they could put their minds together and come up with something.

"But …"

Her nose scrunched. "What?"

"But I think there would be value in telling your story. Not for anyone else's sake. Not even for New Dawn. But for yourself."

"I just don't want people to see me like that, you know? As a victim." Needing something to do with her hands, she fiddled with the top button of his jacket.

"What people? There are only a handful of people in that audience that even know you—and just a few you might call friends. Who cares what they think?"

"Okay." She lifted her chin. "I don't want *you* to see me that way. Like I'm … weak." Her voice strained as she turned from him and walked to the edge of the bluff. Wind blew at her skirt and hair, whipping them into who knew what kind of shape. All of Gwen's work unraveled around her shoulders.

Kara ran her hands up and down her upper arms. If she didn't return to the house soon, she'd become an icicle. But she couldn't quite face the task in front of her. Not yet.

She'd given him a chance to slink away, but no, there Warren came, beside her once more. Before she knew it, he'd placed his jacket over her shoulders, encasing her in warmth. "I've already told you what I think—you're not weak. You're strong, Kara. You left one of the most powerful men in Boston. That took guts."

"I tell myself that, but the lies sometimes are so strong. And I'm tired of fighting them."

"My grandma used to say that lies lose their power when exposed to the light. I'm not a therapist, but I do think there's power in telling your story. And maybe some of that fear, that shame, that you still feel will lose its potency if you speak it out loud."

"Maybe you're right."

They stood there together for a few moments in silence.

Then, "Kara, I don't know what it's like to be you. No one has lived your life, and no one has the right to judge you for any part of it. We all have our demons."

"Even you?"

He laughed. "Are you kidding? Definitely me."

"Prince Charming has demons? I've got to hear this."

"Prince Charming, huh? I like that." Warren hip bumped her. "Who does that make you?"

She tapped her chin with her pointer finger. "I'm still figuring that one out."

"Let me know when you do?" And there was something so unguarded—wistful—about the way he asked that she took his hand and squeezed.

"You'll be the first one I come to." She smiled, then squinted up at him. "Seriously, though. What demons?"

Warren rubbed his jaw, then nodded. "I guess I can't really

ask you to get up in front of a bunch of people and talk about your painful past if I'm not willing to share mine with you."

"You don't have to." Biting her lip, she reached for his hand. "But I'd like to hear ... if you want to tell me." Sure, the tips of her ears and her nose were freezing, but she didn't want this moment to end. Kara had a feeling that he was about to give her a very rare glimpse behind the curtain of who Warren Kensington really was.

He squeezed her fingers and stared across the dark sea below. "About seven years ago, I was engaged."

"Really?" She didn't remember hearing anything about that. Of course, she'd been in the throes of new motherhood, so a lot of society news had evaded her notice. Plus, Warren had lived in New York at the time, hadn't he?

"Yeah. We actually met in grad school, and I liked the fact she didn't come from money. She wasn't like the other women I had dated—well, I didn't think she was anyway."

What did that mean? Kara leaned her cheek against Warren's arm.

Turning his body slightly toward her, he looped his arm around her shoulders and drew her closer. Despite the whoosh of the ocean, she imagined she could hear his heartbeat too. "A few weeks before our wedding, I heard her talking to her mom on the phone—discussing all the ways that marrying me would help her career, all the things she was going to buy once she got access to my money." He cleared his throat. "Her voice, it sounded so ... I don't know. Cold. Calculated."

Oh, Warren. "What happened?"

"After I ended the engagement, I graduated with my master's, threw myself into my family's business, and moved to Boston to get away from the memories. But they followed me."

No wonder he'd stayed single for so long. "I'm sorry."

"It's nothing compared with what you've endured."

"One isn't worse than another." Kara's hand slid to his tie, tugging on it so he'd look down at her. "We were both betrayed by people we loved."

"True." Warren's gaze held fast to hers. "It's certainly made me reluctant to date again … until now."

Kara swallowed hard. "Why me, Warren? You don't … you don't know how messed up I am." And after she gave her speech, after he heard the details of what she'd endured, maybe he'd realize just how much baggage she really carried and run for the hills. "Being in a relationship with me would not be easy."

"Easy is relative." He turned and his other arm came around her, enclosing her fully once again. Both of his hands cupped her cheeks, bringing life and warmth to her skin, igniting something inside of her. "I would never worry about *you* wanting me for my money or family connections. That's just not who you are."

"That's certainly true. In fact, I was determined to avoid ever becoming involved again with a man who *had* money and family connections. You know, because of my stepdad. Because of Jeff and the people who protected him." She took a deep breath. "But Warren, you're different. And I'm sorry I ever lumped you into the same category as them."

"I understand why you did."

"Still. I was wrong." She paused. "I can't promise that I won't get scared again, or that I'll be able to trust completely right away." Kara blinked. "But I'm willing to try. With you. That is, if you still feel the same way."

"I do." A pause. "Kara, may I … may I kiss you?"

She froze. But then, the warmth of his hands seeped into her skin and she gave the tiniest of nods.

Warren's lips on hers silenced all her excuses. All her fears. The kiss was short, chaste, and over before she could register it —but it had been nice.

Fine, more than nice.

Much more.

"I hope that answers your question," Warren said. "I *do* still feel the same way, and I don't anticipate that changing anytime soon. If ever."

Okay, then. She smiled. "I like the way you answer questions."

He winked. "There's more where that came from." Then he snagged her hand. "But right now, we should probably get you inside."

"Oh. Right." The speech. Something sharp twisted in her gut. "Ugh. I'm so nervous."

"I know." He brought her hand to his lips and kissed her fingers, which had begun to go numb from the cold. "But I'll be right there the whole time. I'm not leaving."

Kara only prayed he'd feel the same way once he heard what she had to say.

❄

She was going to be sick, right here, in front of everyone.

Kara stood off to the left of the raised platform where Sarah currently was talking about all of the great things New Dawn had accomplished in Boston. Placing a hand against her stomach, she commanded it to stop roiling like a ship in the middle of a storm. At least there wasn't much in there in case her stomach decided to rebel—between the excited flutter leftover from her kiss with Warren to the panicked butterflies over her impending doom, she'd only taken a few bites of the food she'd so carefully selected for the evening's menu.

As Sarah shared the particulars of a few especially trying cases from the last year, Kara's eyes wandered the dining room. Dozens of round tables had been draped with shimmering silver and blue tablecloths and topped with hurricane vases and gorgeous floral arrangements. Icicle lights strung above the tables gave the effect of melting water frozen in mid-air.

It was all breathtakingly beautiful.

But it was the people that caught Kara's gaze the most. Guests from all over Britain—dressed to the nines in gorgeous reds, silvers, and greens—faced the front, their attention on Sarah.

And soon, on Kara.

Oh, goodness. Was she really going to do this? She was not a public speaker. She was the one behind the events, not the face of them.

God, help.

Now where had that come from? She knew from experience that God didn't answer her prayers.

But maybe she really could use some divine intervention. She was so far outside of her wheelhouse in this moment.

"And now, it's my extreme pleasure to welcome our very own special events coordinator, Kara Gentry, to the stage." Sarah turned toward Kara, arm extended. A smile lit her face, and even from here, Kara saw the clear love and acceptance in her friend's eyes.

With a deep breath and the memory of Warren's encouragement on repeat in her mind, Kara forced her feet to climb the small stage while the audience clapped politely.

Sarah stepped forward and embraced Kara. "You've got this. I'll be right in front if you need a friendly face."

Kara nodded, tight, quick, then released Sarah and moved behind the podium. The applause died down and she swallowed, her hand shaking as she adjusted the short microphone upward just a tad. "Thank you, Sarah." Oh man, her voice sounded like she'd been smoking her whole life. She attempted to clear the dryness away. "I am not usually one to speak in public. In fact, Sarah just asked me to do this a few hours ago because our wonderful guest speaker had a little fender bender.

Thankfully, she's all right. We don't need to worry about her. Although she would have been a great speaker, so I'm sad you'll all miss out on her."

Stop rambling! Less than a minute in and she was already botching this. Her heart rammed against her ribcage as if begging for release. Kara closed her eyes for a brief moment, then peeked out again at the crowd. The lights blinded her, but then her eyes finally adjusted again—and they found the spot they'd been seeking.

Warren sat at one of the front tables, Sarah and Michael beside him—but Kara only had enough room in her gaze for him alone. At the sight of him, her heart rate slowed.

"Lies lose their power when exposed to the light."

Right. This was her chance to tell her story. And maybe, along the way, to sway a few hearts as well.

"I'll be honest. I didn't want to be up here. I didn't want to rehash my story for you all. I didn't want to relive it." She chewed her lip. "But who am I kidding? I relive it every day, when I see my daughter struggling to understand why her parents aren't together anymore. When I wake up in cold sweats after a nightmare." Her gaze stayed steady on Warren, who had leaned forward in his chair. "When I meet a wonderful new man but, because of my past, I struggle with giving him all of my heart."

His hand fisting his tie, he gave her a sad smile, nodded. He understood. He accepted her, faults and fears and all. His reaction bolstered her, giving her the strength to look away from him, to connect her gaze with others' in the crowd.

To keep talking.

"I spent my life hiding who I was. Then I spent it hiding what had happened to me. But I don't want to hide anymore." Her voice shook, but no, she wouldn't stop in embarrassment.

Peace like she'd never known flooded into her heart.

She spoke for several more minutes, telling the crowd about

the horrors Jeff had put her through—and the ways she was still dealing with the repercussions of that today.

And with every word, her shoulders straightened. Her head lifted. Her lungs took in new breath.

New life.

Was she making an impact among the crowd? Maybe that didn't matter so much as the fact she was making an impact on ... herself.

Still, she wanted to reach them, wanted to implore them to keep giving, keep fighting the evil. "I want to end tonight with an apology. I'm sorry—I misjudged the lot of you."

A rustle went up through the crowd.

Kara tilted her head. "For a long time, I thought that those who had money had it made. That being wealthy was something to aspire to. Then, I lived in your world for a time—and I discovered that it has just as many problems as mine did. But someone quite intelligent reminded me that it doesn't matter how much money you have."

She found Sarah in the crowd. Her friend was nodding along, her cheeks slathered in tears. How could Kara ever have held anything against the wealthy class—assuming all rich people were the same—when this woman had fought her own father in order to help Kara? And then there was Warren, a man who had done nothing but show her kindness and encourage her.

"He told me that what counts is what's on the inside, that it's what we do with what we've been given that matters most." Her gaze swept the crowd, which seemed to lean forward collectively as she pressed her speech toward its final moments. "It was because of my own strength—and the support of those around me—that I was able to leave my ex-husband. But it was people like you who gave me the resources to keep my daughter, to keep standing, and to keep fighting. You see, it's a partnership. One cannot exist without the other. You are an integral part in the cycle, and I'm so very grateful for each one of you. Thank you."

As Kara swiped the tears from underneath her eyes and swiveled to exit the stage, the crowd erupted into applause—this time not polite, but strong. Exuberant.

And then, they did something she never expected.

They stood.

They were standing to show their support—but more than that, they were standing *with* her.

Kara pressed her face into her hands, soaking in the applause, the love, the support.

It was too much.

Arms and the scent of lavender surrounded her. Sarah whispered in her ear once more, her voice ragged, "Well done, Kara. Well done." With a squeeze, she let go and hurried up onto the stage. "Thank you so much for that moving speech, Kara. I think what just happened was what some might call a divine appointment. I know I needed to hear it."

There was that word again. *Divine.*

And so maybe, just maybe, God was standing with her too.

Kara walked on wobbly legs back to her seat, but when she reached it, Warren wasn't where he'd been. She looked around the room, where the guests had started to retake their seats, and caught a glimpse of him standing in the back corner, his eyes on her.

Did he want her to join him?

"Someday, you're going to have to learn to trust men again." Cindy's voice popped into her mind. That conversation seemed so long ago, even though it had just been a little over a week.

But sometime between then and right now, a miracle had occurred.

She'd never thought she would trust a man again—but she trusted Warren. Was she a fool, or was this a gift?

Stop second-guessing everything and trust yourself.

Okay, then. Kara snatched a handful of her dress and lifted it so she could walk more quickly and bustled toward the back doors. Warren had moved into the hallway and she followed him to where he studied a painting of a huge oak tree. The wind blew the leaves, some of which tumbled to the ground and every which way—but roots sprouted underneath the soil, digging deep into the earth, holding the tree firm despite the buffeting winds.

That could be her. She wanted that to be her. But she didn't have to do it alone. And the man in front of her just might have a role to play in making that happen.

The sound of Sarah speaking into the microphone faded as Kara approached Warren from behind. She stopped, her heels sinking into the plush rug beneath her feet as she waited for him to turn. What had he thought of her speech?

Finally, he must have sensed her presence, because he pivoted. "Kara." He spoke her name with such reverence, such adoration, that she couldn't do anything but step forward into his arms. Warren hugged her close, his nose sinking into her hair. "You were …"

The close press of his body against hers, his arms surrounding her, his warm breath on her neck—they all made her shiver in a new and thrilling way. "I was …?"

"Brilliant."

She pulled back. "Yeah?"

"More than yeah."

That tugged a grin across her lips. "Did you like the part where I quoted you?"

"You quoted me? I hardly noticed." But his returning smile showcased his teasing. "Seriously, Kara. I am very sorry for all that man put you through. I wish …" He swallowed, his Adam's apple bobbing.

"I know. Me too." Kara studied the contours of his face—his cheeks, his brow … his lips. "That's my past, and while it will probably continue to haunt me in certain ways, I don't want it to define who I am anymore. I am not a victim. I'm a survivor."

"And an amazing one at that."

She stared at him for three, two, one, and then she couldn't stand it anymore. She needed to kiss this man. And not some two-second buss on the lips either. Kara wanted to get lost in him, in this magic and connection pulsing between them.

So, lifting up on her tiptoes, she brushed a kiss against his lips. Then, with eyes closed, she wrapped her arms around Warren's neck. He caught her around the waist, one hand on her hip, one in her hair, and kissed her back with the power of all they'd been holding back.

Together, their mouths moved in a dance that, somehow, they both seemed to know. A heady fog consumed her.

So this was what she'd been missing. What she'd almost missed, because of fear.

Pulling back slightly, Kara let loose a sigh. "Wow."

"You've got that right." He seemed a bit dazed as he played with one of her earrings, brushing his fingers against the side of her neck.

Mmm. Not sure she would ever tire of this—whatever this was. And because he'd been quite the gentleman, leaving the ball in her court, it was up to her to clarify. "So … what now?"

Somehow, he understood her question that wasn't really a complete thought. "Now, we go back in and dance the night away. And then, I'm taking you on a proper date on Monday night. How does that sound, Snow?"

Her brow scrunched. "Snow?"

"As in Snow White? I mean, if I'm Prince Charming …" He shrugged, and they both laughed. "Besides, it seems only appropriate, given the weather at the moment." Warren nodded at the window a few feet away.

There, against the dark night, snowflakes fluttered from the sky. The snowfall wasn't heavy or rushed. It was almost tender in its descent, allowing an invisible hand to move it to and fro until it landed below.

"Hmm. Snow. I like it." She kissed him once more for good measure. "And I would like nothing more than to go out with you on Monday, my prince."

CHAPTER 9

Kara hadn't known the Port Willis crowd long, but she already felt like she belonged more among them than she ever had among the wealthy set.

Though, as she was learning, perhaps it was less about wealth and more about allowing herself to be ... well, herself.

And here, tucked into a booth at the Village Pub—Michael's family restaurant where they'd eaten on her first day in town—with a handful of women, Kara was finally ready to be open. Vulnerable.

Because she majorly needed some advice.

Clearing her throat, Kara flicked a finger down the moisture gathering on the outside of her water glass. "I was wondering if I could ask you ladies a question."

The conversation around the table halted and Kara found four sets of eyes focused on her. When Sarah had suggested a girls' night after the last Pendolphin House guest had left this morning, Kara had been on too big a high—from the massive success of the fundraiser to her upcoming date with Warren and, yes, THOSE KISSES—to say no.

But over the last few hours, doubt had wriggled in. She'd

dialed Jeff's phone five times in a sudden and desperate attempt to talk to Rose, her grounding point, but of course they must already be on their ship, which was set to sail tonight.

So … yes. Advice.

Sarah dragged a fork through her mashed potatoes. "Well, don't leave us all in suspense," she teased. Behind her, a collection of pastel-painted seashells decorated the wall. In fact, the entire restaurant consisted of vintage oceanside decor. That, along with the cozy fireplaces and the wooden beams spaced along the ceiling, created the perfect environment for this conversation. "What's the question?"

Where to begin? "Well … um." Kara's legs fidgeted under the table and the seat of the booth groaned a bit as she shifted. "I kind of have a date tomorrow night—"

"I knew it!" Ginny pumped her fist in the air. Beside her, a smiling Sophia rolled her eyes and gave her friend a little shove.

Joy grinned at Kara from across the table. "Warren's a lucky guy."

Kara shook her head, smiling. "How did you know it was with Warren?"

"Oh, please." Ginny snapped. "The two of you are as obvious a pairing as pasta and cheese, as salted caramel and chocolate, as—"

"We get the picture, sister dearest." Sarah laughed, then turned back to Kara. "I'm really happy to hear that. I've thought for a few years now that you two would make a cute couple. Of course, I knew you had a lot to work through first."

"That's the problem. I still feel like I do." Kara nibbled the edge of her crusty roll before continuing. "And I can't help but wonder if I'm making a mistake. I don't want to be this wishy-washy person. I want to trust him. I do trust him. But …"

"But it's hard to forgive and trust *yourself*." Sophia's words were soft, so quiet that Kara had to strain to hear her, which was strange, since they were some of the only patrons here this late on a Sunday evening.

"Yes, exactly." Kara cocked her head. "How did you know?"

The other women eyed each other, as if they knew a secret Kara didn't. But before she could slink back into herself, sure she'd never really be part of the group, Sophia spoke again. "Before William, I was engaged to a man who emotionally abused me. And I was a domestic violence therapist, of all things. If anyone should have 'known better,' it was me."

Whoa. Kara sat back, the slats of the upper booth hard on her shoulders. "I'm so sorry." With her pause came a charged electricity in the air. "How … how did you learn to trust again, if you don't mind me asking?"

"Of course I don't mind." Sophia fiddled with her long silver necklace, which perfectly matched her stylish soft sweater. "It took time, but eventually William proved to me that he was nothing like David. And God proved to me that he'd been there with me all along, despite the fact I had dismissed his help for so long."

"I'm not sure he's very interested in my situation." Kara tried for a laugh, but it fell flat. "Or me." Then again, her speech *had* gone really well last night. But was that because of him, and her desperate last-minute prayer, or would she have been fine on her own all along?

"I thought that too." Giving her an understanding smile, Sophia nodded. "But ultimately, the abuse was David's fault and no one else's. So, even though God's protection didn't look exactly the way I thought it would—or should—it was still there. *He* was there."

A shiver raced along Kara's arms. Maybe she'd have to think on that one a bit more. "Just hearing from you that it's possible to move forward and have a healthy relationship after such a hard past gives me hope."

"Oh, girl," Ginny chimed in. "All of us here have had to overcome something difficult in our past before we were able to find the loves of our lives. Not saying Warren is that for you, but it's awesome that you're willing to try again. That's seriously the first step."

"Yes, you should be really proud of yourself, Kara." Sarah reached over and squeezed her hand.

"I am." And that speech yesterday had given her a freedom she hadn't expected—even though Warren had predicted it.

But back to what Ginny had said. "You mentioned that you each had to overcome something?" Were these women willing to open up to her, somewhat a stranger? If they could do that, surely she could find the courage to do the same.

At her question, Joy gave an effusive nod. "Oliver dropped into my lap when I wasn't even looking for him. Like you, I'd kind of decided I was good being single forever. And then, when I did meet him—and fell hard—I didn't think I could keep him because I was so busy taking care of my mother." She shrugged. "It all worked out in the end, once I was willing to recognize that God wanted to bless me with wonderful things—if I was open to them."

Kara was certainly sensing a theme. Was God at the center of each woman's story? And what did that mean for her?

She turned to Sarah. "What about you?" Kara knew the basic story of how her boss had met Michael, how he'd followed her home to Boston after her month-long stay in Port Willis several Christmases ago, but nothing of a hardship.

Pursing her lips, Sarah furrowed her brow. Then she dove into the story of fighting her dad for control of her own life and assuming that she and Michael didn't have a future because it didn't fit into her plans—or the ones her parents had for her life. "I got so wrapped up in what I thought I should do for everyone else's sake that I didn't stop to consider Michael was a wonderful gift I hadn't asked for." A pause. "I know you're probably hesitant to date again because of Rose, but consider who you want to be in charge of your life—Fear or Hope."

Fear had been Kara's companion for too long. How she longed to break free of its grasp once and for all. Maybe going on a date with Warren tomorrow was the first step.

No, the first step had been leaving Jeff. Then fighting for Rose. Then working for New Dawn.

And telling her story last night.

Every step she'd taken—large or small—had accumulated, like a snowball rolling downhill. Together, they had tipped the scales toward Hope, unbalancing Fear and removing it from the throne Kara had allowed it to take in her life.

She just couldn't allow Fear to take over once more. And being honest about her struggles was a big part of that. "I'm inspired by all of your stories. I just … I'm so afraid of failing again, you know?"

"I totally get that," Ginny said. "After my first husband left me, all I could dwell on was my failures."

"So how did you overcome that?"

"I'm not saying I don't still struggle with it, because there are times I do." Ginny glanced around the table at each of the women, who nodded in turn—like some sort of solidarity linking them, rising between them.

Here was a group of women who had fought their pasts … and won.

Kara wanted more than anything to be like them.

"But," Ginny continued, "it turns out that my past didn't make me a failure. The things I've been through helped to shape me into who I am now, and I had a choice—I could either wallow in those low points or I could use them to help others and learn from my mistakes. I could either take on the label of Failure or find my value in the fact that God loves me no matter what I do or don't do. He loves me simply because I'm his."

It wasn't the words—though those were powerful too—but

the peace radiating from Ginny's eyes that seared Kara in the gut.

She wanted that.

And, she realized with a start, she'd had it … during her speech. The peace had been otherworldly. But now, it was gone again. Maybe in order to make it a permanent fixture in her life, she'd have to figure out where she stood with God.

Kara was just learning to trust herself and men again. Learning to trust God too? That might be too tall an order at the moment.

There was definitely a lot to think about—but first and foremost, and most pressing, her date tomorrow night.

"Thank you for sharing all of that, ladies. I really appreciate your insights." She took a sip of water and smiled. "Now, for somewhat of a lighter subject—got any tips for going on my first first date in forever?"

CHAPTER 10

Had it really been three days since she'd officially gone out with Warren for the first time?

Since he'd picked her up from her room at Rebecca's B&B—where they were both guests again, although not the only ones—and taken her to a small Italian-inspired restaurant in town where they'd talked until the place closed …

Since, despite the cold snap and snow, they'd walked hand in hand along the bluff overlooking the Port Willis harbor quay and talked about her passion for New Dawn and his passion for charities involving work in third-world countries …

Since they'd returned to the bed and breakfast and eaten Rebecca's pie in front of the fireplace until two in the morning …

Since he'd walked her back to her room and given her another spine-tingling kiss …

Now, two days before Christmas, Kara hung up after a brief call with her daughter—heart full and at peace. Rose was having a wonderful time on the cruise going to the children's club every day. Despite their distance, at least Kara had been able to consistently talk with Rose once a day.

The idea of being apart on Christmas still didn't sit well with her, but next year would be different.

In fact, if the last three days spent in constant company with Warren—exploring an old lighthouse just outside of town, taking a driving tour of the surrounding villages and countryside, digging through antiques at Mavis Lincoln's shop, and making cookies together in Rebecca's kitchen—and the intense emotions Kara already felt were any indication, next Christmas could very well be life changing.

A shiver of pleasure coursed through her at the thought just as a knock sounded on her door.

"It's unlocked," she called as she sat up on the bed and smoothed down her hair.

Warren stuck his head in. He had a pizza and some napkins in his hand. "Is your call done?"

"Yep. Come on in."

He hesitated, cocking his head. "Did you want to eat this downstairs?"

"And have Rebecca yell at us for preferring this over her mince pies?" Kara waved him into the room. "Plus, a large group of loud men checked in earlier today and I'm peopled out."

Chuckling, Warren closed the door behind him and walked toward her, setting the pizza and napkins on the side table. "I completely understand." Then he tugged a chair over from under the window and lowered himself into it.

"Don't want to sit next to me?" she teased.

But instead of an answering smile, a look of desire flashed in his eyes. "Believe me, that's not it."

"Oh." Somewhere downstairs, the sound of muffled laughter carried through the floorboards. "I was just kidding."

"I know. But Kara, I like you a lot. I like what we have right now. And I don't want to do anything to mess this up, including moving too quickly." Warren scratched behind his ear. "Does that make sense?"

Yes, it made perfect sense. Because he respected her, he didn't want to rush their physical relationship—something that had never given Jeff any qualms.

And *this* was just one of the many reasons why she was half in love with Warren already.

Wait. What?

Whoa.

But repeating the sentiment to herself didn't make it any less true. Kara flipped open the pizza box lid and removed a slice, which she placed on a napkin and handed to him. "I like you a lot too. In fact, I was just kind of thinking about what next Christmas might be like if …"

Was she being super forward in admitting that?

"I—" Warren frowned, then pulled his phone from his pocket. His face blanched, turning red before he stuffed the phone back where it had been.

"Everything okay?" Taking a slice for herself, Kara bit into the tomato and cheese mixture. The flaky crust was cooked to perfection.

"Yeah, just a work thing. No big deal." He took a bite of his pizza and chewed, his brow furrowed as he stared at the carpet.

The charged air between them had gone cold, flat.

"Warren? You okay?"

"What?" His eyes darted up. "Oh, yeah. Fine. I'm just tired, I guess. Was up early working."

"And then you spent all day carting me around." She said it with a smile, but once again, he didn't respond in kind.

Her skin prickled. He wasn't … hiding anything from her, right?

No. *People are allowed to have off days, Kara.*

"I understand if you need to go to sleep early tonight," she offered.

"Huh?" Warren blinked. "Oh. No. I'm okay. Right where I want to be." But the frown he made as he snagged another bite of his pizza said differently. He polished off the piece and wiped his mouth. "Now where—"

Grunting, he pulled out his phone again and read an incoming message. Ran his hand down his face and sighed.

Okay, that was it. Something was clearly bothering him. And just like he'd been there for her when she had to give that speech on Saturday night, Kara wanted to be there for him. Standing, she circled the bed and squatted beside his chair, placing a hand on his knee. "Talk to me, Charming. What's going on? How can I help?"

He glanced up from the phone and his expression slackened. "I'm sorry. I'm being terrible company." Then Warren flung his phone onto her bed and tugged Kara onto his lap. "It has nothing to do with you, okay? Nothing you need to worry about."

Nothing you need to worry about. Kara winced. Had he really just used the exact words Jeff used to say when he'd "work" late?

But it was just an unfortunate coincidence. Warren would never betray her or lie to her. He'd said it was merely a work thing, and he was the vice president of a company. Surely there were a lot of fires to put out daily, matters that could be frustrating and easily explain the reaction Warren had had to whatever text or email he'd just received.

Kara looped her arms around the back of Warren's neck and nestled against him. "Okay."

His breathing seemed to even out and she wondered for a moment if he'd fallen asleep. But then his lips connected with her forehead and his hand tightened around her waist. "So … next Christmas."

The air was warm again—and crackling. "Yes?"

"Is it …" He paused, his lips brushing her temple again. "Is it too much for me to admit that I hope we're still together?"

She sat up slightly, pressed her nose lightly against his. "No, it's not."

"Kara … I'm feeling things for you that I didn't think I would ever feel this soon."

She played with the hair at the base of his neck. "Me too, Charming."

"Does that scare you?"

"Surprisingly, no. Because it's you."

And then Warren pressed his lips to hers, long and slow, his kiss full of promises—promises too beautiful to fully grasp. Perhaps Kara's friends had been right. God was giving her an unexpected gift, if she could only open her eyes to see it. To be falling in love so quickly sounded absurd, but Warren wasn't a stranger. She'd known him for years. And Kara was no longer a young girl, easily starstruck by riches and good looks.

She knew what mattered, what counted—and the connection between them was not something that came along every day.

When the kiss grew more fervent, Warren finally pulled back. "I think I'd better say good night before my heart—and my good sense—runs away from me."

Giggling like someone much younger than her thirty-eight years, Kara nodded. "I suppose so. See you in the morning?"

"Unless you're sick of me."

"Hmmm, let me think about that." She popped a kiss on his jaw.

"Snow," he growled, shaking his head and grinning. Then he stood with her still in his arms and set her on her feet. "Have I told you lately that I've got it bad for you?"

"I may have inferred that."

"Good." His voice, low and throaty, did something to her insides. They walked to the door and he leaned down, giving her one more kiss before heading back to his room.

Kara closed the door, sighed, and flopped back onto her bed.

Something vibrated on the mattress next to her. Her hand felt around and found a phone. Oh, shoot. Warren had forgotten it. She grinned. Guess she had an excuse to give him another kiss tonight after all.

But as she sat up, her eyes caught sight of her own name on the screen.

In a text.

From Warren's father.

What in the world?

She really shouldn't snoop, but Warren wouldn't keep secrets from her. And he'd understand—given her past—the need for her to just make sure all was well, right? It wasn't an invasion of privacy if he would willingly tell her if she asked. And if he really hadn't wanted her to see it, he would have locked his phone.

Right?

Kara...

She quieted her inner critic. Because, well ... she couldn't go through what she'd experienced before. No more betrayal. No more lies. No more being made to feel worthless.

Her hand shaking, she clicked through to the text.

Dad: *See if your new friend Kara has any insights into her ex. She will be of great use to us as this merger with Gentry moves forward. Great work, son.*

What?

She scrolled up to find a few similar text messages, and her whole body grew hot, her hands clammy. It sounded ... but it couldn't be how it sounded.

Because how it sounded was that Warren was just using her. Getting close to her in order to put through some merger between his company and Jeff's.

After all the things she'd told him about her ex-husband, Warren wanted to join forces with the man? Really?

"It has nothing to do with you, okay? Nothing you need to worry about."

On top of it all, he'd lied. Because this had everything to do with her.

Or … Kara inhaled. Maybe she was panicking for nothing. Yes, there had to be a good explanation for this, right? But with the evidence staring her in the face, she didn't know what it could possibly be.

Either way, she wasn't sitting around wondering. Not this time. She leaped off the bed and scurried down the hallway, hesitating only a moment before knocking on his door.

The door swung open. "Kara. Hey."

Ignoring his wide grin and curious expression, she held up his phone. "You left this in my room." Her voice spit at him, the accusation clear.

"Oh, thanks." He tilted his head. "Everything okay?"

"Sure, if you call a text from your father *about me* okay."

The blood drained from his face. He glanced up and down the hallway. "Want to come in so we can talk about this?"

"Oh, am I being too loud for you? Don't want to ruin your sterling reputation." Yikes, fine, that was a dig that maybe he didn't deserve. Jeff always said she got "hysterical" when upset. So maybe she should hear Warren out before employing her shrill voice. "Fine." Stepping past him, she entered his room, which smelled so good—like him—that she immediately fought the urge to run.

But she held her ground. "You got a text from your father after you left."

"And you read it?"

"Don't start with me on that. Maybe I shouldn't have, but after everything Jeff did …"

"I thought we established that I'm nothing like your ex." Warren leaned hard against the wall.

"I didn't think you were. But …"

Maybe you're wrong.

But I have to know.

"Regardless of whether I should have looked at the text or

not, I did." Phone still in hand, she crossed her arms over her chest. "Can you please tell me what's going on?"

He studied her for a moment before nodding. "I found out my father is considering a merger with Gentry Pharmaceuticals. Of course, I immediately told him there's no way we can trust a guy like Jeff Gentry. He said he knew that, but there were certain advantages to merging anyway."

Ugh. Business and politics—two things Kara despised. "Why is your dad asking about me?"

"Because he isn't listening to me. He's moving forward with the merger anyway and he wants leverage on Jeff so he can get a better deal or something. I don't know."

He sounded sincere. Still … "You told me this had nothing to do with me. You lied."

"I didn't …" But then he tilted his head back against the wall and groaned. "I can see how it looked that way to you. Maybe I shouldn't have said it like that, but I just meant that it was a moot point because I would never go along with it. I would never use you like that. Kara, don't you know how I feel about you?" His voice had grown desperate as he speared her with a look to match. "I'm … I'm falling in love with you."

If looks could melt a person from their warmth, Kara would be a puddle on the floor. But she couldn't ignore the red flags. Not this time.

If she didn't stand up for herself, if she didn't show her strength now, then she was just the same woman she'd been. A victim.

And that was one thing she'd never be again.

If standing up meant standing alone forever, then so be it.

"Jeff told me that too, once upon a time. But love doesn't lie." Kara shoved the phone into Warren's chest and flounced back to her room, head held high.

It was only once the door was firmly shut—and locked—that she sank down against the wall and cried.

CHAPTER 11

At least she wasn't spending Christmas Eve alone. Sarah and Michael had made sure of that.

Kara forced a smile as she settled against Ginny and Steven's bright yellow couch holding a mug of Ginny's cider and listening to the carolers at the front door, where Ginny, Sarah, and their husbands stood listening. The sun had faded long ago, the moon hidden behind clouds, casting shadows across the tiny Cornish village. Outside, the streetlamps burned dim, granting the whole place a mysterious aura.

But also, a calm.

Which was the exact opposite of the raging river of emotions flooding Kara's whole body.

All day, she'd tried to put off thinking about her fight with Warren. Joy and Sophia had invited her over to bake treats. Little Emily had "helped," and Kara's insides had nearly exploded with missing her own daughter. The magic of Christmas felt empty, destroyed, without Rose here.

Without Warren.

She'd ached to belong somewhere, with someone, and Sarah

and company had been very kind to include her this evening in dinner and lovely conversation. But being included didn't mean she belonged.

Once again, she was alone.

The carolers stopped their jaunty tune and Ginny whooped and thanked them, supplying them with cookies she'd baked before closing the door. All four of them returned to the living room, laughing and chattering about some of the youngest carolers and how cute they'd looked in their mittens and knit hats.

Kara smiled, only half listening as her gaze swept the room. The fireplace and mantel, where Ginny and Steven's wedding pictures showed a casual affair set in a green, blooming garden. A modest-sized Christmas tree, decorated beautifully with an array of silver and pink ornaments. The couch, a rocking chair, and a coffee table.

To many, it wouldn't seem like much, but the whole house was like this. Charming. Small, but full.

That's what Kara wanted in a home. She didn't care about the trappings anymore, because trappings really were just that—a trap, something to lure a person in, to make her think she was secure.

When really, she was a captive.

If only Kara could get up the courage to create such a home for herself and Rose. Maybe it would be enough. She'd always thought it would.

But now, there was the *what-if*—because she'd pictured Warren there too.

Warren, who was supposed to come today as well, but had backed out at the last minute.

"Kara?"

She startled, sloshing a bit of cider over the edge of her cup onto the couch. Hissing, she jumped up and set the mug on a coaster on the coffee table. "I'm so sorry. Let me get a towel."

Despite Ginny's protests, she raced into the modern-looking kitchen with granite countertops and a small eat-in table and chairs. Snagging a towel from the oven handle, she wet a corner of it.

When she came back into the room, the men were putting on their jackets.

"Where are you guys going?"

Michael smiled. "Sarah had a craving for old-fashioned lemonade, so we thought we'd run over to Mavis's house and snag some since the stores are closed. She always has some on hand."

"Oh. Okay. Well, in case I'm not here when you return, thanks for letting me join you."

"Of course," Steven said and he covered his red hair with a beanie. "According to our wives, you're family—and that's good enough for us."

And with that, they ducked out the front door, leaving Kara standing there, dumbstruck and holding the limp towel.

Family.

Her lip trembled as she continued toward Ginny and Sarah, who had taken up residence in the recliner and on the non-stained side of the couch, respectively. "A craving, huh?" Kara looked pointedly at Sarah as she squatted beside the sofa and scrubbed the spot her cider had left behind, praying it wouldn't stain.

"Pregnant women get cravings all the time."

"Yeah, but you don't strike me as the kind of woman who would send her husband out on Christmas Eve to satisfy a craving. Not unless you were up to something." Kara arched an eyebrow at Sarah.

From the recliner, Ginny laughed. "She has you there, big sis."

"Fine." Sarah's fingers made absentminded figure eights on

her stomach. "When Warren canceled, he gave some lame excuse about work. But of course I pushed him—"

"You? Pushy? Never." Ginny's eyebrows wagged.

"Hush, you."

Their banter eased some of Kara's own tension. These women *had* become like family, opening their homes and lives to her when they didn't have to. This was a safe place. And she could use some feedback. Cindy would have been willing to give some during their short call earlier today, but Kara hadn't wanted to take her sister away from time with her kids to wail about her misfortunes.

She got off her knees and sat back on the couch, avoiding the wet spot. Grabbing her mug of cider again, she breathed in the sweet apple scent. "Did he tell you what happened?"

"No." Sarah's hands stilled. "Only that he didn't think you'd want him here."

"He was right." And not just because she was upset with him—but also, with herself. And she was embarrassed. Confused.

"So what happened?" Ginny's gentle question floated across the room, as soft as the snow falling outside.

"He betrayed me. Or … I think he did." Kara took a deep sip of her drink before putting it back on the coaster. Then she buried her head in her hands and shook her head. "I might have screwed everything up."

The whole story spilled from her lips. "I just don't know which way is up. Who I can trust and who I can't. I don't even know anymore if I can trust myself."

A hand rubbed her back and Sarah's sweet voice broke through Kara's sorrow. "'When I am afraid, I put my trust in you. In God, whose word I praise, in God I trust; I shall not be afraid.'"

Kara stiffened at the words and she straightened, lips twisted into a frown. "You all talked the other night about God—how he loves you, how he gives you good gifts. But how do you know you can really trust him?"

"He's the only one who will never fail us, Kara. Even the best humans in the world aren't perfect. If you're looking to other people, or even yourself, to be your foundation, it will shake and crumble every time. But God, well, he doesn't change. He is not only a firm foundation—He is the *only* foundation worth building our lives on. And he's always been there, loving you."

The idea of not having to stand on her own, ever again ... was glorious. And also, a bit unbelievable. "I just haven't always seen that."

Ginny leaned forward and placed a hand on Kara's knee. "It can be difficult when you're only looking at the bad. But look at all the good in your life—like Rose. New Dawn. Even Warren."

Yes, those were all good things. Still ... "I don't want to think about him." Because maybe she *had* been too harsh. But how did she know when to trust and when to run?

"Look, Kara, it sounds to me like Warren messed up by not being completely honest with you," Sarah said. "And it makes total sense that you would have doubts, even compare him to Jeff. But do you honestly, deep in your heart, believe that he and Jeff are anything alike? That they have the same heart and intentions?"

"No." The word came out a squeak. "I just don't want to make the wrong decision again."

"Good thing you don't have to make it alone." Sarah gave her a hug, pulling her close. Then Ginny left her spot on the recliner and pushed her way into the group hug, leaving all three of them laughing.

"We aren't meant to do life alone."

All this time, she'd blamed herself for not being strong enough, not being good enough, not being smart enough. But really, it had been her intense desire to belong to something—to someone—that had driven some of her most desperate acts. From the time she was little, she'd craved security. Identity.

Could it really be true that she could find both of those somewhere she'd never looked before?

Instead of pushing Sarah and Ginny away, Kara allowed herself to be held, to accept the gift of their friendship—and to finally, finally, open her heart to One who had been the giver of all these good things in the first place.

CHAPTER 12

It was almost midnight.

The streets were quiet, the air still. Even the snow flurries had stopped for a time.

Kara walked down High Street toward the park, the gazebo —the tree that she could see lit up even from here. Above her, the clouds had cleared away, bringing starlight and moonshine to rest on her skin.

She'd gone back to her room at Rebecca's a few hours ago, but hadn't been able to sleep—not after the revelations earlier tonight. Her whole body felt lighter, her spirit hopeful and as bright as the tree she approached.

The only thing troubling her was Warren. She'd knocked on his door, eager to mend what she'd broken. To see if they could make things work again. But after a full minute of knocking, Rebecca finally peeked around the corner and told her that Warren had checked out earlier in the day.

He was gone.

Of course, she was bound to see him again in Boston, but she didn't want to wait that long. And what if he decided that dating her—taking a chance on loving her—was too much work?

Then you'll be okay.

The sweet words wafted on a sudden breeze, one that wrapped around her like a hug. Yes, it would sting if she had to say goodbye to Warren, a good man who she could see spending the rest of her life with. But she would survive … and she wouldn't be alone.

The tree now loomed large in front of her. This time, she walked right up to it and touched one of the branches, the spindles cold and stiff. But the lights glowing from inside softened it, taking a thing that was partially dead—it was a cut tree, after all—and granting it new life. Purpose.

Tucking her hands back into the pockets of her coat, Kara stood there for a while, breathing in the scent of pine, of hope. It must be Christmas by now, and even though Rose wouldn't be there this morning to open presents, this may just be the best Christmas Kara had ever experienced.

Because she'd never felt like this before.

Once her nose and lips were near frozen, she sighed. "Goodbye, Mr. Tree. I'll see you tomorrow."

Then Kara turned—and stopped, a gasp on her lips.

Because she wasn't alone. And not just metaphorically speaking, but actually, physically, alone.

A man stood inside the gazebo, watching her.

Warren.

It was like déjà vu as Kara walked toward him, her boots trudging through the snow-littered grass, breath puffing in the air. And when she finally went up the steps, she had to reach out and touch him to be sure he was real. "You're here."

Warren snatched her hand and held it between his own. "And you're freezing. You'd think a woman named Snow would know to wear gloves outside right now."

The affection in his voice—as he said her nickname—almost undid her. "I forgot them at the bed and breakfast and didn't feel like turning around." Her toes curled as he blew into his hands, catching hers in a swirl of warmth. "What are you doing here? I thought you'd left."

He shook his head, where he'd placed a knit cap that covered his hair and the tips of his ears. "I'm staying with Oliver and Joy at Mavis's house until tomorrow. I ... I didn't want to make you uncomfortable by staying at Rebecca's any longer."

"Oh." She took one step closer. "But why are you here, at the gazebo? Is that just some weird movie-like coincidence?"

He laughed. "No, Rebecca called me. Woke me up from a dead sleep and told me that you'd come knocking on my door, that you'd gone out walking at midnight, and that I'd better get my rear out of bed ASAP if I didn't want to be an idiot."

"Sounds like Rebecca, all right." She scrunched her nose. "I didn't know she heard me leave. And I didn't tell her where I was going."

"I guessed that part." His eyes roved her face. "Kara, I'm so sorry about the whole thing with my dad and the company. I should have just been straight with you, but I thought I could handle it without having to bring you into it at all."

"I appreciate and accept your apology. But I have one too." She closed the final few inches between them and wrapped her arms around his neck. In response, he slid his around her waist. "I completely overreacted. I compared you with Jeff again, and that just wasn't fair. You're a different man with a different heart—and I can see you're nothing alike. I was just afraid. Afraid to let myself fall for you. But fall, I have."

"I've fallen for you, too." He brushed a hair out of her face. "Even though it feels really fast, I'm old enough to know exactly what I want, and that's you, Kara. I've been searching all my life for you. Will you let me give you all the affection and adoration you deserve? I know I'm not perfect, but—"

She held a finger up to his lips. "Charming."

"Sorry, Snow." He turned his head and kissed the palm of her hand. "Am I talking too much?" His face moved closer to hers.

"A little, but it's adorable." She shut her eyes, ready for his kiss—a kiss that didn't come.

Because at that moment, Warren pulled back and reached into the inner pocket of his coat. He pulled out a small silver object, about the size of Kara's palm. It was a bit tarnished, but still in pristine condition.

She squinted in the dark. "A bell?"

"My grandfather's bell, to be exact." Warren held the bell between them and rang it, the chime wending sweet music through the air.

"Does that mean you're happy?"

Warren put the bell back into his jacket and resumed his position fully embracing her. "Happy doesn't begin to describe it. I'm not sure words can."

"Then why don't you find some other way to express yourself?" Kara flashed him an impish grin.

And with a chuckle, Warren bent down and kissed her—proving that sometimes the best gifts really did come when a person least expected them.

And that Love conquered all, in the end.

EPILOGUE

ONE YEAR LATER

"Wake up, wake up, wake up!"

Kara groaned and rolled over in bed. "What time is it?"

"Seven in the morning, mommy." Rose shook her shoulders. "That's when you said I was allowed to wake you up. Warren's already got the coffee made for you."

Forcing herself onto an elbow, Kara blinked up at her daughter, who was going through a growth spurt. "He does, does he?"

"Mm-hmm, and even though I've been up for an hour, he reminded me that I had to wait to wake you up. So I've been in my room listening to *Magic Tree House,* but now it's seven and time for presents. Let's go, Mommy, let's go!"

"All right, all right." Kara chuckled, but her whole body was still sluggish from sleep. "I know you're excited." And as the sleep fog cleared from her brain, Kara remembered—she was excited to hand out the presents too.

One in particular.

Rose skipped out the door, yelling toward the kitchen that Mommy was up now and present unwrapping would be starting soon. Kara couldn't help but smile at her youthful enthusiasm, remembering how much she'd enjoyed Christmas mornings herself as a child.

She dragged herself from the bed, pressing cold toes against the wooden floors and shimmying toward her closet to grab her robe. She emerged to find Warren standing in the doorway, looking impossibly handsome in his own fluffy gray robe and flannel pants, eyes sparkling behind his glasses.

He held out a mug of coffee toward her. "Merry Christmas, Snow."

Moving toward him, she gave her husband a quick kiss and took the mug in hand. "Merry Christmas, my prince. You ready for your first Christmas with a daughter?"

"I was born ready." He winked and, laughing, they moved together down the short hallway.

It had only been a year since that magical Christmas in Port Willis, but so much had changed. When they'd returned home, Kara and her sister had gone house hunting, and Kara and Rose had moved into this modest three-bedroom not far from Cindy and Travis.

After only three months of dating, Warren had proposed, and they'd married in July.

Though teasing that she was too old to be a wedding attendant, Cindy had served as Kara's matron of honor, and Sarah and Joy as bridesmaids—though being only two months after the birth of little Judah meant Sarah couldn't join in all of the wedding festivities.

Kara had invited Sophia and Ginny to be bridesmaids as well, but they were too busy with their little ones—Sophia with another little girl on the way and Ginny with her newly adopted toddler, Macy—to make the journey overseas.

Still, the day had been everything Kara could have hoped for, albeit much simpler than Warren's parents had wanted. But they doted on Rose and had softened in their treatment of Warren, and he'd forgiven his father for trying to go behind his back with the Gentry merger, which hadn't ended up happening. Their father-son relationship had actually improved greatly when Warren left the family business and started his own charity organization building wells in Africa.

The sun had only just peeked over the horizon as Kara settled on the couch. The smell of coffee wafted from her mug and her stomach roiled. But that was to be expected, if she remembered correctly from last time. She'd need to switch to decaf now anyway.

Kara set the mug on the side table without taking a sip.

Warren switched on the radio and Kara's favorite Michael Bublé playlist started on low, filling the small living room that reminded Kara so much of Ginny's back in Port Willis. Only here, pictures of her and Warren's wedding day filled the mantel, along with some of her favorite memories of Rose in photo form.

By this time next year, God willing, they'd be adding even more memories.

Speaking of her daughter, Rose was currently kneeling at the tree, sorting presents into piles based on recipient. Rose's and Kara's piles were much larger than Warren's.

But even though his pile was smaller, one present was worth more than them all. She'd wrapped it in tissue paper and placed it in a bag under the tree at midnight, after Warren had gone to bed.

Still, Kara tsked at him. "I thought we weren't going to spend that much this year."

He sat down beside her and flung his arm around her shoulders. "It's my first Christmas with both of my girls." Leaning into her, he nuzzled her neck, and she poked him in the side, giggling. He really was too good to her. He'd even agreed to move into their house instead of buying something larger, even though he could easily afford it. But this was home, and it was exactly as she'd pictured it. Charming and full of love. "I couldn't help but spoil you, Snow."

"Hmm, I guess I'll forgive you then."

"Are you guys going to kiss again?"

Kara snorted as she turned to find Rose standing in front of them, hand on a hip and the other clutching a present. When had she turned into such a little sassy pants? "Come here, you." She snatched her daughter onto her lap and started tickling her. Warren joined along and Rose's shrieks filled the room.

This—this was the gift she'd been waiting for all her life. God had been good to her too.

And to think, there was even more to rejoice over.

Suddenly, Kara couldn't wait any longer.

"Rose, there's a present hidden just behind the tree. Go get it and give it to Warren, please."

Eyes wide, Rose leaped up and obeyed.

While she searched, Warren turned his gaze on her. "Hiding presents from me, are we, Wife?"

"I have to keep the mystery alive." She smiled sweetly. Truth was, their marriage hadn't been all sunshine and unicorns. Some of her deepest issues hadn't come out until they'd said "I do," but they were working through those together in couples therapy. Kara continued to see her counselor on her own as well.

And she was making progress. The mere act of seeing Jeff didn't set her off like it once had. Maybe it helped that Warren went along for drop-offs in case Kara needed backup. Something about his presence had Jeff on his best behavior.

Small gift bag in hand, Rose skipped across the room and plopped it in Warren's lap. "Here you go."

"Thank you, Rosie-Posie."

Rose beamed at his nickname for her. "Can I help you open it?"

Warren glanced at Kara, who nodded. "Sure."

Kara's heart beat a bit harder in her chest. Would Warren be as excited as she had been?

Rose yanked at the tissue paper so hard that the present flew out and clattered onto the floor. She stooped and picked up the white stick, her nose wrinkling. "What is it?"

But Warren's head whipped toward her. "Is that what I think it is?"

A grin burst from Kara's lips. "If you think it's a positive pregnancy test, then yes. It is."

"Really?" His cheekbones lifted as he smiled and leaned forward, placing a hand tentatively on Kara's stomach. "We're having a baby?"

"A baby?" Rose pumped her fist in the air. "Yes, yes, yes!" Then she twirled around like a ballerina, spinning and spinning out her joy.

As for Warren, he leaned closer, pressing his forehead to Kara's. "I can't believe it."

"Are you … happy?"

"Are you kidding?" He kissed her softly. "This is amazing. A dream come true." Then he lifted his head and pointed to the mantel. "Rose, grab the bell. Quick."

Their daughter lifted up on her tiptoes and snatched Warren's grandfather's bell, then stepped through the crinkled tissue paper on the ground as she brought it over.

And together, Warren and Kara lifted it between them, ringing out the good news.

CONNECT WITH LINDSAY

If you enjoyed *The Port Willis Holiday Collection* (or any of my books, for that matter!), would you do me a favor and leave a review on Goodreads, Bookbub, or your favorite retail site?

Also...I'd love to connect with you. Sign up for my newsletter at www.lindsayharrel.com/subscribe and I'll send you a FREE story as a thank you!

Want more sweet romance from Lindsay? Check out my Walker Beach series, starting with Tyler and Gabrielle's story in *All At Once*.

BOOKS BY LINDSAY HARREL

The Barefoot Sisterhood Series

The Inn at Walker Beach

A Refuge by the Sea

Walker Beach Series

All At Once

All of You, Always

All Because of You

All I've Waited For

All You Need Is Love

Port Willis Romance Series

Like a Winter Snow

Like a Christmas Dream

Like a Silver Bell

Standalones

The Joy of Falling

The Heart Between Us

The Secrets of Paper and Ink

One More Song to Sing

ABOUT THE AUTHOR

Lindsay Harrel is a lifelong book nerd who lives in Arizona with her young family and two golden retrievers in serious need of training. When she's not writing or chasing after her children, Lindsay enjoys making a fool of herself at Zumba, curling up with anything by Jane Austen, and savoring sour candy one piece at a time. Visit her at www.lindsayharrel.com.

facebook.com/lindsayharrel

instagram.com/lindsayharrelauthor

Published by Blue Aster Press